This
Calder
Range

Other books by Janet Daily in Thorndike
Large Print:

This Calder Sky

This Calder Range

Janet Dailey

Thorndike Press • Thorndike, Maine

Library of Congress Cataloging in Publication Data:

Dailey, Janet.
  This Calder range.

  Sequel to: This Calder sky.
  1. Large type books. I. Title.
  [PS3554.A29T49 1983]   813'.54   82-19534
  ISBN 0-896-21420-6

Large Print edition available through arrangement with Simon &
Schuster, a Division of Gulf & Western Corporation.

Cover design by Andy Winther.

I

Free grass for the taking —
My luck's gonna change,
'Cause there's nothing left in Texas
To match this Calder range.

September 1878

1

It was a country of benchlands and breaks, coulees and cutbanks – and grass that stretched a hundred miles in every direction. The dominating expanse of blue sky overhead seemed to flatten it, but this vast northern range undulated like a heavy sea. The lonely grandeur of it gripped at the heart of the strong and intimidated the weak.

A pair of riders leading packhorses topped a crest of this virgin Montana Territory and reined in. From the stout, double-rigged saddle to the shotgun chaps and the low crown of their cowboy hats, their clothes and their gear marked them as Texans. They were covered with a thick layer of travel dust.

They walked their horses partway down the gentle slope and stopped again when they were no longer skylined by the plain's swell. Saddle leather groaned as the taller of the two men swung to the ground in a fluid motion. The chalk-faced bay he was riding blew out a snort and dipped its nose toward the grass.

Rawboned and lean, Chase Benteen Calder

carried his near-six-foot height with the ease of a shorter man. His weight was distributed in hard muscles that lay flatly across his chest and broad shoulders and the long girth of his legs. The twenty-six years of his life had beaten a toughness into his boldly spaced features. It showed in the quickness of his dark eyes, the small break along the bridge of his nose, and the pale track of an old scar on his right temple. Experience had made him close-mouthed and vigilant, and the sun had darkened him.

He kept a hold on the reins to his chalk-faced bay while it lowered its head to graze. The rattle of the bridle bit briefly drew his glance to the horse tearing at the curly, matted grass growing close to the ground.

It was native buffalo grass, more nutritious than any other kind. Heat and drought couldn't kill it; cold winters cured it into hay; the trampling of hooves couldn't destroy it. It was said this short grass could put two hundred extra pounds on a steer at maturity. A few minutes ago they had ridden through some ripening blue joint. Taller than the buffalo grass, its wheatlike heads had brushed the stirrups of his saddle.

The great herds of buffalo that had once roamed this range were well on their way to being exterminated by buffalo hunters and hiders. It was an act encouraged by the government in Washington in a deliberate attempt to break the spirit of the Plains Indians and subdue them once and for all. A year before, on October 5, 1877, Chief Joseph of the Nez Percé had surrendered over in the Bear Paw Mountains. Most of the Sioux and the Cheyenne were corraled on reservations, and the rest had fled to Canada with Sitting Bull and Dull Knife. After years of pressure from clamoring ranchers and railroads, the government was finally throwing open the last isolated island of open range. All this land was going to be free for the taking.

Chase Benteen Calder scanned the limitless expanse of the plains with sharp and knowing eyes. His glance stopped on the wiry rider sitting loosely on his horse. Both men were seasoned veterans of a half-dozen trail drives of longhorns north to the railheads in Kansas and beyond. They had just come off a drive Benteen had bossed for the Ten Bar ranch south of Fort Worth, Texas, to deliver a herd to an outfit in the Wyoming Territory. The horses they were riding and the ones that carried their packs all had the 10- brand burned on their hips.

It was on the trail during a stopover at

Dodge City that they'd heard the first talk about the Indian country of Montana Territory and Benteen's interest had been aroused. Then, the ramrod of the Wyoming outfit had mentioned the free grass opening up to the north. Instead of heading directly back to Texas, Benteen had taken this side trip to get a look at the country, and Barnie had tagged along.

This vast rolling grassland was all that they had claimed it to be, and more. Its lower altitude made it more desirable than the plains of Wyoming and Colorado, and its grasses were rich — capable of putting hard weight on cattle.

There would be a stampede into the territory. Free grass was like whispering "gold." Right now, it looked like a sea of gold. Summer had ripened it to a rich yellow and autumn's cool breath was bronzing the heavy-headed grasses that covered hundreds of square miles. Its location wouldn't stay a secret for long. Soon the place would be overrun with people arriving to make their big chance. Would-be ranchers and speculators would come crawling out of the woodwork like cockroaches to try to make a quick buck and run. But Benteen made up his mind to be here before the cockroaches came.

"I think this is it, Barnie." His narrow smile was cool and sure.

"Yep." Barnabas Moore didn't need an explanation of that statement.

Three things were required to make a good cattle range — grass, water, and natural shelter from winter storms. There was grass aplenty; plum thickets and chokecherry trees offered brush shelter; and just ahead there was the wide course of a riverbed meandering through the heaving plains.

Looping the reins around the horse's neck, Benteen swung into the saddle and turned his mount and packhorse toward the cottonwood-lined banks of the river. The taciturn Barnie Moore followed, swaying loosely in rhythm to his horse's gait.

"Look there." Barnie nodded, the rolled front brim of his hat pointing to a cutbank where erosion by water and wind had exposed strata of rock and earth in the slope. Close to the surface, a wide seam of shiny black coal gleamed in the autumn sunlight. "Won't lack for fuel."

Surrounded by virtually treeless ridges, it was an important scrap of information to be tucked away for future use. Benteen made a mental note of it as both men continued toward the river without slacking their horses' pace.

Summer had reduced the river's flow to a sluggish current. It was well within the banks carved by spring melts, the shallow water running crystal clear. But it was water — life-giving, life-sustaining water.

Benteen let the reins sag on the saddlehorn. Beside him, Barnie reached into the deep pocket of his vest and fetched out his tobacco sack and paper. Certainty eased through Chase Benteen Calder. There was no longer any need to search this stark, lonely Montana land.

His eyes were filled with the enormous land-scape, the sprawling plains valley with its shallow river flowing through it, the upthrust of range beyond it — and the high blue sky. This range reached from here to forever.

And it sang its promise to him. It sounded crazy to think the land was singing to him, but it was. The low murmur of the water set the rhythm while a keening breeze swept down the slope, playing a melody in the grasses and the dry leaves of the cottonwoods and willows bordering the river.

In his mind's eye, Benteen could see it all as it would be, herds of cattle growing fat on the native grasses, big barns walled with thick wood beams, and a big house sitting on that knoll from which he could view it all. Not in the beginning, but someday. In the meantime, there was plenty of room in these wide-open spaces to think and breathe and dream — and work like hell to make the dream a reality.

Benteen knew about work. He'd been working all his life for somebody else, but always watching and learning, putting aside money for a place of his own. All of it had been preparing him for this day when he rode onto this land where his knowledge and skill would be put to use. These trackless plains were going to carry his mark. Here he would build something that would endure.

The conviction that he'd found his home range swelled in his chest. This was his. This would be Calder land. "I'm filing on this stretch of river," he stated as Barnie licked his cigarette together.

Every cattleman knew that laying claim to a narrow stretch of the allowed 160-acre homestead tract gave control of an entire region — a minimum of ten miles on either side, or as far as a cow could walk to water. Elbow room increased it by at least another ten miles, and sometimes more. Barnie had already agreed that if Benteen found the right rangeland, he'd file on the adjoining stretch and turn it over to him, which was a common practice of the day. The additional 160 acres would give him breathing room — with more to come.

Texas had given Benteen his fill of being hemmed in and crowded. He'd been a boy at the close of the Civil War, but he'd seen the changes that had come with Reconstruction — few of them good. There had been too many lost causes in his young life. Here was the place for new beginnings.

"Come spring, I'll bring up a herd," Benteen stated in a spare, even tone while Barnie cupped a match to the hand-rolled cigarette and bent a little toward the flame. "If all goes well, I'll be back before the end of next summer. Do you think you can hang on here till then?"

"Reckon," Barnie drawled. He was younger by two years than Benteen. "What do you suppose yore pa'll do?"

Benteen looked into the distance, a net of crow-tracks springing from the outer corners of his eyes. "I don't know." The sun-browned skin became taut across the ridgeline of his jaw. "The Ten Bar's got him choked off the range. But he's a stubborn man."

His father, Seth Calder, was a good man — a strong man. It was possible he could have been an important man, but he had a blind spot, a fatal flaw. He didn't know when to let go of a thing that was dead. The War Between the States had ended years ago, yet his father con-

14

tinued to argue the South's cause, insisting Lincoln had thrown a political blanket over the true issue of states' rights that had prompted secession and turned the war into a question of slavery. That position hadn't made him popular with those in power in a Reconstructed Texas.

His support of the South during the war had left him nearly broke at its end. He struggled to rebuild his modest ranch, only to be wiped out by the Black Friday crash in the Panic of '73. Judd Boston's Ten Bar had survived the crash unscathed. While Seth Calder had to sell cattle, Judd Boston had purchased more, until Ten Bar herds flooded the range, leaving little room for Seth Calder to expand without over-stocking the land. He was crowded into a smaller corner of ground that could barely support a cattle operation, but he wouldn't budge.

And Seth Calder wouldn't let go of the idea that his wife would come back to him. Benteen had spent most of his childhood waiting for a mother who never returned. She had chosen his name at birth – Chase Benteen Calder. Chase had been her maiden name, and Benteen the name of a cousin. His given name was rarely used by those who knew him. Even as a child, he'd been called Benteen.

When he was six years old, his mother had run away with a so-called remittance man – a ne'er-do-well paid a regular allowance by his moneyed English family to stay away from home. His father had always claimed that he'd lured her away with his talk of New Orleans, San Francisco, London, and Europe, of fancy gowns and jewels. After twenty years, Seth still believed she'd return to her husband and son. Benteen didn't. And, unlike his father, he didn't want her to come back.

There were times when a man should stand and fight – and other times when he should cut and run. Benteen saw that, but he doubted that his father would. In Texas, they were outnumbered by memories of the past and a series of present circumstances. Tomorrow was here in Montana Territory. "What about Lorna?" The closeness that had developed between them allowed Barnie to ask the personal question.

"We'll be married in the spring before the herd starts north." There was no more reason to wait. Benteen had found the place that would give them a future. And that was all that had been keeping him from setting a date for his wedding to Lorna Pearce. His gaze was sure and keen, a little on the reckless side. "The next time I leave Texas, it will be for good." He was going to cut all ties, and whatever was left behind . . . was left behind.

2

Fort Worth, Texas, was the jumping-off point for herds heading north on the Chisholm Trail. It was a boisterous, bawdy cow town, catering to the needs of the cowboy. Merchants sold supplies of flour, sugar, coffee, molasses, prunes, cigars, and other items to the trail outfits. There were saloons, dance halls, and sporting women to make sure the cowboy didn't get bored before he left.

It was a town with growing pains. Main and Houston streets were paved, although many argued "paved" was not the right term to describe them. The El Paso Hotel was a three-story building of gray limestone, so things were looking up. But there was a definite lack of sidewalks. No one in Fort Worth was too concerned about the rival Western Trail taking the trail herds away from the much-traveled Chisholm.

But the trailing season was over for this year. Fort Worth was quiet on the November afternoon Chase Benteen Calder rode in. His clothes were stiff with trail grime, gathered over the long miles from the Montana Territory. A scratchy beard growth shadowed his rawboned features, making him look tougher. The edges of his hair had a dark copper cast. It was rough hair – heavy hair, curling thickly into the scarf tied around his neck and knotted loosely at the throat.

With the packhorse in tow, Benteen walked his mount to the livery stable. He wasn't a man to let his eyes be idle, thus his restless gaze continued its survey of the surrounding streets and buildings and the people in town. He halted the bay in front of the stable's open doors and dismounted, stepping onto hard-packed ground. The smell of dust and the rank odor from the stable rose strongly around him. A man with a gimpy leg hobbled out of the shadowed interior.

"Hey, Benteen," he greeted. "I thought you'd quit these parts."

"In time, Stoney." He gave him a thin smile, weary like the man.

The rattle of an approaching buggy drew his glance to the street. Benteen recognized Judd Boston at the reins, accompanied by an escort of riders. The owner of the Ten Bar was dressed in a dark suit and vest, the starched white collar of his shirt circling his throat. The bowler hat atop his head further distinguished him from the riders. The power that came with prosperity was evident in the studied arrogance of his posture.

For all the dandified appearance of Judd Boston, Benteen didn't make the mistake of seeing softness. Beneath those Eastern clothes, the man's burly frame was put together with hard muscles. Benteen knew the instant Judd recognized him. The line of his mouth became long and thin as he pulled within himself.

After the long journey, Benteen was tired, dirty, and irritable. He wanted nothing more than to take a bath, have a cold beer, and see Lorna — in that order. He wasn't in the mood for a conversation with Judd Boston, but he had little choice.

He had never liked the man, but he didn't figure it was necessary to like the person he worked for. Benteen couldn't pinpoint the reason he didn't like Judd Boston. Maybe it was because he was a Yankee or because he was a banker — not a true cattleman. Or maybe it was his clean white hands that caused Benteen to distrust him — so clean and white, as if they'd been washed too many times.

The buggy pulled up close to the livery stable, the escort of riders fanning protectively along the street side. Other ranchers rode into town alone, but Judd Boston never went anywhere without a mounted guard. It was another thing that raised questions in Benteen's mind. Was it a guilty conscience, or did the banker-rancher like the implied importance of possessing a retinue of underlings?

"Calder!" It was a stiff command for him to approach the buggy.

The ordering tone straightened his shoulders slightly, but Benteen allowed no other resentment to show. He walked to the buggy with the loose, unhurried stride of a rider, each step accompanied by the muted jangle of his work spurs. He stopped beside the buggy, saying nothing because he had nothing to say.

His silence didn't set well with Judd Boston. The man had eyes as black as hell. They burned with what he saw as rage. "Where the hell have you been?" he demanded. "I expected you back two months ago."

"I had some personal business." It was a flat answer, showing neither respect nor disrespect. Benteen was aware of the man's dangerous patience. It was the cunning kind, content to wait until the right moment. Benteen was reminded of an alleycat he'd once watched while it played with a mouse.

"I hired you to do a job, Calder." The statement insinuated that he had failed to do it.

It ran raw over his travel-weary nerves. "Your herd was delivered to the Snyder outfit with only ten head lost on the drive." His sharp glance picked out Jessie Trumbo among the escort of riders. "I sent the money from the sale back with Jessie. You've got no complaint coming."

"It was your responsibility to bring that cash to me. Not Jessie's," Boston insisted coldly.

"It was my responsibility to see that you received it," Benteen corrected the phrasing. "You did." There was a rare show of irritation. It didn't seem to matter anymore whether he offended Judd Boston or not. "I hired out to boss your herd and drive it through to Wyoming. After that I was to pay off the drovers with the proceeds of the sale and return the balance to you. The job's done. You may have paid my wages, Boston, but you don't own me. No man owns me."

A coldness hardened Boston's broad features. "The job is done and you are done, Calder," he stated. "I have no use for a man who disappears for two months. You aren't going back on the payroll."

"Good." A half-smile skipped across his face. "It saves me the trouble of quitting."

Their eyes locked, hardness matching hardness. Then a glint of satisfaction flickered in

Judd Boston's eyes. "Baker," he called to one of the riders. "Those two horses in front of the stable are carrying the Ten Bar brand. Catch them up and take them back to the ranch."

The order seared through Benteen like a hot iron. "You damned bastard." His voice was low and rough. "In this country, you don't take a man's horse and leave him on foot. I'll bring them out to the ranch myself in the morning."

"I want them now." Judd smiled. "I could report them as stolen, Calder." Without taking his eyes off Benteen, he prodded the hesitant rider. "You heard me, Baker."

Benteen shot a hard glance at the young rider reining his horse back to walk it behind the buggy. Jessie Trumbo swung his horse to follow him. "I'll give you a hand, Baker," he murmured. Whether the men agreed or not, they were obliged to obey orders. It was part of riding for the brand. Benteen knew that, and didn't hold their part in this against them.

His attention swung back to the man in the buggy. "I'll get my gear off the horses so you can take them," he said. "Maybe now I'll have the time to check some of the brands on your cattle. I've always thought how easy it would be to change my pa's brand from a C- to a 10-. A running iron or a cinch ring could handle that in nothing flat."

Judd Boston stiffened. "You're finished around here, Calder. If I were you, I'd clear out."

A remote smile slanted his mouth. "I planned on it, Boston."

With a flick of his wrist, Judd Boston snapped the buggy whip close to the ears of the chestnut mare. Benteen stepped back as the harnessed mare lunged forward and the wooden wheels of the buggy began their first revolution. The two remaining riders of the escort fell in behind the buggy.

Turning back to the stable, Benteen walked to the packhorse to unload it first. "You made yourself an enemy, Benteen." Jessie Trumbo spoke quietly. Benteen still counted the rider as a friend.

A reply didn't seem necessary but he stared after the buggy disappearing down the street. Most of the men at the Ten Bar were his friends, but there were some who weren't. It was this tangled weave of friendship and enmity in a rough, short-tempered land that kept the aloof interest in his dark eyes. "Is it all right if I stow my gear inside, Stoney?" he asked the stablehand instead.

"Sure." The aging, semi-crippled man nodded.

Benteen carried the pack inside the stable

and into a small office dusty with hay chaff. Opening the pack, he slung the holstered revolver over his shoulder for the time being and removed his rifle. He went back outside to unsaddle the chalk-faced bay.

"Where's Barnie?" Jessie asked, leaning over his saddle horn. "I thought he went with you."

"He did." Benteen hooked the stirrup over the saddle horn and began loosening the cinch. "I left him up in Montana Territory north of the Yellowstone. He's lookin' after my homestead claim until I can bring a herd up in the spring."

"Montana." Jessie sat up, whistling under his breath in surprise. "Then you are pulling out. You didn't just tell Boston that to be talking."

"Nope." Benteen lifted the heavy saddle off the horse's back, a glint of pride flashing in his dark eyes.

"Where you gonna get a herd? Are you takin' your pa's?"

"I thought I'd spend the winter beating the thickets and putting together a herd of mavericks." Benteen wasn't counting on his father pulling up stakes and going with him, taking what was left of his herd. "I could use somebody good with a rope to come along."

Jessie grinned. "It'll be pure hell chasin' down longhorns in all that scrub, but it sounds better than 'yes-sirring' Mr. Moneybags."

Benteen hefted the saddle onto his shoulder and carried it into the stable to leave it with the rest of his gear. When he came out, Jessie and the young cowboy had ropes around the necks of his two horses and were leading them away. Stoney limped up to stand beside him.

"You can have the gray gelding in the first stall," he said. "Jest turn him loose when you're through with him. He'll find his own way back. Always does."

"Thanks, Stoney." He picked up the rifle he'd leaned against the side of the stable and started down the dusty street.

Several blocks down the street, he came to one of the few wooden sidewalks. His footsteps were heavy with fatigue, his spurs rattling with each leaden stride. Although his body was bone-weary, his eyes never ceased their restless scanning of the streets. But they paid little attention to the store buildings he passed, except to note customers going in or out.

"Benteen?" a female voice called out to him, uncertain.

He stopped, half-turning to glance behind him. A rawly sweet wind rushed through his system as he saw Lorna poised in the doorway of the milliner's shop. The hesitancy left her expression and a smile curved the soft fullness of her lips. She seemed to glide across the sidewalk to him, the lightness of her footsteps barely making any sound at all. A blue ribbon swept the length of her long dark hair away from her face and left it to cascade in soft curls down her back. She was like spring, fresh and innocent in her long dress of white cotton with small blue flowers.

The top of her head barely reached his shoulder. Her brown eyes sparkled with the pleasure of seeing him. "I thought it was you." Her voice sang to him.

His eyes drank in the essence of her like a thirsty man long without water. He'd forgotten what a little thing she was. Not so little, perhaps, Benteen corrected as his gaze noticed her firm young breasts pushing at the demure front of her gown that covered her all the way to her neck.

"Where have you been?" she asked as she scanned his haggard and disreputable appearance. "I was beginning to worry about you. The others came back from the drive months ago. Where have you been all this time?"

A surging warmth gentled his rough features. Benteen stroked her smooth cheek with his forefinger, wanting to do more than just touch her. "You sound just like a wife already," he teased softly. He was conscious of his trail

26

grime and unshaven face. The public street didn't make this meeting any easier.

His remark made Lorna lower her gaze, betraying her excited shyness. At times, Lorna Pearce seemed to be a living contradiction. There was a Madonna-like quality to her features, yet her brown eyes could be bold and spirited, revealing an intelligence that she usually concealed in a womanly fashion. She was sometimes as gay and full of laughter as a young girl, and other times, very calm and self-confident. At the moment, she looked incredibly young — too young to be a wife; but she was seventeen, soon to be eighteen, definitely a marriageable age.

She slanted him a look, a sauciness behind her proper air. "If I were your wife, Chase Benteen Calder, I'd take after you with a rolling pin for being away so long without writing me a single word."

He chuckled softly at the threat, not believing she was capable of anything that remotely resembled violence. His features were so solidly composed that when he smiled, the change in his expression was always complete and surprising. He looked over at the shop she'd come out of. "What are you doing here?" Her father's general store — Pearce's Emporium — was several blocks down the street.

"Spending your father's money on another hat?"

"No: I'm waiting to spend your money," Lorna retorted. "I was visiting a friend." She glanced toward the door, where a rather plain brown-haired girl was standing. "You remember Sue Ellen, don't you? We went to school together," she reminded him, and discreetly motioned for her girlfriend to come forward. "Her mother owns the millinery shop."

The girl approached them timidly. "Hello, Mr. Calder," she greeted him in a slightly breathless voice.

"Benteen," he corrected, and wondered what the two girls had in common, besides Miss Hilda's School for Young Ladies. "How are you, Sue Ellen?"

"Fine, thank you," she murmured, barely opening her mouth.

Lorna confidently faced him and challenged, "You still haven't told me where you've been all this time."

"It's a long story. I'll come by the house tonight and we'll talk." He rubbed a hand over his chin, whiskers scraping his rough palm. "Right now, I need a shave and a bath."

"Come for dinner," Lorna invited.

"Six o'clock?" That was the usual time the Pearce family dined.

"Yes," she nodded.

The smile he gave Lorna was for her alone, but he turned and politely touched the brim of his hat in deference to her girlfriend. His stride wasn't quite so heavy when he continued down the street.

The first time he'd seen her was two years ago in her father's store. Even then Benteen had been attracted to her, but of course she'd been too young. From that day on, he'd become a regular customer of Pearce's Emporium, hoping to catch glimpses of her. During trailing season, her parents didn't allow her to come to the store. Cowboys on the town, even those with the utmost respect for the gentler sex, could sometimes get offensive when they'd had one too many glasses of red-eye. The Pearces naturally wanted to protect their daughter from such regrettable advances.

When Lorna had turned sixteen, Benteen had asked her father's permission to come calling. With some initial reservations about his ability to provide a good living, his request had been granted. Benteen had never doubted from the moment he saw her that he would someday make Lorna his wife.

Before he'd left on the trail drive last spring, he'd asked for her hand in marriage. He hadn't wanted to set a wedding date until he'd found a place for them. Benteen had always known his father would have welcomed him and his bride at the ranch, but there was no future. The Cee Bar was gradually being squeezed out by Judd Boston. It was only a matter of time before Boston acquired it on a tax sale. The ranch couldn't support his father, let alone Benteen and Lorna.

For the last three years he'd been saving every dime he could. He'd rounded up mavericks and added them to the trail herds he'd taken north. He'd managed to put almost a thousand dollars aside, with the thought of buying a place where they could build a future. Now that money could go into putting together an outfit to trail north with a herd of maverick longhorns from the Texas brush, since the land in Montana Territory was going to cost him only a filing fee.

Lorna would make him the perfect wife. Her head wasn't filled with dreams about big cities and fancy clothes like his mother. She was sensible and practical – and beautiful. The blood ran strong through his veins.

Lorna's nerves were all ajumble when she heard the footsteps on the front porch. She didn't have to look at the clock to know it was Benteen. Her pounding heart told her to run to the door to meet him, but a girl shouldn't appear too anxious. It wasn't proper – and, Lord knew, there were times when Benteen made her feel very improper.

She pretended to straighten a setting of silverware on the table, covered with her mother's best linen cloth. There was a knock at the door. She caught her father's faintly amused glance as he looked up from the day's issue of the Fort Worth *Democrat*.

"It must be Benteen," she murmured.

"Must be," he agreed dryly and managed to keep the pipe clenched between his teeth as he spoke.

The long skirt of her china-blue dress rustled softly as she moved slowly toward the door. When she passed the oval mirror in the small foyer, Lorna stole one last glance at her reflection. Her dark hair was swept atop her head, making her look much more adult than she had when he'd seen her that afternoon. She hated for him to think her immature, as he sometimes did, she knew. She definitely looked older – all of eighteen, at least.

When she opened the door, Benteen stood for a minute just looking at her. The bold inspection disturbed her in a way that Lorna wasn't quite sure she should feel. Or maybe it was the change in his appearance that was affecting her.

His hat was in his hand, leaving his head uncovered. Thick brown hair gleamed with polished mahogany lights in the rays of the setting sun. His lean cheeks were freshly shaved, revealing the natural strength of his features. He was wearing a clean white shirt and a string tie. But nothing seemed able to dim that innate power she sensed in him.

"You're a little early," Lorna said. She felt the need to conceal her pleasure, and she knew the clock hadn't chimed the hour yet.

"Shall I leave and come back?" Benteen mocked her.

"Of course not." She reached for his hand to draw him into the house.

She was conscious of the pleasant roughness of his fingers as they closed around her hand, holding it firmly. His dark eyes continued to focus on her. Their intensity was something she was never certain how to handle.

"Daddy's in the parlor." Lorna walked with him to the doors. "You can talk with him while I help Mother in the kitchen."

"Don't be too long," he said. "I'm starved."

He released her hand without objection. As Lorna slipped away, she had the crazy feeling he wasn't talking about food. It excited her the way he looked at her sometimes. Other times, she was glad her parents were in the next room. Even now that she and Benteen were engaged, they were seldom left alone for any long period of time. Usually they sat on the front porch while her parents sat in the parlor. Anytime there was a lull in their conversation, her mother invariably came out to offer them lemonade or refreshments of some sort. Lorna was glad that Benteen respected her too much to suggest they go anywhere without the chaperonage of her parents, partly because she was afraid she might be tempted to agree.

They sat across the table from each other at dinner. At times like this, it was easy for Lorna to imagine how it would be when they were married and lived in a house of their own. She looked forward to having her parents over to dinner.

"Did you say you went up into the Montana Territory, Benteen?" her father inquired as he passed him the bowl of potatoes.

"Yes." He helped himself to an ample portion. "They're opening up the Indian country to the east. The grass up there is stirrup-deep, ideal cattle range. I'm staking a claim on a choice section of it."

"You are?" Her father studied him with interest and apparent approval. Lorna brightened with pride.

"It's just what I've been looking for — a place

where Lorna and I can build a future," Benteen stated, sending a brief glance at her. "I figure we can be married in March and leave with the herd I'm driving north in April."

"Leave?" Lorna repeated. She had the feeling she had missed something. "Where are we going?"

"I just explained," Benteen replied with a patient smile. "I've found a place in Montana for us. I even have the spot all picked out where we will build our new home."

"Oh." It was a small sound to mask her confusion. She pretended an interest in the food on her plate, hardly hearing any of the discussion between her father and Benteen.

Part of her couldn't believe that he was really serious about living in Montana Territory. It was so far away. She couldn't imagine leaving Texas. Benteen had never mentioned this to her before. The idea was more than a little frightening.

Benteen didn't appear to notice her silence or her lack of enthusiasm for his plan for their future. Lorna was conscious of her mother's gaze, but she wasn't willing to meet it. Not yet. Not until she was clear in her own mind.

"That apple pie was delicious, Mrs. Pearce." Benteen leaned back in his chair, his dessert plate empty.

"Lorna made it," her mother appropriately gave her the credit, but this was one time when Lorna wasn't proud of her cooking accomplishments. Her mind was too preoccupied with this Montana news. "Would you like more coffee, Benteen?"

"No. Thank you," he refused, and Lorna felt his eyes on her.

"I'll help clear the table tonight, Clara," her father volunteered. "I'm sure Benteen and Lorna have a lot to talk about."

"Yes, of course," her mother agreed.

The others were already standing by the time Lorna pushed out of her chair. Almost immediately, Benteen was at her side, curving a hand under her elbow. "Shall we sit in the parlor?" He took her agreement for granted and escorted her into the adjoining room.

Once inside the room, Lorna turned to face him. "Are you really serious about going to Montana, Benteen?"

He seemed slightly taken aback, a dark brow arching. "Yes."

"But . . ." Agitation and uncertainty twisted inside her. "Don't you think we should talk about it?"

"What is there to talk about?" He frowned, his gaze narrowing on her. "We've already discussed that I was going to look for a place."

"Yes, but you didn't say anything about Montana," Lorna protested. "I thought you were going to buy a place in Texas."

"There's nothing around here, Lorna," he stated. "Up there, the sky's the limit — and what a sky it is! Wait until you see it. It's beautiful country."

"I'm sure it is," she murmured. "It's just that it's so far away."

A smile touched his mouth. "You have to leave your parents sometime." He was beginning to understand her hesitation. He'd forgotten she was so young. Her attachment to her parents was still very strong. That would change once they were married. Her loyalty would shift to him then.

He reached out to take her in his arms. She offered no resistance but she didn't come to him as eagerly as she had in the past either. But Benteen took no notice of that. It had been too long since he'd seen her, and his body was hungry for the feel of a woman's softness.

The numbness caused by his announcement didn't last long under the demand of his kiss. His mouth moved hotly over her lips, a vague roughness in its possession. When his encircling arms pulled her body against him, she felt the burning heat of his hard flesh. Little tremors quivered through her, shaking her.

The intimacy of the embrace alarmed her, because it was arousing desires that seemed sinful.

With an effort, she turned away from him, her heart thudding heavily against her ribs. "I don't think you should kiss me like that." She sounded out of breath.

He curled a finger under her chin and turned it so she faced him. "You're going to be my wife," he reminded her lazily. He seemed amused by the flush in her cheeks. "Aren't you?"

"Yes," Lorna whispered. Suddenly she was filled with all sorts of uncertainties about the intimacy marriage would bring.

Did it mean he would kiss her like that? How was she supposed to act when he did? She tried to calm her jittery nerves and regain control of the situation. After all, she was an adult – soon to be a married woman. She had to start behaving like one. It was perfectly natural for a future bride to be nervous about the wedding night. It wasn't as if she didn't know all about the birds and the bees.

But she didn't know the answers to all her questions. Surely she could discuss this with her mother. Maybe she was supposed to feel the kinds of sensations she had when Benteen kissed her. Maybe it wasn't wrong.

"Is something wrong, Lorna?" Benteen studied the changing expressions that crossed her face.

"Wrong?" She had the uncomfortable feeling that he was reading her mind. "No, of course not," she lied. "We should decide on a wedding date."

"You pick it. I'll be there."

The promise sent her pulse spinning again.

3

It didn't seem to matter how close her relationship was to her mother, Lorna had difficulty bringing up the subject of the way Benteen made her feel sometimes. She had so little to use in comparison, since she hadn't been attracted to any of her other suitors. She had fallen in love with Benteen right from the start.

"What was it you wanted to talk to me about, Lorna?" her mother prompted.

Lorna turned from the window, a little startled by the question. She had been searching for a way to lead up to the subject. "I . . . was thinking about what Benteen said last night — about moving to Montana." It seemed the best place to begin.

"It seems so far away, doesn't it?" Her mother's eyes looked misty. "Your father and I are going to miss you terribly."

"I think I'm a little scared," she admitted. "I thought we'd live close by. I'm not sure I want to go there."

"A woman's place is with her husband," her mother reminded her gently. "You still want

39

to marry him, don't you?"

"Yes." Lorna didn't have to hesitate about that. "It's just that . . ." She touched her fingertips to her lips, remembering the rough pressure of his kiss. "There're so many things I don't know," she sighed at last.

"Every bride feels the same way." Her mother smiled. "And we all seem to have to learn on our own. I remember I was the worst cook when your father and I were married. It's a miracle he survived that first year."

"I think I can manage to cook and keep house. But what about when we have a baby?" That uncomfortable feeling ran through her again. "I mean, presuming that we do have a baby."

"I hope you will. I hope you have several."

"I don't know." Lorna turned away in vague agitation. "Sometimes when I think about . . ." She stopped, unable to finish the sentence.

"It probably won't be easy in the beginning," her mother said. "But after you are married awhile, I think you'll be more able to accept the idea, especially if you want children."

"I . . . suppose." Lorna was troubled by her mother's reply. It seemed to confirm the girl talk at school. Sex was something a proper lady endured. There wasn't any enjoyment in it, not unless the girl was immoral.

It was better if she didn't mention to her mother the way Benteen had made her feel. The excitement that sent those funny little tremors through her body. She'd simply have to learn to overcome them. She wanted to be a proper wife.

It was midmorning when Benteen reached his father's Cee Bar Ranch. Once they'd talked about a partnership, but the Crash of '73 had wiped out that dream. The hard facts of earning a living had forced Benteen to work elsewhere while his father continued his attempt to save the ranch. Last winter's blizzards had virtually written the end to that dream — the blizzards and Judd Boston.

Benteen had had only a vague suspicion about worked-over brands until he'd voiced it yesterday to Boston. Benteen was fairly sure now that the banker had been taking a cow here, a steer there. There were a couple of un-scrupulous characters on his payroll, and Benteen believed he'd found the reason why. It was unlikely he could prove it. He wasn't even sure how much difference it would make if he could. At the most, his father had probably lost fifty head over the past five years. The trouble was, his operation was so small, fifty head hurt him. Numbers — that was the secret.

Benteen had observed closely Judd Boston's operation at the Ten Bar. He'd learned a lot, and he knew cattle. Judd Boston had inadvertently taught him business sense, growth, and markets.

Halting the gray gelding in front of the barn, he dismounted and stripped his saddle and gear from the horse. He slapped it hard on the rump, sending it down the rutted lane they had just traveled. The horse would show up in a couple of days at the livery stable, wanting its ration of oats and corn.

After putting the saddle and bridle away, Benteen carried his gear to the house, a simple white frame house that was beginning to show its age. There were only four rooms – a kitchen with a wood-burning range and an inside well pump to provide running water in the house; a front room with a stone fireplace for heat, a pecan desk, and a horsehair sofa; and two small bedrooms.

Benteen set his rifle in the rack by the desk and took his bedroll and saddlebags into the smaller of the two bedrooms – the one that had always been his. There was no sign of his father, but he hadn't expected to find him home in the middle of the day.

It had been months since he had been home, yet nothing had changed. He looked at the picture occupying the honored position on the fireplace mantel. The ease went out of him as he walked over to the blackened hearth and took down the ornately carved oval frame containing the photograph.

The woman was beautiful. There was no doubt about that. Benteen suspected that the prim pose and the faded daguerreotype didn't do her justice. Her hair was blond – the color of wild honey, his father had claimed – and her eyes were as dark as her hair was light. It was a bold combination that was even more striking when combined with her strong, yet feminine features.

But Benteen didn't see the beauty of the woman who was his mother when he looked at the picture. He noticed the self-centered determination and the hunger for something more out of life in her eyes. Was he bitter? Yes.

If it had been his choice, the framed photograph of Madelaine Calder would have been used for kindling a long time ago. But it hadn't been his choice. He returned the picture to its proper place on the mantel and entered the kitchen to boil some coffee.

His father rode in just before sundown. Not a demonstrative man, Seth Calder greeted his son with reserve, despite the long separation. There was a strong resemblance between the two in their height and coloring, but Benteen had a lot of rough edges yet; his father had been worn and polished smooth.

Few words were exchanged while his father washed up and Benteen put their supper on the table. Not until the meal was over and his father had leaned back in his chair was there any serious attempt at conversation.

An occasional cigar was one of the few luxuries Seth Calder permitted himself to enjoy anymore. He lit one now and puffed on it, rolling it between his lips in a silent savoring. His attitude and appearance seemed to indicate prosperity rather than the edge of bankruptcy. No matter how futile Benteen considered the struggle to keep the ranch, he admired his father's lack of self-pity – the front he continued to display even if it was false.

"How was the drive?" Seth Calder took the cigar out of his mouth long enough to ask the question.

"Fine." Benteen swirled the black coffee in the tin mug. "How many head did you end up losing this past winter?"

"By tally, it came out to thirty missing. I found the carcasses of half that number," his father admitted.

"Did you check any of the Ten Bar herds to

see if some of your cattle might have strayed in with theirs?" Benteen didn't want to come right out and voice his suspicions, not yet.

"I did." It was a simple answer, yet its tone encouraged Benteen to continue along the same track.

"It sure would be easy to work over a Cee Bar brand into a Ten Bar. It would be hard to spot." He eyed his father over the rim of the mug as he took a swig of the strong coffee.

A dry smile twitched one corner of his father's mouth. "Not if somebody botched the job."

"Then it's true?" Benteen lifted his head, regarding his father with narrowed surprise. "I only guessed it yesterday. How long have you suspected what was going on?"

"I happened across a steer with a fresh Ten Bar brand over an old Cee Bar this fall," he said through the cigar between his teeth.

Benteen's expression darkened with a narrowed look that was hard and uncompromising. "Why didn't you do something when you found out? Go to the sheriff."

"How could I?" His father removed the cigar from his mouth and studied the gray ash building on its tip. "When my own son was working for the man rustling my cattle."

"I'm not drawin' Ten Bar wages now."

45

Benteen set his cup down on the table. "You should have said something to me. Told me what you found."

"You'd left for Wyoming on the drive. And I didn't have any proof that it wasn't the work of some overzealous cowboy, done without Boston's knowledge."

"Nothing goes on at that ranch that he don't know about. No order's given without his knowledge," Benteen stated.

"That's the way I figured it." But he seemed unmoved by it. "He ain't laid his hands on any more. I've kept what's left of the herd close in where I can keep an eye on 'em and run a daily count. The next time one comes up among the missing, I'll know who to see."

"Sell out, Pa," Benteen urged, and leaned forward to make his point. "What's this place ever brought you but grief? I staked out a piece of range in the Montana Territory that makes Texas look like a picked-over cotton field. Barnie's sittin' on it now till I can come back with a herd. We can trail the Cee Bar stock up there and turn 'em loose on all that free grass."

Seth Calder shook his head. "Nope, I ain't quittin' just 'cause things got tough."

Impatient and irritated with his father's blind stubbornness, Benteen held in his temper. "You don't understand, Pa," he replied with contained force. "Up there, we can carve out a spread that will make the Ten Bar look like a squatter's camp. It's all there for the taking, and it can be ours!"

"It may look green to you, but it looks like runnin' to me." There was no give in him, and his eyes were dark with disapproval. "No one's gonna drive me off this place, least of all a carpetbagger like Boston."

The chair legs scraped the floor as Benteen shoved away from the table and walked with restive energy to the cast-iron stove, refilling his cup with coffee from the metal pot.

"How much longer can you last?" he demanded. "Another bad winter, a dry summer, and you'll be finished. Boston won't even have to lift a finger. Time's gonna do it for him." It was so obvious, even a blind man should be able to see it.

"The fight ain't over till the shootin' stops."

"What then?" he challenged with thinned lips. "What happens when it's over and you've lost?"

"I'm not leavin' here." Seth Calder held firm to his convictions. "I built this ranch for Madelaine and me. I'll be here when she comes back."

Bitterness splintered through Benteen. "She'll never come back," he snapped. "Not

47

today. Not tomorrow. Not next year. You're lying to yourself if you think she will. If she's not dead, then she's probably somebody's whore."

Seth came to his feet, anger burning in his face, the cigar gripped between his fingers. "I won't have you talking like that about your mother!"

Benteen closed his mouth on all the things he would have liked to say. They were wasted on his father, who wouldn't allow a bad word spoken against her. There was a silent battle of wills that ended when Benteen backed off and looked away.

"I'll be spendin' the winter in the brush making myself a herd from the wild stock. A couple of boys from the Ten Bar are going to help," Benteen announced flatly. "Come spring, I'm going to marry Lorna and move north with the cattle."

It was a statement of his decision, not a request for his father's approval or his blessing. He'd already asked him to come along once, and Benteen wasn't about to repeat himself. His father had to do what he thought was right — just as he did.

In the dining room of the Ten Bar ranch house, Judd Boston held a private court with

48

his foreman, a narrow, spare-fleshed man named Loman Janes. Loman had the huge hands of a man good with a rope and the weathered toughness to his pocked complexion that spoke of his hours in the sun. His light gray eyes were flat with resentment at the rebuking tone of the man who possessed his unswerving loyalty.

"I'm telling you" — Judd's voice had a hard edge to it — "there has to be a reason for Calder to suddenly suspect something after all this time. Someone let it slip about those brands. One of your so-called hand-picked men, probably while he was likkered up."

"No." Loman Janes stood gaunt and tall in the middle of the room, his pride unbending. "They know better than to breathe a word if they want to keep their tongues. He was only guessing when he said that to you."

Judd Boston didn't like that answer. All his plans had been flowing along smoothly until Chase Benteen Calder had muddied the waters with his suspicions.

"I had the feeling the old man had gotten wise to what was going on when he bunched his herd close in to the ranch." His mind went back over the recent events before he turned the force of his hard eyes on his foreman. "He waited until Benteen came back before showing his hand. Now you say Shorty Niles and Trumbo are drawing their pay to go to work for Calder."

"They claim he's putting a herd together to take north," Loman explained stiffly. "As many trail drives as he's made, he's probably got his eye on makin' a big profit with a herd of his own."

"And if he makes a bundle, what will he do with it?" The question was asked aloud, but Boston wasn't interested in Loman's opinion. He didn't trust any man's judgment but his own. "Dump it into the Cee Bar," he concluded grimly.

"Trumbo was spreadin' talk about Calder stakin' claim to some land in the Montana Territory," the foreman inserted.

"Talk." He showed his contempt for cowboy gossip. "There's nothing up there but Sioux and Cheyenne. It's only been two years since they wiped out Custer and his men. He's just trying to throw us off the track." That's what Boston would have done in his place, so he could believe nothing else.

"They're talkin' about free grass up there." Loman knew cattle and cattlemen — and the magic of that phrase.

"And they've got grass right here — and water and cattle," Boston retorted. "I've waited ten years to get my hands on that water on Calder's ranch. With it, I'll have the whole area sewed up."

He had directed a lot of behind-the-scenes maneuvering to get Seth Calder in his present desperate situation. Judd Boston had coveted the Cee Bar land since he'd arrived, but he had soon learned that no amount of gold could buy it. Long ago, he had learned to bend with the wind or run with it. He knew when to push and when to bide his time. Patient and inscrutable, he had waited. The Cee Bar was on the verge of collapse. This was the time to push.

"I want you to find out where Benteen is now, how many men he has with him, and what he's doing," he ordered.

"And the old man?" Loman asked.

"He hasn't got much of an operation left." A cold, humorless smile lifted the corners of his heavy mouth. "Soon he's not going to have any."

Loman knew better than to ask what his boss planned. He was in awe of Boston's intelligence and respected the ruthless determination in the man. There was a perverted sense of pride in being associated with the kind of power Boston held. Loman Janes was content to be the brawn to Boston's brains. He knew Boston needed someone as closemouthed

51

and merciless as he was to carry out his plans. In Loman's mind, they were a team. Boston gave the orders and he took them, but they were dependent on one another. The more powerful Boston became, the more powerful Loman became by association.

4

There were no trails in the brush country of Texas. There wasn't any room for trails. The brush grew in a dense thicket, defying the passage of man or beast and choking to death the prairie grass that had once covered these millions of acres of Texas land.

It was downright unfriendly country, with every plant baring its forbidding set of clawlike thorns and needle-sharp spines. Among the scrubby mesquite trees dominating the land-scape grow the palo verde, its green-black thorns more visible than its leaves, and mounds of prickly-pear cactus. There's the cat-claw that the Mexicans call "wait-a-minute," a much more descriptive term, as anyone snared by its thorns would testify.

No one claimed that God had a hand in making this black chaparral. It was said He gave the land to the devil as his playground.

The short-tempered and sharp-tusked javelinas called it home, as did the rattlesnakes. No horse and rider ever rode the thickets without the constant company of a rattler whirring its warning. There wouldn't have been any reason to venture into the brush if the cunning and wild Longhorn cattle hadn't hidden themselves in it.

The hardy Longhorn wasn't much to look at; flat-sided, narrow-hipped, with a swayed back and big drooping ears, it was a caricature of a cow. The long, sweeping set of horns that gave the breed its name would normally span four feet but they were rarely straight. One tip might point down and the other up. They drooped, twisted, and spiraled in unusual convolutions. The Longhorn came in all colors: washed-out earth colors, dull brindles and blues, duns and browns, and drab clay-reds — solid, speckled, or spotted.

Slow to develop, a Longhorn didn't reach its maximum weight of eight hundred to a thousand pounds until it was eight years old or better. But the tall, bony beast could travel for miles, fight off wolves, bears, and panthers, endure the droughts and blizzards, and adapt to the wildest land and roughest climates.

So cowboys penetrated the thorny ramparts of these boundless thickets in search of maverick cattle that belonged to anyone who was man enough to catch them and drive them out. Cowboys fought the vicious brush country, cursed it, and acquired a healthy respect for it.

With Shorty Niles riding beside him, Benteen walked his line-backed dun horse into a sparse section of the chaparral. It was late afternoon, time for one last sashay through the area before they lost the light. Two days before, they'd spotted a couple of cows with yearling calves in this vicinity, but they hadn't been able to put a rope on them. Benteen wanted to make another try for them.

Winter was the best time to search these thickets. The sharp-edged leaves had fallen, enabling a rider to see farther. The weather was cooler, so horses could run longer without becoming wind-broken, and there was less chance of cattle dying from overheating.

Cow hunting in the brush country required clothes and equipment that offered the most resistance to the thorny vegetation. The leather chaps protecting Benteen's legs were smooth and snug, without any ornamentation that could be snagged by a prickly branch. *Tapaderos* hooded the stirrups of his saddle to prevent a limb from poking through to gouge his boot or prod his foot from the stirrup. His jacket fit snugly around his shoulders, ribs, and waist, leaving no loose folds to be snared by the spiked brush, and his hat was low-crowned.

Benteen wore leather gloves to protect his

hands from the skinning thorns, but Shorty didn't, claiming they choked him. His hands, littered with painful scratches and scars, paid the price.

Being a small man, Shorty always figured he had a lot to prove. He was ready to risk life and limb at the blink of an eye. There were some who wondered how he managed to reach the age of seventeen and still be alive. His short, stocky build had the iron muscles of an older man, and the experience of countless frays was etched in his broad-featured face. Shorty was always the first to volunteer and the last to quit. He was a fiesty friend, but Benteen wouldn't have wanted him for an enemy.

Neither man spoke as they slowly walked their horses through the brush. Talking required effort, and energy was saved for the chase. They rode past a coma bush with dirk-like thorns. Its winter blossoms of small white flowers scented the air with a cloying fragrance; even that couldn't cover up the stench of the four-foot-long rattlesnake lying in their path, trampled to death two days before. It was a sickening but familiar smell to any man who frequented the thickets, emitted by angry rattlers in their death throes.

The line-backed dun hesitated in its stride and stopped. Benteen was immediately alert to the signals of his brush-wise mount. The dun's nose and pricked ears pointed toward a solid wall of mesquite. As the horse trembled eagerly beneath him, Benteen spotted the almost camouflaged roan cow, and the twisted horns of a second. The animals remained motionless, hunkered down in the brush, until they were certain they'd been seen.

Beside him, Shorty let out a Texas yell, a piercing sound that crossed a Comanche war whoop with a rebel yell. With the nerves released, both riders spurred their horses at the hidden Longhorns. Nature bred the Longhorns with the agility of a deer, enabling them to bound to their feet in one leap and be in a dead run by the next.

There didn't seem to be any opening in the thicket, but where a cow could go, a horse could follow. It was up to the riders to stay on board the best way they knew how.

Benteen took after the roan cow while Shorty split away after the second Longhorn. They hit the brush at a run and tore a hole through it — a hole that seemed to close up the instant they were through. Branches popped and snapped; thorny limbs raked his leather leggings and tore at his clothes. To avoid being scraped off his horse, Benteen was all over the saddle, dodging and ducking, flattening himself along the dun's neck, then stretching along the opposite side. He used his arms, his legs, his hands, his shoulders, his whole body, to shield his head from the thorny branches trying to gouge out his eyes. Benteen didn't dare close them or he'd lose control and not see the next limb. Like the tawny horse he rode, Benteen was oblivious of everything but the curved horns of the roan cow racing through the brush ahead of them.

It was a brutal, hair-raising race to catch up with the red roan. In this dense growth, there wasn't room for long ropes and wide loops. As the dun gelding closed in on the wild cow, Benteen waited until he had a small opening in the brush the size of a saddle blanket. With a short rope, he reached over and cast his loop up to circle the cow's head, taking advantage of the sparse plant growth close to the ground.

The dun horse bunched and gathered itself to absorb the yank when the cow hit the end of the rope. When the loop tightened around its neck to pull it up short, it let out a bellow of fear and anger. Plunging and fighting at the restraint, the roan cow hooked its horn at the rope, but didn't charge the rider, as some of her breed did.

After an initially lengthy struggle, the cow turned out to be one of the more amenable ones, and grudgingly obeyed the pull of the rope, permitting Benteen to lead her from the thicket. Sometimes the wild cattle had to be left tied to a tree for a few days until they were tender-headed enough to lead. In extreme cases, the eyelids of outlaw cattle were sewed shut so they would blindly follow another animal to avoid treacherous branches.

With the reluctant cow in tow, Benteen turned the dun gelding in the direction of the main camp, where they penned their catch. He didn't wait for Shorty. The young cowboy was on his own. It wasn't uncommon for brush riders not to make it back to camp before night fell, in which case they bedded down wherever they happened to be.

Shorty caught up with him, though, about a mile before Benteen reached camp. Both horse and rider bore the marks of pursuit. There was a gash on the right wither of the bay horse where a horn had slashed through its hide. Like Benteen's mount, the horse's legs were scratched and studded with dislodged thorns. Shorty was sporting a long cut on his cheek, the blood from it starting to dry and cake.

"I had to leave mine back there necked to a tree," he told him, grinning widely. "I'll go get her in a couple of days."

Benteen nodded and glanced at the broken

pieces of branches sticking out of the fork of Shorty's saddle. "You've got enough wood there to start a small fire."

"Reckon I do." Shorty laughed, and began pulling it out.

By the time they reached camp, the yellow light of dusk was filtering over the brushland. Jessie Trumbo already had a cook fire going. Steaks from a steer they'd butchered the day before were frying in a skillet. The coffee had already boiled, and the pot was sitting near the warming edge of the coals. When he saw Benteen leading in the maverick cow, Jessie stuck a branding iron in the fire.

In front of a mesquite-pole pen, Shorty roped the hind legs of the animal. With Benteen at the head and Shorty stretching out the tail, they put the cow on the ground, flankside-up. The glowing iron was curved in the shape of a C. Jessie stamped it three times onto the cow's hide, burning through the hair into the hide just deep enough to leave a permanent scar that read Triple C.

In Jessie's absence, another cowboy named Ely Stanton took over the cooking chores. In a cow camp, everyone pitched in to do whatever tasks needed to be done, without complaint. Counting Benteen, there were five riders working out of the camp. Four more, Andy Young and Woolie Willis and two others, were holding a herd of twelve hundred captured cattle on the prairie. There was a sizable bunch in the pen, enough to be driven out to the herd.

After the cow was branded, Benteen turned it loose in the pen and unsaddled the dun gelding. Before turning it out with the cavvy, he extracted the thorns from its legs and treated cuts that needed attention.

Night was thickening the sky when he finally joined the other riders at the campfire. Bruised and battered from the day's work, he paused wearily to pour a cup of pitch-black coffee, then settled cross-legged on the ground. After three grueling months, it was almost over. He had a good-sized herd of mixed cattle carrying his brand. With the eleven hundred dollars he'd managed to accumulate these last three years from a combination of trail-boss wages and money from the sale of maverick cattle that he'd roped, branded, and driven north with the Ten Bar herds, he'd have enough to buy a remuda, a couple of wagons, and trail supplies. At Dodge City he could sell off some of the prime steers and get enough money to pay the drovers' wages and have a good chunk left to carry him through the first lean years — if he was lucky.

His glance swept the faces of the other men

around the fire. "Anybody seen Spanish today?"

The half-breed Mexican cowboy had been absent for three nights, but Spanish had practically been reared in the brush. He knew all its secrets. Of all the riders, Benteen was least concerned by the prolonged absence of Spanish Bill, but he took note of it.

"Nope." Ely stabbed a knife into the steak sizzling in the skillet's tallow and turned the meat over.

"I cut his sign this morning," Jessie said. "But it was two days old."

"Where'd you cross his trail?"

"Over by that draw of white brush."

"I'll ride over that way tomorrow." Benteen drank down a swallow of the scalding coffee, strong enough to stiffen his spine and bitter enough to waken his senses.

Something rustled in the brush, attracting all eyes. The firelight flickered, throwing grotesque shadows through the thicket. Before any of them had time to reach for a weapon, a man called out in an accented voice, "It's I, Spanish."

A lanky form separated itself from the shadows and approached the campfire on foot, lugging the bulky shape of his saddle. When Spanish Bill entered the circle of light, his dirty and ripped clothes told a lot of his story. His limping walk said a bit more.

"Where's your horse?" Shorty asked. No one mentioned the fact that Spanish had been absent for three days. His reception wasn't any different than if they'd seen him that morning.

"Back there." Spanish indicated the brush with a nod of his head and set his saddle on a barren piece of ground. Dragging his left foot, he limped to the fire and poured himself a cup of coffee. "I thought I would have to spend another night in the bush, until I smelled those steaks."

"They're just about burnt." Ely indicated the meat was nearly done.

Spanish limped back to his saddle and lowered himself to the ground stretching his injured left leg in front of him and leaning against his saddle.

"I swung my loop on a *ladino*," Spanish said. He used the Mexican word, which has no true equivalent in the American language. "Outlaw" comes closest to describing a wild cow that will fight to the death for its freedom. "When the rope started to tighten around its neck, he switched ends like a cutting horse. That *ladino* had a horn spread five feet across, maybe six. He charged my horse and hooked a horn into its breast, twisting and pushing. I never had time to throw away the rope. The horse died right underneath me. It was a good horse." He shook his head briefly. "But the *ladino*, he takes off with my rope."

Horses were more easily replaced than good rope.

"Was it a big ole red devil?" Jessie asked.

"*Sí*." Spanish nodded.

"I tangled with him a week back. That animal isn't about to be taken. Don't waste your time tryin'. You're better off shootin' him."

No one disagreed.

Supper consisted of steaks and beans, sopped up with cornbread made out of meal, tallow, water, and a little salt. No one pretended it was delicious. It was food that stuck to the ribs and that was the important thing.

After they'd eaten, each man scrubbed his own plate clean with sand. Water was too valuable in this country to waste as dishwater. There was still some coffee left in the pot. Benteen poured some of the thick black liquid into his tin cup and sat on the ground in the shadowed fringe of the firelight. When he took the pouch of Bull Durham tobacco from his pocket, he noticed it was nearly empty.

"Hey, Benteen." Shorty broke the weary silence that had settled over the camp. "Are you going to invite us to your wedding?"

"I was thinking about asking all of you to come along with us on our honeymoon," he replied while his fingers tapered off the rolled cigarette.

"You serious?" Stretched out on the ground with his saddle for a pillow, Shorty lifted his head to frown narrowly at Benteen.

"Sure I'm serious." He leaned forward to take a burning limb from the fire and hold the glowing end to his cigarette. "Lorna and me could use some help trailin' that herd up to the Montana Territory."

"Are you takin' her on the cattle drive?" Jessie Trumbo sounded incredulous.

"I'm not going to marry her and leave her behind," Benteen replied. "The offer stands. Any of you wantin' a job taking these cattle north are welcome to sign on."

"You can count me in." Shorty was the first to speak up.

"I got nothin' keepin' me in Texas," Jessie included himself.

"Spanish?" Benteen glanced at the Mexican. He wanted his experience on the drive.

"I go with the cattle," he agreed, and grinned when he added a quick qualification, " – as long as you get the herd there before it gets cold. My blood is too thin for such weather."

The Mexican's dislike of the cold was well-known and greatly exaggerated. It brought a lazy curve to Benteen's mouth as he turned to the last man in the group. Ely Stanton was always the quiet one, the last to speak up, slow to decide anything until he'd thought it through. He was also the only married man present. He'd tried his hand at almost everything – from farming to storekeeping – but he wasn't happy off a horse.

"What about you, Ely?" asked Benteen.

"I don't think the idea would sit well with Mary," he answered slowly, with reference to his wife. "She's got relatives in Ioway. She's wantin' us to go there and see if I can't find me a place with some good rich dirt."

"Aw, Ely, you ain't gonna walk behind a plow and look at the back end of a horse all day when you could be ridin' one, are you?" Shorty declared with a cowboy's derision of a farmer.

"I been thinkin' about it." There was a stiffness in the man as he poked at the campfire's coals.

"If you decide to pull up stakes for Iowa, you might consider throwin' in with the herd as far as Dodge City," Benteen suggested. "Lorna might like the idea of havin' another woman along for part of the journey."

"I'll let you know about that," Ely said.

The cattle milled in the pen, horns rattling together. The men around the campfire were immediately alert, expecting trouble, but the disturbance was only a minor shifting of positions. Within minutes the bunch had settled down and all was quiet.

"You been away an awful long time, Benteen," remarked Shorty. "How do you know yore gal'll be waitin' there to marry you? Maybe she changed her mind an' run off with somebody else."

Unwittingly he touched a sore spot. Benteen had never forgotten his mother's defection.

"Lorna isn't that kind," he snapped.

"Hey, I didn't mean nothin' by it," Shorty protested. "You been in the brush too long. You're as prickly as a cactus."

Benteen took the last drag on his cigarette and tossed out the butt into the dying fire. "We'll be headin' out of here in the next couple of days. Soon as we got that last penful, we'll join up with Willie and the main herd and head for Fort Worth.

Within a week, the cattle were thrown together and pointed toward Fort Worth. The first few days of the drive were critical, getting the herd trail-broken. The cows' natural instinct was to return to the brush country that had been their home. The drovers were kept busy turning them back and keeping them moving in the right direction.

Some trail bosses believed in pampering the animals, taking it slow the first few days. Benteen elected to push his mixed herd of cows, steers, and bulls – young to old – so they'd be tired when they were bedded down for the night and less inclined to become restless and stampede. Those first days, they averaged better than fifteen miles a day.

Luck seemed to be on Benteen's side. The herd was only a few miles from Fort Worth and there hadn't been a single stampede. Herds had been known to get into the habit of stampeding on a daily basis. But if stampedes could be avoided the first ten days, a herd was normally easy to handle on the remainder of the drive.

Benteen was riding with Spanish Bill on the left point. A long-legged brindle steer had assumed leadership of the herd, striding out in front of the others.

A bareback rider on a big horse crested a rise in the prairie ahead of the herd. Benteen sat straighter in the saddle, ready to curse the slim rider if he spooked the herd. The big chestnut horse was reined in the instant the rider saw the herd strung out before him. Benteen relaxed a little when the horse and rider made a big sweeping arc to approach from the side.

Without appearing to do so, Benteen kept a close eye on the young rider as he approached. The chestnut had a lot of draft horse blood in it to give it that size, and the lanky kid on its back looked as though he had ridden straight off the farm.

It seemed there were more farmers showing up each year, plowing up the range grass and fencing in land. That was all the more reason to be leaving Texas, as far as Benteen was concerned. He'd heard about that new barbed wire, and he didn't like the sound of it.

"Can you tell me where I can find Mr. Calder?" the boy asked as he rode up. His voice had made the transition to manhood but the body hadn't grown into itself yet. He reminded Benteen of a gangly colt, all arms and legs, with a skinny body.

"You're looking at him." He slowed his horse, letting Spanish continue on without him while the boy came alongside.

The big horse was plow-reined into a walk, giving Benteen a better look at its rider. Hatless, the tall, lanky boy had a mop of dark brown hair, cropped close to his neck. He tried to appear older than he was, but Benteen guessed his age was somewhere in the vicinity of fifteen.

"I heard you had a herd to take north this year." The boy studied the animals walking by with what was supposedly a critical eye. "Look like they've been travelin' good."

"Yeah." Benteen had been away too often to know who the boy's family was, but there were a lot of new farmers moving into the area.

"It occurred to me that ya might be needin' some more drovers." The remark was delivered with only a mild expression of interest, but the eager glance he sent Benteen ruined his cool pose.

"Could be," Benteen admitted. "What's your name?"

"Joe. Joe Dollarhide," he said quickly. "I been raised with animals all my life. I know everything about 'em. I'm a hard worker. You can ask anybody. An' I learn fast, too."

"Your folks have a farm around here?" Benteen let his hands rest on the saddle horn and swayed loosely in rhythm with his walking horse.

"Yes, sir." It was a reluctant admission.

"And you wanta be a cowboy?" he guessed.

"I'll make a good one," the boy named Joe Dollarhide insisted firmly. "I already know about cows and horses. I can ride. And I'm a good shot. I been huntin' since I was seven."

"Seems to me your pa could probably use a strong boy like you at home." Most of the time Benteen kept his attention on the herd, only occasionally letting his glance stray to the kid.

"I got six brothers and sisters at home. They're most all old enough to help." First, he assured Benteen that he wasn't needed at home, " 'Sides, it's time I was strikin' out on my own an' makin' my way in this world."

"How old are you?" Benteen had already made his guess, but he was curious what the boy's answer would be.

"Seventeen," he said quickly.

Amusement lurked in Benteen's dark eyes, but he didn't confront the boy with his doubt. He used a more subtle tactic. "I remember the first time I got a job workin' somebody's else's cattle. 'Course, I was only fifteen," he declared, then looked straight at Joe Dollarhide. "It was really somethin', gettin' paid to do work that my pa had been havin' me do for free," he drawled. "How old did you say you were?"

The boy bit at his lower lip, then admitted, "I'll be sixteen in April."

"That's old enough to draw a man's wages, don't you think?" Benteen asked with a half-smile.

"Yes, sir." The boy grinned, then tried to contain his excitement to be sure he understood. "Does that mean you'll hire me?"

Benteen didn't say yes or no. "We're gonna be holdin' this herd outside of Fort Worth for about a week while I get supplies and take care of a few personal matters. I'll be needin' some extra help to spell the boys. They'll have to be dependable."

"You can depend on me. I can do whatever needs to be done," the boy promised eagerly.

"It wouldn't be easy," Benteen cautioned.

"Work's never easy. I can handle anything, though," Joe Dollarhide boasted.

"Have you got a saddle?" His pointed glance drew attention to the chestnut's bare back.

"No," he admitted on a grimly reluctant note, then asserted, "But I'm gonna buy me one when I draw my first pay."

"I think you're gonna need something in the meantime," Benteen murmured dryly. "It's kinda hard holdin' on to the end of a rope when there's an eight-hundred-pound steer on the other end who doesn't want to be there."

"I'll manage," the youngster insisted, determined not to lose his chance at the job.

It was a fool's brag, but Benteen let it slide by without comment. "I'll give you a try for a few days. If you work out, I'll sign you on for the rest of the drive. Does that sound fair, Joe Dollarhide?"

"You bet!" he exclaimed. "You won't be sorry. I promise."

"If you stay on, I'll pay you thirty dollars a month and found. But you can't cowboy without a saddle. Until you get your own, I better see if we can't find a spare one for you to use." There was an old one in the barn, if Benteen remembered right. It was the worse for wear, but better than nothing.

"I'll pay for the use of it," Joe Dollarhide insisted proudly.

"Ride on home and get your possibles together. I'll expect you right after daybreak tomorrow morning," Benteen stated. "If I'm not here, report to Jessie Trumbo. He'll tell you what to do."

Joe Dollarhide pushed his hand to Benteen to shake on the agreement. "I sure do want to thank you for considerin' hirin' me to go north with the herd. I'll do good for you. It's time I was seein' somethin' more of this world 'sides Texas."

A smile pulled at the corners of Benteen's mouth as he shook hands with the boy. That thirst for excitement and adventure ran hot in the young. Despite Joe Dollarhide's inexperience, there was something about the boy he liked.

Dollarhide started to turn the draft horse's

head and ride off, then seemed to remember something and kept the animal parallel with Benteen.

"I meant to say that I was right sorry to hear about your pa, Mr. Calder." There was a stiffness to his words as he tried to show proper respect.

Benteen's eyes narrowed to become hard and probing. "My pa? What do you mean?" He had a way of looking at a man that made him wish he was somewhere else, just as the boy was wishing now.

"Just that . . . him fallin' over dead was so sudden-like and all." The movement of the boy's shoulders was an uncomfortable gesture.

Benteen showed nothing in his face, but the blood inside him ran quick and cold. A heaviness pushed on his chest until he couldn't breathe.

Dimly he heard Dollarhide say, "I'll be here at daybreak."

The nod of his head was automatic, and the kid dug his heels into the broad sides of the big chestnut horse and rode away. For several more minutes Benteen struggled with the icy unreality of the news. There was a mix-up. The kid hadn't meant his father. Everything in him fought against accepting it.

The uncertainty was intolerable. He wheeled

his horse around and cantered it back along the herd to where Jessie Trumbo was riding flank. Reining his mount in, Benteen kept the tension on the bit and the horse skittered along in a dancing walk.

"I'm riding to the Cee Bar," he informed Jessie without explanation. "You're in charge till I get back."

"Sure." Jessie eyed him with sharp curiosity. Trouble was always riding nearby in this land. His instinct sensed its closeness now. He'd seen that look in Benteen's face a few times before, and it never meant anything good.

A twist of the reins and the goad of a dull work spur sent Benteen's horse bounding into a gallop, veering away from the herd. Benteen kept the mustang at a run, driven by a sense of urgency. When the ranch buildings came into sight, a tightness wound inside him like a clock spring.

His horse was snorting and blowing hard as Benteen pulled it down into a slower gait and approached the house at a cantering trot. A bad feeling ran along his spine. It didn't get better when Benteen spotted the roan horse in the corral. A Ten Bar brand was burned in its hip.

He started to ride over to the corral for a closer look, when the front door opened and a man stepped onto the porch, a rifle held at the ready. Benteen swung his horse around to face the man.

"You're trespassing on private property, Benteen." The man's voice rang out harsh and clear.

"Since when is this Ten Bar land?" Benteen challenged. He thought he knew most of Boston's riders, but this bearded man was a stranger.

"Since Mr. Boston said it was." The rifle was shifted to turn its black muzzle on Benteen. "I got orders to shoot trespassers if they won't move on."

"More of Boston's orders?" There was nothing reasonable in Benteen. He was all cold and reckless inside as he walked his horse straight at the rifle barrel. "You know who I am — and you knew I was coming."

"I was told to expect you, Calder." The man with the rifle didn't waver. "This ranch belongs to the Ten Bar now. Mr. Boston felt you might need some convincin' of that."

"And how did he convince my pa?" Benteen demanded, flicking a cold glance at the rifle. "With that, too?"

"Can't say." There was a small negative move of the man's head, but he didn't take his eyes off Benteen for even a fraction of a second. "No more talk. I ain't paid to talk. Ride out, Calder."

Benteen felt a hard, raw desire to charge the man and ram that rifle barrel down his throat. He never took kindly to a gun pointed at him. He liked it even less now.

But it would have been a stupid move. He stopped the mustang. It grated hard on his pride to turn his horse away and ride out of the yard. But there were too many questions unanswered. Benteen swung his horse onto the road to Fort Worth.

5

Benteen's herd wasn't the only one being held outside of Fort Worth that early spring. The cattle town was crowded with rowdy cowboys and trail outfits stocking up with supplies for the drive north when Benteen rode in.

There was a leaden anger inside him as he slowed the mustang to a stop in front of the Pearce house. Dismounting, he tied the reins in a half-hitch on the post ring and walked to the front porch. His footsteps sounded heavy as he crossed the board floor and knocked twice on the door. When it opened, Benteen let his hard gaze search Lorna's face.

After an instant of startled recognition, she went white. "You know," she whispered.

"Pa's dead." His voice was flat as he read the confirmation in her expression.

Lorna nodded once, her lips parting, but no words came out. Benteen lowered his gaze to the door's threshold, physically numbed to the fact. He clenched his hands into fists, trying to accept the truth of the words he'd said, but protest raged inside him.

"When?" The one-word question rumbled from a deep pit within himself.

"The first week of January."

Benteen shut his eyes briefly, barely conscious of the rustle of her long skirt. He stiffened at the touch of her hand on his arm, the quiet offer of sympathy. Briskly he moved to reject it.

"Come inside," she invited.

He brushed past her to walk inside, burning with a raw kind of energy. There was a noise from the dining room. Benteen turned and saw Lorna's mother. She took one look at him and didn't have to be told a thing.

"Come into the kitchen, Benteen, and have some coffee," she invited calmly, as if this visit from him were no different from any other.

It seemed automatic to follow her into the scrubbed freshness of the kitchen. His blank gaze watched her pour a cup from the metal pot on the wood range. She set it on the table.

"I don't imagine you've eaten anything, have you?" Mrs. Pearce guessed.

His hand lifted in a vacant gesture that said food wasn't important. "What happened?" Benteen continued to stand, making no move to sit in the white enameled chair at the table or drink the coffee.

Behind him, he heard Lorna's footsteps as

she entered the kitchen. His mind wasn't able to think about her, perhaps because his heart was incapable of feelings at this moment. He had to keep them shut out.

"The doctor said it was his heart," Mrs. Pearce replied with a somber attention to the fact without embellishment. "By the time the doctor arrived, it was already too late to help him."

"Where was he when it happened?" Benteen questioned.

"He had come to town for supplies – to my husband's store," she answered, being more specific.

"Was your husband with him when he died?" He jumped on the information. Instinct told him that Judd Boston had played a role in his father's death, and Benteen was determined to find out how significant it had been.

"Well, not exactly." Mrs. Pearce displayed patience in the face of his sharp cross-examination. "Your father had given my husband a list of the items he wanted. Arthur thought your father didn't look well, so he suggested that your father use his office in the back room where he could sit and rest while the order was being filled."

"Then he was alone?"

"Yes." She nodded. "He'd taken a cigar and

80

told my husband to include it on his bill. Arthur said your father was in the back room only a few minutes when he heard a loud noise — like something had fallen. When he went back to see what had happened, your father was lying on the floor by his desk. Arthur immediately sent someone for the doctor, but of course it was too late."

"Did he say anything about Judd Boston?" There was a cold cynicism in the question.

Clara Pearce showed a trace of unease at the question. "It wasn't until later that we learned Mr. Boston's bank had instructed the sheriff to serve a foreclosure notice on your father's ranch . . . for nonpayment of notes that were due."

"And Pa didn't mention anything about it to your husband?" The ridgeline of his jaw stood out sharply.

"I . . ." She hesitated, then reluctantly said, "I believe my husband did make a comment about the amount of ammunition your father wanted. He jokingly asked if he intended to start a war. Your father smiled and said only a small one."

Turning his face from her, Benteen swore savagely under his breath. He'd known the day was coming when his father's situation would come to a head, but this wasn't the way he had expected it to end.

"Please sit down and drink your coffee, Benteen," Mrs. Pearce urged. "It's getting cold. You're probably hungry, too. Let me fix you something to eat."

"No." Impatience thinned the hard line of his mouth. He was irritated with her female belief that food could solve things and provide solace to something that was inconsolable.

An inner rage made him leave the kitchen and the feminine attempts to comfort him. He didn't want a soothing hand to ease the hot grief burning away his numbness. A seed of anger was growing inside him, and he wanted to feel it. Again he walked past Lorna as if she wasn't there, and kept going until he reached the parlor.

Lorna had expected Benteen to be upset, but not like this. She would have been shocked if he had cried, yet she thought he would show more emotion than that cold anger. Instead he'd built a wall around himself that shut her out. It hurt to think he didn't want her, and that's the impression he was giving. They were to be married. She was to be his wife. It was her duty to be at his side during times like these, to try to ease his pain.

"What's wrong, Mother?" Her bewildered

voice was quietly pitched. "He looks right through me and he was rude to you."

"Do you remember the puppy you had when you were little?" The understanding that came from experience and maturity was in her mother's gentle expression. "It was kicked by a horse, and when you tried to help it, the puppy was in so much pain that it bit you. The puppy didn't mean to hurt you but it didn't know what it was doing."

"Are you trying to say that Benteen is like a wounded animal?" Lorna was taken aback by the suggestion.

"I'm trying to say that his pain runs very deep," her mother explained. "Men seem to think they have to hide such feelings — that we'll think less of them if we see they can be vulnerable, too. Benteen doesn't want to admit it, but he needs you, Lorna." She silently encouraged her daughter to go to him.

Lorna hesitated and finally accepted the risk of being rebuffed again. She didn't have her mother's insight into a man's thinking, but it was something her mother had probably obtained after years of living with her father.

When she entered the parlor, she saw Benteen standing next to the boxes of personal belongings that she and her mother had taken from his ranch. Judd Boston had given them permission to remove the personal articles from the house. They had kept them here for Benteen's return.

Lorna was struck by how old Benteen appeared. His sun-browned features looked haggard and drawn, showing an age that came from brutal experience rather than the accummulation of years. Even when the dirt and dust from the trail were washed away, it would still be there.

Lorna felt dreadfully innocent and naive. How foolish she had been to think she knew the words that would comfort him, when Benteen had seen so much more than she had. What did she know about death and hardship? It had all happened on the periphery of her life.

His dusty, low-crowned hat was held at his side. The tight hold of his gloved fingers was curling the stained brim. He reached down to pick up the framed daguerreotype lying on top of the folded clothes and various other articles that had belonged to his father. Lorna crossed the room to stand slightly behind him. Her tenderly compassionate gaze wandered over the jacket, stretched tautly across the wide set of his shoulders. The air was almost electrified with his tension.

"We tried to find you when your father

died," she told him, and was cut by his hard glance. "Mr. Boston sent out a couple of his men, but they weren't able to locate you."

"I don't imagine he tried too hard." Benteen's voice was stiffly dry as he continued to stare at the tintype.

"Daddy said it would be hard to find anybody in that rough country," Lorna murmured, and glanced at the picture of the woman in the frame, barely visible from her angle. "That's your mother, isn't it?" Lorna remembered one of his neighbors mentioning it. So many had come to the funeral and offered their sympathy that she didn't recall which one. "She was very beautiful."

"Yes." It was a clipped answer.

In an effort to understand what Benteen was feeling, Lorna tried to put herself in his place, imagining what it would have been like to be raised without a mother, then losing the one parent that remained. She had been so loved by both her mother and father that she couldn't imagine a life without them.

"Your mother died when you were very young, didn't she?" she commented, in the hope he might talk about his mother and eventually release some of the grief for his father bottled inside him.

When Benteen swiveled to look at her, Lorna

was shocked at the bitter hate in his dark eyes. "She isn't dead." His mouth curled over the words like a snarling animal. "She ran off with another man and left us."

"I didn't know." Lorna recoiled a little from this frightening side of him, so utterly ruthless and unforgiving.

That look was finally directed at the daguerreotype. "Pa kept waiting for her to come back, but she never did." The pitch of his voice was absolutely flat, containing no emotion. "He never heard from her once in all these years, but he waited anyway." There was a slight tremble in the gloved hand holding the picture. It was in his low voice, too, when Benteen spoke again – a tremble of anger. "He doesn't have to wait anymore."

A small fire was burning in the fireplace to take the nip out of the springtime air. With a sudden turn, Benteen hurled the daguerreotype and carved wood frame into the fireplace. Glass splintered and broke as it crashed against the andirons holding the smoldering embers of a burning log. Lorna flinched in shock, and recovered immediately to grab for the iron poker and rescue the picture before it caught fire.

The instant Benteen recognized her intention, his hard fingers circled her wrist in a painful grip. "Let it burn, Lorna."

"No." Her eyes were smarting with tears, not understanding him at all. For the first time in her life, she defied male authority. "I'm not going to let you burn your mother's picture, regardless of what she did."

"It's a picture of *my* mother," he snapped. "I'll say what happens to it."

"No, you won't." She switched the poker to her other hand and raked the wooden frame away from the tiny flames licking at it. "It's a picture of the grandmother of *our* children. We're going to keep it."

Lorna was trembling at the anger boiling around her. Any second she expected Benteen to strike her, the feeling of imminent violence was so intense. Her hand was shaking badly, but she continued her frantic effort to save the picture.

His grip had nearly cut off the circulation in her fingers when he suddenly let go of her wrist. "She deserves to burn in hell!" He rasped the condemnation. "Keep it if you want, but I don't want to ever see it again!"

Her knees gave out as his long strides carried him away from the fireplace. Lorna knelt weakly on the hearth, the daguerreotype saved. The front door banged shut behind him as he strode out of the house.

"What happened?"

Lorna glanced over her shoulder. Her mother was poised just inside the parlor, concern in her expression. Unaware of changing loyalties within her, Lorna didn't answer the question. The angry and bitter feelings Benteen had revealed to her were something private that shouldn't be told, not even to her mother.

Laying the poker aside, she turned back to the smoldering fire and gingerly picked the heated wooden frame out of the gray ashes. Part of the frame was charred on the edges, and a corner of the daguerreotype was scorched a yellow-brown. The dark-eyed blond woman in the picture smiled back at Lorna, unscathed by the flame. Lorna blew away the fine dusting of ash and stood up, no longer weak.

"Would you put this in my little chest?" She handed the framed picture to her mother without answering her question. "I'm going to keep it for Benteen."

"Yes, I'll put it away for you." She frowned at the burn marks, her questioning glance sweeping Lorna's face. A sadness drifted across her expression as Clara Pearce noticed the new trace of maturity in her daughter's eyes. She was growing up — and growing away. There was only that one glimpse before Lorna turned away to pick up her heavy shawl from the sofa arm.

"I'm going after Benteen," she said, and walked to the door.

As Lorna came out of the house, she saw Benteen at the hitching post, untying his horse's reins. She pulled the wool shawl more snugly around her shoulders and hurried down the steps to the picket gate.

Except for one glance when she reached the gate, Benteen took no notice of her. She knew he'd mount and ride away if she didn't stop him. With the freshness of his father's death on his mind, she didn't want them to part on a quarreling note.

"Would you help me hitch Dandy to the buggy, Benteen?" she asked to break the silence between them. "I'd like to go with you to the cemetery and show you where we buried your father."

When he finally looked at her, there wasn't any trace of the anger he had directed at her earlier. Lorna breathed easier. But his expression remained hardened, shutting in his feelings so they couldn't be observed.

"Yes." He agreed to harness the bay gelding for her.

Leading his horse, Benteen walked around the picket fence enclosing the front yard of the house and headed for the rear of the dwelling, where a small shed housed the Pearces' buggy and a horse stall. Lorna followed, cutting through the yard.

A silence flowed between them. While it wasn't an easy one, it wasn't uncomfortable either. Lorna watched quietly as Benteen tied the buggy horse in its stall and began buckling on the harness. Activity seemed to provide a release for some of his simmering tension. There was less suppressed violence in his movements as they became smoother, more natural.

With the harness in place, Benteen backed the gelding between the buggy shafts and hooked the traces. He turned to help Lorna into the spring seat, treating her with a measure of aloofness. She made room for him on the seat, hoping he would ride with her, but he passed her the buggy reins and mounted his horse.

Benteen rode alongside the buggy, escorting her along the town's rough streets to the small cemetery. Dismounting, he tied his horse to the back of the buggy and came forward to lift her to the ground.

"His grave is under that big oak," she pointed. "I hope that is all right."

"Yes." His tight-lipped reply revealed nothing.

There was an instant when Lorna thought

Benteen was going to reject her silent wish to accompany him to the grave site. Then his arm curved behind her, his gloved hand flattening itself near the base of her spine. Together they walked along the well-trodden path through the cemetery, past wooden markers and headstones, to the large oak tree dominating the area.

Winter had stripped the leaves from the tree, exposing its symmetrical skeleton of spreading branches and limbs. There was only a hint of green buds. A breeze whispered through the scattered piles of fallen leaves, a lonely sound made poignant by the simple wooden cross standing at the head of the elongated mound of earth. Its dark shape stood out sharply against the mixture of winter-brown grass and new green sprouts pushing up around it.

When they reached the grave, his guiding hand fell away from her. Out of the corner of her eye, Lorna saw him take off his hat and hold it in front of him with both hands. The breeze ruffled the ends of his dark hair as he stared at the cross. The lettering read simply: "Seth Calder. RIP."

"We didn't know your father's birthdate," she explained quietly. "We thought you could add whatever you liked to the marker when you came back."

"That's fine."

"A large number of your father's friends and neighbors came to the funeral." Lorna thought he'd like to know that.

"I'm glad he never lived to see Boston take possession of his land." A muscle flexed in his jaw.

"Mr. Boston felt very badly about the position his bank was forced to take." Lorna wasn't sure why she felt the need to defend the banker's action.

His glance pierced her. "Did Boston come to the funeral?"

"No, but he came by our house that evening to offer his condolences," she explained. "Mr. Boston was upset by the possibility that the foreclosure proceedings precipitated your father's death."

"I'll bet he was upset." His voice was dry with sarcasm.

A frown gathered in her expression. "You surely don't blame him for what happened? I'm sure it was a decision that was forced on him. And I know how much it bothers my father when he has to refuse a longtime customer credit because of a past-due account." Lorna glanced away, vaguely irritated by his attitude. "I'm sure he waited as long as he could."

"Are you?" Benteen murmured.

"Yes, and I don't see why you're acting like

this," she admitted finally. "He and your father were neighbors, and you worked for him several years. I'm sure he found himself in a very awkward position, as a banker."

"Boston has wanted the Cee Bar's graze and water for years. He's been slowly squeezing my father out all this time. Now he's got what he wanted all along. The Cee Bar is his." Benteen pushed his hat onto his head, pulling it down low in front and back. "I've known he wanted it for years, so did Pa. Boston is only pretending to be upset so he'll look good in the town's eyes. Don't believe him."

Taking her by the elbow, Benteen turned her away from the grave and started back toward the buggy. He sounded so certain about the banker's motives that Lorna wondered if she hadn't been too ready to believe the best. She was used to trusting people.

"Have you been to the ranch since you got back?" She tried to watch him and where she was walking at the same time.

"Yes." His faint smile had an unpleasant look to it. "Judd Boston had a reception committee waiting for me."

"He did?" She was confused by his choice of words.

"A man and a rifle were there to make sure I didn't trespass for long," Benteen explained.

When they reached the buggy, he paused to glance back at the graveyard. "The last reason I had for staying in Texas is buried there. It's the last time a Calder is going to be put in Texas dirt."

There was something morbid about his vow, and it frightened Lorna. This was a side of him that she didn't know or understand. She wound her arms around him and hugged him close, pressing her check against his jacket to hide her face. "Don't talk like that, Benteen," she murmured. Now she was the one who needed to be comforted.

His hands took a firm hold of her upper arms to force her away from his chest. Lorna kept her hands around his middle and her gaze lowered. His hands moved to her neck and into her long hair at the sides, forcing her head up.

"How soon can the wedding be arranged?" he asked with a quiet urgency. "I want us to leave as soon as I've got the supplies and horses we'll be needing for the drive."

They had waited so long that Lorna didn't understand why it all had to be rushed now. She had tried to think about leaving the secure world she'd always known. The leather gloves were rough against the delicate skin of her cheeks.

"Why are you so anxious to go?" she whispered.

94

"You are the only good thing I've ever found in Texas," Benteen murmured. Just for a minute, the mask slipped to reveal the pain and bitterness in his expression.

Then his dark eyes seemed to absorb her whole into his system. She was only half-conscious of being slowly pulled into his arms. He lowered his mouth to her lips and took them with a rough force. She curled her arms around his lean waist, warmed by his enveloping body heat.

Benteen could feel the pulsing life in the soft female form pressed against him. Surrounded by all this death, he needed the renewal her body offered. He fed on her lips, eating them with a hunger that forced them apart. His hard tongue probed the space he'd created.

Lorna stiffened at its invasion. The sensation was new, and vaguely thrilling. She relaxed a little, sensing that it gave him pleasure, that it filled a need he had at this moment. Ultimately, that was her objective in the embrace.

There was an instinctive reciprocation of the intimacy. With it came a gradual change in her desires, into something more self-centered. There was less giving and more taking as inner needs began to dictate her wants. As her mouth mated with his, she was beginning to feel hot all over, burning with a fire she didn't know how to extinguish.

The hardness of his leanly muscled body was beginning to assert its pressure on her, trapping her against the unyielding boards of the buggy. The long skirt of her dress was whipped around his legs by the wind. There was an insistence about the thrusting angle of his hips that she didn't understand. His hands were under her shawl, pressing her spine to arch more completely against him. Lorna was on tiptoe, straining to achieve the closeness he was demanding, and feeling a raw frustration when she failed.

His arms relaxed their hold. She was momentarily confused, not wanting the embrace to end. A hand slid along the side of her rib cage. She pushed against its touch, thinking Benteen was going to force her out of his arms. Instead, his hand moved to cover her breast, taking full possession of its ripe fullness, straining against the material of her dress.

An inferno of emotions seemed to erupt inside her. For a split second she yielded to them, until she recognized the sinful lust that was possessing her. She tried to pull free of his arms, but there was no place to go. The buggy was behind her, pushing her into his male wall.

There didn't seem to be any strength in her

fingers when she tried to push his hand away from her breast. She was breathing hard, as if she'd run some great distance. Her cheeks were scarlet with shame at her loose behavior. Lifting her head, Lorna searched his face in alarm, afraid he would be shocked that she had practically invited him to treat her like this — like one of those soiled doves she'd seen around the saloons. But the ache she saw in his eyes almost made her wish she hadn't stopped him.

Benteen took a half-step back so the lower half of his body no longer pinned her against the buggy. His gaze dropped to the hand on her breast, and he slowly brought it down.

"I shouldn't have let you do that," Lorna whispered anxiously. "I don't know what got into me. You're probably thinking —"

"— that I want to bury myself in you," Benteen finished the sentence for her, the sexual significance of his remark lost on her innocence. He seemed to realize it, as one side of his mouth became twisted in a rueful smile. "We'd better get married damned soon, because I need you, Lorna."

"I need you too," she murmured, but she was speaking emotionally.

"The things you do to me, woman." The cryptic phrase was accompanied by a slight shake of his head. "I'll be a solid stone by our wedding night."

A shudder trembled through her at the greater intimacies that night would bring, and her possible reactions. The shawl had fallen down around her arms. Benteen reached to gently pull it up around her shoulders.

"It's getting cool. We'd better get you home before you catch a chill."

"Will you have dinner with us tonight?" she asked, not wanting him to leave her now that he had returned.

"I need to go back and check on the herd," he refused gently, then promised, "I'll be in town tomorrow. I'll see you then."

He assisted her into the buggy. This time, he climbed onto the seat beside her, taking the reins and driving the horse to the Pearce house.

6

On a trail drive the cook was second in importance only to the trail boss. Most of the drovers considered him to be more important, especially if he knew how to cook. Besides fixing the meals and keeping a pot of hot, strong coffee going all the time, he doctored men and horses, was entrusted with personal belongings and money, pulled teeth on occasion, and trimmed hair. The cook could make life pleasant on the drive or turn it into sheer hell.

There was only one man Benteen wanted — a cantakerous old sea dog who claimed to have been the personal cook of an admiral. His name had long been forgotten, probably even by him, ever since a cowboy had claimed that his coffee tasted "rusty." "Rusty" emptied the pot on the cowboy's head. No one ever made the mistake of claiming his coffee was rusty again, but the name stuck.

Rusty had been cook on two of the outfits Benteen had bossed. He allowed himself to be persuaded to accept Benteen's offer to trail with him a third time. He claimed that it wasn't that he liked working for Benteen so much as it was a desire to see the Montana Territory, blaming the wanderlust in his soul.

Together Rusty and Benteen picked out the chuck wagon, since it would be Rusty's domain for the next few months. The man who sold it gave Benteen the name of a man who had a covered wagon for sale. He slipped the piece of paper in his pocket and walked over to Pearce's Emporium with Rusty.

After he had introduced Rusty to Arthur Pearce, he explained to Lorna's father, "Rusty is the cook for my outfit. He'll tell you what provisions he needs. I'll be back later to pay for them."

The quickest way to get on the wrong foot with Rusty was to tell him how many pounds of sugar, bacon, and assorted items he'd need. So Benteen gave Rusty the authority to purchase what he felt he needed.

"Lorna asked me to tell you, if I saw you today, that she wanted to talk to you," her father passed along the message.

"A man named Davies has a wagon for sale. I'm going to see him first, then I'll ride over to the house to see Lorna," Benteen agreed.

"She won't be home this afternoon," Arthur Pearce quickly corrected that impression. "She and my wife are going to the milliner's shop this afternoon to pick up her wedding veil. Then they were stopping by the church to speak with the minister."

Amusement lightened Benteen's eyes. "What am I supposed to do? Run all over town trying to catch up with her?" He shook his head at the vagaries of the female sex.

"I'm just passing on the message." Arthur Pearce smiled in understanding.

Leaving the store, Benteen first went in search of the man who had the wagon for sale. There seemed to be a never-ending number of things to buy. His pockets kept getting lighter.

The wagon was needed to carry the items for their new home in Montana as well as personal possessions. Also it would afford Lorna some privacy and the luxury of a bed. He didn't expect her to rough it like the rest of them.

After the wagon, Benteen still needed to buy another twenty head or so of horses. He wasn't comfortable with less than eighty horses in the remuda. Yates was wrangling for him and claimed to have found a fair-looking group to finish out the string. More money spent, not to mention the wages to the boys on the cowhunt. When he had started putting his plans in motion, eleven hundred dollars had looked like an ample amount of money to fund the drive. Now Benteen wished he'd taken the extra time last spring to catch another twenty head of wild cattle to throw in with the Ten Bar herd he'd trailed to Wyoming for Boston, instead of settling for just thirty steers of his own. He'd have two or three hundred dollars more to play with now.

It was a good thing he planned to sell some of the steers from the herd when they reached Dodge City, provided the beef prices were respectable. He'd need the money to pay off the drovers when they reached Montana Territory. He wondered briefly about Barnie and how the winter had been. The knowledge Barnie gained with one Montana winter behind him would be invaluable, come the next.

Benteen weaved his way across the street, dodging horse-drawn wagons and galloping riders. The dust constantly swirled about him, kicked up by hooves and wheels. The livery stable was just ahead. Benteen could see it through the haze of mixing dust and people.

The clang of a blacksmith's hammer banging a horseshoe into shape added to the din of the streets. As Benteen neared the stable, he saw the gimpy-legged man holding a bald-faced roan for the shoer. He angled toward the blacksmith's lean-to.

"Hey, Stoney," he greeted the man.

"Hey, Benteen," Stoney raised a hand to

him. "Sad thing about your pa. Heard yore gonna be pullin' out soon."

"Three days." That was his plan.

"Right after the weddin', huh?" Stoney grinned, a ribald twinkle lighting his eyes. "Think you'll be in condition to fork a horse?"

Benteen smiled and let the comment pass without reply. "I heard a man named Davies had a wagon for sale."

"Yep." Stoney nodded and yanked on the horse's head when it started to fuss at the smithy's approach. "Another one of them farmers," he said, and spit into the dust. "They're getting thick up north. Heard they was fencin' in the water."

"Is that a fact?" He filed the information away, part of the storehouse of knowledge about trail conditions. Trail drives went from one watering hole to the next. "What about the wagon?"

"It's over behind the barn," Stoney replied, gesturing toward the stable with his head. "Davies left it here. He's hopin' to sell it to get seed money. I told him he should pack his things and move on. They're a stubborn bunch, those farmers."

"What kind of condition is it in?" Benteen was going to look for himself, but it never hurt to ask.

"Hell, it's like new. He brought it from Kansas. Swears he'll never go back." Stoney chuckled. "Can't blame him."

"I'm gonna take a look at the wagon," Benteen stated.

"It'll go cheap. Like I said, the fool needs money for seed."

Benteen could use a bargain. Crossing to the corral, he started to hop the rail and cut through to the rear of the stable. He thought he heard someone call his name, but there was so much racket in the streets it was hard to be sure. He glanced around.

"Hey! Calder!" A wagon rattled toward the stables, a man and woman perched on its seat.

Benteen stepped back on the hard-packed ground as he recognized Ely Stanton. Ely whoaed the pair of horses to a stop in front of the stable and set the brake.

"Howdy, Ely," Benteen greeted the man and touched his hat, nodding respectfully to the woman sitting beside him.

"I was just coming into town to look for you." Ely was smiling, a rare occurrence in Benteen's memory. "This is my wife, Mary. I don't think you've met her. This is Mr. Calder, honey."

"I'm pleased to meet you, Mrs. Stanton," Benteen responded to the introduction.

"It's an honor, Mr. Calder," she replied. She was a plain-looking woman, strong with a no-nonsense air about her. She was the kind who could wind up henpeckin' a man if he wasn't careful. But there was a solidness about her, too, that Benteen liked. "Mr. Stanton has told me a great deal about you. If only half of it was true, you must be quite a man."

Ely sent her an impatient look to shush up, but Benteen chuckled at the bluntness of the woman — after all, he wasn't married to her. Mary Stanton wasn't about to be intimidated by a man's superiority.

"Ely has mentioned you several times, too," Benteen replied, and the woman looked a little uneasy, as if her outspoken nature was a trait that her husband found objectionable, but she concealed her feelings well.

"I came to tell you that I have decided to take you up on the offer for Mary and me to travel with you on the drive," Ely stated, putting a little bit of emphasis on his role in the decision-making process, asserting his position as head of the house.

"But only as far as Dodge City," Mary inserted. "From there, we're going to Iowa, where I have relatives."

"Ely mentioned that before," Benteen assured her, but suspected Ely wasn't in favor of that journey. Benteen hated to see a man with Ely's cow sense turn to dirt farming, but it wasn't his life.

"I just wanted to be sure you understood." But her reply was directed more to her husband than to Benteen.

"I do." He pretended to be unaware of the interchange between husband and wife. "We're planning to pull out in three days. You and your wife are welcome to join up with the herd whenever you get loaded up."

"We'll be there the day after tomorrow," Ely stated, and his wife didn't dispute it.

"Benteen!"

He recognized Lorna's voice and pivoted. A smile broke over his features when he saw her wave to him from the middle of the street where she waited with her mother for a buckboard to pass. He had a tantalizing glimpse of a well-turned ankle as she lifted her skirts to hurry a few steps out of the way of another horse-drawn vehicle. There was a silent groan inside him at the thought of waiting two more days before she belonged to him, and there would be no more "glimpses" of things.

"Hello." For all her ladylike demeanor, there was a vivid sparkle in her brown eyes. "We stopped by the store on our way to the millinery shop. Daddy said you were coming over here."

"I came to see about a wagon to haul all of your 'precious cargo,' " he said mockingly, referring to all the embroidered linens and household articles she had accumulated for their new home.

"It had better be a big one." Lorna smiled.

He tucked a hand under her elbow and turned her to face the Stanton wagon. "Lorna, I'd like you to meet Ely Stanton and his wife, Mary. They'll be traveling with us part of the way." Then he reversed the introductions. "This is my fiancée, Lorna Pearce, and her mother, Mrs. Clara Pearce."

Benteen was too busy watching Lorna to notice how subdued Mary Stanton was during the exchange of greetings.

"You didn't mention there would be another couple traveling with you and Lorna," Clara Pearce remarked, pleased by the turn of events.

"The decision was recent," he admitted. "But I thought Lorna might like the company of another woman for part of the journey. When Ely mentioned his plans, I asked them to travel with us."

"I'm glad you did." The idea that she'd have another woman to talk to made Lorna feel just that much easier about this trip they were undertaking.

Her mother shared that relief for a different

reason. Although she was confident Benteen would look out for Lorna, she had been worried about her daughter being the only woman in a campful of men — drinking, carousing cowboys. She'd heard about their wild sprees on a town, the bloody fights, the shooting, and the womanizing. A lady wasn't safe on the streets of Fort Worth at night — some streets at least. Her husband had insisted there was no cause for concern, but Clara hadn't been so sure. Now, with another respectable woman along, Lorna wouldn't be alone.

Lorna turned to smile at the woman on the wagon seat. "I'm going to look forward to us getting acquainted." She paused an instant and asked, "May I call you Mary?"

"Please do," Mary Stanton murmured, and measured her with a veiled look, taking note of the white skin, always protected from the damaging rays of the sun, and the white gloves that covered smooth hands.

Having been raised one of a brood of farmer's children, Mary Stanton knew all about hard work and hard living. She was a good, God-fearing woman. She bowed her head to no man, but there were members of her own sex that made her feel self-conscious about her lack of education and refined manners. Lorna Pearce was one of those. So her feelings toward the young woman were ambivalent. On the one hand, Mary pitied the girl's innocence of the hardships ahead of her, and on the other, she envied her ladylike airs, cultured speech, and unblemished looks. Which explained the silence of her tongue. She didn't want Lorna to discover she wasn't her equal.

"Your father said you needed to speak to me this afternoon." Benteen reminded Lorna of the message he'd received.

"Yes. Reverend Matthews wants to meet with us tomorrow morning at the church." The demure curve of her lips seemed somehow provocative. "I think he intends to lecture us on the sanctity of marriage and our respective duties."

"Is it necessary?" Benteen breathed heavily, irritated because there were so many other things essential to their departure that needed to be done.

"Chase Benteen Calder, you are going to be there," she stated. "The reverend is half-convinced that I'm marrying a heathen. If you don't come tomorrow, he's liable to refuse to perform the marriage ceremony."

"Good." His smile mocked hers. "Then I'll just carry you off and he'll have to marry us to make an honest woman out of you."

A faint blush heightened the color in her

cheeks. "That isn't amusing," Lorna protested, but there was a sparkle of humor in her eyes.

"I'd let him 'save' me in the process," Benteen assured her, and felt the rush of heat through his veins when she laughed in spite of her attempt to appear so proper and devout. God, how he wanted her.

"I'll meet you at the church tomorrow morning at ten o'clock," Lorna replied, and laid her gloved hand on his arm, an acceptable display of public affection. "Mother and I have to go. There's still a thousand and one things that have to be done before the wedding." She politely included the couple on the wagon in her farewell. "It was a pleasure meeting both of you. And I look forward to seeing you again, Mary."

It was getting harder to let Lorna leave his side. Benteen struggled with the longings that burned inside as he watched her walk away with her mother. The need to possess her totally — to bind her to his side — was gaining strength with each passing minute that brought the hour of their marriage closer.

"Your lady is a very lovely girl," Ely Stanton remarked, also watching Lorna with respectful admiration. He didn't notice the hurt that flickered in his wife's expression at his choice of words and the attention he was exhibiting to another woman.

Benteen pulled himself together and dragged his gaze away from Lorna's figure and the tantalizing sway of her long skirt. He took pride in Stanton's compliment of Lorna.

"Yes, she's very beautiful," he agreed.

"But will she be when the sun and the wind get through with her?" Mary Stanton challenged briskly. "Forgive me, Mr. Calder, but I don't think you have considered how difficult it's going to be for someone with your bride's background. She's used to . . . soft things."

"Lorna is strong. She can take it." Benteen stiffened at her questioning his judgment and Lorna's character.

"Mary didn't mean anything by it," Ely apologized for his wife and elbowed her to keep quiet. She closed her mouth tightly, irritated with men, who thought they were the only ones who knew anything.

"I understand, Ely," Benteen murmured with a cool look. The man had his hands full keeping his wife in line, so he left it to Ely to straighten her out. Benteen wasn't sure if he liked the idea of Lorna spending very much time with Mary Stanton. It might turn out to be a mistake. "I've got to go look at that wagon. See ya in a couple of days," Benteen said, and took his leave of the couple to inspect the wagon behind the livery stable.

In the millinery shop, Lorna stood in front of the mirror, turning her head this way and that to admire the lace veil and its cluster of white beads to conceal the combs securing it to her hair. She loved the contrast of the white lace on the sable brown of her hair. It made her feel absolutely stunning. She couldn't resist preening a little, even if it was being vain.

"Sue Ellen, isn't it just too beautiful for words," she murmured excitedly to her friend. "I know I should take it off before something happens to it, but ..." She breathed in, expressing her reluctance with a negative shake of her head.

"Just imagine what it's going to look like with your wedding gown." Sue Ellen couldn't help being a little envious of Lorna's natural beauty. While she, herself, wasn't exactly homely, she lacked the vividness of Lorna's personality. She always felt drab in comparison.

"I can hardly wait until Benteen sees me in my wedding outfit," Lorna declared with a quick turn to her friend. "Just think, Sue Ellen. In a couple more days, I'll be Mrs. Chase Benteen Calder."

"Aren't you ... getting a little nervous?" Every time she thought about marrying a man like Benteen, Sue Ellen felt little shivers of alarm. He was so male. He wouldn't have been her choice at all. She would have picked someone quieter, more reserved. It was almost scandalous the way Benteen looked at Lorna sometimes. "I mean . . . about the wedding night . . . and all."

Lorna glanced away to avoid meeting her friend's curiously intent look. A quick warmth burned her cheeks. "Yes . . . a little," she admitted.

It was something she tried not to think about because it seemed improper to let her imagination dwell on it too much, as it tended to do. Nothing she had seen or learned in her young life had taught her to regard passion as a virtue. It was practically the complete opposite. To even let her thoughts stray in that direction was considered shocking.

"Do you suppose . . . I mean, I've heard . . . it's very painful for a woman." Sue Ellen lowered her voice and glanced apprehensively toward the back room, where her mother and Mrs. Pearce were having tea. "It . . . sounds degrading to let a man do . . . those things to your body, doesn't it?"

"Maybe it won't be so bad." Lorna felt hot and trembly all over, embarrassed yet excited in a frightened kind of way.

"I guess you eventually get used to it," Sue Ellen offered as consolation. "I've even heard that you can get to where you can pretend it isn't happening. You can think about something else instead, and block it out altogether."

"Really," Lorna murmured, and tried to laugh away her uncomfortable feeling. It came out forced. "I guess I'll be finding out for myself soon enough."

"Oh, Lorna." Sue Ellen's chin quivered when she gazed sad-eyed at her friend. "I wish you weren't going away. I don't want you to leave."

"Don't start crying, Sue Ellen, or I will," Lorna warned.

"But you're going so far away," her friend protested. "Maybe we'll never see each other again."

"Yes, we will," she insisted with a determined tilt of her chin. "And we'll write each other — regularly."

"If I were you, I'd be scared of living way up there in that Indian country." Sue Ellen shook her head, silently marveling at Lorna's courage."

"Benteen will be with me," Lorna asserted.

"But he'll be away sometimes, looking after the cattle. What if the Indians come while you're alone? They might capture you and take you prisoner." Her alarm grew in proportion to her expanding imagination. "I've heard stories about what those savages do to white women. They take turns with her, making her commit all sorts of vile, unspeakable acts."

"Sue Ellen, stop it," Lorna demanded, struggling with her own growing fears.

"I'm sorry." Her friend was immediately contrite. "It's just that I get so worried when I think about you all alone — with no doctors for hundreds of miles probably." She realized that she was doing it again. "I won't say anything more. I promise."

Lorna hoped she meant it. She already had enough misgivings about leaving her home, her parents, her friends, and the only kind of life she'd ever known.

The shop bell above the door signaled the entrance of three customers. Lorna's glance was absently drawn to the sound, and immediately she recognized the heavily rouged women and their bright-colored gowns. Her reaction was an instant withdrawal of obvious interest. A respectable female didn't acknowledge the presence of "scarlet ladies of the night." They dressed to draw attention to themselves — "attract business" was the way they put it. Lorna was aware they frequented the millinery store for the latest creations in outrageous hats and bonnets. In the past, Sue Ellen had whispered many of the conversations she'd overheard, censoring the foul language and guessing at the definition of terms neither she nor Lorna had ever heard before.

"I'd better go get Mother," Sue Ellen whispered, too reticent to wait on them herself. "You can come in the back room, if you want, and wait until they're gone."

"No, I'll be fine." Lorna turned back to the mirror and lifted touching fingers on the lace veil.

She was slightly amused by her friend. Sue Ellen acted as if she would be contaminated by the presence of the three sporting ladies in the same room with her. Although Lorna didn't admit it, she was a tiny bit curious about these women who were shunned by respectable members of the community. As long as she ignored them, she saw nothing wrong with remaining where she was.

Reflected in the mirror, she saw a henna-haired woman waylay Sue Ellen before she could escape into the back room. "Excuse me, miss. I've stopped to see if the hat I ordered has arrived yet." Her voice had a cultured sound to it.

Sue Ellen turned red all the way to the roots of her hair. "I'll get my mother." She backed hurriedly away from the woman.

Lorna heard the titter of laughter from the other two when Sue Ellen disappeared in a red-faced panic. "Lordie, Pearl," one declared. "You embarrassed the lady. I'll bet her knockers turned red."

"She was embarrassed by her own imagination," retorted the henna-haired woman named Pearl.

Just for a second Lorna wondered if that was true. Sometimes Sue Ellen seemed very preoccupied with the intimacies between a man and a woman. She didn't have to dwell on the thought, distracted by a glimpse of a black-haired prostitute who had wandered over to look at some hats displayed near Lorna.

"Pearl. Jenny. Come look at this," she called to the other two.

With all three gathering near her, Lorna concentrated on her reflection in the mirror. She didn't want to appear to be taking any notice of them.

But the red-haired Pearl didn't find it necessary to ignore Lorna. "That is a beautiful veil," she declared, and came over for a closer look.

"Thank you." Lorna's response was coolly polite and nothing more.

"You must be getting married," Pearl guessed as she was joined by her two compatriots.

"Yes, I am," Lorna admitted, and caught a hint of envy in the woman's look. She experienced a small twinge of compassion because no decent man would ever marry women of their profession.

"You'll make a lovely bride," she declared, and turned to her friends. "Won't she, girls?"

"Indeed," agreed the black-haired girl.

The third, named Jenny, didn't look any older than Lorna, even with the rouge and painted mouth. "Who's the lucky man? Maybe we know him," she suggested with an arching smile.

Lorna almost didn't tell them, but she changed her mind. "Benteen Calder." Part of her said she shouldn't be talking to these women at all.

"Benteen Calder," the black-haired girl repeated with a quick glance at Pearl. "I think I have seen him around.

Lorna stiffened, but the red-haired Pearl quickly explained the blurted comment. "Don't worry about it, honey. Dixie just means that she's seen him in one of the saloons, having a beer. Girls like us don't forget when we meet men like Benteen Calder."

It sounded like a compliment. Despite Pearl's assurance that she had no cause for concern, Lorna couldn't help wondering if they didn't *know* Benteen better than she did.

"Let me give you some advice, honey," Pearl said with a melancholy smile. "If you don't want your man slippin' away to see our kind on the sly, you'd better be wilder in bed than he is."

Such talk first drained the color from her face, then sent it flooding back. Lorna wanted to shut her ears, but she couldn't. Somewhere she lost her voice, too.

"I've learned a lot about men over the years." The woman made it sound like a long time, yet she didn't look any older than her mid-twenties. "They may want a lady on their arm, but they want a whore in bed. I know that shocks you, but, honey, there's a helluva lot of truth in what I'm sayin'. If wives took that advice, we wouldn't have so many married men for customers."

"Miss Rogers!" The shocked voice of Liza Mae Brown, Sue Ellen's mother, brought a quick end to the conversation. What was worse, Lorna realized the shopkeeper as well as her mother had overheard the last bit of Pearl Rogers' advice.

But the bold woman wasn't intimidated by the outraged look. "Don't waste your breath lecturing to me, Mrs. Brown." She turned away from Lorna, completely unabashed. "I wasn't corrupting the child. In fact, I might have saved her a lot of heartache in the future." Her attitude became strictly business. "What about the hat I ordered?"

"It hasn't arrived as yet," Mrs. Brown began.

"Then we'll come back in a few days," Pearl replied, and with her two companions, made a dignified exit from the shop.

"Sue Ellen, why did you leave Lorna here by herself?" Mrs. Brown rebuked her daughter, and quickly apologized to Mrs. Pearce. "I am sorry this happened, Clara. I feel dreadful that Lorna was exposed to such indecent talk. I probably shouldn't even allow those women in my shop, but unfortunately I can't afford to refuse their business."

"It wasn't your fault, Liza." Her mother magnanimously removed all blame from the woman. "I know my daughter well enough to be reassured that she wouldn't pay any attention to what was said. They were only trying to justify their loose morals by putting the blame on respectable women."

"How true," Mrs. Brown agreed fully.

"Let's put the veil away, Lorna." Her mother came over to help her remove it. "We still have to go by the church."

The conversation was skillfully turned to other subjects. Lorna thought the matter was going to be dropped, but her mother brought it up again after they had left the shop.

"I know you have never had any contact before with that element of our society," she began. "Perhaps it's just as well that this happened. Instead of always turning a blind eye, we should take a stand against that element and convince the town fathers they must be abolished. It will be a problem wherever you may live, so it's best that you see it now."

"Yes, Mother." But Lorna's mind was still lingering on that shocking advice she'd been given. "What kind of . . . men seek their company? It wouldn't be someone like . . . Daddy or Benteen?"

"Of course not." The answer was quick, followed by an attempted qualification. "That isn't to say that men don't sometimes sow wild oats before they settle down with a wife and a family. And there could be circumstances that would prompt a man to seek out that kind of woman to supply his needs."

"What kind of circumstances?" Lorna asked.

"If a wife isn't capable of occupying the marriage bed, because of illness or" – her mother hesitated – "when it wouldn't be wise for her to become in the family way. A man has to understand that there comes a time when a woman might not want any more children."

"Then you and Daddy . . ." Lorna didn't finish the thought. It seemed too much an invasion into her parents' private relationship.

"That's right," her mother admitted. "And your father understands it's the only way a woman can prevent such things."

"And he doesn't mind?" She wondered about that in the light of what the prostitute had told her.

"No."

"Does it bother you that you don't have the closeness anymore?" Lorna chose her words carefully, not wanting to be offensive.

"Naturally not," her mother replied with a quick smile of assurance. "After all, its purpose is the conception of children, not for the sake of itself."

"Yes, I know," she murmured.

"Don't let it be a source of concern," her mother advised. "You'll come to know all this yourself. One day, you'll be telling your daughter the same things."

"Yes, one day," Lorna agreed with a faint smile, but she was still troubled by some of the sensations she felt in Benteen's arms. It was becoming apparent that wasn't normal, especially when the only one who indicated it was, was herself a fallen woman.

7

The wagon turned out to be in better condition than Benteen had hoped to find it. He struck a deal with the farmer named Davies and hitched a team of horses to it. Late that afternoon, he drove it to the Pearce home so Lorna could load her possessions in it. She knew nothing about packing it to evenly distribute the weight through the box, so he stayed to help.

There were so many nonessential things she wanted to take. Benteen disliked the role of forcing her to choose, but it had to be done.

"What's this?" He frowned when he picked up two thorny twigs partially wrapped in damp cloths.

"I'm not going to believe you if you claim those are too heavy and bulky to take," she retorted, placing her hands on her hips to silently dare him.

"But what are they?" Benteen asked.

"They're cuttings from my mother's rose-bush," Lorna explained. "I want to plant them beside our new home."

"Lorna, they'll die." He tried to be patient.

"You're just wasting your time to take them."

"You wouldn't let me bring my grandmother's chiffonier or the oak table my uncle made for us," she reminded him. "I'm going to have something to remind me of home. Those rose cuttings are going with us. I don't care what you say, they will live."

Benteen sighed heavily. "Take them if you're so determined."

"I am."

"Where shall I put them?" he asked. "Under the seat?"

"Yes, I can get to them easily there," Lorna agreed.

He slipped them under the wagon's seat, where they would be in the shade and less likely to be crushed by shifting baggage in the canvas-covered wagon box.

"I hope that's all," Benteen said.

"All except a few things I'll have with me," she replied. "My wedding dress and such. And don't tell me I can't take that with me."

"I'm sorry. I know it seems that you're leaving a lot behind." Benteen smiled grimly. "But there's only so much the horses can pull."

"I know." She lowered her chin and turned away.

Benteen saw the shimmer of a tear in her eye

and caught her chin in his hand. "What's the tears for?"

"It's so easy for you to pack up and go," she murmured. "You're not leaving anyone behind."

"You can't be getting homesick," Benteen chided. "We haven't even left yet."

"Don't make a joke of it," Lorna protested.

Exercising control, he put an arm around her and brushed his mouth against her forehead. "I promise that you'll grow to love our new home in Montana as much as you do here."

"I know." She sniffed back the tears and moved out of his arms, because she didn't want Benteen to think she was being childish. She should be looking forward to their new life together, not crying about leaving home, but it wasn't easy. Partially turning so he couldn't see, Lorna furtively wiped away the dampness of her cheeks. "You won't forget to be at the church tomorrow morning at ten to talk to the reverend, will you?"

"I'll be there," Benteen stated. "I'm not going to let anyone throw a last-minute hitch in our wedding plans."

Just for a little second, Lorna wished it could be postponed for a short while — until she could get over these jitters. But she didn't mention it to Benteen. Several times she had sensed his impatience that the wedding wasn't going to take place sooner.

It was dark when Benteen reached the camp, located near where the herd was being held. The two night riders on the first watch were circling the herd, riding slowly in opposite directions. The cattle were lying down, chewing their cuds. Benteen could see the moonlight shining on their horns. Somewhere off in the prairie, a coyote howled its wailing cry. A steer blew out a soft snort, but it was a sound of contentment rather than alarm.

An ease went through Benteen as he listened to one of the night riders crooning "The Texas Lullaby" to the cattle. Its quavering melody drifted over both ends of the scale, keeping to the slow, steady rhythm set by the walking horse. Dismounting, Benteen unsaddled his horse and tied it to the picket line where the night horses for the next three watches were staked. Carrying the saddle on his hip, he walked to the flickering campfire.

The chuck wagon was set up for business, the rear board lowered and supported by a pole propped in the ground. It exposed the partitioned cupboard with shelves and drawers for food and utensils and provided a worktable for the cook. Benteen noticed the tongue of the wagon was pointed at the Big Dipper, as it always would be for the rest of the drive. Just one of the many duties that went with the cook's job. At every night camp, the tongue of the chuck wagon would point to the north, so no matter the weather the next day, the trail boss knew the direction to take.

The Big Dipper was the cowboy's compass and his clock. As it revolved, its positions told the cowboy what time it was and marked off his two-hour watches on night herd. On cloudy nights, he had to guess at the time unless he was riding a night horse that had its own clock in its head and would head for camp when its tour of duty was up.

Leaving his saddle in the shadows just beyond the firelight where he would bed down for the night, Benteen crossed to the chuck wagon for a tin cup to fill with coffee. His seemingly idle glance took note of which riders were present and which were not.

"Shorty's got first watch, does he?" he remarked to Rusty, and blew on the coffee he'd poured before he took a big sip. "I thought I recognized him singing to the cattle."

"Shorty and Hank," Rusty confirmed, and named the second rider on night herd.

"That Shorty sure as hell can sing," a drover named Jonesy declared, and paused in his whittling of a stick to listen.

"What would a sonuvabitch like you know about it?" challenged a mocking voice from the shadows. "I'll be goddamned if you could carry a tune in a crooked damned jug."

"Oh, yeah?" Jonesy bristled at the criticism of his singing voice or lack of one. "I sure as hell hope someone's taught you another damned verse of 'Sweet Betsy.' If you sing that same sonuvabitchin' one all this drive like ya did that last time, I'll fix it so you don't sing no more."

"I didn't get no damned complaint from any sonuvabitchin' cow," Zeke Taylor shot back.

A heat was building, and Benteen stepped in before tempers could flare. "Instead of arguing about your singing, both of you better start watchin' your language." He paused to let his hard glance make a sweep of the other riders at the camp circle. "That goes for all of you. When this drive gets under way, you're going to have ladies in the camp. There's some of you that can't say a single sentence if it doesn't have a 'hell,' a 'damn,' or a 'sonofabitch' included somewhere — and sometimes all three and one or two more. Save your cursing for the cattle. If you can't do that, maybe you'd better keep your mouths shut around the womenfolk."

"Hey, flapjaw, do you think you can manage

that?" Jonesy taunted the talkative drover, Zeke Taylor.

"I know a helluva lot more about how to talk to a lady than you do," he retorted.

"Pass the word to the others," Benteen ordered. Besides the riders on night herd, four of the drovers had been given permission to spend the night in Fort Worth, with the understanding they'd be back at first light in condition for work if it meant being tied in the saddle. "No cursing around the women unless you want to ride drag for a month."

The threatened punishment drew a grumble from the ranks, which Benteen ignored. On a cattle drive, three riders were usually assigned positions at the rear of the herd to prod the laggards and weaker steers into keeping up with the rest of the cattle. It was hot, dusty work, the least-wanted duty. In most cases, the drovers rotated the positions of drag, flank, and point so that each man fared equally.

Jessie Trumbo was leaning his slight frame against a rear wagon wheel by the chuck box. Benteen wandered over to a stand beside him and drank the strong coffee.

"Everything been quiet?" Benteen asked.

"Quiet as you can ask," Jessie replied. There was a lengthy pause as he straightened to bite off a chaw of a plug and fit the wad into the inside pocket of his cheek. "The Ten Bar's got a big herd together to drive north. They got 'em bedded down 'bout five miles from us. Bull Giles is bossin' it."

"You talk to him?" Benteen swirled the swallow of coffee in the tin cup to mix in the dregs.

Jessie gave a slow nod. "Bull just happened to ride over this way. Claimed we'd be eatin' his dust all the way to Kansas."

"S'pose it would upset him if it was the other way around," Benteen mused with a dry smile.

"Might." There was a gleam in Jessie's eyes.

Lorna's mother accompanied them to the church the next morning. While the wedding couple met with the reverend, she saw to some last-minute details regarding the decorations. Nothing was being spared to make her daughter's wedding, their only child, a special event. Clara Pearce filled all her time with preparations for the wedding so she wouldn't have time to think about the empty days that would follow when her daughter was far, far away.

It was successfully blocked from her mind when Lorna and Benteen had been instructed to the minister's satisfaction as to their respective roles in a Christian marriage. She walked to the rear of the church to rejoin them.

"Are you ready to leave, Mother?" Lorna asked. "Benteen has some errands he needs to do, but he wants to see us home first."

"I'm ready," she agreed, "but I need to stop at the store just for a moment and speak to your father." During trail time, Clara Pearce didn't like being on Forth Worth streets without a male escort, especially around the business section, where so many of the cowboys gathered. "It won't take long," she told Benteen.

"I can spare the time." Politeness and a sense of duty dictated that he take the time whether he could spare it or not. Women needed the protection of a man. That was an accepted fact.

Outside the church, Benteen assisted Lorna's mother into the rear seat of the buggy and helped Lorna into the front seat. Walking to the back, he stopped to tie his horse on behind, then climbed onto the seat with Lorna, taking up the gelding's reins.

The streets were crowded with cowboys and drovers, as they always were at trail time. Few of them failed to notice the young, attractive female in the seat next to Benteen. He was aware of the kind of comments that were made, but he didn't feel the need to defend her honor.

No harm was intended, and most remarks were made out of Lorna's hearing.

In front of Pearce's Emporium, he stopped the buggy and handed the reins to Lorna while he assisted her mother. "We'll wait here for you," he said.

"I won't be long," she promised again.

Benteen moved back to stand next to the buggy seat on the side where Lorna sat. "Tomorrow is the big day. Do you think your mother will be ready?"

"I hope so." Lorna permitted a small smile to show. "She's been running around like this for days. You'd think she was the one getting married, instead of me."

There was too much activity going on around him for Benteen to ignore it. Vigilance was an instinct born of experience. A man never completely relaxed his guard, so his eyes were always taking note of the faces and movements of those around him. He saw Judd Boston walking briskly down the sidewalk toward his bank before Boston saw him.

Despite his personal dislike of the man, Benteen admired Boston's iron nerve. There wasn't the slightest change in Boston's expression when he spied Benteen standing beside the buggy. A lesser man would have ignored him or gone out of his way to pretend not to

132

have seen him, but not Judd Boston. He brazenly altered his course to come over to speak to him.

"Good morning, Benteen. Miss Pearce." He politely tipped his bowler hat to Lorna.

"Boston." Benteen inclined his head briefly in the banker's direction in silent acknowledgment of the greeting, a coolness in his eyes.

"I haven't had an opportunity to offer you my sympathies for your father's death, although I'm sure you'll doubt my sincerity." Boston immediately confronted Benteen with his own thoughts.

"Since you already know that, I don't have to say anything." Benteen didn't pretend otherwise.

"I'm not surprised you feel that way," Boston said. "After you returned, I did expect you to come by the bank for an explanation of the circumstances leading up to your father's death."

"Why? It was obvious. You foreclosed, my father died, and you confiscated all his property and cattle."

"Perhaps I thought you would be more upset over that than you are," Boston suggested.

"It was inevitable. I saw that even if my father didn't," he replied. "The deck was stacked against him, but he refused to see it."

"I'm glad you are being sensible about this,

Benteen." He smiled, but it was the smug smile of a man who believed he was facing an inferior.

"No. I'm just smart enough to throw in my hand and ask for a new deck before I sit down again to play at the same table with a snake," Benteen countered.

It rankled Boston, but only briefly. "I understand you're driving a herd of your own north."

"That's right."

"That's quite a financial undertaking" — he paused to glance at Lorna — "especially when you have a new bride. I understand the wedding is tomorrow."

"Yes."

"It's a pity to leave such a beautiful bride so soon after the wedding," Boston murmured, turning his flattering attention to Lorna.

Benteen felt his hackles rise. "Lorna will be coming on the drive with me," he stated shortly. "We'll be making our new home in the Montana Territory."

"I heard rumors to that effect" — Boston eyed him with new interest — "but I didn't take them seriously. You are actually leaving Texas for good?"

"There's nothing left in Texas for me." Benteen thought of his father. Seth Calder would turn over in his grave if Judd Boston believed a Calder was running from a fight. It was a family pride that made him speak. "You haven't run me out, Boston. My decision was made before you moved against the Cee Bar. Understand that if our paths ever cross again. My father wouldn't stoop to your level of underhanded dealing, but I will fight dirty."

"Your hostility is unfounded, Benteen. I never had anything personal against you or your father," Boston insisted calmly.

"I believe that," Benteen replied. "He was just in the way of something you wanted. And I'm warning you to stay out of my way."

Boston laughed silently, as if it were preposterous to think there was any cause for Benteen's suspicions in the past or future. "I have an appointment to keep. You will excuse me." He formally took his leave from them and paused to add, "My best wishes to you both." The last was really directed at Lorna, a subtle attempt to remain in her good graces and cast doubt in her mind about Benteen's opinion of him.

A grim, inflexible line ridged his jaw as Benteen watched Judd Boston walk away with the slow, measured stride of a king inspecting his domain. The buggy springs creaked under Lorna's shifting weight. Benteen glanced sideways, reading the thinly veiled disapproval in her expression.

"You weren't very courteous, Benteen."

"His kind doesn't listen to courtesy." His reply was abrupt.

Lorna's mother came out of the store. Benteen moved forward to take a small parcel she was carrying and give her a hand into the buggy. Then he was in the seat beside Lorna, turning the bay gelding toward its home stable.

On his way home to the Ten Bar headquarters that evening, Judd Boston made a rare detour that took him out to the herd of beefs scheduled to take the trail north in two days. There was an additional mission he wanted his trail boss to carry out, after the cattle were delivered to the railhead at Dodge City.

One of the drovers spotted the buggy bouncing across the prairie with its escort of riders alongside and passed the word to Bull Giles that the boss was on his way. Bull Giles rode out to meet him. Bull came by his nickname honestly. He had the neck, shoulders, and chest of a purebred Durham bull, and a punched-in face. By nature he was as argumentative as a bull on the prod, testy at the best of times. He liked giving orders better than taking them. He had the talent and the know-how to be top man on any ranch, but not the ability to say "yes, sir" to the owner. So he bossed trail herds, which kept enough distance between himself and the owner.

The Ten Bar foreman, Loman Jones, was riding alongside the buggy. Bull Giles had no love for the man, and ignored him to speak directly to Judd Boston.

"Is something wrong, Mr. Boston?" The question was almost a challenge as Bull struggled to sound courteous and respectful.

"Benteen Calder will be pulling out with his herd in a few days." Judd Boston went directly to the point.

"Yes, and they'll be tastin' our dust all the way to Dodge City," Bull announced.

Boston wasn't concerned who was first or second on the trail. "Just get those beefs to market with some extra weight on them. It isn't a race."

"I know about trailin' cattle," Bull asserted.

"You'd better," he stated. Bull Giles hadn't been his choice, but Loman Janes insisted he was the best man available. "Calder claims he's taking his herd all the way to the Montana Territory. I want to know if that's where he really goes."

"That's where he's headed, all right," Bull stated. "I talked to Jessie Trumbo yesterday. Barnie Moore's up there waiting for him with a section of range all staked out."

"I've heard the story." Boston was impatient with the man's impertinence. "I want to make sure that's his intention."

"You ever been up in that country?" Bull challenged. "I hunted buffalo around the Little Missouri a few years back. It's grass; nothing but miles and miles of grass." Bull knew the story behind the takeover of the Cee Bar, and his eyes became sly. "Why would Benteen want to come back here and squabble with you over a little chunk of ground when he can lay claim to a range that would make the Ten Bar look like a pauper's outfit?"

"Once that herd is delivered in Dodge City, you find out what Calder's up to," Boston ordered, and popped the buggy whip to send the team bounding forward.

8

The wedding ceremony itself didn't seem to take any time at all. There was one moment, just before she walked down the church aisle on her father's arm, when Lorna wanted to call it off. Then she had seen Benteen standing at the pulpit waiting for her, so handsome in his broadcloth suit. He didn't look at all nervous. In fact, he appeared so confident and sure that Lorna felt childish for having even a moment's doubt.

She expected to feel some change inside herself when the minister pronounced them man and wife, that some new maturity would overcome the butterflies in her stomach. But Mrs. Chase Benteen Calder felt the same as Lorna Pearce had. Even with the reverend's blessing, she blushed when Benteen placed a chaste kiss on her lips. He was her husband now, which gave him certain rights to her that she couldn't deny him. With his arm constantly around her, holding her and touching her, how could she not think about that?

The marriage ceremony was followed by a

reception and a wedding supper at the Pearce home. Benteen had no relatives to invite, and the Pearces had only some elderly cousins living in the area, but there were enough friends on both sides to make up for the lack of family. Alcohol was not part of the refreshments offered by Mrs. Pearce, but some was stashed outside the house. Somebody was always slipping out for a little nip. The conversation and the laughter grew more boisterous with each "little nip."

"I think it's time we left," Benteen murmured close to her ear during a lull between congratulating friends.

"Maybe we should stay a little longer." Lorna was reluctant to leave the reception just yet. She was the center of attention. She wanted to savor the moment just a while longer because she'd never be a bride again. Also, she was slightly uneasy about being alone with Benteen.

"No." He was firm, a restlessness showing about his features. "Let the guests keep your parents up until all hours — not us."

A wife wasn't supposed to argue with a man's decision, so Lorna gave in. They weren't allowed to slip away quietly. The minute the guests realized the bride and groom were leaving, they were showered with rice and occasional phrases of ribald advice.

Since they wouldn't have a home of their own until they reached Montana, Benteen had reserved a suite at one of the better hotels in Fort Worth. He set the small case Lorna had brought with her inside the room and turned back to see her hovering by the threshold.

"Shall I carry you in?" he asked with a half-smile.

The possessive darkness in his look was a bit more than Lorna's shaking nerves could handle. She stepped quickly into the room before he could come back to pick her up. Benteen closed the door and Lorna stiffened at the click of the turning lock key.

"It's a very nice room." She looked around and walked over to a tall chest of drawers, mostly because it was the opposite corner of the room from the bed. She ran a gloved hand over its oak wood. "It's good solid furniture."

When she turned, Lorna found Benteen watching her with warm amusement. "The bed is solidly built, too," he murmured.

A scarlet heat burned her face and neck. Nothing she had learned at Miss Hilda's School for Young Ladies had told her the proper behavior and procedure on her wedding night. She knew all about setting a fine table and arranging flowers and embroidering the linen, but she knew nothing at all about what was expected of her on this night of all nights.

"I'm sorry, Lorna. I shouldn't have embarrassed you." Even as Benteen apologized, amusement continued to deepen his voice.

"I don't know what to do," she admitted with a slightly bowed head. "You'll have to tell me. Am I supposed to go into the dressing room first? Or . . ."

When she hesitantly lifted her gaze, Benteen was shaking his head to the side. She thought it was in answer to her question. When he started across the room, she thought he was going to the dressing room. Instead, Benteen walked to her. Very lightly, his hand cupped her chin.

"I've waited a long time, Lorna. Too long to waste time with playing musical chairs with the dressing room."

Her heart was beating so fast that she couldn't speak. She had been waiting for tonight, too. Not dreading it as a proper girl should do, she realized. She wasn't afraid of what Benteen was going to do to her. She wanted it to happen. If anything frightened her, it was this clawing need to find out what it was like, because passion was something respectable women shouldn't feel.

There was a wild fluttering inside while Lorna watched the strong line of his mouth make its descent toward hers. A flare of excited panic held her completely still as his mouth touched her own. It moved slowly and sensuously, exploring the stiff curve of her lips until they softened under his gentle insistence.

Then the kiss was ending and Benteen was slowly lifting his head, studying her expression with eyes that were three-quarter-lidded. Lorna hoped he couldn't see what she was thinking or feeling. A glint of satisfaction appeared, and she drew a breath of relief that she hadn't been too forward.

He took her by the hand and led her to the bed, his gaze never breaking contact with hers. Before he let go of her hand, Benteen slipped off the glove and took her other hand to do the same. There was a controlled deliberation in his actions as he laid them on the stand beside the bed and turned down the covers.

When he faced her again, Lorna was captivated by the quiet strength etched in his features, a solid assurance that he knew exactly what he was doing. It helped, because she didn't. For a small second, she felt some of his confidence. Then his hands touched the first button of her gown, and the sensation fled. She dropped her gaze to the starched-stiff collar of his shirt, so white against the tanned column of his neck.

All her senses became charged. She stood stock-still under the brush of his fingers, making no attempt to interfere while Benteen slowly unbuttoned her gown. With each shallow breath, Lorna caught the scent of bay rum from his lean and closely shaven cheeks. Her heart was drumming in her ears at a forbidden tempo, too excited by the removal of her dress. She closed her eyes.

Layer by layer, her petticoats were removed and spread on the chair with her gown. All that was left was her chemise and her stockings. Lorna hadn't moved. When his hands didn't return to remove the last garments, she raised her lashes to look at him in uneasy curiosity.

The jacket of his broadcloth suit was off, and Benteen was unfastening the boiled collar to remove his shirt. At the first glimpse of the breadth of his naked chest, darkened with curling brown hairs, a fluttering weakness attacked her stomach. Lorna was shocked by her reaction, because she wanted to see more of his lean, hard body that until now she had only felt pressed against her.

The impropriety of that desire forced her to turn away so she wouldn't see how he looked unclothed. The tightness in her stomach was increasing, until it was almost an actual pain. A lamp was burning next to the bed, throwing a steady light over that corner of the room. Lorna wished for darkness. At least, then, if she was tempted to look at him, she wouldn't be able to see.

"We should turn out the lamp." The disturbed pitch of her voice revealed too much of her inner feelings.

"Then we couldn't see each other," Benteen pointed out, and came up silently behind her. "And I want to see my wife."

She breathed in sharply when his lips touched the curve of her neck and nibbled at the pulsing vein. She closed her eyes tightly, fighting the violent storm of sensations breaking over her. Her knees went weak when she felt the steady pull on the ribbon tie of her chemise. Benteen lifted it over her head, discarding it with a careless toss.

Suffused with heat, Lorna could hardly breathe when his strong hands began rolling down her stockings, traveling down her thigh and over her knee and calf and gently lifting her feet to peel the stockings off completely. She was shaken with tremors that she rigidly tried to conceal from him. All her underclothing was gone.

"Will you look at me, Lorna?" The firm insistence of his voice made her open her eyes, but she fixed her gaze steadfastly on his face.

In the periphery of her vision, she was conscious of the muscled width of his shoulders and the dark hair on his bare chest. The dark light in his eyes burned down her body with ravishing force before it came back to her face.

His hand circled her wrist to pull her in the direction of the bed. Overcome by a surge of modesty, she resisted its pressure.

"I'll need my nightgown," she whispered.

"No, you don't," Benteen stated in husky denial. "Nightgowns are for sleeping. We aren't going to sleep for a while. Not for a long while."

A little sound trembled from her throat as she allowed herself to be drawn to the bed. The soft mattress offered blessed support for her shaking limbs. Her gaze clung to the contoured planes of his face as the bed took his weight as well as her own. The taut, queasy feeling in her stomach became worse, but she couldn't let Benteen know the extent of lust in her flesh. She didn't want to shame herself in his eyes.

With her head on the feather pillow, Lorna was careful to keep her body stretched out straight and her arms at her side. She didn't want to show any awareness of the heat that radiated from his body across the few inches that separated them. Benteen was lying on his

146

side, angled toward her. His breathing had thickened. The look that smoldered in his eyes contained a potent force that shook Lorna all the way to her toes.

When he let that look wander to her high, firm breasts, the tense flatness of her stomach, and even lower, Lorna couldn't suppress a shudder. Again she closed her eyes, trying to shut out her brazen thoughts.

"It isn't wrong for me to look at you. I'm your husband," Benteen reminded her needlessly, because she was fully aware of the multitude of rights the gold band around her finger gave him. The anticipation of them was tearing her apart. He reached over and dragged the pillow from under her head, then remained partially leaning over her, the hair-roughened texture of his chest brushing the naked curve of her breasts. A tingling sensation started over her skin, prompting Lorna against her will to look at him. His face was very close to hers, filling her vision until she could see the pores of his tanned skin and the faint scar on his temple.

"I'll be as gentle as I can be." His warm breath fanned skin that was already hot. "There's no need to be frightened of me."

Her mute nod of understanding was a hesitant movement of her chin. She heard his breath catch as his dark eyes probed hers. Her own glance drifted to the hard male lips, waiting for their touch with a fast-beating heart. Then they were coming down.

His mouth moved onto her lips in an unhurried and sensuous exploration, warm and without pressure. It teased her for a response, lightly brushing her lips, going away and coming back until her lips parted to invite the kind of deep kiss that had so thrilled her once before. The taste of him filled her mouth.

The flat of his hand spread itself onto her rib cage, so warm against her bare flesh. She felt the swelling thrust of her breast anticipate the possessive encirclement of his hand. When he took its weight, the sensation was so much sharper, skin against skin, without the protective barriers of dress and undergarments.

The solid outline of his male body was pressing along her length. She didn't dare touch him as she ached to do, so she curled her fingers into the mattress cover to keep them from sliding up and down the sinewed flesh of his rib cage where his heart was thudding so strongly.

When his mouth slid hotly down her throat, Lorna turned her head aside, pressing her cheek against the mattress and biting her lip to silence the moan of raw pleasure. But the downward journey continued, and she stiffened in vague alarm when his lips moved onto the peak of her breast.

Babies suckled a woman's breast, but it had never occurred to her that a man did. A spasm of erotic quivers splintered through her as his mouth opened to take her nipple into it. His tongue turned it into a hard point of pulsing sensation, until Lorna was driven nearly mindless. When he did the same thing to her other breast, his thumb rubbed the wet peak of the abandoned nipple, keeping it aroused.

A keening sweetness nearly shattered her control. She felt the moan building in her throat and pressed a tightly curled fist against her lips to smother it. His hand came to drag it away as Benteen shifted his attention back to her face, roughly brushing his mouth over her cheek.

"Don't hold it in, Lorna." There was a groaning quality to his half-mumbled words. "Let me hear you."

"I can't." It was a moaned response that contradicted her answer.

She turned to seek his kiss and let his demands hold sway with her. The need to withhold her touch was forgotten as her hand curled into the thickness of his hair. Her sanity seemed threatened when his hands began to stroke and manipulate other parts of her body.

Primitive instinct held sway, wiping out the discretion that had dictated her reactions. Lorna yielded to the fiery sensations burning her loins and let her hips arch against the stroking pressure of his hand and the release of raw tension it offered. Sensation built upon sensation, until there wasn't room for conscious thought in her mind. No directive was sent to keep her legs tightly together, so the space was invaded.

A wildness gathered force inside her, lifting Lorna into a frenzy. Distantly she heard Benteen murmur, "Enjoy it, my love." Then she was convulsed by an eruption within, so intensely pleasurable that it rocked her.

Several minutes passed before she could open her dazed eyes. She lay there panting and exhausted, yet feeling absolutely wonderful. Benteen was smiling at her while his hands made slower work of their caressing moves. Lorna was conscious of a faint sheen of perspiration covering her skin. She wasn't sure what had happened to her, but he seemed to know.

"Lorna, you have so much to give," Benteen declared thickly, and began kissing her.

She had thought she was beyond feeling anything again, that all ability for sensation had been drained from her. Yet as Benteen started kissing her lips, her throat, and her breasts again, and his skillful hands resumed their stroking caresses, the threading excitement began knotting inside her again.

This time, his knees forced their way between her legs to spread them as he raised himself atop her. There was a vague awareness that the moment of coupling had come. Something warm and hard rubbed against her moist valley in search of its entrance. Unconsciously her gaze was drawn to the lower part of him.

A tingle of alarm ran down her spine at the sight of him. He wasn't soft and small like the little boy baby she'd seen once. She hadn't realized that part of his body grew over the years as well. The discovery was followed by a moment of panic, certain that she was too small to ever mate with him. The initial probe seemed to confirm it.

"No, please." Her hands pushed at him, trying to lift his weight off her.

"It will be all right, Lorna," Benteen tried to calm her, but she sensed his inability to control his lust as he continued to hold her down.

"No." Her eyes appealed to him not to go through with this. Hot color filled her cheeks as she tried to explain what should have been obvious to him. "It's . . . it's too big."

151

"No, it isn't." The corners of his mouth twitched before lust overruled the attempt at a smile and dragged a groan from his throat. His mouth opened her lips with hungry force and smothered any further protest.

There was a stab of pain as he miraculously entered her, but it gradually lessened under the rhythmic thrusting of his hips. Soon the pain was forgotten as those waves of sensation began to build to a climax within her again. His tempo increased to a faster rate, driving Lorna to that crazy, golden moment of explosive pleasure. There was a shower of aftershocks. Then a series of violent shudders quaked through Benteen before he relaxed onto her, breathing hard.

After a minute he rolled onto the mattress and opened his eyes to look at her. His serious expression made her uncomfortable. When his hand reached over to idly cup the underside of her breast in his palm, Lorna became shy about his wandering gaze. She groped for the bedcovers and pulled them partially across her body and his.

There was a crooked slant to his mouth. "We are married, Lorna," he murmured. "You don't need to be ashamed to look."

"I know." But it was hard to break long-ingrained habits of modesty.

"How do you feel?" he asked, and let his hand slide onto the quivering muscles of her stomach.

"All right." Lorna was conscious of blushing at his frank question.

"You were wrong, weren't you?" His hand moved possessively onto her hipbone as he quietly mocked her. "I wasn't too big for you."

"Please." She didn't think she should be talking about such things, even if they were married.

"You liked it, didn't you?" It was more statement than question, and Lorna was immediately worried that she had found the lovemaking too enjoyable. She didn't want Benteen to think she was a common street tramp.

"No," she lied.

"What?" He levered himself onto an elbow and studied her with a narrowed skeptical look. "I didn't get that impression."

"I can't help that." She tried not to look at him.

"If you disliked it, why did you seem so willing . . . so eager?" Benteeen challenged quietly.

"You are my husband. I can't deny you the rights of the marriage bed," Lorna murmured.

He caught her chin and forced her to look at him. "Why are you lying?" he demanded with curious intensity. "I was watching you the first time. You're too innocent to fake a climax."

She turned red with shame and tried to squirm away from him, but Benteen held her fast, quickly pinning her to the mattress. She tried to hide her face from him, but he wouldn't permit it.

"I didn't mean for anything like that to happen," she whispered tightly. "I didn't know how to stop it."

"Why would you want to?" he asked incredulously.

"Because . . ." Lorna hesitated, confused by his question. "I don't want you to think that . . . I'm bad."

His gaze narrowed still further, probing deep into her eyes. "You surely don't think that feeling passion makes you bad?" The accusing question was barely spoken when his features smoothed out. "My God, you do," Benteen murmured. "Who put that thought in your head?"

"It's what I thought." She remained wary and unsure. "Although it was never said in so many words."

"I knew you were young, but . . ." The rest of the sentence was dismissed with a shake of his head. "Passion is a feeling that occurs naturally between a man and wife — or a man and woman, for that matter. It isn't wrong to like sex." Her glance fell at his blunt use of the word. "Can you even say it?"

"Of course." But a heat invaded her.

Benteen tipped his head down to look at her, a warm amusement lighting his eyes with patience. "Then say it. Better yet, say that you enjoyed having sex with your husband."

"I . . . enjoyed having sex with my husband." After a faltering start, Lorna rushed through the sentence.

"Did you?" he asked.

"Yes," she admitted in a faint murmur, still doubting that it was something she should acknowledge.

"Maybe if I had you say it a thousand times, it would sound more like an expression of love instead of a confession of guilt," Benteen suggested dryly.

"I do love you." Lorna never intended for him to think otherwise.

"You damn well better not love anyone else," he declared on a mock threat, and reached over to turn down the lamp's wick.

"Wait." Lorna stayed his hand. "I have to get my nightgown."

"No." He turned the wick down and cupped a hand to the glass chimney, blowing out the flame. Then he was gathering her naked body into his arms and pillowing her head on his chest. "We're going to sleep in the raw tonight. I don't want you to be self-conscious about your body – or mine."

"I'll try." But it wasn't easy when his body was so vitally hard and warm. She doubted if her awareness of it would ever permit her to relax enough to sleep.

His hands rubbed over her. "You don't belong anywhere else but right here, Lorna." It was a firm statement of ownership. "This is only the beginning, with a lot more to come. Woman was made to give a man pleasure."

Something in his remark prompted Lorna to remember the advice given to her by that sporting lady, Pearl Rogers. It started a whole chain of thoughts.

"Benteen?" Her hand made an absent exploration into the curling hair on his chest. "Have you had . . . sex with many women?"

"What's this?" There was a smile in his voice. "An investigation into my sordid past?"

"Have you?" Lorna persisted.

"I've known some women in my time," he admitted.

"What kind?" she asked.

"I don't see that it makes any difference." He attempted to avoid the question. "You're my wife now. My woman."

"But these women, were they respectable?" She had to know if he was comparing her to the right kind of women.

"I respected them," he stated. "That's all you need to know."

"But . . ." She lifted her head to question him further, suspecting that she was really like the loose women he had known.

"No more questions." He covered her mouth with his hand, then let it slide down to rub his thumb across her lips. "We're going to have a long day tomorrow. It's time we both got a little shut-eye."

A minor debate was waged in her mind before she shelved the subject for the time being and rested her head on his chest again. His arm tightened, to snuggle her closer to his side. Lorna started to crook a leg over his to get comfortable, but she jerked it back when she brushed something soft.

"What's the matter?" Benteen asked.

"Nothing," she lied in confusion.

"You can put your leg over mine," he invited.

"No, that's all right," she insisted nervously.

"What is it? I know there's something." The determined tone was in his voice. "What is it that you're too embarrassed to say?"

"It's . . . small." She couldn't help feeling

self-conscious about noticing that.

Her discomfort wasn't lessened by his low chuckle. "It's only hard and erect when a man is aroused. You'll soon learn how it's done," Benteen assured her.

It seemed there was a great deal she had to learn. Lorna had always considered herself to be well-educated. She could read and do numbers, as well as sew and cook and keep house. She had thought she was moderately well-versed in the facts of life, but it seemed she wasn't aware of the fundamentals. She didn't like feeling ignorant.

II

Get them cattle movin'.
Honey, dry your eyes,
'Cause that Calder range is waiting
Under blue Montana skies.

9

The first light of dawn glinted through the dusty glass of the hotel window. In the street below, there was a small stirring of activity. Benteen lay awake in bed, watching Lorna sleep. The covers were down around her hips, exposing her high, firm breasts. Until last night, he hadn't realized how much passion was locked inside that beautifully slender body, but he hadn't been shocked by it. "Delighted" was a closer description.

His gaze traveled down to her flat stomach and the bones of her hips. My God, how she had drained every ounce of life juice from his body! Just remembering made him grow stiff with desire. His eyes returned to her face, its innocence touching him as her modesty had last night. There was a slight curve to her lips as they lay warmly together, a hint of the pleasured satisfaction she'd also known last night. She stirred, turning a little toward him.

It was time they were getting up, but he didn't want to waken her. He wanted to look at her, study every detail that he had missed last night and a few that he hadn't. His hand moved to the bedcovers to inch them down a little farther, not wanting to disturb her slumber just yet.

Her lashes fluttered, then were slowly dragged open. Benteen watched the sleepy confusion across her features as Lorna tried to place where she was. Her glance swung to him, startled recognition flaring in her eyes.

"Good morning, Mrs. Calder." The lazy smile matched his slowly drawled greeting. He saw the rush of modesty when she realized she was uncovered, and pulled up the covers that he was going to pull down. It was a pity, but in time she'd get over this self-consciousness.

"Good morning." Her voice was soft, a little husky with sleep.

"Do you know you snore?" Benteen teased.

"I don't!" She was aghast at the thought, her fingers tightly clutching the bedcovers to her breastbone.

"Yes, you do. And very prettily, too." He leaned over and rubbed his mouth over her lips. Their instinctive response almost made him forget the late hour. Grudgingly he drew back. His control was tested when he saw the hesitant desire flicker in her eyes. He had to turn away or give in to the urge to erase the hesitancy. "It's time to get up, so we can be on our way."

When he swung out of bed, Lorna's head turned on the pillow so she could look at him, a little disappointed that he hadn't wanted to make love to her again. For a brief second she had forgotten Benteen was as naked as he was, but the sight of him was a sharp reminder. Her first impulse was to look quickly in the opposite direction, but her curiosity was stronger. It made her feel a little bit wicked to run her gaze over his tapered back and the hard, lean flanks of his hips. Benteen didn't bother with the privacies of the dressing room, pulling his clothes on right there in the bedroom. Not his wedding suit, but tough, durable workclothes.

Benteen turned to glance at the bed as he tucked his shirt inside the close-fitting denim pants. "Get out of the bed and get dressed." It was more prompting than an order.

"Do we have to leave this morning?" Lorna asked. "Can't we wait one more day?"

He came back to the bed and leaned down to place a hand on either side of her. "If I thought we could wait one more day, I'd be in bed with you now." His look seemed able to see her body beneath the covers, and Lorna felt that stirring of passion within her. "But we can't hold the herd on that ground any longer. They're out of graze, and they have to be moved."

"But just one day . . ." she began, some female instinct telling her that he could be tempted the way Adam had been in the Bible.

"No." It was a decisive answer, followed by decisive action as Benteen slipped his hands under her shoulders and lifted her out of bed. "The plans are set and the boys have their orders to have the cattle ready to move out no later than midmorning." Once she was standing naked in front of him, his hands wandered absently over her ribs and waist. "I'll be leaving as soon as I've shaved and cleaned up. If you're coming with me, you'd better get a move on."

One look at the interest flickering in his otherwise determined features, and Lorna wasn't at all intimidated by his idle threat that he would consider leaving her behind. Before it could take hold, he was letting her go, to turn abruptly away.

"Get your clothes on," Benteen ordered gruffly.

And Lorna had her first hint of how easily aroused a man could be by a woman's form. The thought barely had time to register before it was crowded out by more immediate considerations that included getting packed and dressed for the journey.

After a quick breakfast in the hotel's dining

room, they went by the Pearce home so Lorna could see her parents one last time before they left. A restless part of Benteen made him impatient at the delay, but for Lorna's sake he controlled it, aware that he couldn't expect her to leave home without a farewell parting from her family. But when it threatened to stretch into a lengthy and painful good-bye, he stepped in.

"Lorna, we have to go." His hand gripped her elbow, his voice firm.

"Can't we stay a little longer?" She turned to him, the tears now starting to fall steadily.

"No." Benteen didn't try to temper his refusal, although the tears made it difficult.

When she saw that her appeal wasn't swaying him, she turned back to hug her mother tightly. Mrs. Pearce was crying as well, more emotional than Benteen had ever seen her. There was even a sheen of dampness in her father's eyes as Arthur Pearce stepped forward to clasp Benteen's hand in both of his.

"You take good care of my little girl." There was a stiffness to the man's smile and the rigid set of his chin.

"I will, sir." Benteen pretended not to notice the huskiness in the man's voice.

Then Lorna was pulling out of her mother's arms and looking tearfully at her father. "Oh,

Daddy," she sobbed, and wrapped her arms tightly around his neck. For a minute Arthur Pearce hid his face in her dark hair and hugged her close.

"You be good, now, ya hear?" It was a gruff admonition to mask his pain.

"I'll miss you so much, Daddy," Lorna declared in a sobbing voice.

Benteen knew there wasn't any easy way to end this. "I'm sorry, Mr. Pearce," he intruded firmly on the emotional scene. There was a reluctant nod of understanding as Arthur Pearce tried to set his daughter away from him. Taking her by the shoulders, Benteen pulled her the rest of the way back. Her hands remained extended, reaching involuntarily toward her parents. "It's time, Lorna."

"I . . ." But the words were choked off as she turned quickly away from the sight of her mother crying and the pained look on her father's face. She practically ran toward the wagon, covering her mouth to hold back the sobs trembling through her whole body.

Grimly Benteen helped her climb up to the wagon seat and followed her up. It hurt him to look at her anguished, tear-filled face, so he kept his eyes averted. She was barely seated and she was already turning to gaze longingly at her parents. The reins to the horse team were wrapped around the brake handle. Benteen unwound them.

"Good-bye!"

"Good-bye!"

"Don't forget to write!"

"We'll miss you!"

"Good-bye!"

Benteen didn't attempt to separate the voices calling after each other as he slapped the horse with the reins and chirruped to the team. The jangle of trace chains, the pounding shuffle of digging hooves, and the rattle of the covered wagon combined to drown out the voices. Beside him, Lorna waved frantically, straining and twisting in the seat to keep her parents in sight as they drove down the street. The tears kept falling, and Benteen kept a tight-lipped silence, understanding yet feeling the anger of frustration, because there was nothing he could say or do. Her desolation was beyond comforting, so he didn't try.

They were nearly out of town before her shoulders quit shaking with sobs, but the tears didn't stop. Benteen slid a short glance at her pale, strained face, partially turned from him, and looked again to the front. With one hand he untied the kerchief knotted loosely around his throat and silently offered it to her.

She took it and wiped at her tear-drenched

cheeks, while holding on to the sides of the wagon seat to keep from being bounced out by the rough road. When she had dried her face, she clutched the kerchief in her lap.

"I can't help it," Lorna defended her tears.

"I know." His voice was tight. She dabbed again at her eyes, bowing her head and sniffling. Purposely or not, she was making him feel like a bastard for taking her away from her parents. It rankled him, because she was his wife. She belonged with him, not them. Benteen stifled it as best he could, but some of his agitation crept through. "Those tears aren't going to make you feel any better." He was conscious of her stiffening and cursed himself for not offering her some comfort.

When he tried to put his arm around her, Lorna pushed it away. "You don't understand," she accused, the tears building again in her eyes. "I'll probably never see them again."

In all likelihood, she was right, so Benteen didn't attempt to argue the point. But her eyes were on him, waiting for him to deny it and allay her fears. Her chin started quivering at his silence.

"It's true, isn't it?" she whispered.

"I don't know." He was honest as he could be with her, a grimness to his profiled features.

He expected her to burst into tears, but the

outpouring of grief didn't come. Tears continued to slide silently down her cheeks as Lorna stared at the road ahead. That was harder for him to endure than the wild weeping he had anticipated.

All was in readiness to take the trail when they reached the camp at nine that morning, three hours of sunlight gone. The horses were hitched to the chuck wagon; Ely Stanton's wagon was ready to pull out; the wrangler had the horse remuda bunched; and all the cowboys were in the saddle, waiting for the word to move out.

Pulling in the team, Benteen set the brake and wrapped the reins around it. He cast a glance at Lorna, noting the tears frozen on her face. A heavy sigh broke from him as he swung down from the wagon seat to the ground. He walked to the rear of the wagon and untied his saddle horse.

Jessie Trumbo rode up as Benteen stepped into the saddle. "All set whenever you give the word," he said, and received a short nod.

Benteen rode past without looking at Lorna and cantered his horse to the Stanton wagon. He touched his hat in a silent greeting to the plain woman sitting alone in the wagon seat, a bonnet covering her hair. She met his look squarely.

"I'd be obliged, Mrs. Stanton, if you would drive my wagon this morning," he requested stiffly. "My wife would be grateful for your company. The wrangler's helper will drive yours."

"Of course, Mr. Calder," Mary Stanton agreed, and gathered her long calico skirts to climb down from the seat.

Pivoting his horse, Benteen trotted it over to the chuck wagon, where Jessie was talking to the cook, Rusty. "Tell Joe Dollarhide he'll be driving the Stanton wagon this morning."

Both men had noticed the bride's white, teary face, but both men knew better than to mention it to Benteen. With a nod, Jessie wheeled his horse away from the chuck wagon and galloped out to the remuda to fetch the young rider.

When Mary Stanton crawled onto the wagon seat beside Lorna, she felt a surge of pity for the young bride. "Your husband thought we could keep each other company this morning," she explained with a quiet smile.

Lorna nodded stiffly but didn't speak. Her fingers had wadded the kerchief into a tight ball on her lap. Across the way, Mary saw the cranky old cook preparing to start his team out, so she unwrapped the reins and adjusted them in her hands. The chuck wagon would lead the way to the day's nooning, a little off the route the herd would take.

"We'll be following the chuck wagon," Mary said. Her glance rested on the sunbonnet hanging loosely down Lorna's back. "You'd better tie that bonnet on your head," she advised. "Else the sun'll ruin your pretty skin." In time, it would anyway, but she kept that knowledge to herself.

In her present state of anguish, Lorna didn't particularly care, but she numbly pulled the bonnet onto her head and knotted the ties snugly under her chin. A young boy rode by and dismounted to climb aboard the second covered wagon after tying his horse behind. When the chuck wagon rattled into motion, Mary started their team of horses. Lorna grabbed hold of the wagon seat again as it lurched forward. She looked for Benteen, catching a glimpse of him just as he signaled to move the herd out.

"It's hard leavin' home that first time," Mary remarked after they'd traveled a short distance. "Not knowing when you might see your family again."

"Yes," Lorna admitted, finally looking directly at the woman only a few years older than she was. She sensed that Mary Stanton actually understood what she was feeling.

"Have . . . you seen your parents since you left home?"

"No," Mary admitted. "My ma died last year. I'm hoping we can go to her grave when we get to Ioway."

Her answer gave Lorna no reassurance that her fears were groundless. Yet the words were more bearable coming from Mary than from Benteen.

"A woman's lot in this world is a lonely one," Mary said. "You'll find that out — and find a way to make the best of it."

"I don't feel so sure about that," Lorna murmured.

"Right now, you're thinking about what's behind you, but when you get to your new home and there's babies to raise, you'll be looking ahead. Grief passes. That's the way it is."

"I suppose." But it was very fresh for her now, too fresh to accept so philosophically.

"A woman doesn't have much choice in this world. When she's being raised, her parents tell her what to do. And after she's married, it's her husband."

"It isn't fair," Lorna replied, not truly realizing what she was saying.

"Life isn't fair, but it can be good." Mary smiled faintly. The girl had a little more pluck than she thought.

It didn't seem possible to Lorna, not when she might never see her parents again. Married life wasn't turning out to be what she thought it would be. From what Mary said, it wasn't going to get any better. It was so hard to think with the noise of bawling cattle and the clatter of the wagon hammering at her eardrums as they bounced and jolted over the rough prairie ground.

All her thoughts were turned inward. Lorna didn't notice that the Texas prairie was garbed in its best dress to see her off. Spring had brought green grass to the land again, and the few trees were swelling and bursting with green buds. Wildflowers gave color to the rolling hillsides. Purpling blue patches of bluebonnets, yellow clusters of wild mustard, and the scarlet-orange stands of Indian paintbrush dotted the land.

It was a season that reached out to the restless. Benteen felt its call. He'd answered it enough times in the past. From the vantage point of a high knoll he watched the Longhorns string out. The brindle steer had already shouldered its way to the front, assuming leadership of the herd. It was characteristic for individual animals to keep the same position in a trail herd every day. Some would always be in the middle, some closer to the front, and others lagging behind. No matter where they started at the beginning of a day's drive, by the time it ended, they would have established their habitual position.

Spanish Bill and Jessie Trumbo were the point men, riding in the lead on either side of the herd to guide in the right direction. The swing, flank, and drag riders would rotate their positions each day, but not the point men. It was a critical position, requiring experience and skill. Benteen had given the responsibility to the two men he trusted most.

The herd wasn't driven so much as it was drifted in the right direction – always at a leisurely walk. The long-striding cattle could eat up ground without losing weight as long as they were kept out of a trot. In most cases, the Longhorns gained weight on the trail north to the railheads if there was plenty of water and graze along the way.

Ahead, the wagons were disappearing into a crease in the prairie. Benteen watched the canvas-topped wagon that carried Lorna, until it dipped out of sight. He hoped he'd done the right thing – having Mary Stanton ride with her. He hadn't wanted her to be alone, yet he had the responsibility of the herd.

The trail boss of any drive had one motto that he lived by: Look out for the cows' feet and the horses' backs, and let the cowboys and cooks look after themselves. That partially applied to his new bride as well. These cattle represented their tomorrow. She had to understand that. He put the spurs to his horse and galloped to the point.

Because of the late start, Benteen let the herd drift north an hour longer than usual, until the sun was straight up, before letting them stop to graze on a midday break. The spot had been preselected, so the chuck wagon was waiting with a light meal for the drovers. The cowboys ate in shifts, a few always staying with the herd.

Benteen carried his plate over to where Lorna was seated by the wagon. Her cheeks were dry, but she still looked numbed to her surroundings.

"How about something to eat?" He crouched down beside her, pushing his hat to the back of his head.

"I'm not hungry." She didn't look at him.

"Suit yourself." Sitting on his heels, he started eating. He glanced around, again seeing the wildflowers and the bursting of spring green. "It's a pretty day."

"Here." She dug his red bandanna out of her pocket and handed it to him.

"Are you and Mary Stanton getting along all

right?" For the time being, Benteen tucked the bandanna in his shirt pocket.

"Yes."

"I can arrange for her to ride with you this afternoon if you want," Benteen offered.

"I can manage the team," Lorna retorted.

He set the plate down, unable to eat with all this cold tension in the air. "Lorna, I'm sorry about your parents. I know you feel bad, but there isn't much I can do."

"There isn't much you *want* to do." She stood up and walked over to the Stanton wagon.

Picking up his plate, Benteen started eating again, but he didn't taste a thing except anger. It was a hell of a way to start the first day of married life, but he'd be damned if he'd apologize again.

When the Longhorns had grazed long enough, they began to lie down. That was the signal to start them back on the trail. It was easier driving the herd in the afternoon, because they were thirsty and willing to walk to water.

This part of the trail, Benteen knew well. Ordinarily he wouldn't ride ahead at this point to check out the night's bedding ground, except he remembered Stoney at the livery stable mentioning some of the water holes had been fenced by farmers. Sure enough, he found new barbed wire fencing off the water.

Spanish had ridden with him. "A man selling this wire built a fence with it in San Antonio. He stampeded some Longhorns into it to show how strong it was. They knocked a post out of the ground, but the wire held."

"Cut it," Benteen ordered.

"The farmer isn't going to like it." Spanish turned a curious pair of black eyes on the man.

"Neither will a herd of thirsty Longhorns," he replied. "Cut it."

By the time the herd had nearly reached the night ground, the riders had gathered the cattle into a more compact herd so they weren't strung out so far. Taking them to water, they spread the Longhorns into bunches to avoid crowding and pushing.

Benteen and Spanish had the barbed wire down by the time the herd reached the watering place. All hell started to break loose when the downed wire began tangling with hoof and horn.

Benteen cursed when he saw what was happening. "Stampede!" He recognized the warning signs a second before the first steer made its mad plunge that sent the whole pack on the run.

The ground rumbled with the thunder of

their hooves. Horns popped and rattled as they clashed together. All other duties were forgotten. Benteen took time only to make certain the cattle were headed away from the wagons as he whipped his horse after the stampeding herd. Jonesy was racing just ahead of him, singing at the top of his lungs, "Rock of ages, cleft for me. Let me hide myself in thee." Many cowboy sinners saw "the light" in the midst of a devil's stampede. Some superstitious drovers believed a stampeding herd would respond only to hymns.

With Jonesy on a faster horse, Benteen let him overtake the leaders and ride alongside to begin turning them in a slow, wide circle. Luckily, it was a short run, lasting no more than five minutes – the thirsty cattle willing to be brought under control. The bawling started as they began to mill loosely, the riders taking care not to crowd them too tightly in the event of cattle in the center going down and being trampled.

Just when the herd seemed to have settled down, barking dogs started them moving nervously again. Benteen jerked his head toward the sound and saw a bunch of farmers rushing toward the water hole. His mouth thinned into an angry line.

"Jessie! Shorty!" He waved the two men to

come with him and wheeled his horse away from the herd toward the oncoming farmers.

The rifle was in his scabbard. Benteen pulled it out and levered a shell into the firing chamber, taking aim at a slick-haired dog leading the pack. A rifle shot was likely to stampede the cattle again, but so were the dogs. He fired, knocking the first one back into the others. Behind him, Shorty and Jessie were pumping bullets into the pack. Within seconds, those that could still move had turned tail and were kiyipping back the way they'd come. Benteen faced his horse at the wagon-load of farmers.

"You killed our dogs!" one cried.

"Did you put that fence up?" Benteen ignored the outraged protest.

"That's our water!" a farmer shouted.

"Like hell it is. Trail herds have been watering there since the first steer was taken north."

"You owe us for that fence you cut — and for every steer that took a drink," another demanded.

"I'm not paying you to water my cattle," Benteen snapped.

"We'll see what the marshall has to say about that," the first one threatened.

"You do that."

There was a grumbled exchange among the farmers before the team was finally turned around. Benteen watched them go, not turning until they were out of sight. When he shoved the rifle into the scabbard of his saddle, he heard Shorty and Jessie do the same.

"Damn farmers!" Shorty spit. "We shoulda put a couple bullets in them."

"Let's get back to the cattle." Benteen reined his horse toward the restless, uneasy herd milling nervously.

The wagons had reached the night's campground well ahead of the herd. By that time, Lorna was deeply regretting that she had ever boasted to Benteen that she could manage the team. The four horses pulling their wagon were not the tractable animals that hauled her father's freight wagon, and her arms ached until they were trembling from holding the reins. There weren't any roads across the prairie, and after a day of being bounced all over the wagon seat, her body seemed so bruised and battered that there wasn't a part of her that didn't hurt. Grimy dust covered her face and clothes, adding to the discomfort.

She was in agony because she hadn't relieved herself since the noon stop. Lorna climbed carefully down from the wagon seat, not jumping the last two feet, afraid the jar of landing would cause her to humiliate herself. She looked anxiously around. At the noon stop, there had been a small stand of trees where she'd been able to hide herself, but here there was nothing but grass in all directions. She couldn't even see any bushes.

"I'll unhitch the horses for you, Mrs. Calder," a young voice said.

Turning with a start, Lorna saw the dark-haired lad standing on the other side of the team. She recognized him as the one who had driven Mary's wagon that morning. He couldn't have been more than two years younger than she was. Lorna felt very young and foolish at the moment, younger than he was, but she was a married woman, so she couldn't let him know.

"Thank you." Her smile was hesitant. She doubted if she could have unharnessed this headstrong team without something going wrong.

Walking stiffly, Lorna crossed to the Stanton wagon. She felt less inadequate when she saw Mary being helped by the horse wrangler. The bow-legged man drove the team free from the wagon tongue, handling them from the ground.

"Mary," Lorna called to her newfound friend and adviser.

The stocky woman came to meet her; a sharpness in her look that was somehow gentled by her tired smile. "How are you feeling?"

"Fine." If her other matter wasn't so urgent, Lorna would have continued the idle chatter. Instead, she lowered her voice so none of the three men in camp could overhear. "What do we do about relieving ourselves?"

For an instant there was silence. Lorna dropped her gaze to the prairie sod, certain she had disgraced herself by speaking of bodily functions, but she hadn't known what else to do.

"You just go off a way and do it," Mary said.

Lorna's glance ran back to the woman in shock. "But it's so open." She cast a furtive look at the wrangler unharnessing the horses. "Anyone could see me."

"Out here, Lorna, there's times to be modest and other times when it just isn't possible," Mary explained gently. Her glance made a swing of the area. "There's a little hill right over there. Maybe you could go behind it. You're not exactly out of sight, but it's as close as you'll get."

Under the circumstances, there seemed little she could do except what Mary had suggested. Lorna had never felt so selfconscious in all her life as when she pretended to idly stroll behind that little hill. No one appeared to notice her, or at least they weren't looking. Lorna tried to make herself as small as possible when she knew she couldn't wait any longer.

Her long skirt and petticoats provided a degree of covering. When she heard someone walking in the grass, they were also a hindrance, getting in her way when she tried to hurriedly pull up her undergarments. Her back was to the sound, which made it worse, because she had no idea who was coming. She darted a furtive glance over her shoulder and recognized the cook. Apparently lost in thought, he was studying the sky as he walked.

Standing up, Lorna frantically smoothed her skirts and started swiftly for the campsite. Red-faced, she slid a quick look in his direction, hoping he would ignore her. Humiliation was doubled when she discovered he was not. She couldn't bear the thought that he knew what she had been doing out here.

"I came out for a closer look at the wild-flowers." Lorna came up with a desperate lie to explain her presence.

A twinkle leaped into his eyes. "I reckon I got the same idea, ma'am." He touched the drooping brim of his hat and walked on by.

Lorna wished the ground would swallow her

up. She hadn't fooled him for a minute. And she hadn't really wanted to know that his intention was the same as hers had been.

When she reached the wagons, neither the wrangler nor his helper paid any attention to her, but it felt like a hundred eyes were watching her. She heard the din of the approaching herd. Benteen and another rider were at the water hole, cutting the wire that fenced it in.

10

Lorna shared a small pan of water with Mary to wash some of the grime from her face and hands. Bathing was out of the question. The cook had returned from his stroll on the prairie and was adding a few dead limbs to the already blazing fire. The wood had been gathered along the trail that day by the wrangler and stowed in a hammocklike contraption stretched under the bottom of the chuck wagon, called a cooney. The metal coffeepot was already set out to boil for its usual half-hour.

"I think we should offer to help with supper, even if it won't be accepted," Mary suggested with a faint grimace.

"Why not?" Lorna wasn't too anxious to face the cook, but she didn't understand why anyone would refuse help in the kitchen — even a prairie kitchen.

"Ely says that cooks on these drives jealously guard their positions. They don't like being given advice about anything related to cooking," she explained. "But let's make the gesture anyway."

With Mary for moral support, Lorna walked over to the chuck wagon. The end gate was down, making a small worktable. Satisfied that the fire was burning well, the cook had returned to his outdoor kitchen. He was taking sourdough batter out of a keg for the requisite biscuits that accompained nearly every meal, and adding more flour, salt, and water to ferment with the remaining batter to keep the starter going.

"Is there something we can do to help?" Mary asked.

"Nope." He didn't even turn around to answer.

A rumbling started and grew into a roar. "What's that?" Lorna turned toward the sound in alarm.

"Stampede." The cook stopped his work to look. "They ain't comin' our way." He turned back to the table.

Lorna stared at the mad rush of cattle, a quarter-mile distance giving her a view of the entire scene. She had heard tales about cattle stampedes and riders being trampled under their hooves. Her heart was in her throat at the sight of riders racing pell-mell, stride for stride with the thundering herd. Benteen was out there somewhere, but in the haze of dust and the mass of running bodies, she couldn't pick him out. Fear for him paralyzed her, rooting her feet to the ground and riveting her eyes to the scene.

Rusty continued his work, but kept one eye on what was happening. Until he found out whether he was going to be cook, doctor, or undertaker, there were biscuits to be made. When he saw the cattle slowly circling back into themselves, he nodded his approval. "They got 'em turned," he announced. "It's all over but the shoutin' now."

It wasn't until Lorna heard the loud bellowing of the cattle that she realized the animals hadn't made a sound during the panicked run. The din was awful. Dust boiled to encapsulate the milling herd and hide the riders. She still couldn't see Benteen anywhere.

From the far side of the herd came the baying bark of dogs, or so Lorna thought. She jumped at the rapid-fire explosions that followed, and glanced in alarm at the cook.

"Are those gunshots?"

Rusty nodded. "I reckon Benteen met up with the folks who strung the wire. He's probably explainin' the situation to 'em."

The gunfire stopped seconds after it had started. But Lorna knew she wasn't going to draw an easy breath until she saw Benteen again — safe and unharmed. She continued to scan the area, trying to pick out horse and rider from the churning mass of longhorned beasts.

"There's Ely," Mary breathed, standing next to her.

Lorna hadn't considered that her friend was experiencing the same anxiety she was. Her hand closed on the woman's arm in a silent expression of gladness that Ely Stanton had made it unscathed.

"But where's Benteen?" Lorna murmured.

It was an eternity of minutes before she spotted him with the other cowboys surrounding the herd. Her legs started shaking and she felt almost sick with relief.

"The excitement's over for a while," the cook stated, eyeing both women discreetly. "Why don't you sit yourselves down and have some coffee?"

"Thank you," Mary said. "I think we will."

The coffee was so strong and black that Lorna nearly gagged on the first swallow.

"Ely always said my coffee was weak." Mary's laugh was thin. "I didn't believe him when he said you could float a pistol in trail coffee."

Untying the bow to her bonnet, Lorna slipped it off and smiled her agreement to Mary's remark. She felt emotionally drained. At least the strong coffee partially revived her, despite its appalling taste.

Benteen stayed with the herd until it had been watered and thrown off the trail to graze awhile before bedding down for the night. When he rode to camp, the wrangler Yates was bringing the cavvy in so each rider could get his night horse for his two-hour watch. He dismounted at the chuck wagon.

Rusty handed him a tin cup, knowing he'd want coffee first thing. "Anybody hurt?"

"Nope." Benteen held the cup while Rusty poured it full of coffee from the pot. "Taylor's horse stepped in a prairie-dog hole and went down, but he went off clear of the herd. Says he's all right." He drank the coffee down, not giving it a chance to cool.

"All that commotion gave your bride quite a scare." Rusty passed on the information carelessly, but noticed Benteen's quick glance toward the wagon.

Lorna stood poised at the back of the covered wagon, an uncertainty in her manner as she stared at Benteen. He set the cup on the makeshift worktable of the chuck box and crossed the camp circle. Her gaze went over him from head to toe, inspecting him for damages. Unconvinced, she searched his face when he finally stopped in front of her.

"Are you all right?" she asked.

"Not a scratch." The corners of his mouth deepened at this concern for him.

She swayed toward him, then slid her hands around his middle to hold him close, his solidness more reassuring than his words. "I was so worried," Lorna admitted, and felt a hand on her hair.

"It's all part of a day's work," he said. She shuddered that he could be so nonchalant about it. "Besides, something good came out of it."

"What?" It seemed impossible.

"You're not angry anymore."

Keeping her head down, Lorna pulled reluctantly away from him. "I wasn't angry before." But she didn't try to explain the hurt she'd felt at his lack of understanding about her parents and the indifference he'd shown for what she was going through. "We heard some shooting." She changed the subject.

"A bunch of farmers sicced their dogs on the cattle." Benteen shrugged, making light of the incident.

"Were they the ones who fenced in the water?" she asked, to see if the cook had been right.

"They said they were."

"I suppose they were upset about it," Lorna

guessed. "Wasn't it wrong to cut it down? I mean, you shouldn't destroy other people's property, should you?"

"A man doesn't have any right to fence thirsty cattle away from good water." His lids were shielding his eyes, but she sensed his displeasure at her questions.

"But shouldn't you have asked before you cut it? The farmers probably wouldn't have been so angry if you had."

"While I sent somebody to look them up and ask permission, what was I supposed to do with twenty-five hundred head of thirsty Longhorns? They would have torn the fence down to get to that water, and cut themselves up bad." Benteen was curt with her, and she saw the hardness in his eyes. "This isn't Fort Worth, Lorna. Life is different out here."

Behind them, Rusty banged a metal pan. "Come an' get it or I'll throw it out!"

Benteen half-turned at the sound, then faced Lorna again. "Supper's ready. Are you hungry?"

"Yes." Actually she was starved, but he had made her feel young and ignorant again. She resented that, and retaliated by shutting him out from her private thoughts.

He curved a hand under her arm. "I want to introduce you to the men. Some of them you know, but the others haven't met you."

While the cowboys waited in line for Rusty to dish up their plates of stew, Benteen identified them individually to her. Two of the shyer ones turned red when she was introduced to them. Shorty Niles flattered her outrageously, making her laugh, but all of them treated her with the utmost respect. They weren't at all like the foul-talking, loud trailhands she'd seen on the streets of Fort Worth.

There was no order to the meal, no formality observed. The men sat on the ground, leaving their hats on and shoveling the food into their mouths as if there might not be another meal for days. Lorna found it difficult to appear at all ladylike when she was sitting cross-legged on the ground with her skirts billowing around her and holding the plate of stew she was eating. Rusty came around with the coffeepot to refill the cups.

"This stew is very unusual." She had been taught to compliment the cook. Since she hadn't eaten anything that tasted quite like it before, it seemed logical to mention it. "What's it called?"

There was a lull in the conversation. Rusty glanced at Benteen. Everyone was fully aware of his orders about swearing in front of the women.

"It's called . . . son-of-gun stew," Rusty said finally, and a few of the cowboys chuckled aloud.

Lorna didn't understand the joke and slid a questioning glance at Benteen. His mouth was slanted in a half-smile, but he kept his gaze down.

"It's made with beef, isn't it?" Lorna guessed.

"Well, yes, ma'am." Rusty seemed to hesitate before admitting it. "It's made from beef parts — the heart, liver, tongue. 'Course, it gets its flavor from the marrow guts."

"Marrow gut," Lorna repeated, and let her fork rest on the plate. "What's that?"

"It comes from the tube that connects a cow's two stomachs." Having spent a great deal of his life at sea, Rusty knew sailors had to have some greens in their diet to keep from getting sick and diseased. So did cowboys on the trail. Meat and beans alone weren't enough. Since cattle ate grass, the necessary nutritious elements were in the marrow of the tube connecting their stomachs. If a cowboy ate it, he got the benefit of the greens. "Son-of-a-bitch stew," as it was more widely known, usually contained it.

"Oh." Lorna stared at her plate and wished she had never asked. There wasn't any way she could eat another bite. And the food that was in her stomach didn't feel like it wanted to stay there. She looked across the way at Mary, but she didn't appear to have been listening.

As if she hadn't been through enough that day, here she was eating animal guts. It was too much. She set her plate on the ground, not caring that the cutlery clattered off the side, and scrambled to her feet.

"Excuse me," Lorna mumbled, conscious of Benteen's frowning look.

Gathering her skirts tightly around her, she ran from the campfire area and sought refuge in the back of the wagon. She sprawled the length of the quilt-topped mattress and started to cry. She just couldn't take any more.

A guilty look of regret stole across Rusty's lined face. "Sorry, Benteen. I fergot such talk offends a lady's delicate sensibilities."

A hush had settled over the men at Lorna's flight. Benteen was conscious that they were waiting to see what he was going to do. He was irritated at the awkward position Lorna had put him in.

He forced himself to smile. "Don't worry about it, Rusty. There's a lot of things she's going to have to learn to accept."

He put his plate aside and rolled to his feet. Crossing the camp with slow deliberation,

Benteen raised the canvas flap of the wagon and ducked his head to climb inside, aware of the smothered sounds of Lorna's crying. He struggled to control his impatience. She lifted her head from the quilt long enough to look at him, then turned it quickly away.

"What is it this time, Lorna?" There wasn't room to stand in the cramped quarters of wagon bed, so he sat down on the mattress.

Immediately she moved, turning and pushing herself into a sitting position. Her legs were crooked under her skirt to avoid any contact with him.

"Animal guts," she declared in a choked voice. "How can you expect me to eat animal guts?"

"It isn't the gut. It's the marrow, and you liked the stew well enough before you found out what was in it," he reminded her.

"It isn't just that," Lorna protested, and scrubbed away the tears with her hand.

"Then what is it?" Benteen demanded.

"It's everything. You never told me it was going to be like this," she accused.

"You knew it was going to be rough." His eyebrows were pulled together in a dark frown.

"Rough, yes." She nodded. "I can take being bounced all over a wagon until I'm black and blue. I can stand being dusty and dirty because there isn't enough water for bathing. But it's the rest."

"The rest?"

"Don't you know how humiliating it is for a woman to relieve herself where others can see her?" Lorna sobbed, turning pink again at the embarrassing memory. She buried her face in her hands. "I wish I were back home with my parents where they eat regular food."

"What do you want from me, Lorna?" There was a steely quietness to his voice. "Do you want me to turn the wagon around tomorrow morning and take you back?"

"No."

"Then what do you want?"

"I don't know." She shook her head, confused and overwrought by the whole situation.

"I hadn't realized how difficult this trip was going to be for you," Benteen admitted. "I understand how embarrassing certain things can be. But you're going to have to come to terms with them."

"That's easy for you to say," Lorna retorted, finally bringing down her hands to look at him with bitter reproval.

"It isn't easy. And it wasn't easy to sit out there with all my men watching while you go running off to hide in the wagon and cry," he informed her roughly. "You were crying when you came this morning, and you're crying tonight. Doesn't it matter to you what they're thinking right now?"

She cast an uneasy glance at the canvas side of the wagon, realizing that all the cowboys knew Benteen was in here with her now.

"I hadn't thought about it," Lorna admitted.

"I imagine their opinion is the same as mine," he stated. "I thought I married a woman, but instead I find I've got a spoiled child on my hands."

She swung at him as hard as she could. The flat of her hand cracked against his cheek, the force of the blow turning his head. Lorna was shocked by her own physical violence and stared at Benteen with fear as he slowly turned his head back to look at her. No man had ever laid a hand on him in anger and got by with it, but she was a woman — his wife. Benteen controlled the urges within him.

"I'm sorry," she whispered, and eyed the white mark left by her hand as it slowly turned red.

"I swear to God I don't understand you." The angry words were forced through clenched teeth. "You have enough guts to hit me, yet you cry over the lack of privacy."

"You made me angry when you said that," Lorna defended her action.

"You're going to have to grow up. I haven't got time to hold your hand," he declared tersely.

"I don't want you to hold my hand, and I am not a child." That was the cruelest implication. Lorna couldn't help bristling at it. "I may not know as much as you do about things, but that doesn't make me a child."

"This trip is going to be hard. I'm not going to lie and tell you it will get better. Today is just a sampling of what's to come," Benteen warned. "You have a choice. You can either cry over every little thing that happens and wallow around in misery the whole time, or you can accept the way things are — like the rest of us. Mrs. Stanton isn't in her wagon crying her eyes out. The same thing happened to her today."

It wasn't a totally fair comparison, and Benteen knew that. Mary Stanton had not led the sheltered city life that Lorna had. But he mentioned the woman as an example to challenge Lorna.

"What are you going to do? Stay here in the wagon and feel sorry for yourself? Or come outside by the fire with the rest of us?" he questioned.

"I'm coming out." There was a flash of anger in her dark eyes.

"Good." He held out his hand to take hers.

Grudgingly she laid hers into his grasp, resentment for his bluntness and lack of concession to her femininity still smoldering under the surface. Benteen wasn't sure whether her attitude would change to please him or to show him out of spite. There was fire in her; his smarting jaw could attest to that. It would carry her through this journey in better condition than wrapping her in cotton wool.

When she shifted her weight to climb off the mattress, it brought her closer. An awareness sang out to him of all that was woman about her. His other hand curved itself to her neck to stop her movements, and felt her head stiffen in resistance to his touch. Benteen ignored her unwillingness for his kiss and brought his mouth down to the straight line of her lips. He was irritated when she wouldn't yield to him, and increased the pressure until she did.

But submission wasn't enough, not when he'd previously tasted the fullness of her response. He began an investigation of individual curves in her lips, chewing at the lower one and wandering over the top until he felt her leaning into him. He answered the desire she was signaling with a hard, brief kiss, and drew back.

Her mouth was softly swollen, tilted toward

him in silent invitation. She was breathing quickly, at a disturbed rate. Her eyes were dark with need. She looked pliable and a little flushed with eagerness.

"That's the way a bride should look," Benteen murmured in satisfaction. "No tears, and no sulking."

Something flickered in her expression as she suddenly regarded him with a thoughtful look. "When I was a little girl and I did something my daddy didn't like, he'd sit me down and talk to me real stern," she said. Benteen lifted a brow, not seeing the relevance of her childhood memory. "After I promised to behave and be a good girl, he always gave me a piece of rock candy. Do husbands give out kisses as rewards for good behavior?"

Benteen frowned, wondering if he had imagined the little sting in her question. He couldn't be sure. Something told him it was best if he ignored her query.

"Let's go outside," he said, "before everyone starts wondering what we're doing in here."

The remark achieved its desired effect. She didn't pursue an answer to her question and followed Benteen to the rear of the wagon. He swung down and turned to lift her to the ground.

There was a studious attempt by the cowboys to take no notice of her return to the camp circle, but it didn't make it any easier to rejoin them. Everyone had finished eating, and the dirty plates and cutlery were piled in the "wreck pan" to be washed. Lorna noticed the tubful of dishes. Without offering a word of explanation to Benteen, she moved away from his side and walked to the chuck wagon, where the cook was putting some beans to soak.

"I will wash the dishes for you," she stated, and saw his head jerk, a refusal forming in his expression, so she quickly continued with more poise than she felt. "You may not want any help with the cooking, but I can't imagine any man wanting to wash dishes. So I'll do them for you."

"Usually the wrangler or his helper does them," the cook explained. "But I reckon they won't object to losin' the job."

"Thank you, Mr. Rusty." Lorna began rolling up her sleeves to tackle the tubful of dishes. Benteen had indicated everyone regarded her as a spoiled child. She intended to show them that she wasn't above doing menial tasks and that she intended to pull her own weight.

Her new role as cook's help was duly noted by the cowboys as they came to the wagon to get their bedrolls stowed in the front. Benteen noticed, too, but with mixed reaction. He wanted her accepted by the men as his wife, but he didn't want her to associate with them too closely. Over the long haul, it would invite trouble. For the time being, he let it stand.

After assigning men to the four sets of guards drawing night herd duty, Benteen saddled his night horse for his own final check of the cattle. He led it to the chuck wagon, where Lorna was busy scouring the tin plates. Her glance was faintly defiant.

"I'm riding out to the herd," he said.

She nodded, rinsed the plate in her hand, set it aside, and reached for another. Benteen briefly met Rusty's glance, then looped the reins over his horse's neck and swung into the saddle.

The herd was bedded down not far from camp on a stretch of level ground — an area the Longhorns would have picked for themselves. With their thirst quenched and their bellies full, the cattle were lying down. Despite the stampede earlier, they showed no signs of being restive. As Benteen walked the dun horse in a wide circle around the herd, he picked out the brindle steer in the moonlight, resting a little off from the main bunch. Willis and Garvey had pulled the first watch. A rider approached, making his slow circle and hunching loosely over the saddle. Benteen recognized Garvey's musical, crooning voice singing a stanza of "The Old Chisholm Trail."

I'm up in the mornin' afore daylight
And afore I sleep the moon shines bright.
Come a ti yi yippy, yippy, yay, yippy yay,
Come a ti yi yippy, yippy yay,
No chaps and no slicker, and it's pouring
*   down rain,*
And I swear, by God, that I'll never night-
*   herd again.*
Come a ti yi yippy . . .

Garvey let the song trail off in mid-chorus as he drew even with Benteen, both horses stopping for the riders' brief palaver.

"They're as contented as ticks on a dog," Garvey said.

"Let's hope it stays that way," Benteen replied, and kneed his horse forward. Behind him, Garvey picked up the chorus where he'd left off.

. . . yippy yay, yippy yay.
Come a ty yi yippy, yippy yay.
I went to the boss to draw my roll,
He had it figured out I was nine dollars
*   in the hole.*

There was a score of verses or more. Benteen knew Garvey was likely to sing them all and make up a few of his own before his two-hour shift was through. Rounding the herd, Benteen angled the dun horse toward camp. To the south he caught the winking light of another campfire. Bob Vernon had been one of the three drag riders today, and he'd mentioned to Benteen that the Ten Bar herd was behind them.

He left the dun tied at the picket line and carried his saddle to the camp circle. Lorna was sitting by the fire, staring into the flames, something no range-wizened cowboy would do because it blinded him when he looked into the night and its differing textures of darkness.

Knowing the night might be short and the following day long, most of the trailhands were stretched out on the ground, a "soogan" — quilt — cushioning its hardness. Many of them still had their hats on or were using them to cover their faces. Bob Vernon, the scholar of the bunch, was reading a dog-eared copy of Plato for the fifth time.

A cowboy's bedroll was more than just a soogan and a tarp. It held nearly all his possessions that he didn't carry on his person. Everything from tobacco sacks and cigarette papers to a spare cinch and a rope, from a change of clothes to a picture of his family or his girl, from old letters and reading material to a marlinespike, was kept in it.

Young Joe Dollarhide was sitting with Lorna, too green to the trail to know that the sleep he was missing might be all he'd get for two days or more. It happened like that sometimes when herds got it into their heads to stampede. They could keep a man in the saddle for days with no sleep and only dried jerky to eat.

"I'm plannin' on havin' a big spread of my own someday," Joe Dollarhide was bragging to Lorna when Benteen walked up. "I already got my brand all picked out. A dollar mark for my name — a dollar mark on a cowhide." He liked his cleverness in coming up with the association and wanted Lorna to notice it, too. Then he was absently modest. " 'Course, it'll be a few years before I get a place of my own."

"And a girl of your own?" Benteen asked to make sure the boy understood that Lorna was private property.

"Mr. Calder." He stood up quickly, almost snapping to attention.

Benteen took the challenge out of his voice. "Thanks for keeping my wife company." There was still a slight emphasis placed on her marital status.

"Yes, sir." Joe Dollarhide awkwardly bowed to Lorna. "Night, ma'am."

When he started to retreat, Benteen said, "I want you to look over the remuda tomorrow, Dollarhide, and see if there's a gentle horse in the lot — something a lady can ride sidesaddle. If there isn't, I want you to pick the most likely one and break it for my wife. Let me know whose string the horse is from and I'll put it right with him."

"Yes, sir." the young man's shoulders were pushed back, proud that he had been trusted with the responsibility.

As the lad moved into the shadows around the fire, sidestepping bedrolls, Benteen reached for the coffeepot on the fire's edge. "If we can find a gentle horse, you won't have to spend all your time bouncing in the wagon," he said to Lorna as he filled an empty cup left near the pot. "Want some coffee?"

"No, thanks." She shook her head, the glow of the firelight flattering her clear features. "I don't see how you can drink it when it's so thick."

"That's when it's good." He smiled and crouched on his heels beside her, amused by her grimace of distaste. When he took a swallow, his glance ran beyond the tin rim to sweep the camp area. "Where's Mary?"

"She and her husband have already retired for the evening," Lorna answered.

He glanced at the Stanton wagon, and said nothing, letting the silence run between them. From a distant prairie ridge there was the yap-yapping howl of a coyote, trailing off on a thin, wavering note.

"Coyotes?" Lorna asked.

"Yes."

"I heard them once before, when I was a child," she said. "I never realized how lonely they sound."

"You're not used to the quiet."

She huddled closer toward the fire, as if seeking its warmth. The shawl was pulled tightly around her shoulders to keep out the coolness of the Texas night. There was a strange mixture of vulnerability and strength in her profile.

"You'd better turn in," Benteen suggested. "Tomorrow's going to come quick."

There was a second of hesitation as she glanced at him. "What about you?"

It was difficult to read her look, half-thrown into shadows by the firelight. But something in her attitude fanned his close-held needs. She did that to him, making him want to open up and let her into his most secret thoughts.

"I'll be along." Benteen took another drink of

coffee, breaking contact with her look, guarding himself with an aloofness that he didn't fully understand.

Another second went by before she stood up and adjusted the ends of her shawl more closely around her middle. Her long skirts made a soft swishing sound in the tufted grass as she walked to the rear of their wagon. Benteen kept his back to it, listening to the strike of a match and catching the brief flare of light from the lantern wick. He thought of the long journey ahead of them and the cattle land that waited for them in Montana. The picture of it was burned in his mind — the thick grass, the limitless sky.

This Texas sod he stood on was part of the past he was putting behind him, the lost causes that had been his father's and the Southern code of chivalry that had often tied his father's hands. But not his. Nothing was going to stand in his way.

"Holy Jesus." Shorty Niles swore under his breath somewhere in the collection of bedrolls.

Benteen was snapped out of his inward-turned thoughts by the sudden electricity that swept through the night. His first thought was the herd, until he saw Rusty pivoting abruptly so he wasn't facing Benteen's direction. Which was also the direction of his wagon. He jerked his glance over his shoulder, where it was caught and held by the lantern backlighting the canvas covering and a woman's silhouette. Her arms were rising above her head, taking with them a layer of clothing that changed the shape of her silhouette. The roundness of the upper part of her body had its effect on him, filling Benteen with a second of intense desire.

But he wasn't the only one seeing this. Springing upright, he discarded the cup and crossed the short distance with long, reaching strides, outrage vibrating through every sinew. He yanked the canvas flap loose and swung into the wagon bed all in one move. Startled, Lorna swung around to face him, half-undressed.

"Blow out that lantern," he snapped in a low growl.

"But I can't see." She blinked in innocent confusion.

He reached past her to do it himself. "You'll undress in the dark. You and this light are putting on a show for the whole camp!"

His accusation was met with silence; then her embarrassed whisper came from the wagon's darkness. "I didn't know."

"Now you do." Benteen turned to leave, angered yet aware she hadn't known. He paused, fighting down his temper. "It's all right, Lorna," he said, to let her know he wasn't putting any fault with her. "Just be more careful."

He swung down from the wagon and tied the flap back in place. His gaze made a circle of the camp, but all the trailhands were on their side facing the other direction.

Walking back to the fire, Benteen scooped up the cup he'd dropped and carried it to the chuck wagon. Rusty was winding his alarm clock so he could rise before any of the others and have breakfast going by the time the first light touched the sky.

"Havin' women along presents all sorts of difficulties that ain't even thought of," Rusty said without looking at Benteen.

"So I'm learning."

The cook glanced sideways, a whiskery white growth beginning to show up on his face. " 'Pears to me it might be smart to set them wagons back a bit at night." His glance slid down to the bulge in Benteen's pants. "I don't have to ask if you'll be sleepin' with your bride. 'Tween you and Stanton, them cowboys' imagination is going to be workin' overtime without hearin' anythin'. "

Benteen didn't disagree. "Wake me before the others," was his only reply.

"I will — unless the wagon's rockin'," Rusty murmured.

Instead of going directly to the wagon, he walked out to the picket line and had a smoke. Before the cigarette was half gone, Benteen was crushing it under the heel of his boot. A couple hundred miles up the trail when his tobacco ran low, he'd be wanting that wasted cigarette, but it wasn't what he wanted now.

The wagon was dark and silent when he reached it. He climbed in and peeled off his clothes down to his underwear. Feeling his way to the mattress, his hand encountered Lorna's quilt-covered form near the edge.

"Move over." His voice was low, but the wagon springs creaked under her shifting weight.

When he slid beneath the quilt, he discovered that Lorna was hugging the side of the wagon, taking pains not to touch any part of him. For several long minutes he lay on his back and stared at the ribbed canvas roof. Then he reached over and ran his hand along her arm.

"Lorna." It was a request for her to roll over to him.

"No." She was rigid under his touch. "They'll hear us," she whispered.

Benteen shifted to his side and applied pressure to force her shoulders onto the mattress. Her hands came up to push at him, her face faintly outlined in the darkness.

"They'll be thinking we're doing it whether they hear us or not," he reasoned, and curled an arm across her stomach to pull her more closely against him.

"No, I don't want to." She turned her head away from him when he bent to kiss her, so he nuzzled her throat instead. The little vein in her neck was pulsing madly, assuring him that she was lying.

"We're going to be on the trail nearly six months, Lorna. That's six months' worth of nights." His hands were moving over her, discovering her rounded shape despite the loose-fitting nightgown. Her hands were still between them, but she wasn't fighting him. "There's no way I'm not going to make love to you between now and trail's end. And I don't care who listens to us."

"I do," she whispered.

"Then we'd better start learning how to make love quietly," he countered. "After last night, do you want to go that long without it?"

"No." It was a reluctantly moaned answer.

A second later, her lips were under his. He felt that long rush of heat go through him — sweet and wild. There was that same immense shock, that same feeling of a deep need finally satisfied. Lorna could fill his emptiness in a different kind of union that was just as complete.

The nightgown went all the way to her feet. He tugged at the material to work it up around her hips so his hands could get under it and make contact with her woman flesh. It was a rude discovery to find more clothes.

"Do you always wear so many clothes to bed?" Benteen grumbled, and tried to find how her drawers were fastened. "Will you take these things off?"

"Not so loud," she whispered.

"Take them off." He breathed the words into her mouth.

By the time she was through, the nightgown was around her waist and his hands felt the silken heat of her bare skin. He warmed himself with it, letting his roaming hands wander over her rounded buttocks and hips to the source of the heat.

"Your body is hot," he murmured.

"So is yours." Her lips were open against his cheek, the moistness of her mouth turned to him.

When he shifted onto her, a soft sound trembled from her throat. "We're supposed to do this quietly, remember?" Benteen liked the expression of desire she hadn't been able to contain, and eased himself into her.

Instinctively her legs tightened around him. He took it slow, dragging it out to make it last, aware of her hips urging him. Her face was turned away from him, as if to hide the wild need her body was already showing him. His hand forced her face around, his thumb seeking her parted lips to open them more. As the first quivering spasm began to shake her, his kiss filled her opened mouth with his hard tongue. His own shudders drove him deeper into her.

Afterward he gathered her satisfying body into his arms and hugged her to his side. "You are a shameless woman," he murmured against her dark hair.

"Don't say that," Lorna protested in an alarmed whisper.

"It's true." He breathed in the warm, musky smell of her. "You leave me with nothing."

"I thought you meant . . ." She didn't finish it, closing her mouth before the rest came out.

"Feel how small you've made me." He took her hand and showed her.

She brought her hand quickly back to his chest. His chuckle was a silent one, amused by her persistent attempt at modesty when she had been anything but modest a few minutes ago.

"Did I do something wrong?" Lorna murmured.

"You pick the oddest times to be bashful about certain things. That's all," Benteen assured her, and kissed her temple. "You'd better close those dark eyes and try to sleep. We're going to be rising with the sun."

"Good night." She snuggled against him, all soft and warm against his rock-hard frame.

11

They'd been on the trail over three weeks and still hadn't left Texas. Monotony had set in. One day was little different from another as they traveled across a rolling prairie that seemed nonending. The only variation came from the weather. Most of the time it was clear and hot, with the sun making its glaring track across a cloudless sky. When there was a wind, it didn't bring relief. Instead it whipped Lorna's face, burning her cheeks and sending its particles of prairie dust through all her clothes.

The first time the gray clouds darkened the sky, she thought rain would be a blessing, but she soon learned it wasn't. For four days it was dismal and wet, drizzle alternating with a steady downpour that saturated everything. She ate and rode in wet clothes, and shivered and slept in them, too. And the men were in the saddle almost around the clock, the night watches doubling, and on bad nights when the herd wouldn't lie down, all of them rode.

Lorna saw little of Benteen. He was always

up and often in the saddle before she awakened, checking the herd. Sometimes a whole day would go by without her seeing him at all. Many nights she was asleep when he came to bed. She had not seen this compulsive side of him before. Benteen pushed himself harder than he pushed anyone else. She'd mentioned it to Mary once, when Rusty was within hearing — the crusty cook allowed them to help with some of the camp chores but not the cooking.

Rusty had supplied the explanation: "He's the trail boss. It's part of his job to be first up in the mornin' and assign each drover his duty. He has to ride ahead and see where water is, know where to stop at noon and make camp at night. He's gotta keep a tally of the cattle to know if any is lost. If there's any dispute among the men, his word is law. A trail boss always rides three, four times the distance the herd covers."

With Benteen absent so much of the time, Lorna doubted that she could have endured the loneliness if it weren't for Mary Stanton. In such a short time, she had become closer to the woman, telling her things that she wouldn't have dreamed of saying to her mother or Sue Ellen. But neither her mother nor Sue Ellen had experienced trail life. Having Mary for a friend was like having an older sister. Lorna felt free to discuss things that once she considered unmentionable. There were a lot of things she wanted to know about married life, which would make her sound too ignorant if she asked Benteen all of them. Most of the answers, Mary knew, and others they jointly speculated on. Mary was very frank and open – no subject was taboo.

Mounted on fresh horses, a trio of drovers rode out of camp to relieve the cowboys watching the nooning herd so they could come in to eat. Lorna paid scant attention. There were always comings-in and goings-out at camp. Soon there would be dishes to be done. In the meantime, she was busy moistening the cuttings from her mother's roses. She didn't even look around when she heard the pounding hooves of a cantering horse approach the camp. It gave a blowing snort as it was reined in.

"What are you doing?" The voice belonged to Benteen, and Lorna turned, lighting up inside at the way he was studying her. He was leaning an arm on the saddle horn, mindless of his head-tossing horse.

"I'm watering my rose slips," she said, and showed him the cuttings. "Do you see how well they're doing? And you said they'd die," Lorna reminded him.

Benteen didn't comment. "I told Dollarhide to saddle your horse. I thought you might like to ride ahead with me this afternoon."

It was a rare invitation which Lorna was silently delighted with. Feeling provocative, she tipped her head to the side and showed him a look of feigned surprise. "Do you mean that you're actually going to spend some time with me? It's so seldom that I see you for more than five minutes."

His gaze narrowed, but a smile was showing. "You're getting a bit saucy, aren't you?"

"I don't understand why you would say such a thing," she declared innocently, then laughed.

"I'm going to grab a bite of food. I'll see *you* later." His tone indicated the subject would be brought up again, but with a certain bemusement in it that said he wasn't upset. It was a reaction to the way she was flirting with him.

There was a gleam in her eye when Benteen reined his horse away from the wagon and walked it to the chuck wagon. Within seconds after he'd left, Lorna was hurrying over to tell Mary of the afternoon outing.

When Mary had expressed her pleasure for Lorna's sake, Lorna asked the same question she'd asked before. "Are you sure you don't want me to speak to Benteen about a horse for you?"

Mary's answer was the same. "No, I'm sure. The only way I know how to ride a horse is astraddle. That was all right when I was a little girl on the farm, but it's definitely not something a married woman should do."

"But I could teach you to ride with a sidesaddle," Lorna persuaded.

It was a tempting offer, because Mary fancied looking as ladylike as Lorna did, but it was for that very reason that she refused. She didn't want to admit to envying Lorna. She doubted that she would ever be able to achieve Lorna's skill or grace, and what good would it do her if she did? She had better things to do with her time, she convinced herself.

"No, thanks. I get enough bumps and bruises from the wagon seat. I don't need to get more falling off a horse," she refused firmly.

With a sigh, Lorna turned away. Even if she had been able to persuade Mary, there was still only one sidesaddle, which meant they wouldn't be able to ride together, and that would have been half the fun.

Unless she was accompanied by Benteen on one of his forays in advance of the herd, her rides were restricted to staying with the wagons. The wind whipped her long skirts, spooking the cattle, so she wasn't allowed to ride anywhere near the herd or to venture out of sight of the wagons. Despite the strict limits, just the change from driving the wagon all the time made it more than worthwhile.

Her mount was a buttermilk-colored buckskin. By nature, it was a calm, steady animal, but with plenty of life. There was nothing plodding or sedate about its way of going. He seemed more surprised than uneasy with the unusual saddle on his back and the many layers of skirt and petticoats constantly brushing his side, but he settled down to it quickly. Lorna named him Sandman because of his color and his gentlemanly ways.

As she cantered the buckskin alongside Benteen's mount, the prairie gave way to rough, broken country that marked the Red River Valley and the Texas boundary. Lorna was awed by the wild land. There was certainly nothing like it around Fort Worth, but she'd never ventured more than a day's drive from there in her life until now.

When they reached the Red River, its sluggish water was thick with the clay-red silt that gave it its name. Stopping on a knoll overlooking the river, Benteen studied the river like a general looking over a battlefield before the battle starts.

"Is something wrong?" Lorna asked.

She wasn't aware how treacherous river crossings could be to cattle and men. So far, they had forded only tame streams that had offered them no trouble. Benteen didn't enlighten her about the difference.

"No." His gaze traveled beyond the river to the land on the opposite side. "Once we cross that, Texas will be behind us."

The satisfaction in his voice sobered Lorna, because she didn't share his desire to cut all ties with this country. There were many things she didn't allow her mind to dwell on; missing her parents was one of them. She had tried so hard to get through each day without complaining, to show Benteen that she was game enough to take it. She kept telling herself that everything would be all right when they finally reached Montana and they had a real home instead of a covered wagon. But would it?

"Wait here," Benteen ordered. "I'm going to ride down for a closer look."

Checking the buckskin's attempt to follow, Lorna watched Benteen ride down to the fording place. It seemed he was always thinking about the cattle and the trail ahead. There was hardly room for anything else. Even when he took her along, like this afternoon, it seemed to be a token gesture — just like when she was a little girl and her father used to let her come to his store as long as she promised to sit and be very quiet and not make a nuisance of herself. The only time she had Benteen's undivided attention was at night — and that hadn't been very often lately. In irritation, Lorna realized he was saving his strength and energy for the trail drive.

Benteen had swum his horse to the other side and was on his way back when she heard the sound of a horse and rider approaching the river. Lorna turned, not recognizing the burly man on the sorrel horse. It wasn't anyone from their outfit. Lorna was more curious than alarmed by the sight of the stranger riding up to her. He was only one man, and Benteen was within shouting distance.

When he stopped his horse a few yards from her, he swept off his hat in a gallant gesture of respect and held it to his chest. He seemed to be all chest, shoulders, and neck. Lorna inclined her head in a silent acknowledgment of his action.

"Good day to you, Mrs. Calder," the stranger said, taking her by surprise when he used her name. There was a boldness about him as he smiled. "We've never met, but you've been described to me, so I recognized you right off."

"You have the advantage, sir," she murmured.

"My name's Giles. My friends call me Bull," he introduced himself. "I'm bossin' a herd a few miles back down the trail."

"I'm pleased to meet you, Mr. Giles." Lorna had heard the men talking about one herd following them, although there were many ahead and behind. "Would you be driving Mr. Boston's cattle?"

"That's right enough, ma'am." He was blatantly admiring. "You not only sit a horse pretty, but you got a bright mind, too."

No one — not even Benteen — had complimented Lorna for her intelligence and ability to think. Ever since her marriage, she'd felt incredibly ignorant and naïve. But this man had just made her feel clever and smart. It did wonderful things for her self-esteem.

"You're very kind, Mr. Giles." She was glowing.

"How can a man be anything else in the company of a beautiful lady?" His gallant flattery seemed such a contradiction to his muscled, pugnacious appearance. Perhaps that's what made it seem so sincere, Lorna thought.

Cantering hooves signaled Benteen's approach. The man named Bull Giles gave a considering look in her husband's direction and shoved his hat back onto his head. The smile went from his face as it took on that closed-in expression Lorna had noticed men wear when they met each other. When Benteen halted his horse, it was positioned between Lorna and the Ten Bar trail boss.

"Giles." Benteen greeted the man with a nod of his head.

"How's the river?"

"A little soft on the other bank, but otherwise it's in good shape." River water dripped from Benteen, and his horse was shiny wet with it.

"When're you figurin' to cross?" the big man asked.

"Tomorrow morning."

"Don't be all day at it," Giles said. "Else I'll have to push you aside to take my cows across."

"I don't push too easy," Benteen replied. On the surface, the exchange seemed to be an idle one, holding no heat, yet Lorna sensed some undercurrent running between them.

"That's the way I always had it figured," the big man agreed. " 'Course I had thought Boston would get some opposition over the Cee Bar."

"It wasn't my play, and Pa had already cashed in his chips before Boston picked up his winnings," he stated.

"Yeah, I heard you was headed for Montana Territory." Giles nodded. "Reckon I might take another look at that country after I deliver these cows in Dodge City." But he was looking straight at Lorna when he said it, leaving the impression that she was what he'd be going to see.

Lorna blushed a little, feeling the sharpness of Benteen's gaze upon her. She felt the fluttering of her pulse and didn't know which man to blame for it. When Giles glanced at Benteen, there was something in his eyes that dared Benteen to object.

"Have you met my wife?" Again there was emphasis on the possessive word.

"Yes, I introduced myself when I rode up," he admitted. "I hope you're taking good care of her, 'cause there's bound to be somebody else around willin' to do the job."

"Namely you?" Benteen challenged in a cool, smooth voice.

"An ugly brute like me?" Giles laughed.

Lorna failed to notice that he didn't deny it, although Benteen did. "I'm sure you underrate your own worth, Mr. Giles," she insisted. It reminded her too much of the way Sue Ellen was always putting herself down because of her plain looks.

"Now you are being kind, Mrs. Calder." Such flawless manners seemed so incongruous coming from such a rough-looking man. His attention swung back to Benteen. "I think I'll take a look-see at the river myself." He backed his sorrel horse up a few feet, then reined it toward the river ford.

When the Ten Bar trail boss was out of hearing, Benteen demanded, "What did you say to him before I came?"

"Practically nothing. Why?" Lorna frowned.

"You must have said or done something. A man doesn't look at a married woman the way Giles looked at you unless he's been given a reason to think his interest was welcome." His gaze was narrow, punching holes in her newly found self-esteem. "You were looking quite pleased about something when I rode up."

"He had paid me a compliment — something I rarely hear anymore," she retorted a little snappishly.

"In case you haven't noticed, I have been busy lately." He matched her testiness.

"Why? Because you've been bossing this drive?" Lorna gave him a cool look. "Mr. Giles has been busy bossing a drive, too, but that didn't keep him from saying something nice to me."

"It's probably been three weeks since he's seen a woman."

"And I suppose it makes a difference because you've seen me every day and he hasn't," she challenged. "Or maybe Mr. Giles knows how to make a woman feel good about herself and you only know how to make her feel foolish and ignorant."

Lorna slapped the buckskin with the reins and sent it galloping back over the route they had traveled to the river. She knew Benteen was angry, but so was she. She hadn't encouraged Bull Giles and she resented the implication that she had.

That night, Benteen assigned himself to the second shift of night herd and spread out a bedroll on the ground outside the wagon so he could be easily wakened. Lorna hadn't spoken to him since they'd reached camp, and he was damned if he was going to make the first move. The next morning he blamed his irritability on the shortness of the night.

The wagons were sent ahead to cross the Red before the herd. Once the Longhorns had the morning stretch and grazed a short while, Benteen made a circling wave of his hat over his head to signal the men to move them out. The point riders picked up the motion and passed the signal down the line.

The brindle steer quickly shouldered his way

to the lead. It wasn't long until the herd was nicely strung out, a multicolored ribbon of hide and horn moving along. The cattle were walking freely toward the water, at this point drifting, not driven. There had been no water at last night's bedground, and this morning they were thirsty.

When the brindle and his immediate followers waded in to drink, the drovers tightened ranks to shove the rest of the herd after them and force the lead group into the river. Jessie Trumbo on right point swam his horse in front of the brindle to show him the way to the other side.

"Come on and follow me!" Benteen heard Jessie call to the steer. "Come on, you captain of this sea of horns!"

The swimming Longhorns made a strange spectacle. The mud-red river hid their bodies under the water, leaving exposed only the heads with their sweeping rack of long horns. The cowboys pressed to keep the herd compact, not allowing a gap to appear in the flow of horns.

The first steers reached the opposite bank while the swing men, Jonesy and Andy Young, rode into the river on either side of the swimming cattle. The flank and drag riders continued to push from behind. From his vantage point on the riverbank, Benteen watched the proceedings, alert to anything that might threaten this smooth crossing. Sometimes cowboys never knew what would startle a cow — an eddy, a submerged tree branch, or the cry of a whippoorwill. Andy was letting his side of the herd drift too far downstream, where there were patches of quicksand that could swallow a horse or steer in minutes. Benteen shouted to him above the din of bawling beefs. It was acknowledged with a wave.

Something went wrong in midstream. Benteen never saw what it was. Suddenly the cattle started milling in a circle, trying to turn and swim back to the bank they'd left, but the rest of the herd was being pushed into them.

It had happened quickly — and it had to be broken up just as quickly, or the animals in the middle would be drowned in the crush of churning bodies. Jonesy had already seen it and was swimming his horse directly at the tangled mass, hitting and yelling at the excited beasts to turn them toward the north bank. Benteen spurred his horse into the river as Andy Young turned his mount toward the mill. A steer, swimming in a blind panic, rammed into Andy's horse. It floundered, unseating its rider.

"Andy's down!" Jonesy shouted.

Benteen saw the cowboy hat floating downstream, then caught a glimpse of Andy's head as he bobbed to the surface. The coil of cattle was between him and the rider. Jonesy was closer.

From the north bank, water splashed as Spanish rode his horse into the river to come to their aid, while Jessie held the part of the herd that had already made the crossing.

When Jessie threw a rope for Andy, Benteen directed his efforts to breaking the mill. There wasn't time to think of the personal risk or danger. There was only the cattle and saving them. Spanish rode his horse close to the center and slid off to begin climbing across the backs of animals to the middle. With border curses and flailing fists, he began driving a wedge in the circle of horns. Benteen's pressure finished the job, and the steers were once again heading in the same direction toward the north bank.

Benteen's horse labored onto the bank, trembling and snorting. He was breathing hard, too, but his mind was still on the cattle and getting the rest of the herd across. Two of the flank riders accompanied the stream of horns across. As Shorty Niles rode by Benteen, his face was white and strained.

"The sonofabitches didn't make it. The stupid sonofabitches," he cursed, but it was a pain-filled voice.

Benteen looked at the last place where he'd seen Jonesy. His riderless horse was on the south bank, shaking itself like a wet dog. There was no sign of Jonesy or Andy Young. Benteen drank in a deep breath and held it, shutting his eyes before he let it out in a long, wavering sigh.

No attempt was made to look for the bodies of the cowboys until the entire herd had made the crossing and been bunched a half-mile from the river. When they searched downstream, they found the bodies floating a mile away. In all, the mill at the river crossing had taken a heavy toll. Two riders dead and seventy head of cattle drowned.

The bodies were wrapped in tarp and carried to a bluff overlooking the river to be buried. It was a solemn service; by necessity, a brief one, too. Lorna stared at all the emotionless faces of the men standing by the graves, hats in hand. Ely Stanton had fashioned a pair of crude crosses out of tree limbs and rawhide to mark the burial sites, but no names were carved into them. Someone had plucked their hats from the river, and they were hanging on the upright beams of the crosses. No cowboy went anywhere without his hat. He ate with it, slept with it, and died with it.

As trail boss, it was Benteen's duty to say a few words over them. "They were good men, but You know that. Give them good horses to ride and a clear sky overhead. Amen."

"Amen," Lorna repeated, but she was the only one.

Her eyes were bright; a thread of fear trembled over her at the mortality of humans. She didn't know Jonesy — no one had told her his full name — or Andy Young very well, but they'd both been alive at breakfast this morning, bringing her their plates to be washed. Now they were dead. Yet she seemed to be the only one affected by it.

There was a head-down shuffling-away from the graves. She heard Vince Garvey murmur to another drover, "When I cross over an' hear some angel singin' off-key, I guess I'll know it's Jonesy. Never could sing a note."

"Hey, Shorty, would you teach me another verse to 'Sweet Betsy'?" Zeke Taylor asked.

"Sure." Shorty nodded.

Lorna watched them filing to their horses. "Doesn't it bother them?" She hadn't realized she'd murmured the question aloud until Rusty spoke up.

"Nearly everyone here has ridden out to see the elephant," he said. "He's come close to shakin' hands with Death many a time. They just don't let their feelings show when one of their kind meets his Maker. They know about dying, but they know about living, too."

Rusty walked away without waiting to see if she understood his explanation. Mary paused by the graves and laid a bouquet of wildflowers on each of them, and bowed her head in a silent prayer.

The flowers would die. The elements and the animals that roamed the wild country would soon knock down the crosses, and the grass would cover the graves. Lorna turned and ran to the wagon at the bottom of the slope, unaware of Benteen's approach or the tightness of his jaw when she turned and fled.

Resolutely Benteen went after her, prepared for another emotional display over the death of the two cowboys. There were tears in her eyes when he reached the wagon, but determination sharpened her tightly drawn features.

"Lorna."

"You needn't worry. I'm not going to cry like a child." She climbed onto the wagon seat and began searching frantically for something. The minute she found it, she hopped to the ground.

"What are you doing?" Benteen frowned.

"I'm going to plant two of the cuttings from my mother's roses on their graves so they'll always have a marker." Her dark eyes challenged him to object.

The gesture made his voice husky. "Make it quick. We've got to be moving out."

12

With Texas and the Red River behind them, the drive began its trek through the Indian territory. This section of the Chisholm Trail between the Red River and the Cimarron had been notorious for the raids on cattle herds by Indians and white renegades alike in the early years of the trail's history. Although the risk of an attack had lessened, the men kept a sharp eye out for trouble just the same. With the deaths of Andy and Jonesy, the drive was shorthanded, which meant extra duty for everyone.

A week into the Indian nation, Lorna was washing dishes from the noon meal. The arduous life was beginning to show its effects. She had lost weight, taking the girlish plumpness from her cheeks. In spite of the bonnet she wore most of the day, her complexion had lost its milky-white color, burned by the sun and wind to a golden brown. Her hands were chapped and rough from being immersed in water often high in alkali. Sometimes when she looked in the small mirror in the wagon, she doubted if her own mother would recognize her.

It was a small consolation that Mary's dresses were loose around her waist, too. But Lorna noticed that her sisterly friend appeared to be weathering it better than she was. With a sigh, she turned back to the wreck pan, washed another dish, and handed it to Mary to dry.

There was a vague awareness that someone was watching her. She looked up. Terror leaped through her blood. A half-naked Indian was standing by the chuck wagon, his face and chest smeared with warpaint. All those frightening stories Sue Ellen had told her about white women being taken captive by Indians came rushing to her mind. She dropped the half-washed plate into the water and screamed.

Benteen had just left Spanish on the point to ride ahead when he heard the scream come from the noon camp. Dragging the rifle from its scabbard, he reined his fresh mount toward the distant wagons and buried his spurs in its belly. It had been Lorna who screamed, although he didn't know how he knew that.

Horses were running behind him. Benteen took one quick look to verify it was Spanish and Shorty Niles from the flank position, coming to support him, as had been preplanned if there was trouble. There weren't two better men if it turned into a fight.

His suspicions were confirmed when he saw a half-dozen bucks straddling skinny ponies between the herd and the wagons. They all had rifles, two of them brand-new repeating rifles, Army issue. Benteen slowed his horse as he neared them, feeling their stony eyes watching him. He rode past them toward the noon camp, not knowing how many Indians were there, and trapped between the two.

That initial scream of terror seemed to shock Lorna to her senses. The savage had made no threatening move toward her. She was frozen beside Mary and staring at the first real "wild" Indian she'd ever seen. She saw he was old, his scraggly hair nearly gray. He was skinny and leathered, not quite as alarming as she had thought. Lorna dragged her gaze away from him to look more and saw two on horseback, holding the string to a third horse.

The old Indian started talking. Lorna couldn't understand a word he was saying, but he seemed to be making a very eloquent speech, judging by the graceful gesturing of his hands. She half-turned her head toward the cook.

"Do you understand what he's saying, Mr. Rusty?" she asked.

"It's just a bunch of mumbo-jumbo to me," he admitted.

The Indian stopped talking and gestured to his mouth. "I think he wants something to eat," Mary said.

"Are there any beans left?" Lorna asked.

"Yep," Rusty answered.

"Hand me a plate, Mary." Lorna's hand was shaking when she took it. Smiling widely at the Indian, she held it out to Rusty. "Put some beans on it — and any biscuits you have." She glanced at the other two Indians on their ponies. "Fix two more plates, Mary."

She made the same gesture of her hand to her mouth that the old Indian had made and offered the plate to him, stretching her arm to the limit of her reach. He took it and began shoveling the beans into his mouth with his fingers.

"I don't remember anybody takin' such a likin' to those Pecos strawberries," Rusty commented, and scraped the last of the beans onto a plate.

Mary set the two plates on the edge of the worktable and motioned for the other two Indians to come eat. Then she and Lorna backed away to stand closer to Rusty as the two vaulted from their horses and rushed toward the chuck wagon, setting their rifles on the ground.

"They must be starving." Lorna frowned at the way they crammed the beans into their mouths.

It saddened Lorna to watch the old Indian lick the tin plate to get the last of the beans. He held out the plate and gestured again to his mouth, wanting more.

Rusty made an empty motion with his hands. "No more. All gone." In an aside, he murmured to the women, "I hope they don't ransack the wagon, or we won't have no more."

Lorna realized that the situation was still precarious. Then she heard the pounding of horses' hooves and looked around to see Benteen riding up, followed by the Mexican and Shorty.

Peeling out of the saddle before the horse came to a full stop, Benteen made a quick assessment of the scene — the empty plates and the three Indians turning to face him. It was going to be up to Shorty to keep his eye on the other six between the camp and the herd. He kept the rifle gripped in one hand at his side.

"They seem to be hungry, Benteen," Rusty said.

Spanish came up beside him, all quiet and

alert. "What do they look like to you?" Benteen asked. "Kiowa? Osage? Do you speak their lingo?" Benteen walked slowly forward, all his muscles coiled and ready. Spanish followed a half-step behind.

"No Kiowa. A little Cheyenne. A little Comanche. Maybe they know Spanish," he suggested.

"Try it."

Spanish greeted the old Indian, the obvious spokesman for the band, and received an answer. He translated it to Benteen. "The old one is Spotted Elk. He says you are trespassing on his land." There was a pause as the Indian spoke again and Spanish replied. The Indian said something else. This time Benteen recognized the word "wohaw," which was what the Indians called the Longhorn cattle. "He says" – Spanish paused – "you must pay him one hundred beefs or you cannot cross his land."

"Tell him the price is too high." Benteen had bargained with Indians before. "Tell him I will pay him one wohaw for a toll price to pass through his land."

There was a lengthy haggling exchange between Spanish and the Indian while they tried to agree on terms. Spanish glanced at Benteen. "He says he will settle for twenty beefs — no less."

"Rusty, what have you got in the wagon? Any geegaws?" Benteen asked, not taking his eyes from the gray-headed Indian. "Any supplies you can spare?"

"Got some red bandannas. Those red devils ought to go for them." Rusty walked to the front of the wagon and pawed through the contents until he found what he was looking for.

"Lay them on the ground," Benteen advised, then said to Spanish, "Tell him we will give him five steers, those bandannas, and some tobacco. And tell him" — he reached in his shirt pocket and took out his tally book and pencil — "there's a big herd a day's drive behind us. They will pay him twenty steers if he gives them this paper."

Moistening the lead point, he wrote a quick note: "To Whom It May Concern: This is a good Indian. Pay twenty beefs for passing through his land." And Benteen signed it "Judd Boston." It was a dirty trick, but Boston had a few coming. He had no qualms about letting those Indians become Bull Giles's problem. It was a way of getting back at the rival trail boss for being so forward with Lorna. He tore off the note and handed it to a grinning Spanish, who loved a good joke at someone else's expense as much as the next cowboy.

Spanish relayed the message. The Indian considered it, then came back with a counter offer that widened the Mexican's eyes. "While he waits for the big herd, he says he will take ten steers and the young squaw to look after him."

Lorna's mouth opened in shock. Benteen didn't blink an eye. "Tell him the squaw's no good. She complains too much."

"Benteen Calder . . ." She breathed his name in outrage.

"Just shut up and stay out of it, Lorna," he ordered. "Tell Spotted Elk what I said and repeat the last offer."

When it was done, the old Indian looked at Benteen with a sidelong glance. "He says you insult him. If you don't give him ten steers, he will have his braves stampede your herd tonight and you will not have any cattle."

"Tell Spotted Elk if his braves stampede my herd, I will attack his village and kill all his warriors. Then ask him how his women and children will eat when there are no men to hunt for them."

Lorna was stunned by Benteen's threat. The Indians were only hungry. All they asked was for him to pay for crossing their land with his cattle. The old Indian had not said anything about attacking them, only stampeding the cattle. In her opinion, Benteen's threat was much too harsh.

There was a long silence while the old Indian held Benteen's hard gaze and weighed his words. Finally he nodded his head once.

"He will accept the offer," Spanish confirmed; then a smile twitched at the corners of his mouth. "He says he will take the complaining squaw off your hands, too."

Benteen hesitated an instant. "Spotted Elk can have the complaining squaw, but —"

"Benteen Calder, what are you saying?" Lorna was furious, and a little frightened, too. "How dare you —"

He raised his voice to drown her out. "— but tell him that she has had the spotted sickness."

The instant Spanish repeated Benteen's statement, the old Indian backed away, putting distance between himself and Lorna. A mumbled phrase to the other two braves had them retreating as well. Lorna was too incensed to be relieved.

"Rusty, tie a couple of tobacco sacks up with those bandannas," Benteen ordered. "When you ride out to the herd, Spanish, have the boys cut out those two lame steers and three others. We've got a couple that have been trying to quit the bunch ever since we left."

"Right."

As soon as they had their bundle of loot, the gray-haired Indian and his two braves mounted their horses and waited for Spanish. Benteen stayed in camp while Shorty and Spanish rode together back to the herd.

Rusty walked to the chuck box and reached in a drawer, pulling out a six-shooter. "Guess I'd better be keepin' this within reach," he said. "They just appeared out of nowhere. I didn't have time to get this."

"There wasn't much you could do with three of them," Benteen said, and let his gaze travel to Lorna and Mary. "Are both of you all right?"

"We're fine," Mary replied. "They didn't come near us except to take the food we gave them."

"Do you really care?" Now that it was over, Lorna was starting to tremble, but her anger at Benteen hadn't lessened, regardless of the outcome. "You were going to hand me over to that savage." She didn't believe for a second that he had seriously entertained the idea, but she thought he'd taken a big chance with her life when he had pretended to agree.

"You know better than that," he said tersely. "If a situation like this happens again, Lorna, I want you to keep quiet and let me handle it. I know what I'm doing."

"Just tell me one thing," she demanded, staring at him. "If Spotted Elk had stampeded the herd, would you have attacked his village and killed his men?"

"Yes."

A cold shiver danced over her skin. She believed him. "Why?" she murmured. "He didn't threaten to harm us."

"You don't understand Indians and the way they think," Benteen stated. "They respect strength. I promised a harsh penalty if he came against me — more severe than he would inflict. That's why he agreed to accept five cows, and that's why his braves won't stampede the herd tonight."

"Cattle." Her voice trembled on the word. "That's all you ever think about. You don't care about me or anyone else. Just as long as those damned cows make it to Montana."

"Those 'damned' cows represent our future." He cuttingly emphasized the swear word Lorna had used. "And, yes, that's all I care about! You and everyone else should be able to look out for yourselves. You aren't a bunch of dumb animals. You can think. You've got a mind."

Turning on his heel, Benteen strode to his horse and swung into the saddle.

Hot tears were welling in Lorna's eyes. "I

don't have to ask where you're going," she told him angrily. "You're going out to check on the cattle!"

He gave her a cold look and reined his horse in a half-circle. Her shoulders started shaking, but she wouldn't cry. She glanced at Mary, expecting her sympathy.

"That wasn't fair, Lorna," Mary said. "He does care."

"No, hc doesn't," she retorted. "Not about us. Only those animals. Those stupid animals."

More than anything, she wanted to crawl into the back of the wagon and have a good cry, but it would be just exactly what Benteen expected her to do. She walked stiffly back to the pan of dishes.

"Let's get this cleaned up," she declared. "As my husband would say, we've got to move on."

Behind her back, Rusty and Mary exchanged glances but said no more on the subject. It was between her and Benteen. It never did any good to interfere between a man and his wife, even with the best of intentions.

Before they had the last of the gear stowed away, Benteen rode back into the noon camp, followed by young Joe Dollarhide with Lorna's buckskin in tow. She wasn't in any mood to be placated by being treated to an afternoon ride, but she wasn't given any choice as Joe tied his horse to the back of her wagon and climbed into the seat to take up the reins and drive the team off. She glared at Benteen, cinching the sidesaddle on her horse while the other wagons pulled out.

"I'm not interested in riding with you," Lorna stated when he finally looked at her.

"Come on. I'll give you a leg up." He waited beside her horse until she grudgingly came to him.

With the buckskin standing quietly, Benteen linked his fingers together to make a cup of his hand. She stepped into it and made him take her full weight to lift her up to the saddle, then ground her hard-soled shoe into his hands before drawing her foot away.

Benteen waited until she was settled comfortably in the sidesaddle and had her skirts adjusted, then mounted his horse. "Ready?" His face wore no expression when he looked at her.

At Lorna's stiff nod, he sent his horse forward. They cantered parallel with the herd for a short distance, then passed. Then Benteen veered his horse to the east and Lorna followed. No attempt was made to break the brittle silence between them.

After they had traveled several miles and were well away from the herd, Benteen stopped his horse by a stand of oak trees and dismounted. Lorna didn't know his purpose for stopping here, so she didn't alight until Benteen came over to lift her down. Under the shade of the trees, she loosened the strings to her bonnet and let it fall down her back.

"I suppose there's a reason for us stopping here," she challenged, looking around. If he intended to apologize and romance her, she wasn't going to make it easy for him.

"Have you ever shot a gun before?" he asked. "A rifle or pistol?"

Lorna stared at him, a little stunned that her guess had been so wide of the mark. Her eyes widened when Benteen lifted the long-barreled revolver from the holster belted around him. He began removing the bullets; the click-clicking sound seemed ominously loud.

"Have you?" Benteen repeated.

"No." Her father hadn't even permitted her to touch the weapons in his store, fully aware that her mother would have been horrified if he had.

"I'll show you how it works."

While he began explaining the functions of the hammer, the chamber, and the trigger, Lorna had difficulty paying attention. She didn't see why she needed to know this. What was more, she didn't *want* to know anything about guns.

"Here." He held out the pistol to her. "Get the feel of it."

She hid her hands behind her back. "No." She refused to touch it and eyed him with a wary frown.

Benteen was patient. "Take it. It isn't loaded."

"What's happening, Benteen?" A wave of uneasiness washed through her. "Ever since we left Fort Worth, you seem to be changing right in front of my eyes. When you were courting me, you were always kind and attentive. You never raised your voice to me. Lately, you're always snapping at me about something. You just get harder and harder every day. What happened to the man I knew in Fort Worth — the man I married? I'm sure he wouldn't be insisting that I learn how to shoot a gun."

"There's a big difference between Fort Worth and here. There aren't any sheriffs who will come if there's trouble. There aren't any streets or roads. You can't depend on anyone but yourself," Benteen stated. "This country weeds out the cowardly and the weak. You have to be hard if you're going to survive. You can't fight this land and make it bend to what you want. You have to adapt to it. I'm not really any different, Lorna. The man you knew in Fort Worth was what the town allowed me to be."

Once she wouldn't have understood what he was saying, but she had lived on the trail for more than a month. There were so many things she accepted that would have repulsed her before.

"Maybe it isn't just you," she admitted. "Look at me and how different I am. I've worn the same dress for days without washing it. I haven't bathed since we left Fort Worth. My hands. My face. My hair is practically caked with dust and grime." She lifted her gaze to him, bewildered by her own changes. "I never used to be cross. When you're short with me, I just want to hit back."

"I've noticed." His voice was dry. "Life's tough enough out here without there being trouble between you and me."

For a long second they looked at each other; then, with a little cry, Lorna went into his arms, tilting her head for his kiss. His arms crushed her to his solid male length, the pistol still held in his hand. Their lips moved hungrily together, as if clinging to something they'd almost lost. The sweaty, dusty smell of him was blocked out. There was only the hard vitality of his body and the satisfying pressure of his mouth on hers.

When the kiss ended, Lorna continued to press her cheek against the bristly roughness of his. Her eyes were closed in a holding on to of the moment of closeness.

"Sometimes I'm frightened by what's happening," she admitted in a whisper.

"Nothing can frighten you unless you allow it," Benteen replied, and pulled back his head to look at her, bringing his hands up to push on her shoulders and force her feet onto the ground. The butt of the pistol grip dug into her flesh. "It's time you learned how to shoot."

Reluctantly she withdrew from his embrace and stared at the gun, before finally taking it. It was heavy. Benteen had handled it as if it weighed next to nothing.

"First see if there's any bullets in it," Benteen instructed.

"But you unloaded it."

"Check for yourself," he insisted. "Do you remember how to do it?"

"Yes, I think so." Lorna turned the cylinder as she had seen him do and confirmed the gun was empty.

"Pull the hammer back a few times and squeeze the trigger so you can get the feel of it," he told her. She had to use both hands to hold it. "And remember, *never*," he emphasized, "point it at anyone, even when the gun is empty."

The hammer and trigger were stiff. Coupled with the weight of the gun, they made her attempts feel very awkward. After she had done it a few times Benteen took the gun back and began returning the .45-caliber bullets to their chambers.

"I'll load it with five bullets." He stressed the number and suggested, "Why don't you pick out a target?"

Lorna chose something big. "That tree trunk." She pointed to a large oak not too far away.

He appeared to do no more than swing the gun toward it, holding it with only one hand. The sudden explosion and flash of blue fire from the pistol startled Lorna. She flinched and closed her eyes at the deafening noise.

"That's what it's going to sound like when you fire it," he said, and smoothly shifted his grip on the revolver to hand it to her butt-first. "It will kick back against your hands, so hold on to it firmly. And don't close your eyes."

"Did you hit the tree?" she asked, feeling very nervous and not at all eager to go through with these lessons.

"Yes." Crow tracks of amusement fanned out from the corners of his eyes. Using both hands, she lifted the gun straight out from her and closed one eye to squint down the barrel. Her heart was beating madly in her throat. "Don't try to aim it." Benteen lowered her arms and adjusted the grip of her right hand to lay a forefinger along the barrel. "Pretend you're pointing your finger at the tree and squeeze the trigger."

The instructions sounded very simple. She even thought she had done what he told her. When she squeezed the trigger, the gun exploded and seemed to almost jump right out of her hands. Instinctively she closed her eyes.

"You shot off a leaf on the top of the tree," Benteen informed her. "Try it again, but this time look at the trunk and point your finger at the spot you're looking at."

"I don't know why we're doing this," Lorna protested, wanting to end the lessons now. "I'm never going to shoot at anything."

"I hope you never have to," Benteen stated. "Try again."

Lorna tried again – and yet again – with the same degree of failure. "How many bullets are left in the gun?" he asked.

She had to stop and count how many times she and Benteen had fired it. "One."

"Always leave one bullet in the gun. Never fire that last one at anything." His expression was so serious that it simply made Lorna more uneasy about this whole experience. "Save it for yourself."

"So I won't be taken alive by Indians." Every female in the frontier had heard stories about women killing themselves rather than being captured by Indians. Lorna was no exception. She shuddered at the thought. With today's meeting fresh in her mind, she tried to reason away her fear with the unlikelihood of it ever being necessary. "You don't really believe that Spotted Elk or his band would attack us, do you?"

"I wasn't thinking of these reservation Indians so much as I was the Sioux up in the Montana Territory." Benteen slipped more bullets out of his cartridge belt. "Load it and try again."

"Why don't I practice another time?" Lorna felt shaky inside.

"No. We're gonna stay here until you either hit the tree trunk or I run out of bullets."

It was typically quiet around camp that evening. Most of the drovers lay exhausted, slumped against their saddles, rolled cigarettes dangling from their mouths. Yates was re-shoeing one of the cow ponies over by the chuck·wagon, the tap of his hammer out of rhythm with the song Woolie was playing on the harmonica. Joe Dollarhide was sitting next to two drovers, all ears as they traded tall tales.

Lorna was sitting with Mary. Ely had drawn first watch on night herd and Benteen was out making one last turn around the bedground to see that all was quiet. In the dimming light, the sewing needle made quick flashes of silver as it darted in and out to secure a button to one of Benteen's shirts. Lorna had already related to Mary an account of her first shooting lesson that afternoon, and Benteen's warning about saving a last bullet. That seemed to amuse Mary.

"Why are you smiling about something like that?" Lorna frowned.

"I was just remembering a sad story I heard one time." Mary paused in her mending. "A young wife had just come out from the East to join her husband, who had homesteaded a farm in Kansas. I imagine she'd been filled with horror tales about the Indians before coming. Anyway" — she shrugged and began stitching again — "she'd only been out here a couple of weeks. Her husband was out in the fields, and she was alone in their sod house. She heard someone ride up, evidently looked out the window and saw two Indians. She was probably certain that she was about to be kidnapped and raped, so she ran to the trunk and dug out her husband's service pistol and killed herself."

"And the Indians?" Lorna prompted.

"There's the irony of it. They were friends of her husband. One had been educated in a school back East and had come to visit," Mary said to explain her wry smile.

13

Day after day, the prairie undulated in front of the trail riders and wagons. The sun seared the grass to a shade of gold-brown while ten thousand hooves stirred up choking clouds of dust. The only sounds that made themselves heard were the rattle and rumble of the wagons, the cracking of horses' ankle joints, and the steady thud of walking hooves and the muffled clatter of horns banging into each other. It dulled the senses and the mind.

It was a season ripe to breed violent storms, boiling up suddenly and erupting in a fierce display of thunder, lightning, and rain. On those stormy nights — six different occasions during the drive through the Indian nation — it was every man in the saddle, trying to hold the herd. Twice the cattle stampeded, but they never ran in the right direction, which was north. In total, three days were lost rounding up strays, and the tally still came up short twenty-seven head, but no lives were lost.

Riding ahead, Benteen spotted a young buck antelope. He was far enough away from the herd that a shot wouldn't spook the cattle. After a steady diet of "Pecos strawberries" and "overland trout" — the cowboy slang for bacon — fresh meat would be welcomed in camp. He dropped the antelope with one shot and gutted it on the spot, cutting off a hindquarter and leaving the rest.

Although they were surrounded by tons of beef on the hoof, cattle weren't killed for meat. Too much of the carcass spoiled before it could be eaten, and the animal was too valuable at the marketplace and as breeding stock on the ranges. No cow or steer was butchered unless it was injured and unable to keep up with the herd.

With the antelope's hindquarter tied behind the saddle, Benteen rode a little farther, until he reached the Cimarron River. The other side was the sovereign state of Kansas. His gaze picked out a buffalo skull on the opposite side of the river. It marked the cutoff trail leading to Dodge City. Every half-mile, there would be another skull, he knew from past experience. There weren't any farms on the cutoff, no damages to pay for crops destroyed or fences downed, no fines for trespassing.

But the cutoff meant a dry drive, a murderous hundred miles over virtually waterless country. At their normal pace it would take roughly eight days to cover it. But in eight days, parched cattle could be dead or dying. That meant the pace would have to be doubled. They'd stop here, at the Cimarron, and rest for a couple days, then start the cattle out fresh.

Those two days seemed like heaven to Lorna. There was finally time and an abundance of water to wash clothes and lay them out in the prairie sun to dry, weighted down with rocks. She and Mary were even able to bathe in the river, one of them keeping watch for any errant cowboys while the other washed. The cowboys made use of the water facilities, too, and Benteen teased her for not skinny-dipping like he did, but she had been too modest to remove her chemise, even if Mary was the only one to see her.

Before they started out, everything that could hold water was filled. But there was only a remote possibility enough would be carried to make the hundred miles. It would have to be rationed. Benteen gave orders that no one but Rusty touch the water barrel strapped to the side of the chuck wagon.

Lorna thought her previous experiences on the trail had prepared her for anything, but she'd never gone thirsty before. The grueling pace that had to be set sapped her strength. By the second day, she'd been shown the trick of carrying pebbles in her mouth to stimulate the flow of saliva. The sun broiled down, bleaching the white skulls that marked the dry trail even whiter, until they seemed to glisten with ominous portent. There was no relief from the heat. Choking dust covered everything and sweat turned it to mud on Lorna's skin and in her hair. That night the thirsty cattle started bawling, and she couldn't sleep.

The heat on the third day was oppressive. Some of the cattle were going blind from lack of water. Rebellion was growing in the ranks of the Longhorns, well broken now to the trail routine. The animals knew there was water in the Cimarron behind them and kept wanting to turn back, not trusting the riders herding them to take them to water up ahead. The drovers had their hands full, literally driving the cattle, beating at them with coiled ropes or buckskin poppers tied to rope ends.

When they stopped at noon on the fourth day, Lorna felt too weak to climb down from the wagon seat. The Arkansas River was still somewhere ahead of them. Her nerves couldn't take much more of that piteous lowing from the parched herd. She half-fell to the ground and staggered, grabbing a wheel rim for support. Perspiration drenched her clothes, making the material stick to her body and turning the dust into rivulets of mud.

Rusty brought her a cupful of water, and she smiled a weak thank-you. Greedily she drank a mouthful and stopped, wanting to make it last. He eyed her closely.

"You're lookin' peaked. Better get some more salt." His beard had grown into a full set of long white whiskers, grimy now with trail dust.

"I will." Her dry throat rasped her voice.

It was surprising the difference one drink of water could make. Her legs were steadier as she crossed the cracked brown grass to the chuck wagon. The men would be breaking in shifts, two or three coming in at a time to eat while the rest stayed with the recalcitrant herd. The point men, Spanish and Jessie, were the first to come in. Neither waited for the coffee to boil, holding out a tin cup for Rusty to fill with the vile black liquid. Both were too tired to eat, waving aside Rusty's offer of cold beans, to chew listlessly on some jerky.

As she licked at some salt, that bath at the Cimarron seemed a long-ago dream. Lorna wondered how any of them were finding the energy to take another step or go another mile. A bone-weary Jessie Trumbo was rubbing tobacco juice in his eyes, making them burn to stay awake. Why were they going through this hell? The answer was Benteen — and his determination to get the cattle through regardless of the cost.

Suddenly Lorna realized Mary hadn't joined her. She glanced toward the Stanton wagon and saw the woman crouched in the scant shade provided by the rolled canvas roof. Something seemed to be wrong. Lorna forced her hot, tired body across the space to the Stanton wagon. It wasn't until she was standing beside Mary that she discovered Mary was crying, dry racking sobs shaking her shoulders.

It seemed impossible. Mary was the strong one. She knew about hardship, deprivation, and the lack of creature comforts. Lorna hadn't believed anything could reduce her friend to tears. She sank to her knees beside Mary, hesitantly touching her shoulder in concern.

"What is it, Mary?" she asked, but Mary only shook her head, unable to talk. Lorna was at a loss. She glanced at the cup of water she still carried. "Have a drink of water," she urged. "You'll feel better."

She remembered how it had revived her. When Mary shook her head to refuse, Lorna forced the issue by pressing the cup to her lips. She tipped it, a few drops spilling onto Mary's dress. Her heart twisted at the loss of even those precious drops.

"Drink," Lorna insisted, not wanting any more wasted.

Mary managed a couple of sips, then turned her head away. The sobs had stopped, but she continued to draw in deep, shuddering breaths. Her lips were chapped and cracked from the lack of moisture, as were Lorna's.

"Why are you crying, Mary?" She tried to coax the woman into talking. "Did you and Ely have an argument?"

"No." Mary sniffed. "I . . . was just thinking."

When no further word was forthcoming, Lorna prompted, "What were you thinking about?"

Her chin was quivering when Mary finally lifted her head to look at her. "Oh, Lorna . . ." her voice wavered. "My pa's chickens back home have a better life than I do."

It was a combination of heat, thirst, frayed nerves, and exhaustion that worked on Lorna. Mary's remark first made her smile, then chuckle; then she started laughing and couldn't stop. It was so true. Any farm animal had it better than they did. Soon Mary was laughing with her, until both of them were laughing and crying at the same time in mutual misery, collapsing against the wagon wheel's spokes when they could no longer support themselves.

Rusty eyed them anxiously, certain they had gone mad from thirst and not knowing what to do. But it was an emotional release that gradually ended. Lorna rested against the spokes and stared at her friend.

"Mary, I wish you weren't leaving us when we reach Dodge City," she murmured soberly. "I would never have made it this far without you. When I think how far we have to travel yet to get to Montana, I don't know if I can make it without you along to make everything bearable."

"You can," Mary insisted, but there was a longing in her eyes, too.

"Why don't you and Ely come with us to Montana?" Lorna suggested eagerly. "It's new country. You and Ely could homestead some land near Benteen and me. Then we could see each other once in a while."

"We planned to go to Ioway." But Lorna could see Mary was wavering.

"Would you think about it?" Lorna urged.

"I'll think about it." But Mary added a warning to her agreement. "But I'm not promising anything."

"Let's drink to that." Lorna lifted the cup in a toast, took a sip of the water, and offered it to Mary.

Mary's sip turned into a swallow. Remorse twisted through her face. "I've drank nearly all of your water. I'll give you some of mine."

"No." Lorna refused with a small shake of her head. "I've had enough anyway." She glanced at the amount of water remaining in the cup Mary returned to her. "There's enough here for my rose cuttings. I can't let them die now."

She used the wagon wheel to help pull herself upright. Even though she was still hot, tired, thirsty, and a little weak, she felt a little better inside. It was a constant surprise to discover how much strength she possessed — the strength to endure, the strength to go on when she thought she couldn't, the will to survive and still be able to find something to laugh about. Lorna walked to the far side of the wagon, where she'd tucked the cuttings under the seat.

When Benteen rode into camp, he noticed Mary sitting in the shade of her wagon, but there wasn't any sign of Lorna. He dismounted, tying the reins of his sweating horse to the wheel of the chuck wagon. After he'd poured himself a cup of lukewarm coffee he looked around camp again for her, then wandered over to Mary.

"How are you holding up?" he asked with

a gentle look of concern.

"Much better, thanks to your wife." Mary smiled wanly. "I was wrong about her."

"What do you mean?" Benteen didn't recall the comment Mary had made on her first meeting with Lorna.

"I thought because she was used to soft things she wouldn't be able to take it out here, but you said she was strong. And she is. Stronger than me."

His brow lifted in skepticism as he studied the sturdy woman. "I don't know if I'd go that far."

"She just gave me most of her water," Mary said. "When I offered her my share in exchange, she refused it. Can you imagine?" Worry flickered through her eyes. "You'd better see that she drinks some. She's saving what's left for her mother's roses."

"What!" It was a quick, low retort as his gaze swung sharply to the wagon. Benteen could just barely see the top of her head on the far side, the bulk of the wagon hiding her from his view. "Take this." Benteen pushed the cup at Mary. It would have dropped if she hadn't caught it.

He crossed to the wagon and step-vaulted over the tongue and crosstree. When he rounded the high box seat, Lorna was carefully moistening the cuttings to use every precious drop of the water. A rage shook him when she looked up. The ordeal of the last ninety miles had sunken hollows under her eyes, parched and dried her lips raw, and put exhaustion in her face.

"You stupid little fool!" Benteen rumbled and grabbed the rose cuttings from her hand before she could react. His gloved hand tightened into a fist around them. "What do you think you're doing?" He silently cursed the bewilderment in her eyes.

"I was just giving my roses some water," Lorna admitted. "It wasn't very much, Benteen."

"All around you, there's thirsty men and animals — and you're watering plants! Have you lost your mind?" The forbidding set of his features was emphasized by the gritted teeth and the dirt and four-day-old beard darkening his jaw. His dark eyes were burning black. Lorna had seen him angry before, but never like this — never at the point of losing control.

"I couldn't let the roses die," she argued lamely.

"And that little bit of water might be the difference between *you* living and dying. And you wasted it on these!" His doubled fist had a stranglehold on the plants as it made an angry upraised gesture.

"I didn't think," Lorna murmured.

"I swear you never think," he growled, and turned, heaving the rose cuttings as far as he could throw them.

Lorna cried out and grabbed for his arm, but it was too late. "My roses! You had no right to do that!" Tears were welling in her eyes when she turned her accusing glance on him, but Benteen didn't show any remorse. His face was set in cold unyielding lines.

Gathering up her skirts, she turned away from him and hurried in the direction he'd thrown the cuttings. It was a stumbling run, hampered by tiredness and the thickly matted grass catching at her feet. She thought she'd seen where they'd fallen, but her tear-blurred vision made it hard to see anything.

When Lorna reached the area where she thought they were, she was breathing heavily from the exertion in her thirst-weakened condition. She had to keep wiping away the tears to see as she beat at the grass, sweeping it aside in a frantic search for the cuttings. Obsessed with finding them, she looked and looked, failure bringing a wildness to her actions.

She was making so much noise on her own that at first she didn't hear Benteen's approach until his rough voice called her name. When she glanced around, long strides were carrying him through the grass toward her.

"Forget those roses and get out of this hot sun before you collapse," he ordered.

"No." She fell to searching again.

"Dammit, they aren't worth it, Lorna!" Benteen snapped, and grabbed her wrist to force her to obey.

All her anger and resentment for his high-handed tactics boiled over. She yanked her wrist out of his grasp and confronted him with the full weight of her mutiny, trembling with the fury that consumed her.

"You did this on purpose!" Lorna accused. "You never wanted me to bring those cuttings! I don't think you wanted to bring anything from Texas! I'm surprised you don't burn the wagon with all our things in it so there won't be anything to remind you of Texas! You've been wanting to get rid of those roses all along! You've been hoping they would die! And you finally had an excuse to throw them away!"

"Are you going to get out of this sun, or do I have to carry you back to camp?" Benteen demanded angrily, ignoring her tirade.

"I'm not leaving here until I find them! I don't care how long it takes!" Temper was drying up her tears, making her eyes hot. "The wagons can leave without me!"

"You little fool!" He savagely ground out the words.

"Yes, you're always saying I'm stupid, or childish, or a fool." And the words wounded, so she lashed back, wanting to hurt him. "I don't care what you think anymore! Those were *my* roses! And *my* water! You had no right to tell me what I could do with either of them!"

"I'm your husband and that gives me the right to keep you from killing yourself!" Benteen snapped.

"You'd kill yourself for those damned cattle! What's the difference?"

"I'm not going to argue with you. You're coming back to camp with me, and that's final!" This time when he grabbed her, there was no breaking free of his grip.

But Lorna fought him just the same. She knew his superior strength would make him the victor in any physical struggle, but there was still a verbal battle to be fought.

"I'm not going anywhere with you!" Her physical strength was ebbing, flowing from her like the perspiration trickling down her neck. "I'm not one of your cattle to be herded along!"

"They have more sense!" The hands digging into her shoulders gave her a hard shake.

"How would you know?" Lorna demanded,

panting. "Have you ever asked what I thought about anything? I never really wanted to go to Montana. Did you know that? You didn't even care enough about my opinion to ask."

"It's immaterial now. We're halfway there."

Lorna stared at the angry, determined thrust of his jaw. "I hate you, Benteen Calder."

"You're becoming hysterical," Benteen muttered.

To a degree, she was. Her anger and resentment were exaggerated, overshadowing other emotions that, in a calmer moment, would be just as strong. Now the desire to hurt overpowered all others.

"I hate you." It vibrated through her voice. "I rue the day I married you."

His nostrils flared, her arrow finding its mark. He hauled her roughly against his chest, pinning her arms between the crush of their bodies. A black fury turned his eyes cold.

"That's too damned bad." His upper lip curled over the words. "We are married and we're going to stay that way."

"I'm not going to Montana with you." Lorna flagrantly defied him now that she had discovered a raw nerve. "When we reach Dodge City, I'm leaving with Mary."

She felt the wild force building inside him, coiling all his muscles with the tautness of a spring wire. It was so close to being released, it rocked him.

"You try, and I'll drag you back." The threat growled from some dark place inside him. "You're mine and I'll never let you go."

"Then I'll run away again," Lorna declared, to take advantage of this hold she had over him.

It unleashed the violence in him. His leather-gloved fingers forced their way inside her bonnet to grab a handful of hair, loosing it from its matronly bun and pushing the bonnet off her head. His brutal grip pulled painfully at the roots to tilt her head back. Lorna felt the first quiver of alarm.

"Like hell you will." It was a snarl, followed by a cruel violation of her lips.

Lorna struggled in panic, but his arms were like steel binding her against him. Her lips started bleeding under the grinding pressure of his mouth, and the rough whiskers scraped her tender skin. He was exacting retribution for her threatened desertion of him, dominating her physically to destroy the seeds of revolt.

In his mind burned the memory of a mother who had abandoned him and the years of hell his father had endured. It was this black and bitter hatred that drove him to abuse. Even the thought of Lorna leaving him was a pain that

273

ripped him apart, leaving him only with a violence that he couldn't control.

Her whimpers never penetrated the fiery mists that controlled his conscience. Benteen knew nothing of what he was doing when he forced her to the ground and fought his way through folds of material to tear aside her undergarments. He didn't taste the blood on her lips or feel the wet tears against his skin. He was a male animal, basely subduing the female.

When his fury was spent, she was limp beneath him. The mists that had blinded him began to dissolve. His eyes focused on the face turned away from him – the wetness of her cheeks and the red stain of blood on her chapped lips. She was shaking with sobs that made no sound.

Benteen was sickened by what he'd done to her. A violent nausea rose in his throat to choke him as tears stung his eyes. He'd never felt less a man in all his life. It was a wrong that could never be undone.

"Lorna." His fingers moved tentatively to touch her cheek.

"Don't." She flinched from him, shutting her eyes tightly.

If she had stabbed him in the heart with a knife, the pain couldn't have been greater. In sharp contrast to his brutal possession, he tenderly rearranged her clothes, but she continued to lie unmoving on the grass. His tortured gaze was turned skyward.

"God, forgive me." It was a barely audible murmur that he didn't offer to Lorna, because he didn't think she ever could forgive him. Then he turned back to her, unable to walk away and leave her like this. "Lorna."

"Leave me alone." Her broken voice made the request that he couldn't give to her.

"No, I won't leave you," Benteen said quietly. "And I don't blame you for hating me."

"Why did you have to say that?" She opened her teary eyes to look at him, but he couldn't meet them. She felt defiled and humiliated, yet strangely guilty, too.

"I went crazy at the thought of you leaving me. It will never happen again."

Lorna shivered with the sensation that it was more than his anger he was burying; it was his ability to feel deeply as well. His sexual abuse had left her with loathing, but hate didn't describe what she felt toward him, although she couldn't have said she still loved him either. It was all too brutally fresh for Lorna to assess the damage to her feelings toward him.

Only one other time had she seen Benteen

come so close to the violent hatred he had just displayed. She had thought he was going to strike her on that occasion when she had rescued his mother's picture from the fire — a mother who had left him, as she had threatened to do.

Lorna was faced with the knowledge that she was partly responsible for what had happened. She had made her threat in anger, but there was never any real possibility that she would have carried it out. She had found a way to hurt him and used it, never thinking of the consequences. Like Benteen, she discovered there was nothing she could say.

She sat up, keeping her back to him while she wiped the tears from her cheeks with the hem of her grass-stained skirt. He waited silently, making no attempt to help her to her feet. Her hair was loose, falling down her back and tangling with her sunbonnet.

"I'll help you look for the rose cuttings," Benteen said.

"No. I don't want them." They would always be a reminder of what had happened here. It was going to be difficult enough for them to forget.

They walked together back to the noon camp, but they'd never been further apart. It was a gap they both had a hesitant wish to bridge, yet neither knew how to begin. They separated when they reached the wagons. Lorna climbed into the back of the stuffy wagon to fix her hair and think privately.

They held the restless cattle through the noonday heat before starting them out again. Ten miles from the Arkansas, the Longhorns caught the smell of its water. The problem became preventing the herd from stampeding to the river. The brindle steer, dubbed Captain after it had led the herd across the Red River, did its part in checking the mad flight of the thirst-crazed cattle by maintaining a steady pace and hooking its long horns at anything that tried to pass him.

When they reached the river, it became lined with multicolored hides as the cattle waded into the water. The great majority of them stood there, moaning low and absorbing the wetness into their thirst-craved bodies and waited to drink a little. A scant few overdrank and died.

While the cattle drank, the trailhands went upstream and sprawled facedown on the edge of the river to drink their fill. Not far away, in plain view of the camp, sat Dodge City. Lorna hadn't realized how hungry she was for the sight of a building.

In camp that night, she and Benteen said very little to each other beyond what was necessary. She went to bed early and lay awake a long time, waiting for him. When he came to the wagon, she didn't pretend to be asleep, but remained on her side, faced away from him. After he'd undressed, he crawled under the quilt. She unconsciously stiffened when he accidentally brushed against her. Lorna forced herself to relax. In the eyes of God, he was her husband "for better or for worse." She rolled over to lie facing him. His hands were clasped under his head as he gazed at the canvas ceiling.

"We'll let the herd graze and rest here for a couple of days," he said. "Tomorrow we'll go into Dodge City to restock the supplies."

"There's a few things I need to buy," Lorna replied, and realized he was expecting her to reaffirm her intention to leave him there. "I'm going to miss Mary," she said to let him know she was staying.

His chest lifted on a deep breath and slowly went down. "I know you will," was all he said.

It was a small step — a beginning.

14

Dodge City bustled with activity. The hooting whistles of trains clanking over iron rails wavered through the stockyards with its pens of cattle. Cowpunchers prodded cattle up wooden chutes to load them into railroad cars bound for the Eastern marketplaces.

The unpaved streets in the main section of town were churned by horses' hooves, raising clouds of dust to spread over everything. There was the constant sound of footsteps on the wooden sidewalks as cowboys swaggered from saloon house to gambling hall. Sometimes they gathered in boisterous knots on street corners and shouted obscene greetings to acquaintances riding past.

It was into the babble of confusion that Lorna rode, perched on the wagon seat while Benteen drove the team. A pair of barking dogs charged the horses, nipping at their heels and darting out of reach of a kicking hoof. The loudness of it all was vaguely alarming after weeks of the prairie's relative quiet.

"It's so noisy." She glanced at Benteen as two

riders dashed past their wagon in an impromptu horse race. Last night had eased the tension between them, although nothing was back to normal. They were both treading warily.

"It's rowdy," Benteen agreed with a half-glance at her. "We'll stop at the Dodge House. I thought you might welcome a real bath and a couple of nights spent in a regular bed."

"It would be nice, yes." Lorna knew it was an attempt to make up for the creature comforts she'd been missing.

The lobby was crowded with elegantly dressed meat packers from the North, feeders, and an assortment of cattle buyers. They rubbed elbows with dusty, dirty cowboys fresh off the trail. The presence of a female in their midst was quickly noted, making Lorna self-conscious about her appearance. She kept her head lowered so they wouldn't see how her once flawless complexion had been weathered by the elements, and her rough hands were carefully hidden from view as well.

She stayed close to Benteen while he signed the register, and tried to be inconspicuous. "We are pleased to have you back with us, Mr. Calder," the desk clerk welcomed him without glancing at the register. "I believe we have your usual room available —"

280

"I'd like something bigger this time," Benteen interrupted. "Something with a dressing room for my wife."

The clerk glanced at Lorna, then at the register. "Very good, sir. We have just the room." He handed the key to the porter with a murmur of instructions. "I'm sure it will be satisfactory."

"Also arrange to have some water sent up for a bath," Benteen requested, and handed the valise containing Lorna's personal articles from the wagon to the porter. "Will you show my wife to the room?"

"Aren't you coming?" Lorna glanced at him in vague confusion, hesitant whether she should ask why he wasn't.

"No. I'm going to take the wagon to the livery and see to the team." He was reserved in his explanation. "I'll be back in a while."

"If you'd come this way, ma'am?" The porter prompted her to follow him.

Lorna didn't want to ask Benteen to accompany her to the room, although she would have liked the protection of his company when she crossed the lobby full of men. It didn't matter that the cowboys on the trail had seen her looking her worst. These were gentlemen, and she didn't want them wondering about an unescorted lady in their midst.

She kept her gaze modestly lowered as she followed the porter, conscious that Benteen's gaze traveled after her. As Lorna climbed the stairs, she heard the rustle of silk. She looked up, half-expecting to see a "lady of the evening," since the trail town would obviously abound in them.

By no stretch of the imagination was the woman at the top of the stairs a member of that old profession. Her long dress of blue silk had a low neck and short sleeves, styled in the latest fashion. Her pale blond hair was swept atop her head in an elegant style, not a lock out of place. The fine jewelry and the regal carriage of her slim form informed Lorna that this was a real lady.

As Lorna approached the woman standing near the top of the stairs talking to some equally well-dressed man, she noticed the woman wasn't as young as she had first appeared. Her skin was so smooth and her beauty so flawless that it was difficult to judge her true age. If it wasn't for the faint lines showing on her powdered neck, Lorna would have thought the woman was in her twenties.

It was rude to stare, and she tried very hard not to as she followed the porter past them. Her curiosity got the better of her when she heard the woman's voice. It had a foreign accent that quite intrigued Lorna. She slowed her steps to listen, not paying attention to the porter striding ahead of her.

"Your invitation is most gracious, sir, but I was given to understand by the earl that he has accepted the mayor's offer to sit in his private box," the woman was saying.

Earl. The mayor. A private box. The lady was obviously someone very important as well as wealthy. Lorna cast a backward glance for another look at the elegant woman. There was something oddly familiar about her.

"Mrs. Calder?" the porter called to her.

When the woman glanced sharply down the hallway, Lorna quickly averted her head. She didn't want to disgrace herself by being caught rudely staring. She hurried to the door where the porter was waiting.

"Is something wrong, ma'am?" he inquired politely.

"No." She thought about asking him who the lady was, but that would be too forward.

After setting her valise inside the room, he handed her the key. Reluctantly she took it, hoping the porter didn't notice the roughness of her hands. Before she entered the room, she darted another glance at the stairs. The well-dressed man was bowing over the woman's hand, taking his leave of her.

When the fawning fortune-hunter had finally gone, the Lady Elaine, wife to the Earl of Crawford, turned to glance down the hallway. The smile left her lightly rouged mouth as her dark eyes became sharp with curiosity. She knew she had concealed her shock well when she heard that name. It wasn't a common one.

The porter walked toward her, smiling like a silly schoolboy. "Good day to you . . ." He faltered, not knowing the proper way to address her. " . . . your Highness."

"Good day." God, how she loved the way these yokels bowed and scraped to win their way into her good graces. "Excuse me a moment, young man."

"Yes, ma'am . . . your Highness," he corrected, turning a little red but no less eager to serve.

"The young woman. I believe I heard you refer to her as Mrs. Calder. My husband was acquainted with a family named Calder during an earlier visit to America. I was wondering if they might possibly be related to them."

"I doubt it." He turned his head to the side in skepticism. "Her husband has been coming here regularly, bringing trail herds up a couple times a year from Texas."

Lady Elaine stiffened just a little. "Would you know his name?" she inquired.

"I believe . . . his name is Benteen Calder," the porter replied.

"As you said" — she made a small moue of regret — "it is unlikely my husband would know him. Thank you."

"My pleasure, ma'am . . . your Royalty." His bobbing attempt at a bow was awkward.

After the porter had started down the stairs, she remained a moment longer and sent a considering glance down the hallway. A cool intelligence showed as she wondered what problems this might present, if any. Perhaps she and Con should leave immediately for San Francisco. But they had already accepted too many invitations. Besides, there was a part of her that was curious. She almost laughed aloud when she realized that. After all these years, who would have thought that she'd care a damn.

"Laine, my pet, are you coming down?"

With a graceful turn, she looked down the stairs, where her husband stood with one foot on the steps. She looked at him with eyes of long ago and saw the changes — the added weight that had broadened his middle and the receding hairline that had raised his already high forehead. The mustache and muttonchop whiskers emphasized his jowls and weak chin. He had never made her heart beat fast, but he'd given her everything she'd ever wanted — after she'd put the idea in his head.

"Yes, I'm coming, Con."

It was more than two hours since Lorna had entered the hotel room. In that time, she had taken a long bath and washed her hair. She wished for a wrap to wear over her under-garments and chemise. That lady she'd seen in the hall probably had dozens of silk or satin ones. She didn't want to put on her only clean dress until her hair had dried.

Benteen still hadn't come to the room. Lorna wondered what was keeping him as she ran a comb through her damp hair. Her mind kept turning back to the lady she'd seen, her image staying sharp. Lorna was intensely curious about her, wondering who she was and where she came from. The accent had sounded foreign.

There was a light rap on the door. Lorna sat a little straighter on the bed, bringing the comb down to clutch it in front of her. "Who is it?"

"It's me. Benteen."

Crossing the room, she turned the key in the lock to open it, then hid behind it as it swung inward. She caught the scent of bay rum as

Benteen walked past her into the room. Closing the door, she turned the key to lock it.

When she pivoted away from the door, she saw that Benteen was studying her, his gaze running over her bare shoulders, down her length to her slender ankles. Her body reacted to the sensation of being touched. Lorna breathed in, not conscious that the movement pushed her breasts against the cotton bodice, accenting their roundness. She was suddenly uneasy, wondering if he was going to force himself on her again.

A muscle tightened in his jaw a second before he swung away. "I thought you'd be ready by now."

It was suddenly clear that he had deliberately delayed his return to give her time to finish her bath and dress. He hadn't wanted to be here during that time. Lorna had no difficulty guessing why. Benteen had told her on past occasions when they made love that looking at her body aroused him. He had wanted to avoid that happening.

"My hair isn't dry," Lorna explained, and glanced at the comb in her hand.

Walking to the mirror, she began running the comb through the dark mass again to separate the damp strands and hurry the drying process. In the mirror, she could see his reflection. She studied the rough cut of his features and the shaggy hair growing almost down to his collar. There were strength and power etched there, a clearness of purpose and solid will.

Lorna suddenly noticed the clean shirt he was wearing, and the pants. The sunlight streaming through the room's window set fire to the ends of his hair.

"You've bathed," she realized.

"Yes. One of the saloons has bath facilities in back," he stated. "I thought it would save time if I went ahead and cleaned up, instead of waiting until you were through."

Unconsciously she tested the air, catching again the drifting scent of bay rum that indicated he had shaved, too. It was slightly stimulating to her senses. She was becoming too aware of him.

"When the porter showed me to the room, I passed this lady on the stairs." She began talking about the first thing that came to her mind. "She was wearing the most beautiful dress. I'm sure she's someone very important. I heard her say something about using the mayor's private box. And she had a foreign accent, too."

"There are a lot of immigrants here in Kansas," Benteen replied.

He couldn't keep his gaze from straying to

her; the curved shape of her was a magnet. The straps of her chemise drew his attention to her shoulder blades. As she combed her hair, he watched the rippling movement down her spine to a waist so slender his hands could easily span it. Her rounded buttocks and hips tantalized him, fully outlined by the chemise.

"This lady wasn't an ordinary immigrant." Lorna stayed with the topic, although another woman was the farthest thing from Benteen's mind. "I know she's special. She referred to 'the earl.'" She combed the ends of her hair around a finger. "That's a title, isn't it? Like a duke?"

"I believe so." Benteen had an aversion to titled nobility. His mother had run away with a remittance man, a member of that class. "Fancy titles mean nothing. Don't be impressed by them, Lorna."

His abruptness with her brought renewed concentration to combing her hair. Lorna resented the way he'd made her feel wrong for being fascinated by the woman she'd seen. She didn't see the harm in it. The teeth of the comb became snagged by a tangle in the back. Her attempt to tug it free pulled at the roots.

"Ouch!" It was an involuntary exclamation. The snarl was in the back. Lorna tried to twist around so she could see to comb it out, but it wasn't possible.

"I'll get it for you," Benteen volunteered.

Lorna hesitated an instant at the thought of having him so close to her. It hardly made sense when she'd slept with him last night. She handed him the comb and continued to face the mirror, resting her hands on the edge of the dresser with its pitcher of water and basin.

There was something about the touch of his fingers on her hair as they tunneled under its damp weight to hold the snarl that started her heart pattering. After he gently worked loose the tangle, he began slowly running the comb through her long hair. Lorna half-closed her eyes in involuntary enjoyment of his hand following the comb to smooth her hair. When he bent his head closer to hers, she took little notice of it.

"Your hair smells good," Benteen murmured as the comb ceased its movement. His hand settled onto the bare point of a shoulder, his callused skin pleasantly abrasive on sensitive flesh. "You smell good."

When his hand began a caressing movement, Lorna stiffened. Her fingers tightened their grip on the edge of the dresser. Benteen felt her silent protest and immediately took his hand away. The comb was thrust in front of her. The instant she took it, Benteen moved briskly away. She held the comb, looking at it, her breath running shallow.

"Thank you." It was an awkwardly polite expression of gratitude for his help with the snarl.

"It's no good, Lorna." His reflection in the mirror showed a nerve twitching near his mouth. "I'm a man, not a priest. We're going to have to reach some kind of understanding, because I don't know how long I can keep from touching you."

She turned very slowly to face him, aware of the harsh reality of his statement and the choice she had made to stay with him. It was going to be very difficult to say these next words, because she knew it was too soon.

"I told you on our wedding night, Benteen, that I had no right to deny you the privileges of the marriage bed. That's still true." She tried to brace herself to endure what was to come.

Benteen stared at her, his eyes narrowing. "My God, Lorna," he muttered thickly. "Why don't you just call me an animal for expecting you to submit to me, instead of being so meekly dutiful?"

"Because I know what you said is true." She had the intelligence to understand that, even if she wasn't sure she was emotionally ready to become intimate with him again. "I recognize it's a man's need. It's something you enjoy." She couldn't look at him while she explained the reasons behind her acquiescence.

"And you?" Benteen challenged quietly.

"I'm not sure I will without . . ." Lorna had intended to say, ". . . without remembering when you took me in violence." But she left it unsaid, knowing Benteen would read in the rest.

He walked to within a foot of her and stopped. All expression was kept from his face as he hooked a finger under her chin and raised it. There was a panicked acceleration of her heartbeat, but Lorna quelled it and tried to return his steady gaze.

"We'd better find out if you can," Benteen said.

With calculated deliberation, he slowly bent his head toward her, watching closely for any adverse reaction from her. Inside, she was recoiling, but she was able to keep it from showing. When his mouth made its first tentative brush against her lips, Lorna didn't resist. His mouth came back to move gently over them, mindful of their chapped soreness. The kiss was warmly reassuring. Lorna could accept its gentle pressure and find a small degree of corresponding warmth.

His body did not touch hers, but she could

feel its heat radiating from him. If it could stay like this, she could handle it. His hand moved onto her neck, lightly tracing its long curve to the hollow of her throat. She started to feel the tension threading through her nerves. When his mouth tried to coax her lips apart, her mind flashed back to the last time when no such persuasion had been used. She tried very hard to block out the degrading memory, but she felt herself growing rigid under his touch. She didn't want it to be like this. She wanted to feel that raw passion of all the other times before the last.

Although she let her lips part in an attempt to force the feelings, Benteen sensed the difference. The kiss was stopped cold as he slowly drew away to look at her. Her gaze wavered under the deliberately aloof inspection of his.

"You aren't any good at faking it, Lorna." He knew if he let her go through with this charade of desire and made love to her, as he desperately wanted to do, she would ultimately resent this exercising of the privileges she said he had. She would despise him more than she already did.

"Benteen, I'm trying —"

"If it can't come naturally, I don't want it," he broke in roughly. "Be honest about what you're feeling, even if it's hatred."

"I don't hate you," Lorna said, but didn't enlighten him about what she did feel.

"I'll stay away from you for a while. You tell me when you want me to be your husband." And he hoped to God he'd have the strength to wait for that day — and that it wouldn't be too far into the future. He turned from her and walked to the window to look onto the street below. Without looking, Benteen was conscious that Lorna was still standing in the same spot. "Your hair is dry enough now. You'd better put your dress on."

"Yes." Her head was bent. She realized she had been foolish to think she could pretend to feel pleasure. But accepting his advances had appeared to be a way to assuage her guilt for goading him with her threat to run away, which had brought about the rape. She couldn't plead ignorance, because she'd known how violently angry Benteen had become over his mother's picture. She should have guessed he would be overly sensitive to any hint that she might repeat what his mother had done.

Lorna wasn't so generous that she believed it had given him the right to rape her. It was merely an acceptance that a portion of the fault was hers — only a portion. There was an uneasy feeling that she had tried to transfer that small part to Benteen a moment ago by nobly sacrificing herself to his lust.

They spent most of the afternoon at one of the general stores. Lorna had only a couple of small purchases to make, but she went through the entire store with a critical eye, comparing it to her father's store in Fort Worth. The surroundings were so familiar to her that she hated to leave. Benteen must have guessed it, because he took his time buying the supplies needed to restock the chuck wagon. Several of the customers who came in were men he knew, either cowboys who had been on previous drives with him or trail bosses like himself. He stopped to shoot the breeze with them, not hurrying to load the wagon.

That night, they dined in the hotel's restaurant. It was a wonderful treat for Lorna to eat off a table again. Although Rusty was more than a passable cook, the monotony of the trail fare had begun to wear on her. Which made the restaurant meal taste even better. Lorna kept looking around at the other diners, hoping to see that lady again so she could point her out to Benteen, but she never did see her.

Benteen was quietly attentive, willing to indulge her idle chatter, yet keeping himself slightly aloof from her. All the conversation that she could hear going on around her was about beefs, brands, beef prices, and shipping costs. It was very noticeable when a hush fell briefly over the room.

A well-dressed man in a dark suit and vest had entered the dining room. But there was a difference. A huge revolver was strapped to his hip and a shiny badge was pinned to his vest.

"Benteen" – Lorna leaned forward to murmur to him – "do you suppose that man is Wyatt Earp?"

His passing glance made a sweep of the man. "Yes."

"I've heard that when he shoots, he shoots to kill," she murmured, remembering some of the exciting stories she'd heard about the infamous lawman. "But he only kills those who deserve it."

"You didn't hear that from any Texan," Benteen said dryly. "They've put out a thousand-dollar bounty on his head."

Her eyes rounded, shocked that any of her fellow Texans could do anything so cold-blooded. "I don't believe it."

"It's true." His smile was only a half a smile. "As for shooting to kill, a man hadn't better have any other reason for drawing his gun, or he'll be the one who's dead."

He said it so matter-of-factly that Lorna suddenly wondered, "Have you ever killed anyone, Benteen?"

There was a glint of humor in his eye, reminiscent of their courtship days. "None that didn't deserve it." He mocked her with the justification she'd used for Wyatt Earp.

Killing a man was nothing to boast about in his book. Those times he had reason to draw his gun, the men facing him had either been Indians or raiders attempting to take his herd. There hadn't been that many occasions. It was enough to say that he was alive and there were others who weren't.

"I'll bet you've never killed anybody," Lorna insisted, eyeing him with a doubting look.

Benteen shrugged mildly and let her comment ride.

When they had finished and left the dining room, Lorna pulled her shawl a little tighter around her shoulders in a contented gesture. "I'm so full," she sighed, and glanced wistfully at Benteen. "I don't suppose we could take a short walk before going to the room?"

He was well-acquainted with the boldness of a liquored-up cowboy. The dance halls, saloons, and gambling houses would be in full swing, and the bawdy houses would be open for business. The streets in Dodge City were not the place for a respectable lady to be taking an evening stroll, certainly not his wife. He shook his head. "We can step outside for some fresh air, if you like," Benteen offered instead.

"No." It was the walk she wanted, more than the fresh air.

With the impersonal guidance of his hand at her elbow, Benteen escorted Lorna up the stairs to their room. He unlocked the door and pushed it open for her to enter, but he didn't follow her inside.

"A couple of the boys are coming into town tonight," he said. "I want to make sure they stay out of trouble so I won't have to be bailing them out of the hoosegow." He made light of the possibility. "After you lock the door, take the key out. I'll get another one from the desk to let myself in."

Although Lorna couldn't say it, she was relieved he wasn't going directly to bed with her. Then she realized he was making an excuse, saving them both the tension.

"All right," she agreed to his suggestion.

"Sleep well," he said.

After she had closed the door, she turned the key and removed it from the lock. In the hallway, Benteen listened to the sound and felt the trembling urge to beat the door down. He reached into his pocket for the makings of a cigarette instead. His hand shook as he rolled it, spilling tobacco onto the floor. Finally he wadded the whole thing up — paper, tobacco, and all — and tossed it aside to stride down the hall.

After lying awake for a long time, Lorna finally fell asleep. She didn't hear Benteen come into the room in the wee hours of the morning. Half-drunk, he stared at her sleeping face.

"Don't leave me." His voice was half-slurred.

He undressed in the dark and crawled into bed. He passed out almost immediately, the alcohol working its magic to deaden his sexual drive.

When Lorna woke up the next morning, Benteen was gone. Only the rumpled pillow next to hers told her that he had slept there last night. She rose and dressed hurriedly, not certain when he might come back.

As she was smoothing the last strand of hair into its neat coil, there was a knock at the door. She went to it, and paused, noticing the key in the lock.

"Benteen?" she asked.

"Yes."

When she opened the door, his gaze flicked to her dress and back to her face. "I thought you might be awake by now."

"I got up a few minutes ago," Lorna admitted. "Is it very late?"

"After nine o'clock."

It seemed impossible that she could have slept so long. Her exhaustion had obviously been of the mind as well as the body.

"Are you ready to go down for breakfast?" Benteen asked.

"Yes. I suppose you've eaten," she guessed.

He nodded. "I'll have coffee with you. Then I'll have to ride out to the herd. There's a buyer who wants to look over those three hundred head of steers I plan to sell."

"Oh." Lorna wasn't sure why she had expected him to spend most of the day with her. Wasn't it always the cattle? She was sure if it ever came down to a choice between their marriage and the cattle, the cattle would win.

"You'll be all right, won't you?"

"Of course," she declared on an airily sarcastic note that he didn't understand.

The cattle buyer stopped by their breakfast table to see when Benteen wanted to ride out to the herd. Lorna could tell how anxious Benteen was, so she suggested that he leave now, assuring him she would manage fine on her own. Then she was irritated when he accepted it without protest.

She wasn't used to all this idle time, and didn't really know what to do with it. After breakfast she spent some time in the room. But that was too confining. She ventured out of the hotel for a short walk, and returned in time for lunch.

The dining room was full. When she couldn't find a place to sit, she started to leave rather than draw attention to the fact she was unescorted. As she turned, Lorna nearly walked right into the man entering the dining room.

"Mr. Giles." She was surprised to recognize a familiar face after seeing so many strangers.

"Mrs. Calder." He took off his hat and made a little bow to her. "I thought I might bump into you and your husband here. It's his usual hangout in Dodge."

"I guess you brought your herd safely here," she said.

"They're a couple miles outside of town, eating grass and getting fat," he confirmed.

There were some people, Lorna supposed, who would be intimidated by the man's bigness and his brutish appearance, but she felt completely safe with him. He showed his interest in her as a woman, but always with respect. She knew he wouldn't make any overtures unless she invited them.

"Have you had lunch, Mrs. Calder?" he inquired.

"Actually, no," she admitted. "But the

tables are all taken."

"Someone's just leaving over there." He nodded toward a table where the men were standing up to leave. "I'd be proud if you'd join me for lunch. Or are you waiting for your husband?"

"He took a buyer out to look at some steers he's selling. I'm not sure when he'll be back." Eating alone wasn't a pleasant prospect after being left to her own devices all morning. "I'd be happy to lunch with you, Mr. Giles."

15

Lunch with Bull Giles was a thoroughly enjoyable experience. All that brawn masked a man with a keen mind and a cutting wit. In his dry quiet way he mocked the cattle talk going on around them and the well-dressed men engaging in it. Several times his biting comments made Lorna laugh aloud.

When Bull Giles showed an inclination to linger over coffee and stretch out the lunch, Lorna knew she shouldn't allow it to happen. It would be too easily misconstrued. As it was, Benteen would not be pleased that she had spent any time with Bull Giles. She was beginning to understand just how strong that possessive streak was in Benteen.

But she was enjoying Bull's company. It was innocent and harmless, so why should she deny herself of it? That small seed of rebellion had not been completely stamped out. Did she always have to do things to please someone else? Surely she could chat with a person she liked simply because it was what she wanted to do. After all, they were hardly alone, not with a restaurant full of people around them.

Lorna didn't refuse when a waiter stopped at their table to refill their coffeecups. She lifted the china cup, delicately blowing to cool the coffee before taking a sip. Over the cup's rim, she noticed the absorbed way Bull watched her.

"I'm probably keeping you from your business. I'm sure you're anxious to show your herd to cattle buyers." For a vain instant Lorna wanted the reassurance that Bull desired her company, unlike Benteen, who placed a higher priority on the cattle.

"I'm not so anxious that I'm willing to deprive myself of the company of a beautiful lady," Bull declared with his usual charm.

"Why is it that men feel that way before they are married but not afterward?" Lorna had meant it to be a lightly teasing retort. Only after she heard herself saying the words did she realize it revealed her disillusionment about marriage. She tried quickly to cover it with a deprecating remark about her own sex. "I suppose women are that way, too."

"I've never known a beautiful woman, married or single, who didn't want the attention of her man." Bull talked in generalities the way she had, but Lorna sensed he was seeing through it.

She took another sip of coffee, then held the cup and traced a portion of its rim with her finger. Aware she was displaying uncommon interest in a simple cup, Lorna used the opportunity to change the subject.

"Isn't it strange how much better everything tastes — food, coffee — when you aren't having it out of a tin plate or mug?" It was something she could admit to Bull Giles, but she hadn't said it to Benteen. He would have seen it as a complaint, whereas Lorna felt Bull would understand.

"With tablecloths and napkins," Bull added with a hint of a responding smile.

"Two days of this" — Lorna let her glance stray around the room, taking note of so many things that now represented luxury — "will spoil me."

"You deserve to be spoiled," he asserted. "A trail drive is no place for a lady like you."

"It certainly isn't an easy way to travel." She deliberately understated the hardships that had tested her endurance and taken her one step beyond her limits. "But everything will be fine when we reach Montana." She said it without conviction as she studied the polished silver of a spoon against the white tablecloth.

A moment of silence followed; then Bull spoke very quietly. "You don't have to go to

Montana, Mrs. Calder, if that isn't where you want to go."

Her glance lifted to meet his. Bull Giles was much too intuitive, she realized. Lorna smiled, but with a trace of aloofness because he had guessed too much. "My husband is going to Montana. I go where he goes, Mr. Giles," she stated to establish firmly her determination to make their marriage work.

"Of course." But there was doubt in his expression.

It had been a mistake to linger over coffee, so she made it clear to him in a subtly polite way that it was time to leave. Bull made no attempt to persuade her otherwise, and escorted her from the dining room.

"Was there any shopping you'd like to do?" he asked her when she stopped in the lobby to thank him for lunch. "I'll be glad to accompany you."

Lunching with him could be explained by the lack of empty tables, but accepting his company beyond that would not be proper.

"No, thank you," she refused. "Benteen took me to do all my shopping yesterday."

"If you need anything —"

But Lorna didn't want him to extend the offer. "I enjoyed lunch, Mr. Giles. I'm sure you have a great many things to do. I won't keep you from your business any longer."

"Then I'll leave you." His bulky frame made a half-bow toward her. "May I say, though, that I've never enjoyed a meal so much before, thanks to you, Mrs. Calder. Maybe we'll meet again."

She nodded her head slightly at the compliment, but didn't reply. Setting his hat on his head, he walked away toward the street doors. Lorna watched him go and lingered a few minutes in the lobby, loath to go back to the room just yet to wait for Benteen to return.

Just then a murmur went through the lobby, and heads turned toward the staircase. Lorna's curious glance swung to it and saw *her*, the older woman she'd seen at the top of the stairs the day before. This afternoon she was wearing a biscuit-colored traveling suit with a stylish hat to shade her face. She descended the stairs with slow, regal grace, seemingly oblivious of the stir she was creating. Lorna noticed the way the woman never looked directly at people and thus didn't invite them to speak to her.

The woman's wandering course took her to the side of the room where Lorna was standing. She gave the impression she was waiting for someone. When the woman noticed Lorna, she smiled faintly and nodded to her. This recognition by someone as obviously important

307

brought a rush of excitement as Lorna returned the gesture.

With a studied casualness the woman suddenly wandered over to Lorna. The small smile on her lips took Lorna's attention away from the stare of the woman's dark eyes. It seemed impossible that this lady was actually seeking her out.

"We seem to be the only women here," the woman remarked with a brief glance at the male population in the lobby.

"I'm sure none of them are looking at me," Lorna replied in all sincerity.

A soft laugh came from the woman's throat. "How flattering of you to say that."

"It's the truth," Lorna assured her. It would be impossible for her to compete with the woman's looks, clothes or poise. She was the epitome of everything beautiful and sophisticated.

"Let me introduce myself. I'm Elaine Dunshill, wife to the Earl of Crawford."

Then she had been right about the woman being one of the titled aristocracy. "I'm pleased to make your acquaintance, your ladyship." Lorna made a little curtsy, as she had been taught in Miss Hilda's School. An eyebrow was slightly raised by Lady Elaine at the proper reference. "I'm Mrs. Lorna Calder."

308

"From Texas." It seemed more statement than guess.

"I am," Lorna confirmed with vague surprise."How did you know?"

"That soft, drawling accent of yours," she explained. "Nearly everyone in Dodge City seems to be from Texas."

"That's because of the trail herds." She summoned the boldness to ask, "Where are you from?"

"England. My husband and I are on an extended tour of America. When my husband was younger, he spent a year in the West. The stories he tells about his adventures." The woman widened her dark eyes to indicate they were endless. "He's decided to relive some of it. Actually we're on our way to San Francisco."

"I've heard it's an exciting city," Lorna admitted.

"Yes." She seemed indifferent, and glanced toward the street doors. "At the present, I'm waiting for my husband to bring the carriage around. He wants to drive out and look at some of the herds. He cherishes the dream of someday being the proprietor of a large ranch in the West. Are you waiting for your husband, too?"

"Yes." In a way, it was partially true, although it wasn't precisely her reason for being in the lobby. "He rode out this morning with a cattle buyer to show him some steers he wants to sell."

"You and your husband are here in Dodge City to sell cattle?"

"Yes, but we're only passing through on our way to Montana Territory. My husband has some land there that he's going to run cattle on. It will be our new home," Lorna explained.

"Then you have left Texas for good?" The English lady appeared mildly interested by that discovery.

Some of Lorna's regret must have shown in her expression, because the blond-haired woman guessed, "It must have been very difficult to start out on a new life."

"It was." Which was something of an understatement, but Lorna didn't want to confide how painful it had been.

"Do you and your husband still have family in Texas?" she inquired.

"Benteen's father passed away shortly before we left, but both my parents live there," Lorna explained.

"How sad for your husband," Lady Elaine murmured. She lowered her lashes to conceal any hint that the news was of significance to her. The last potential problem was gone. Too many years had passed for her to feel anything but relief. Always keen in her observations of small details, she noticed the rough and reddened hands of the young Calder wife. She experienced a rare surge of compassion, perhaps because her thoughts had briefly turned back to her own harsh years. "I hope you won't be offended, Mrs. Calder, but in the short time I've been in the West, I have discovered how damaging this climate can be to a woman's skin."

Lorna reddened and tried to conceal her hands in the folds of her dress. She was well aware of the contrast between her skin and the woman's creamy smooth complexion.

"I have a lotion that my chemist prepared specially for me. I should like to have my maid bring some to your room. It does wonders, I assure you."

"It's very generous of you," Lorna murmured.

"Women need to look out for each other. Actually, we do a much better job of it than men." Again there was that faint smile. "I'll send my maid to your room with some of my lotion." The street door opened and an elegantly dressed gentleman entered. "My husband is here with the carriage. I must leave. It was a pleasure talking to you, Mrs. Calder."

"Good day to you, your ladyship." Again

Lorna made a small curtsy and received a gracious nod before the woman turned and glided across the lobby.

Lorna had expected the lady's husband to be some dashing and handsome nobleman, but the man Lady Elaine greeted was much older than Lorna believed the woman to be. He wasn't at all handsome. Except for his clothes, he looked dull and ordinary. He ruined Lorna's fantasy that Lady Elaine was wedded to a Prince Charming.

She was so engrossed in the titled couple that she almost didn't see Benteen enter the hotel. The elegantly dressed woman was facing away from him. She received no more than a passing glance from him to ascertain it wasn't Lorna as he walked by. A second later he spied his wife across the lobby. At first he thought the rapt look on her face was for him, and his stride quickened, but it vanished when she saw him.

Benteen didn't realize how many little things in their relationship he'd taken for granted. Like the way she used to turn to him when he touched her, the special excitement in her eyes when he looked at her, and the way she always watched for him. But not anymore. He tried to steel himself not to feel the loss.

Lorna hadn't turned out to be the loving amenable wife he had thought she would be.

At times she was too assertive, too ready to disagree with him, and too critical of his actions. He blamed Mary Stanton's influence for the way Lorna had started talking back to him. Those new qualities in her rankled him, yet he strangely admired her passionate spirit, her strength of will, and her unbending pride. When she angered him, he wanted to break her — as he had nearly done when he'd raped her. Yet Benteen had the uneasy feeling that if he ever succeeded in making her kneel to him, he would cease to care. It was an odd contradiction that he didn't understand.

He was trying not to care for her so much, so he wouldn't be scarred if she left him. If he couldn't hold her, he wanted to be able to turn his back on her and block her existence from his mind. That's what his father should have done.

"I didn't expect to see you in the lobby," he remarked when he reached her. "I thought you'd be in the room."

"I was just on my way there," Lorna replied.

"Who is the young woman?" Con Dunshill asked of his wife. She usually expressed no interest in those of her own sex, so he had been surprised and curious to see Elaine in conversation with a young woman, especially one not of her class.

"I really don't know," she lied, to make it appear that the girl's identity was of no import to her.

Her husband's attention was diverted by the appearance of the man who had volunteered to accompany them out to see the herds of Longhorns. Lady Elaine slid a glance across the lobby at the young woman who was her daughter-in-law.

An alertness stilled her wandering thoughts when she saw the tall, lean cowboy talking to Lorna Calder. Her sharp gaze studied his hewn features. The resemblance was there, a rougher version of Seth Calder, but it was Benteen. Her son whom she had abandoned so many years ago.

She felt no guilt about it. She'd had enough trouble talking Con into taking her away with him. A child would have complicated everything. Besides, Seth had doted on the boy. Benteen had served as an achor to keep Seth in Texas rather than come after her. If she had taken his son, Madelaine knew Seth would have torn up the world until he found him.

Madelaine — Lady Elaine — was convinced that some women were cut out for the role of mother, and others weren't. She wasn't. There wasn't anything associated with Benteen that she had found remotely satisfying or pleasant.

The pregnancy had been terrible. She had nearly ruined her figure. During those long, torturous hours of labor she had cursed Seth repeatedly for planting this child inside her. When she finally expelled the thing from her that was causing so much pain, she was only glad to be rid of it. She had no desire to see it or hold it; only with the greatest reluctance did she let the infant suckle at her breasts. She left it to Seth to see to many of the baby's needs.

In her opinion, no woman should be obliged to have a child when she was only sixteen. It seemed she had never been young or carefree. Always it had been work and responsibility – the kind that threatened to ruin her beauty. She used to dream about fine clothes and jewelry, and tons of money that she could spend any way she wanted. Then Con had ridden up one day to water his horse, and Madelaine had found the way to obtain the riches she'd dreamed about. Madelaine Calder had become Elaine Asher.

It had been relatively easy to manipulate Con Dunshill, second in line of succession to the Earl of Crawford. At first she'd had to be content to be his consort. He had showered her with expensive gifts and clothes, taken her to the finest places in San Francisco and later New York. She convinced him that only his persuasions had prompted her to leave her husband and son, weighting him down with guilt. When she had intercepted a telegram from his family ordering him back to England, she conveniently mislaid it and trumped up a story that she'd gotten hold of a Fort Worth newspaper and learned of the death of her husband and son. By the time she "found" the telegram, Con was ready to take her to England with him as his fiancée. She had already acquired a good deal of sophistication. Together they came up with a background that would convince his family she would be a suitable bride. As the stories go, they lived happily ever after.

She had taken great pains not to have any more children, letting the other Dunshill wives provide the sons to continue the line. Con assumed that he was sterile, which gave her another hold over him. For all his education, he lacked the ability to scheme and maneuver people. Elaine had learned well and had secretly amassed a small fortune of her own.

It was a rather novel experience to know that the man standing across the room was her son. He moved slightly, giving Elaine a better view of his face. He had grown into a virile man. The more she looked, the more she saw. Ruthless determination, ambition, and the drive to succeed. She recognized those qualities in him, because they came from her. What a team they could make, she thought, then sighed.

"It took longer than I thought," Benteen said. "Were you able to keep yourself amused?"

"Just before you came, I was talking to that lady I told you about," Lorna said. "And she is a lady. Her husband is an English earl. She's right over there by the door. You passed her when you came in."

Benteen half-turned to look as the petite, well-dressed woman walked out of the hotel on the arm of a gentleman.

"Why was she talking to you?" he asked.

"I guess because I was the only other female present." Lorna wasn't really sure herself. "She was very kind. She's going to send her maid to our room to give me some of her special lotion for my skin to heal its roughness."

"Can't you get something for it? We don't need charity from her kind," he insisted tersely.

"It isn't charity," Lorna retorted. "It's no different than when Mary lets me use some of her thread to mend your clothes. Women do those things for each other."

Benteen had the urge to order her to refuse it, but he had vowed to himself that he wouldn't assert his will on her.

The minute she mentioned Mary's name, she was sidetracked by the thought of her friend. "Did you see Mary when you rode out to the herd?" she asked. "She said that she and Ely wouldn't be leaving for a couple of days. They are still there, aren't they?"

"Yes. Ely's making repairs to their wagon to get it back in shape."

"I didn't think Mary would leave without telling me good-bye." But she was relieved just the same. "It seems as if I've always known her," she mused. Life seemed to be made up of constant good-byes. "It's hard to accept that I'll probably never see her again either."

"I sold the cattle." Benteen changed the subject, not liking the sense of guilt her remark gave him.

Lorna realized she hadn't inquired about the success of his morning's outing. Cattle, always cattle. "I hope you got a good price for them." It was a perfunctory comment, offered out of duty rather than interest.

"Eighteen dollars a head."

"Is that good?"

"That's what they pay for prime — sometimes twenty," he replied to assure her it was a very good price. "There's a big demand for beef in European markets. That's what is keeping the price up."

His words were reminiscent of other remarks she'd heard at the lunch table. A smile teased the corners of her mouth when she also remembered Bull Giles's biting comments.

"Did I say something amusing?" His gaze narrowed.

Lorna quickly wiped the smile from her face as she decided not to test the extent of Benteen's sense of humor. "No, not at all. I was thinking of something else."

"Have you eaten?"

"As a matter of fact, I did." She wasn't going to conceal anything from him. "All the tables were full except one. Mr. Giles suggested that we share it."

"Giles? Bull Giles?"

"Yes. He's arrived here in Dodge." She included the obvious information.

"As your husband, I have the right to request that you have nothing more to do with that man," Benteen stated.

"I haven't given you any cause to make that request," Lorna replied coolly. "Besides, we're leaving tomorrow. More than likely Mr. Giles is another person I'll be telling good-bye and never seeing again."

"That's the second time you've said that. Is there a particular reason why you keep bringing it up?" Benteen grew stiff.

Lorna wished devoutly that she hadn't. It was too depressing. "No. No reason," she said in a dispirited tone. A wry smile tugged the corners of her mouth up. "I have grown up some, Benteen. Now I can tell people good-bye and not cry all day about it." This time she changed the subject. "Have you eaten?"

"No."

"Shall we go into the dining room, then?" she suggested. "I'll have a cup of tea while you eat."

That evening, Lorna retired to their hotel room after dinner while Benteen again made his excuses not to stay. Too restless to sleep, Lorna sat on the bed and read the newspaper he had bought earlier.

She was surprised by a knock on the door. It seemed unlikely that Benteen had come back so early, and he had a key to let himself in. She doubted that Bull Giles would be so bold as to come to the room. She glanced at the valise near the bed where she kept the pistol Benteen had given her.

"Who is it?" Lorna demanded, and moved to the end of the bed closer to the valise.

"I am Lady Crawford's maid," came the precisely spoken reply. "She sent me by with some lotion for the madam."

Lorna hadn't exactly forgotten about it, but she thought the woman had. She crossed the room and unlocked the door. When she opened it, the maid was standing outside. She wore a black dress with a pristine white apron and a ruffled cap atop her head. She looked as starched and stiff as her clothes, as she made an inspecting glance at Lorna.

"The lotion, madam." She seemed to sniff her disapproval as she presented Lorna with a small jar.

"Will you express my gratitude to her ladyship, and give her my regards?" Lorna requested with equal formality, and clutched the jar tightly in her hands, treasuring the thought that its contents might make her skin as smooth as Lady Crawford's.

The maid appeared vaguely surprised that Lorna was capable of civilized speech. "I will, madam." She made a brief curtsy and turned on her heel to rustle down the hall in her starched dress.

The lotion seemed to be all that Lady Crawford had claimed it to be. Lorna swore she felt a difference the minute she applied it to her face and hands. If she used it sparingly, it would last a long time. She could hardly wait until Mary tried some of it.

Most of her elation faded when she thought

of her friend. She had hoped she'd be able to persuade Mary to continue on with them. But Benteen had said they were making preparations to leave. With the strain of her marriage, it was going to be a very long and lonely journey to Montana Territory.

Again Lorna was asleep when Benteen returned in the early morning. She didn't hear him undress and slide into bed beside her, taking care not to touch her.

The first rays of the sun were shining through the window when he stood fully clothed beside the bed. "Wake up, Lorna," he said briskly.

She stirred and rolled over to blink sleepily at him. For a few seconds there was warmth in her eyes for him; then it faded.

"It's time to leave," she guessed.

He nodded shortly. "I'll bring the wagon around while you dress. I'll meet you downstairs."

"All right," she sighed, but he was already walking to the door.

The ungainly covered wagon lumbered into camp while the morning was still new. The scene awaiting Lorna had grown very familiar to her. The highly functional chuck wagon with its sideboards for storing the cowboys' bedrolls and chuck box at the tail end was set up for business. A couple of drovers were hunkered down by the fire, nursing cups of coffee. Over by the Stanton wagon, Mary was washing clothes. She had assumed the role of camp laundress during the drive, a chore that usually went to the cook.

When the wagon rattled to a stop, Ely put aside the harness he was repairing and came over to give Benteen a hand with the team. With the brake set, Benteen swung to the ground and turned back to place a steadying hand on Lorna's waist as she climbed down from the wagon seat.

"Thought you might want to know, Benteen" — Ely kept busy with the team, not pausing while he spoke — "me and Mary have talked it over. We'd like to go on with you to Montana an' maybe file on a piece of land there. I can run a few cows an' maybe work for you on the side."

"I'll be needing a few riders," was all Benteen said in response.

Lorna heard it all and stared at the two men in numbed amazement. How could they treat such an important decision so calmly? They could have been discussing the weather. She picked up her skirts and hurried across to the Stanton wagon. Mary had squeezed the water out of the last shirt and turned to set it with the others to be spread out on the grass to dry.

"Is it true?" Lorna didn't wait for Mary to turn around. "Are you coming with us?"

Mary's face beamed with a warm smile when she faced Lorna. "It's true."

But Lorna couldn't take the news as calmly as everyone else seemed to be doing. With a laugh of delight, she gave Mary a quick hug.

"I can't believe it!" she declared. "I was hoping you'd come. What changed your mind?"

Although Mary was smiling, there was a serious light in her eyes. "A combination of things," she admitted. "I finally realized Ely would never be happy being a farmer. He was trying to please me because he felt he'd let me down by not providing a home for us. I was a farmer's daughter for so many years that I thought I should be a farmer's wife. All along I've been trying to change Ely from a cowboy into a farmer. A man's work is his pride. You can't take it from him or you haven't got a man anymore."

"I don't believe you really meant to do anything like that." Lorna refused to think ill of her friend.

"Not consciously, but I did. And I discovered I had pride, too," Mary added. "Going back to my relatives in Ioway would be the same as saying we didn't have what it takes to make it out here."

"But you do," Lorna insisted.

"Once I was the one reassuring you," Mary pointed out wryly. "I've never had a real friend before, Lorna. I guess the last reason is you."

Both of them were on the verge of tears. "If the last half of this trip is like the first, maybe we should paint a sign on our wagon like the fortyniners did," Lorna suggested in an emotionally tight voice. " 'Montana or Bust.' "

16

The Western Trail angled north out of Dodge City, cutting across the western end of Kansas and taking aim on Ogallala and its railhead on the southern end of the Nebraska sandhills. From there the trail swung west to Cheyenne and the Wyoming Territory north of it.

The herd of two-thousand plus Longhorns, their numbers depleted by the sale of three hundred steers, was a week out of Dodge City. Since they were handling fewer cattle, Benteen hadn't hired more trailhands to take Jonesy and Andy Young's places. The herd was trailing kindly, so his present crew would be able to handle them.

Benteen was scouting ahead on the trail to choose a site to bed the cattle for the night. It was a sweltering July afternoon in the sun. There wasn't any change on the flat prairie. It seemed they had traveled for miles without seeing a tree. Behind him, the herd made a dust cloud on the horizon.

Off to his left, he heard the distant clatter of a wagon. His gaze swung toward the sound. A pair of mules was pulling a high-sided wagon across the prairie. It looked like a Conestoga with the canvas removed. Some homesteader had probably hauled his family west in it, then converted it for farm use. Not wanting any trouble with farmers if it could be avoided, Benteen reined his horse toward the wagon to intercept it before it reached the herd.

The man pulled in his mules when Benteen rode up. The unrelenting Kansas sun had burned the farmer's face to a ruddy shade. His eyes were sunken and dull, resigned to his constant war with nature.

"Hot day, isn't it?" Benteen remarked idly, and took off his hat to wipe the sweat from his brow with his sleeved forearm.

"Always is. You with that trail herd?" The man spoke in chopped sentences, as if complete ones required too much effort.

"It's my herd," he acknowledged. "The name's Calder. Benteen Calder."

"Got a place off the trail." The farmer gestured over his shoulder. "Water in the crick, and grass. Welcome to bed 'em there. Missus and me be needin' fuel for the winter."

Dried cow and buffalo manure was often referred to as "prairie coal." Where trees were scarce, it was the only source of fuel. With a little bacon rind for kindling, it burned with a hot flame.

"I'll ride over and take a look," Benteen said.

"Hail took my crop a week back." Which explained why he was willing to let the cattle graze on his land. They couldn't damage a crop already destroyed.

Handling the team like the veteran driver she'd become, Lorna followed the chuck wagon to the site Benteen had selected for the night's camp. The wagons were going to be positioned between the herd and the farmer's homestead, a hundred yards away.

Their route took them close to the farmer's home. It was the first time Lorna had seen a sod house, although she'd heard about them. She couldn't help staring at the strange-looking structure with tufts of grass sticking out between layers of earth. The door and windows were framed with wood and the roof appeared to be a combination of brush, earth, and poles.

A woman was standing in the doorway of the primitive cabin, halted in the act of wiping her hands on the long apron around her waist. Lorna raised a hand and waved to her. Suddenly the woman started running toward the wagon.

"Stop!" she cried out. "Please, stop!"

The woman sounded so desperate that Lorna thought she needed help and hauled back on the reins to stop the team. Tears were streaming down the woman's face as she ran alongside the wagon. Her hand was reaching out to Lorna while she continued to sob breathlessly for her to stop.

When the wagon rumbled to a halt, Lorna climbed quickly down. "What is it? What's wrong?" she asked anxiously as the woman stood and covered her mouth with a hand.

"Thank you." It came out in a muffled sob, as her hand made a tentative gesture toward Lorna as if she wanted to touch her.

"What is it?" Lorna asked again, and glanced toward the sod home, wondering if someone was sick or hurt.

"I'm sorry." A laugh bubbled through her sobs. "It's just been so long . . . since I've seen another white woman."

A cold shiver went down Lorna's spine at the explanation. My God, what kind of life was it that reduced a woman to tears at the sight of another woman?

"You probably think I'm crazy." The woman brought her hands together and clasped them in a prayerful attitude at her breast. "But I just couldn't let you go by . . . without talking. Alfred never mentioned there were any women with the trail herd." She glanced sideways as Mary came up to see what was wrong. "Alfred's my husband. I thought I was seeing things when you waved to me. I thought this emptiness had finally driven me crazy."

Her words were tumbling out, rushing over themselves in her anxiety. Lorna was torn with pity for the woman, and a little frightened by the picture she painted, too.

"You aren't imagining things," Lorna promised. "This is Mary Stanton, and I'm Lorna Calder."

"My name's Emma Jenkins." She suddenly raised a hand to the frizzy wisps of hair that had escaped from the carelessly gathered bun. "Gracious, I must look a sight."

Lorna guessed that the woman had ceased to care about her appearance, probably discouraged by the dark hollows under her eyes and the thinness of her face. She made a vow to herself that she would never let it happen to her.

"It's this land, you know," Emma Jenkins insisted with a resentful glance at the lonely prairie that stretched from horizon to horizon. "The wind moans so."

Benteen came riding back to find out what was holding up the two wagons. His horse stopped a few feet short of the women and did a sidestepping dance under him.

"What's the problem?" His glance traveled over the three on the ground.

"Mrs. Jenkins, I'd like you to meet my husband, Benteen Calder." Lorna tactfully ignored his question and introduced them instead.

"Please to meet you, Mrs. Jenkins." With a nod, he touched his fingers to the front of his hat brim.

The excitement of the moment had made the woman so highly emotional that all her reactions were exaggerated. Now it was guilt and remorse that claimed her. "I'm sorry. I'm afraid I detained your wife," she admitted anxiously. "I know you're wanting to set up camp for the night, and I'm keeping you."

"I'm glad you stopped us," Lorna said. "It's given us a chance to thank you for letting us camp here."

"Would you . . . ?" She started to put the question to Lorna, then turned eagerly to Benteen. "Would you and your wife please come eat with us tonight?" Swinging to Mary, she included her, too. "And you and your husband, Mrs. Stanton? It would be so wonderful having company . . . and someone to talk to in the evening. Oh, please come."

"We'd be proud to come," Lorna assured her.

It nearly made her cry to see how hungry Emma Jenkins was for company.

Mary was more aware of the strain feeding four extra mouths could put on the food supplies of a frontier family. "We wouldn't want you to go to extra work for us," she said in mild protest. "Maybe it would be better if we came to visit after the evening meal."

"Please, I want you to come," Emma Jenkins insisted. "We have a nasty old rooster who pecks my little girl every time she goes outside. It's been begging to have its neck wrung for a long time."

"As long as you're sure . . ." Mary accepted with reluctance.

"I am." The woman became happy again.

The thick earthen walls of the sod house kept the interior cool even on the hottest day, yet the air inside was dank and musty, like a cave. There were old newspapers on the walls to add some lightness to the rooms. A thread-worn carpet covered the dirt floor, and a brightly colored patchwork quilt lay atop the straw-filled mattress on the wooden frame in the corner. Muslin was tacked to the windows for curtains, and a large traveling trunk had been converted into an infant's bed. A second trunk was pulled up to a crude table with two chairs.

Additional seats were provided by two boxes.

Despite the little touches that tried to turn it into a home, it seemed a cheerless place to Lorna. There were water stains on the carpet that indicated the roof leaked. And the pieced-together strip of bright gingham on the table looked very much like a skirt from an old dress. But the table was set with beautiful flo-blue china, an odd symbol of luxury amid such rude surroundings.

Emma Jenkins was wearing her best dress, a rather plain dark blue dress made for service-ability rather than looks, and her light brown hair was slicked back in a neat bun. Her tow-headed daughter kept hiding behind her, sucking earnestly on her thumb and peering apprehensively at the four strangers in the house.

"Can't you say hello to our company, Elizabeth?" Emma tried to coax her two-year-old daughter to stop clinging to her legs, but little Elizabeth hid her face. "I'm sorry," Emma apologized to them. "I'm afraid she's shy. She's never seen anybody that she can remember except Alfred and me."

"Children that age are naturally shy around strangers," Mary assured her.

"Your china is beautiful," Lorna complimented.

"Thank you." Emma beamed. "We brought it all the way from Ohio. And only one plate got broken on the trip."

"Missus cried for a week, too," Alfred Jenkins added; even he showed signs of being perked up by the company.

"Please, won't you all sit down," Emma invited.

Alfred insisted that Mary and Lorna sit in the two chairs while Ely and Benteen sat on the boxes. Alfred and Emma Jenkins scooched together on the traveling trunk with little Elizabeth on Emma's lap. In addition to the chicken, there were potatoes, cornbread, and hominy. Before they dished their plates, Alfred bowed his head and said grace.

"Dear Lord, You took our crop, but You gave us fuel for the winter and brought nice folks to our table. We thank You for that. Amen."

The simple words made Lorna feel very humble. The eagerness to share what little they had caused her to look twice at herself. She noticed the small helpings of food they took so there would be plenty for everyone else.

Of course, Emma Jenkins was too excited and too busy asking questions to eat. Alfred seemed just as interested to find out what was going on in the world. There was so much crosstalk going on — man to man and woman to woman — that it was surprising any of it made sense.

After the meal, the men went outside to smoke. Emma was appalled when Lorna and Mary offered to help with the dishes. They were company; she couldn't let them help. She very carefully stacked the china in a pan and insisted she would do them later.

It was dusk when Benteen stepped into the sod house to state it was time they were returning to camp. An emotional Emma hugged them and thanked them for coming. As Lorna walked away with Benteen, she glanced over her shoulder. The woman was standing in the doorway, just as she had seen her the first time. Lorna waved, as she had done before.

This time it was Alfred Jenkins who came hurrying after them. They waited for him to catch up with them. When he did, he spoke low so his voice wouldn't carry as it so easily did on that flat terrain. "I just wanted to thank you for what you did for my missus by comin' here tonight." He spoke in complete sentences, which seemed to show how sincerely moved he was. "She hasn't smiled in a long time. You helped her. Thank you. That's all I had to say." He seemed embarrassed by how much he had said, and turned quickly to retrace his steps to the woman in the doorway.

"Isn't there something we can do for them, Benteen?" Lorna murmured. "Something more than leaving behind a bunch of cow chips?"

Benteen was a long time replying. "We'll see what we can do, come morning."

When they reached camp, Lorna retired directly to her wagon. Besides being all talked out, there were too many things on her mind, mainly a determination that this land wasn't going to do to her what it had done to that woman, mentally or physically.

She slept alone in the wagon. Since leaving Dodge City, Benteen had spread out a bedroll on the ground with the other drovers. The change in the sleeping arrangements hadn't gone unnoticed, but no one speculated aloud about the possible reasons.

When Lorna climbed out of the wagon the next morning, her glance went first to the sod house. The scarlet-orange hue of breaking dawn shaded the roof thatched with dirt and willow. She turned her gaze on the lonely grandeur of the plains with a kind of defiance then walked with a free-swinging stride to the chuck wagon for the morning meal.

"What's with the kid?" Shorty Niles was asking Rusty as she walked up.

Both men slid short glances at Joe Dollarhide, sitting off by himself in a moody silence. Usually he came back for seconds, but the food on the plate balanced on his knees didn't appear to have been touched.

"Beats me." Rusty shrugged, but the grimness of his mouth showed concern. "Last night I offered to let him grind the coffee, but he didn't want to."

There was never a shortage of volunteers to grind coffee, since the Arbuckle Coffee Company put a peppermint stick in its one-pound bags. All the cowboys had a sweet tooth, and whoever ground the coffee got the candy. There was obviously something wrong if Joe Dollarhide had turned down his chance.

"Good morning."

Lorna turned to find Benteen standing behind her, a cup of coffee in his hand. There was an awkward moment when she couldn't quite meet the dark study of his eyes. He lowered his gaze to take a swallow of coffee, and it was gone.

"How are you this morning?" she asked.

"As well as can be expected, under the circumstances." His voice was dry, neither condemning nor complaining. She felt the flash of sexual tension and knew exactly what he meant. But he didn't expect a reply, because he spoke again, this time addressing Shorty. "When you're through eating, I want you to ride out to the herd. Spanish tells me two cows dropped calves in the night. Give the calves to the Jenkins family."

"Right." Shorty nodded and took his plate, moving away to sit on the ground.

"His milk cow should have enough to keep two calves alive," Benteen said to Lorna. "The Jenkins family will have a beef to butcher this winter."

"Food as well as fuel," she said, and smiled. "Thank you."

"Don't thank me. Thank the cows." A sunburst of lines radiated briefly from the corners of his eyes.

"Mr. Calder, sir?" Joe Dollarhide set his plate on the ground when he spied Benteen at the chuck wagon. He rose and rubbed his hands down his thighs in a nervous gesture now that he had Benteen's attention. He approached with a degree of uncertainty.

"What is it, Dollarhide?" Benteen thought he knew. Last night he'd seen the boy gazing at the lighted windows of the sod house with a kind of homesick longing.

"I was just thinking . . . since that farmer let us graze the herd on his land, maybe we should do something in return. A favor for a favor," he suggested lamely.

"What do you have in mind?" Benteen prompted, without telling the kid what he'd already done.

"I . . . thought . . . I could do his morning chores for him — milk the cow and slop the hogs." There was an earnest look in his expression.

"You did, huh?" Benteen took a drink of his coffee, studying the lanky kid over the tin rim. "Maybe you'd better decide whether you want to be a cowboy or a farmer. I never met a cowboy yet who volunteered to slop hogs or milk cows."

"I want to be a cowboy." Joe Dollarhide stiffened, uneasy that Benteen might have guessed being so close to a farm had made him a little homesick for his pa's farm.

"How come you aren't practicing with your rope?" Benteen challenged quickly, because Joe usually practiced off and on all day long, trying to become proficient with that essential tool of the cowboy.

"I been catchin' just about everything I swing my rope at — head or heel," Joe declared. "Ask Yates. I been doin' it regularly."

"In that case, we'll be needin' an extra rider on drag this morning. There's a couple of cows that aren't going to like the idea of us leavin' their calves with a farmer. Do you think you could handle the job?"

"You just give me the job, an' I'll show you." His homesickness was fading now that he was finally getting a chance to be more than just a wrangler's helper.

"Then you'd better be thinkin' about gettin' your breakfast ate and a horse saddled," Benteen pointed out. "Everyone else around here is just about ready to fork leather."

"Yes, sir." Joe Dollarhide was grinning as he went back to pick up his plate and wolf down the cold breakfast.

Benteen shook the dregs out of his empty coffeecup and handed it to Rusty. His glance went briefly to Lorna. "I'm gonna ride out and look over the herd. See you at noon."

As he walked toward the saddled horses on the picket line, Lorna studied him with puzzled interest. "Rusty, how did he know that Joe was homesick?"

"Instinct, I s'pect." The cook, too, turned a thoughtful look on Benteen. "Some men know cattle, but not a darn thing about workin' the men lookin' after the cattle. Handlin' men is something Benteen just knows." He sent a sidelong glance at Lorna. "Now, women's another thing. Your kind is a different breed altogether. Ya ain't so easily 'managed.' "

"Maybe it's because we don't want to be 'managed,' " Lorna suggested.

"Maybe," he conceded with an indifferent nod. "By the by, there's a nice patch of wildflowers in a little ravine that runs behind the chuck wagon here."

A smile trembled on her lips, in spite of the modesty she should have felt. "Why, thank you, Mr. Rusty." Ever since that first occasion, he had always referred to her strolls to answer nature's call with an inquiry about the wildflowers she'd seen along the way. It had become a private joke between the two of them. Who would ever have thought that she'd be able to laugh about bodily functions with a man?

When Shorty Niles and Joe Dollarhide had ridden up to the farmhouse with the two newborn calves across their saddles, Lorna had watched from the camp. She smiled when she heard Alfred Jenkins turn and call to his wife. His voice carried all the way to camp.

"Emma! Emma! Come quick!"

Lorna knew their blessing that night would include a mention of the windfall. It made her feel good.

The sweltering temperatures of early July

showed no sign of letting up after three days of driving the herd over more treeless prairie. Spanish was the only one who didn't seem to mind the hot, sweating ride, joking with the other cowhands and insisting his blood was just getting warm. Heat lightning flashed through the heavens three nights running. It made for uneasy times on night herd.

Benteen slept lightly, bedded on the ground near the wagon. A low voice called him to wake for his turn to watch. It was an unwritten rule that you didn't wake a sleeping man by touching him or shaking him. You were just as likely to find a gun pointed at you.

Pushing back the hat shielding his face, he saw Shorty's outline standing at the foot of his bedroll. The campfire was out, but an overcast sky lit the world of shadows with flashes of sheet lightning. Benteen rolled to his feet.

"It's not good out there," Shorty murmured. "You'd better shuck your metal."

Night guards had a greater fear of lightning in a storm than stampeding cattle. They were sitting targets in flat country for the jagged bolts that rained fire out of the sky. The superstition prevailed that it was metal that attracted the lightning to riders, so on stormy nights a cowboy divested himself of his knife and spurs, and some even hid their guns.

"Wake up Spanish. Tell him he's drawin' an extra watch," Benteen ordered. "Dollarhide's too green if there's a storm brewin'."

Shorty nodded as Benteen moved to his night horse, a grulla he called Mouse, tied to the wagon tongue, saddled and ready. "Hope you know some church songs."

When the three riders rode out to the herd and split up to start their circling route, some of the cattle stood up in a silent acknowledgment of the changing of the guard. A few minutes later, they were lying back down.

It was quiet, too quiet. Benteen stopped the blue-gray buckskin a couple of times just to listen. The warm air was stifling, licked with tension. Flashes of lightning skylighted the cattle, confirming they were all lying down, but he could hear the rumble of distant thunder. And it was coming closer.

When he passed the kid riding counterclockwise around the herd, Dollarhide was softly crooning an old love song. A little farther on, he met up with Spanish. The Mexican reined in, so Benteen paused, too.

"The Captain is up." Spanish passed on the information that the lead steer was on his feet. "He doesn't like this night either."

"Who does?" Benteen murmured, and started his horse forward.

343

The brindle steer was not given to spooking, making a steady and reliable leader for the herd. When Benteen saw the steer, it was testing the air, not liking what was out there any more than Benteen did. He tried to soothe the rest of the herd with "The Texas Lullaby," a tune made up of, not words, but wavering notes. Another steer stood up, motionless and expectant. Then it was by twos and threes they were getting up, until the whole herd was on its feet.

The sky became black as hell, split with bolts of fire. The air was so thick it seemed suffocating. Suddenly a glowing light appeared on the top of every horn. It was an eerie sight that Benteen had seen once before in his life — this phosphorescent light folklore called by many names. He knew it as St. Elmo's fire.

In moments of blackness, there was nothing to be seen but the strange, awesome illumination of more than four thousand horns. Spanish was singing louder from his side of the herd, trying to reassure the beasts that the ghostly lights were nothing to fear. There was a stirring in their numbers as the herd began to mill uneasily.

A great blue ball of lightning ripped from the sky, momentarily blinding Benteen. There wasn't even time for a breath before the ground shook with a mighty clap of thunder. But the reverberations that followed were made by the stampeding herd, at a mad run in one leap.

The grulla nearly jumped out from under Benteen as it bounded in pursuit of the cattle. The sky burst open, dumping buckets of rain and whipping it in sheets. There was no way of knowing where Spanish and Dollarhide were. Benteen couldn't see where he was going and had no choice but to trust his horse and stay with the panicked mob of cattle.

Half-blinded by the darkness and the driving rain, he could catch only glimpses of the herd. The eerie glow seemed to dance from horn tip to horn tip, while the heat from their maddened crush of bodies burned the side of his face. There was no time to think of the danger, of a misstep by the horse; it was spur and ride hell for leather to get to the leaders. One man could turn a herd if he knew how.

Drumming hooves popped and clicked; horn tips clacked together; and the thunder of the storm raged louder than all of it. The little mouse-gray grulla was stretched out until its belly seemed to scrape the prairie grass. They were racing with the leaders of the stampede, running stride for stride. The mustang under him knew its business and pressed into the leaders to force the turn.

Once they had started, the rest of the herd followed. Other riders were skylighted, racing with the herd. What began as a wide circle tightened concentrically into a small one until they had coiled into a bawling mill.

The thunder and lightning rolled on across the prairie, but the rain stayed, pouring down steadily. There was no way of telling how much of the herd had scattered in the mad dash, not until morning. The drovers' job became one of containment to hold the main section of the herd intact.

The Longhorns had run eight wild long miles from camp. Three cowboys were missing – Spanish, Dollarhide, and Woolie Willis. Any number of things could have separated them from the herd – a horse falling or a rider taking out after another bunch. Nobody speculated on the fate of the missing three.

The rain stopped before dawn, the clouds peeling away to show the stars. Before first light, Rusty was hitching the team to the chuck wagon and lending a hand to Mary and Lorna with their wagons. When the soft color of morning was tinting the land, they set out in search of the stampeded herd.

The Longhorns had left a wide trail of trampled grass and churned earth. Along the route, Lorna saw several of the drovers — looking for stray cattle, she presumed. A couple of them stopped, had a word with Rusty, and rode on.

Jessie and Ely were holding the main body of the herd when they arrived. Rusty picked the most likely spot to set up a camp and pulled in the team. Unhitching the horses from the wagon, he left their harnesses on and tied them up.

"You ladies want to give me a hand?" he called to Lorna and Mary. "Those boys is wet and tired. They'll be wantin' coffee and some hot grub as soon as they can get it."

"I'll get a fire going," Lorna volunteered, and hopped down from the wagon seat.

"There's some dry wood and chips in the cooney," Rusty told her.

The coffee was boiling good when the first riders approached the new camp. Lorna could see the steam rising from the horses' wet hides. One of the riders spurred his horse to reach camp before the others. Vince Garvey swung out of the saddle, staggering a bit with tiredness.

"They're bringin' Woolie in. Broke his leg," he informed Rusty, and dragged himself to the fire to pour a cup.

Lorna caught the flicker of relief in Rusty's

face, but he growled cantankerously. "And just what am I supposed to be usin' for splints in this treeless hell?" He quickly bobbed his head at Mary and Lorna. "Beggin' your pardon."

"That's your problem, sawbones." Vince drank down his coffee. "Bust up the wagon, I guess." His horse was still standing where the cowboy had dropped the reins, its head hanging low. "Sure hope Yates gets his remuda rounded up," Vince remarked. "These horses are about to drop."

"What about Spanish and Dollarhide?" Rusty asked.

There was a long pause while Vince poured another shot of the black coffee into his cup. "They won't be needing your help."

For an instant, it didn't sink in. Lorna hadn't been aware the two riders were missing, so the significance of Vince's reply initially missed her, until she saw the long faces of the men riding in.

"They're dead." She had to say it aloud, even then she didn't believe it. "What happened?"

Vince glanced at her, then looked at Rusty and shrugged a nonanswer. The riders entered camp and dismounted, all except one. The injured cowboy was hunched over the saddle, his face sickly pale. Benteen was among the trailhands that carefully lifted Woolie to

348

the ground. His hat tumbled off, revealing the thick mass of curling blond hair that had given him his nickname. He groaned in pain when Rusty probed the length of his left leg.

"This ought to rate me some of your snake-bite remedy, Rusty." Woolie grunted the words in his effort to keep in the pain. The cook was the guardian of the sole bottle of alcohol brought on the drive — for snakebite purposes.

"You got a broke leg, not a snakebite," Rusty grumped. "But I reckon a couple of swallows might help 'fore I set this leg."

When he went to the chuck box to fetch it, he motioned Mary and Lorna to come over. Lorna was still numbed by the news of young Joe Dollarhide's death, and the Mexican-Indian Spanish Bill.

"Do you reckon you two ladies can hold Woolie down while I straighten his leg?" Rusty murmured. "He ain't likely to struggle much with the two of you lookin' on. He'd want to show you how brave he is."

Lorna glanced uncertainly at Mary. "I guess so."

"You just set the leg, Rusty," Mary stated. "Lorna and I will see that he doesn't give you any trouble."

Rusty uncorked the bottle and filled a tin

cup with the liquor. He carried it over and handed it to Benteen, who crouched beside the injured cowboy. While Rusty returned to the wagon to get some rawhide strips and pry off a board, Benteen helped Woolie partially sit up. Woolie gulped down half of it, choked on a cough, then finished it.

"My God, Rusty," he declared hoarsely as Benteen lowered him to the ground. "You sure that stuff ain't to kill snakes?"

"Maybe that's what the label said." Rusty paused to break the board slat in half with his knee. "Never could read too good." He waved Lorna and Mary toward the prone cowboy. "Each of you grab an arm."

As Lorna knelt beside him, Benteen stepped back out of the way. Woolie tried to grit his teeth against the pain and smile at the same time.

"Look at me, fellas," he called to the other drovers. "I got a lady on each arm. Bet you're wishin' you was me."

Lorna had never seen anyone in physical pain before. It was impossible for her to be indifferent. She was tensing in sympathy for him when Rusty laid the wood slats on the ground beside Woolie's left leg, holding the rawhide strings between his teeth.

"Hold on tight," he said through them, and

350

took hold of the left boot.

"I'll try not to swear, ladies," Woolie said, trying again to smile. "But I hope you'll be pardonin' my language if anything slips out."

"We will," Lorna whispered as her hands gripped his arm and shoulder to hold him flat.

Her gaze stayed riveted to his white face. She couldn't bring herself to look to see what Rusty was doing. Beads of perspiration started popping out all over his face as Woolie clamped his teeth shut. His features were contorted with pain. Lorna wished he'd cry out. His body jerked from Rusty's sharp pull; then he let out an agonizing groan and went limp.

"Passed out," Rusty declared. "You can let go of him now."

As Lorna sat back on her heels, she felt weak inside. Benteen's hands closed on her shoulders to help her to her feet. She half-turned to him, a little pale. His glance seemed to run over her with disinterest.

"Better get some coffee," he advised.

When she glanced to see if Mary was coming, her friend was helping Rusty tie the boards tight and straight to keep the leg bone in position. Lorna felt helpless. She thought she had learned to cope with everything that could possibly be thrown at her, yet she'd never had to handle an injury before.

She wandered to the fire, not really wanting any coffee, but she poured a cup anyway. Cupping it in her hands, she drifted to the edge of the circle, away from the silent group of cowboys. It wasn't her intention to eavesdrop, but when they started talking quietly among themselves, she couldn't help overhearing.

"I'll bet Spanish never knew what hit him," Bob Vernon murmured.

"They say the hair stands up on the back of your neck just before lightning hits you," Vince Garvey offered, and Lorna felt her blood run cold. A bolt of lightning had killed Spanish.

"Yeah, well, there's one consolation," Shorty muttered. "Spanish hated the cold. I never liked the idea of bein' fried myself, but it mighta been the way he'd a-chose."

"I sure wish we'd a-found somethin' of the kid to bury." Zeke Taylor shook his head. "It don't seem right."

"Them cattle did the buryin' when they trampled him into the ground." Shorty bolted down a swig of coffee as if it were liquor.

Lorna felt sick to her stomach. She turned and stumbled to her wagon, gripping the side and leaning weakly against it. Her hand covered her mouth. She wasn't sure if she was trying to stem the rising nausea or stifle the sobs choking her throat. She kept remembering the time Joe Dollarhide had told her about the ranch he wanted to have someday, and how eager he had been to become a cowboy. He was just a young farmboy a long way from home. Now there wouldn't even be a grave to mark where he lay.

"Lorna." It was Benteen.

She swallowed hard. "I was . . . just thinking about Joe . . . and how much he wanted to be a cowboy."

"Drink your coffee."

She hadn't realized it was still in her hand until he carried the cup to her mouth and tipped it to force her to drink. Its bitter strength stiffened her. She brought her gaze up to his face, so lacking in emotion.

"He was so young, Benteen," she murmured. "Doesn't his death mean anything to you? Or Spanish?"

"You aren't the only one who has to say good-bye to friends, Lorna." His voice was as flat as his expression. "I think mine have been more final than yours."

When he turned and walked away, she felt both pity and guilt. He couldn't show his grief, because that wasn't part of his code. But it was there, she realized. Why hadn't she seen through his closed-in expression?

Breakfast was being dished up when Yates, the horse wrangler, drove more than half the remuda close to camp. With fresh horses to ride, there was no more reason to tarry over the meal and give tired horses a chance to rest. Over five hundred head of Longhorns had scattered in the stampede. They had to be rounded up and brought back to the main herd. There wasn't time to rest or mourn the dead.

17

The noon meal was a catch-as-catch-can affair. A pot of beans was kept hot, as well as the coffee, for any rider that came in. Usually a driver would ride in, wolf down some beans, wash them down with coffee, saddle a fresh horse, and be gone in less than fifteen minutes.

"It looks like Mr. Willis has woken up," Lorna noticed as the injured cowboy stirred in the shade of the Stanton wagon and attempted to sit up. "I'll take him some food."

After Woolie had passed out, they had carried him to the shade and laid him on his soogan, where he'd slept through the morning and into early afternoon. It was a combination of shock, exhaustion, and alcohol that had kept him out.

Mary added some biscuits to the plate of beans Lorna dished up. She carried the plate and a cup of coffee over to the wagon. Woolie had managed to sit up with the wagon wheel for support, but effort had him sweating again from the knife-sharp throbbing in his broken leg. There was still a pale cast to his tanned face as his breath came in short pants.

"I thought you might be hungry." Lorna bent down to offer him the food and coffee.

"Thanks." He took the plate, but made no attempt to eat the food. His head turned to gaze at the herd. "How are the boys doin'? I'll bet those cattle are scattered all over hell and gone."

"They've brought in several bunches already this morning," Lorna assured him.

Despite the faint glaze of pain in his eyes, there was a determined set to his jaw when he looked again at Lorna. "Could you help me get to my horse? They'll be needin' my help."

"You're in no condition to ride with that broken leg," she protested.

"You get me in a saddle and I'll stay there," he insisted. "They're working shorthanded an' they'll be needin' every rider they can get."

With the loss of Spanish and Dollarhide, there were only six able-bodied riders left, not counting Benteen. Two of those had to stay with the main herd, which left only four to search for the missing cattle.

"You can't go tearing off across the prairie." Lorna frowned.

"Maybe not," Woolie conceded, grimacing in pain when he tried to shift his position. "But I sure can walk a horse around that herd and free up Jess or Ely to look for cattle. It don't take two good legs to do that."

She stared at him, seeing a certain logic in what he was saying. His first thought on waking had been for the herd, not concern for his injuries or hunger. First and foremost, it was the cattle — just like Benteen. The herd represented their future livelihood. Lorna remembered the way her mother worked at the store to help out on busy days, while she had resented the amount of time her father spent at his work and not lifted a hand to help him.

"Missus Calder, I just can't sit here when they need me," Woolie argued.

"You are going to sit there until you've eaten that food." Even she was startled by the ring of authority in her voice. "You're going to need all the strength you can get."

"Yes, ma'am." He obediently took up his fork.

Rising, Lorna turned and walked to the chuck wagon. She opened the sideboard where the bedrolls were stowed. "Rusty, which one of these bedrolls belonged to Joe Dollarhide?"

He came over, a curious frown making a scowl on his features. "Why do you want to know? I was gonna see to it that his property was returned to his folks."

"Just tell me which one it is." She kept the

sound of authority in her voice, not wanting to explain her plan to him.

Just like Woolie Willis, he obeyed. "This one." He pulled out one that didn't appear any different from the others.

"Thank you." Lorna turned away before he could ask any more questions. As she started for her wagon, she called to Mary, "Could you come help me a minute?"

She was inside the wagon and untying the roll when Mary climbed in the back. "What is it?" asked Mary.

Unrolling the tarp, Lorna didn't pause to answer as she rummaged through the contents. "I'm going to ride astraddle, so I need some clothes to wear. These skirts and petticoats will just spook the cattle and there'll be another stampede. Joe Dollarhide was about the same size I am. I thought his pants might fit me."

Mary sat down on a corner of a trunk, dumbfounded. "What are you talking about?"

"Benteen's shorthanded right now. He needs riders to find the missing cows." Lorna found a clean shirt and pair of pants and held them up to study them with a critical eye. "Mr. Willis just said that anybody can walk a horse around the herd. So that's what I'm going to do, which means Mr. Trumbo can look for cows." She turned to Mary and held the pants against her waist. "What do you think?"

"Lorna, a woman in pants?" Mary was certain she'd taken leave of her senses.

"They'll be too long, but we can roll them up," she decided, and ignored the shocked remark.

Her mind was made up, and she began peeling off her clothes. The pants fit a little snug around the hips, but the shoulder seams of the shirt drooped onto her arms. She rolled the pants legs up until the toes of her shoes showed. The clothes felt very strange, made her feel like she wasn't really dressed.

"Well?" She looked at Mary.

"Lorna, those pants show everything. It's scandalous," her friend declared.

"Then I won't tuck the shirt in." Lorna tried to pretend she didn't feel self-conscious, that it was all very natural and right.

"You're really going to go through with this, aren't you?" Mary realized.

"Yes."

"What are you going to do for a saddle?"

"Jonesy's saddle is in the back of the chuck wagon." Lorna had already thought about that. "I'll use it." She picked up her sunbonnet and tied it on her head.

Mary laughed, unable to smother it. "You look silly in those pants and that bonnet."

Lorna grinned, then laughed, too. Both knew the alternative to the sunbonnet was no hat at all, which meant exposure to a blazing Kansas sun. Which was no alternative.

When she swung out of the wagon, unhampered by skirts, Lorna discovered a freedom of movement she'd never known. To cover her nervousness, she walked briskly to the chuck wagon and tried to pretend there was nothing strange about the way she was dressed. There was a shocked and incredulous look on Rusty's face. It was one of the rare times she'd known him to be speechless.

"Would you catch my horse for me, Rusty?" she asked briskly. "I'm going to relieve Mr. Trumbo from herd duty so he can look for the missing cattle."

The cook managed to nod and reached in the front of the wagon for a spare rope. All the while that he walked out to the remuda, confined in a rope corral, he kept looking back over his shoulder at Lorna, as if he believed his eyes were playing tricks on him.

The reaction was the same when she rode out to the herd and relieved Jessie Trumbo. The cowboy was dumbstruck at the sight of a woman in pants and sitting astraddle a horse. He kept twisting in the saddle to stare at her as he rode away. Lorna had discovered there was no real trick to riding astride the saddle. It was still a matter of leg strength and balance.

It was late afternoon when Benteen approached the main herd, driving the fifty head he'd found. The cattle trotted quickly when they saw their own kind. Benteen eased his horse back to let the bunch infiltrate the herd on their own.

With a nod to Ely, he started to turn his horse toward camp for a cup of coffee before heading out to make one last sweep while it was still light. Out of the corner of his eye he saw a strange sight. It looked like a man wearing a sunbonnet. It couldn't be — but it was.

The rider was too slim to be a man — a boy maybe. Benteen didn't recognize the way he was sitting his horse, either. Then he noticed it was Lorna's horse. He set his spurs to his horse to intercept the slim rider making a slow circle of the herd. His horse was pulled to a plunging halt directly in her path. Lorna stopped her mount.

Benteen raked his gaze over the shirt, plastered to her skin by perspiration, and the pants, drawn tightly across her thighs. Outrage simmered somewhere within him, but he was too stunned for it to have any force.

"What are you doing out here — in that getup?" Benteen frowned.

"I'm taking Mr. Trumbo's place so he can look for the cattle." She tried to be calm and very matter-of-fact about the unusual situation. "I knew you were shorthanded, with Mr. Willis laid up and all, so I thought I'd help out. These cattle are just as important to my future as they are to yours." Lorna had been thinking about that a lot while she rode around the herd.

For a long moment Benteen didn't say anything. On only one point could he argue with her reasoning, and that was her flagrant defiance of convention by wearing pants. Yet he saw the practicality, the necessity of such clothes if she was going to help. And he certainly could use it.

"When you're in camp, you wear a dress," he stated. "I don't want you walking around in front of the men like that. It shows too much of your body."

"I will," Lorna promised, and tried to keep the swell of triumph from curving her lips.

But she sobered at the sudden tension that entered his expression as he seemed to involuntarily lower his gaze to let it wander over her body. There was no attempt to voice the desire she sensed that he felt, nor even an acknowledgment of its existence. Then with apparent calm he turned his horse and rode away.

As she lay alone in bed that night, her body was tired but her mind wouldn't stop thinking. Benteen was sleeping on the ground outside the wagon. She wondered if he felt as lonely tonight as she did. Lorna remembered how warm his body had been to curl against, how pleasantly solid.

There were so many things about him that she hadn't understood before. Maybe she had been too inexperienced about life to understand them. He had not been raised as gently as she had. When he got hit, he hit back. He did not threaten idly, as she had done.

She ran a hand over her breast and remembered the way his hand used to claim it and play with the nipple until it was hard and round in his fingers. Gradually she had stopped being shy with him and enjoyed the things he made her feel. Maybe the bad memory was fading. Maybe he could make her feel those things again.

Sighing, Lorna rolled onto her side and tried to close her eyes. There was a brief irritation that Benteen had left the decision for her to make the first move as to when they would be man and wife again. Yet, if he had tried to force it, she would have been angry. It was very confusing.

After two days of wearing pants and riding astraddle, the trailhands became accustomed to the sight and Lorna stopped being an eye-popping oddity. There was a bit more to the work than Woolie Willis had led her to believe, yet Lorna discovered she could handle it. She was really quite proud of herself, too.

It had taken two days to round up the scattered herd. There were ten head they never found. The third morning, they started up the trail again. Benteen assigned Lorna to ride one of the flank positions, while Woolie Willis drove their wagon. He was hobbling around on a makeshift pair of crutches Rusty had fixed up for him. It was hard work, dirty work that tested Lorna's endurance.

Ten days later, they reached Ogallala, Nebraska, on the North Platte River. They stopped south of there for a day so Benteen could ride to see if he couldn't hire a couple extra men. Lorna took advantage of the day's layover to wash clothes.

When she had her things together, she went through Benteen's bedroll to get his dirty clothes. A bright brass coin fell out of the roll onto the quilt. It didn't look like any money she'd ever seen before. Lorna picked it up to examine it curiously.

On one side, a woman's portrait was stamped. The printing on the other side read: "Compliments of Miss Belle, Dodge City." It was a coin of some sort, but it obviously wasn't money or any kind of foreign currency. And who was Miss Belle?

Curiosity got the better of Lorna. Leaving the clothes in the wagon, she climbed out. Three of the trailhands had ridden into town with Benteen, and the others were out with the herd. Woolie Willis was at the river, trying his hand at catching some fish. There was no sign of Mary, but Rusty was over by the chuck wagon. Since he'd been practically all over the world as a ship's cook, it seemed likely that he would know what this coin was, so Lorna went to ask.

"Rusty, have you ever seen a coin like this?" She showed him the brass coin lying in the palm of her hand.

He glanced at it, then sent her a sharp look. "Where'd ya get it?"

Something in his tone prompted her to be vague. "I just picked it up." But she didn't say it had fallen out of Benteen's bedroll. If Rusty thought she'd found it on the ground, that wasn't her fault.

"One of the boys musta dropped it," he concluded.

"What is it?" Lorna repeated her question. "Is it money?"

"It's a dollar token," he replied, and tried to look busy.

"Do you mean it's really worth a dollar?" Lorna studied it again.

"There's places that accept it as legal tender. I don't know as I'd take it into just any bank," Rusty hedged on his answer.

"Who's this woman — Miss Belle? Is that her likeness on the other side?" she asked.

"It probably is." He nodded reluctantly.

The pieces were starting to fit together in her mind. A dollar token. Good in some unmentionable places. A woman's picture.

"Is it a kind of advertisement?" Lorna guessed.

"Yeah, you could call it that," Rusty agreed.

"What is this lady advertising?" A cold anger was starting to chill her dark eyes. "It doesn't state what her business is."

Rusty actually started to turn red. The color crept up under his white whiskers, making his skin ruddy. "Well, now, I don't rightly know," he faltered.

"Do you suppose she might be a 'soiled dove'?" She challenged Rusty, daring him to

366

deny what she had already guessed.

"If you already know, why'd ya ask me?" he grumbled in irritation. "You shouldn't be askin' me questions like that anyhow. It's them pants you been wearin'. They're makin' you forget what's proper."

"I am a married woman," Lorna asserted. "I am not unfamiliar with such women. It would be silly to pretend they don't exist."

"I reckon. There ain't exactly a surplus of women out West, an' sometimes a man gets tired of sleepin' alone." This time his look challenged her.

Her cheeks flamed at his implication that Benteen might be tired of sleeping alone. Pivoting on her heel, Lorna hurried back to the wagon. The brass coin seemed to burn her palm. She dropped it on the mattress, then sat down to stare at it.

Dodge City. He had wanted to make love to her at the hotel when he came to the room after she had bathed. Only she hadn't been able to freely respond to his advances. Both nights they had stayed there, he had been out late. That had to be when he had gotten the coin.

A wild jealousy stormed through her as she was forced to conclude that Benteen had gone to bed with a whore to satisfy his lust. He had been unfaithful to her, and she'd kill him for that. Her hands were trembling with rage as she took the pistol from the valise. He'd regret the day he ever taught her to shoot.

When she checked to make sure it was loaded, another incident forced its memory on her. But Lorna wanted to listen to only the part that said "a whore in bed." But there was a corresponding phrase to it that pushed its way into her consciousness. "Lady on his arm."

The gun was lowered to rest in her lap. That was what the prostitute had said when they'd spoken so briefly in the millinery shop. The redhead named Pearl had advised her that if Lorna wanted to keep Benteen from seeing that kind of woman, she had to be wilder in bed than he was.

During those first weeks of marriage, Lorna had learned that Benteen responded to the passion she once tried to conceal. And she had responded to his. Even though she'd had cause to keep him from her bed, the question was: for how long? If she wanted her marriage to work — which she did — then certain changes had to occur. She had forgiven him for what had happened; now she must forget it.

The gun returned to the valise, along with the brass token of the Dodge City charmer.

She gathered up the clothes to wash and left the wagon.

All day long, she had time to think about her decision. When Benteen returned from town in the late afternoon, Lorna felt quite calm about it. She barely noticed the package he was carrying — if anything, presuming it was supplies — until he offered it to her instead of Rusty.

"I bought something for you," Benteen stated with a bland look. "I had to guess at the size."

Her calmness fled. Lorna hadn't expected a gift, and she was knocked completely off balance by it. She stared at the package, then at Benteen. His jaw hardened at her hesitation, taking it as a rejection of anything that came from him.

Murmuring "I don't know what to say," she reached out to take it from him. "What is it?"

"Open it and find out," he urged.

It was a flat-crowned cowboy hat. At first Lorna could only stare at it. Finally she lifted her sparkling gaze to Benteen.

"You looked silly in that bonnet." Warmth gentled his look. "Every cowboy has to have a hat. You'd better see if it fits."

When she tried it on, the hat was a little

snug, but she'd probably be glad of that on a windy day. Lorna wished she had a mirror handy. For the moment, she had to rely on Benteen's opinion.

"How does it look?" she asked.

"It doesn't go with the dress." His mouth crooked.

"But I promised not to wear pants around camp." She laughed, but he pulled his gaze away from her and she knew she'd said the wrong thing.

"The hat looks fine."

"Thank you for buying it for me," Lorna offered. "I really like it."

"You're welcome." With the present given, he moved away.

It was going to be difficult to make the overture when he was so determined to keep his distance from her. She understood why, but that didn't make her decision any easier to carry out. She hoped she had the boldness to see it through.

Her earlier calmness never returned. It was the approach of her wedding night all over again. All through supper, the little flutterings in her stomach wouldn't go away. While she was washing dishes, Lorna saw Benteen go to the wagon for his bedroll, which she had hidden away.

The last dish was handed to Mary to dry, and Lorna was wiping her hands on her skirt when Benteen walked over. She felt the mad race of her pulse, caused by either anticipation or apprehension. Part of her wasn't sure. She had difficulty meeting the frowning study of his gaze.

"What did you do with my bedroll?" He kept his voice down for only Lorna to hear. "I can't find it."

"I put it away." The casualness was forced. "You won't be needing it."

She hoped he would take the subtle hint and not expect her to be more explicit. When she started to turn away, his hand was on her arm to stop her.

"Why won't I need it, Lorna?" His dark gaze searched her face for the answer.

"Why would you, if you're going to be sleeping in the wagon?" Her attempt at a smile trembled with nervousness.

"Is that where I'm sleeping?" Benteen asked huskily.

"Yes," she said, and took a deep breath. "I want you to be my husband, Benteen."

She felt herself being drawn into him. Lorna thought he was going to gather her into his arms and take her on the spot, the desire for possession was so overpowering in his look.

Then his glance swung impatiently at the sun still hovering on the horizon. She couldn't hold back her nervous laugh. It stopped abruptly when he looked at her again. There was a moment's unease as Lorna wondered if he would be rough and demanding. His sharp gaze seemed to read her doubt.

"I'll make it beautiful for you," he murmured.

The promise brought a hint of pink to her cheeks. This time when Lorna turned away, Benteen let her go. She crossed to the wagon and climbed inside. There were many preparations she wanted to make before he came to her.

Removing the pins from her hair, she untangled its dark length from the coiled bun, then brushed it until it crackled and glistened. She stripped off her clothes all the way to the skin, and sparingly used Lady Crawford's lotion to make her body silken to his touch. Evening shadows were stealing in when she slipped under the quilt to wait for Benteen.

It wasn't long before the tent flap was lifted and he stepped into the back of the wagon. Unable to see in the darkness, Lorna listened to the sounds he made undressing. When he raised the quilt to lie down beside her, she felt a tremor go through her body.

"I hope this night will be as long as all the others have been." His voice was lower than a murmur as he moved to her.

It was too late for any kind of second thoughts as his mouth searched hers with a hunger Benteen didn't try to control. She closed her eyes as her lips parted voluntarily to deepen the kiss. There was no more reason to think as instinct took over and her hands slid compulsively up his muscled shoulders.

His fingers were tunneling under the weight of her hair and spreading down her spine to gather her closer. She felt him stiffen. The demanding pressure of his mouth eased as he muttered thickly against her lips, "My God, you aren't wearing any clothes."

"No. I wanted it like our wedding night — with nothing between us," Lorna admitted in a murmuring whisper.

His hands began to move over her body, down her spine to the slender indentation of her waist and the rounded curve of her hip. Lorna shivered with a raw pleasure, moaning softly. Benteen accepted the silent invitation and abandoned her lips to nibble at the slim curve of her neck.

Inevitably, it seemed, he continued his exploration to the taut swell of her breasts. Where his kiss had been hungry and demanding, he now teased and tantalized. His tongue was like rough velvet on her breast, tracing small spirals around the sensitive rosy peak. Her hands buried themselves into the thickness of his hair and tried to force an end to the exquisite torment.

The moment spun out endlessly as Lorna surrendered to the passion he aroused. His hands and mouth were creating havoc with her senses, disturbing her all anew. She whispered his name over and over.

When he finally responded to her wordless urging and moved onto her, she felt a second of panic under the weight of him, but the warmth of his mouth reassured her that she had nothing to fear. And the coupling became very natural and right, mutually desired and gloriously satisfying.

Yet, when it was over and Lorna was resting in the crook of his arm, trying to breathe normally again, she sensed something hadn't been as it was before. There was a part of him that Benteen hadn't given her. He'd held back the emotional side.

"What's wrong, Benteen?" she murmured, and let her hand glide across his curling chest hairs.

"Nothing."

Somehow, she knew he was lying. "I wasn't

really going to leave you," she said, because it was something she had never told him in so many words. "I just wanted to hurt you, because you threw away the roses. It was childish."

"You feel like a woman." His hand kneaded the softness of her shoulder to confirm it.

"I'm trying to be serious," Lorna murmured.

"I don't want to talk about it, Lorna." His voice was flat and firm.

"But we should be honest," she persisted. "You said it yourself."

"You wanta be honest?" Benteen challenged, and shifted position to lie on his side, looking down at her. "Then tell me what made you decide to hide my bedroll?"

"Maybe I was afraid of losing you to some other woman," she suggested, to see his reaction.

"Try again, but come up with a better story," he mocked.

"You could have been with one of those dance-hall girls all day," she insisted. "What did you do in town, besides buy me a hat? You didn't hire any trailhands."

"I wasn't with any dance-hall girl all day." Benteen smiled and traced his finger along her jaw. "And, if I had known I was going to get this kind of thanks for buying you a hat, I would have come back much sooner."

"Why did you buy me the hat?" Lorna let him sidetrack her, deciding against mentioning the brass token she'd found in his bedroll.

"I hoped it would make you look more like a boy," he admitted, and ran his finger over her lips and against her teeth. "I was going out of my mind looking at you in those pants."

She bit his finger, not too hard, but hard enough. "That's for wanting a boy instead of your wife," she told him.

"Maybe I could have both." His mouth began a descent toward hers. "A wife and a son."

"What if I want a daughter?" she asked.

"Why do you always have to disagree with me?" Benteen muttered. "We'll have a son first, then a daughter."

"How about the other way —?" But Lorna didn't get to finish the sentence, as he closed it off with a kiss. When she did have a chance to speak again, she was too enraptured with the other pleasure to remember what she had intended to say.

III

From right where you're standin'
As far's you can see.
That's Calder range you're lookin' at,
And all for you and me.

18

When the trail herd left Ogallala, they followed the Platte River Valley into the Wyoming Territory and struck north out of Cheyenne. As long as possible, Benteen kept to routes established by previous drives that brought Texas cattle to Wyoming ranges.

Five weeks out of Nebraska they were in new country, the virgin plains that had once belonged to the buffalo. It meant Benteen had to do a lot more riding in advance of the herd, scouting terrain as much as a day or more ahead of the drive for graze, water, and safe places to ford.

Behind him, the Longhorn cattle marched onward along the great pathless solitudes. Sometimes they were strung out for nearly two miles. As Lorna found, it was tedious, harassing work to keep the weary cattle moving without hurrying them. At night she fell into bed bone-tired and snuggled against Benteen, sleeping the minute she closed her eyes.

Woolie's leg was healing, making him all the more anxious to get back in the saddle. Lorna didn't think she'd be sorry to retire her cowboy hat and let him return to the weary, monotonous toil. But she was proud of the part she played, and knew she could do it again if her help was needed.

No visible line marked the boundary between Wyoming and Montana. One evening Benteen rode into camp and announced they were in Montana; the next day they'd cross the Powder River. In two weeks they'd be pitching their final camp. Tears of relief sprang into Lorna's eyes. The trail had seemed endless. They'd been on it four months, and in some ways it seemed like four years.

"I wish you hadn't told us how close we are," she said to him later when they were in bed.

"Why?" He turned his head to look at her, lifting a strand of her hair to idly finger it.

"Because now I'll be impatient to get there. I'm tired of living like this," Lorna admitted. "It wasn't so bad when I didn't know how much longer it would be. Now I just want it to be over."

"Complaining again." Benteen clicked his tongue in mock reproval.

"Yes, I am." She didn't deny it.

"Just wait till we get there. You'll find it was

worth all we've been through," he promised, and pressed his mouth to her temple.

The herd crossed the Powder, Pumpkin, and Tongue rivers, and finally, the Yellowstone in the middle part of August. Less than a week after the crossing, Benteen cantered his horse back to swing alongside Lorna, riding left flank. There was a vital, eager tension about him. It gleamed in his dark eyes when he reined in beside her.

"Wanta ride ahead with me?" he asked. "I'll have Zeke cover swing and flank."

By now the cattle were so well-broken to trail, they'd lost the urge to stray off on their own. They traveled as a unit, knowing when it was time to stop for the nooning and when to start in the afternoon. Only the drag riders had trouble yet with the laggards in the herd.

"Yes." Lorna sensed something in the air. She knew they were close to the range Benteen had claimed, but she didn't know how close.

Easing away from the herd, they put their horses into a steady lope to make a wide pass of the herd. The land rolled out in limitless plains of thick, matted grass. Its flatness was broken with buttes and gouged with coulees, and dominated by a lonely stretch of sky.

A rider was briefly outlined on the crest of a

ridge. It was the first human Lorna had seen in weeks, outside of the trail crew. She pointed out the approaching horse and rider to Benteen, but he'd already seen him. Satisfaction settled over the line of his mouth as he slowed his mount to a trot.

"It's Barnie," he told her.

When the rider pulled up to greet them, Lorna expected a boisterous welcome. But Barnie Moore just nodded. "I figured that was your trail dust. Got any cigarette papers? I'm clean out."

Benteen handed him a pack of papers from his vest pocket. "Keep it."

"Never did take to chewin'." He shook out some tobacco from his pouch and deftly twirled the paper around it, licking it shut. Lighting the cigarette, he sucked in the smoke and held it for a silent, savoring moment.

"How's it been? Quiet?" Benteen waited until he'd exhaled to ask.

"I've had lots of visitors," Barnie said. "Word's gotten around about this free grass. A bunch of outfits have been up lookin' it over."

"I figured that." Benteen wasn't surprised.

"You're gonna have some big boys for neighbors – XIT, the Turkey Track. Kohrs and some of the ranchers in western Montana are headin' this way now that the goldfields are playin' out an' they won't be selling as much beef to the miners. It's gonna get crowded."

All the while Barnie relayed the information, his glance kept straying to Lorna. With her long hair tucked under her hat and the loose-fitting shirt and snug pants, she looked like a smooth-cheeked boy, but she had long ago stopped being conscious of her appearance in men's clothes.

"Who's the kid?" Barnie bobbed his head in Lorna's direction.

Laughter glinted in Benteen's glance to her. "This is my wife. We've been shorthanded, so she's been helping out with the drive." Barnie tried very hard to disguise his shock and not stare. Benteen helped by suggesting, "The herd's about five miles back. Why don't you show them the way while Lorna and I ride ahead?"

Barnie tugged at the brim of his hat and mumbled to Lorna, "Beggin' your pardon, ma'am"; then he swung his horse out of their way.

"It's quite all right, Mr. Moore." She smiled.

Benteen continued to hold his horse in after Barnie rode off. His glance ran sideways to Lorna, bright with a knowing light.

"You never told me we were this close." But she knew he had kept it from her deliberately. "How far is it?"

"About two miles. Are you impatient to get there?" A brow was arched with the mocking query, fully aware of her answer.

"You know I am." Her smiled widened.

"Let's go." He pricked his horse with the spurs to send it bounding into a gallop.

Lorna's horse was a stride behind and stretching out to run. Chunks of grass and sod were torn up by the pounding hooves as they raced the last two miles. It brought a wild exhilaration to the moment of journey's end. Lorna was breathless, her dark eyes shining with excitement when she pulled her horse to a halt beside Benteen.

"This is it." His voice rang proud with possession as he gazed upon the land.

There was a crude log shack sitting close to the river, with a small corral built out of cottonwood. She tried not to feel lost, but there should have been some invisible banner proclaiming this to be their new home. All she saw was a muscular landscape, so big and commanding that it stretched out her stare until her eyes hurt.

Under a summer sun, the harsh land rolled out in uneven waves, an endless sea of dull yellow grass with miles and miles of hazy blue sky overhead. Beyond the treeless ridges, a flat-topped butte poked its dark head above the horizon. Lorna thought back on the long trail they'd traveled to get here — and the price they had paid in lives, in tears, and sweat. For this.

Her jaw hardened. This land wasn't going to beat her with its loneliness. She was going to stand up to it, and turn it into a home. Pulling her gaze from the overpowering breadth of the land, Lorna concentrated her attention on the green trees growing solid along the riverbanks. There would be wood for a cabin. She wasn't going to live in a sod house like that woman in Kansas.

She followed when Benteen walked his blowing horse the last hundred yards to the shack. All his attention was on their destination, his gaze sweeping the surrounding range with proud satisfaction. It gave Lorna time to adjust to the vastness she saw, and attempt to visualize how it could look with a house and some buildings — anything to make it look civilized.

Under the cottonwood trees along the riverbank, Benteen halted his horse and swung out of the saddle with lazy ease. Lorna dismounted to let her horse drink, too. She watched Sandman's black muzzle nose at the water, the bit clanking against his teeth before the buckskin began sucking in the cold river water.

"With this water, we control the range for twenty miles on either side," Benteen began to explain the significance of the location. "As far as you can see, Lorna, and beyond, belongs to us."

"All of it?" She was struck by the immensity of it.

"Yes." He leveled his steady gaze on her, but the burning fire in his eyes was for the land. "And it's just the beginning."

"But Barnie — Mr. Moore — said there were other cattle outfits moving in," she remembered.

"Not onto this range, they won't." He let the reins trail the ground and walked a few steps from the river. Reaching down, he tore off a handful of grass and held it out to Lorna. "This is like gold to a cattleman. And the water is silver. There's always going to be somebody who will want it for himself. Because we got here first and claimed the best, others will try to crowd us out. I won't be crowded."

"Do you really think they'll try?" Her head was tipped slightly back to study him without the obstruction of the hat brim.

"It's the nature of man to want what someone else has." Benteen showed tolerance for her attempt to cling to a belief in the goodness of people. "Call it envy or greed. Some control it.

A few are open about it. And others try to disguise it. The few that are big always want more, and the ones that are little want to be big. Those that are in the middle, neither big nor small, try to pretend that's the way they want to be."

"Which one are you?" Lorna asked, and watched his mouth crook in a smile that held little humor.

"I've always been the one that was little who wanted to be big. I'm going to be big," he stated. "The Calder Cattle Company will be an outfit anyone in these parts will have to reckon with."

"But that isn't wrong." She frowned. "That's just being ambitious."

Smiling faintly, Benteen brushed the blades of grass off his glove and put an arm around her slim shoulders. "Ambition is a kind of greed, too." They left the horses to walk in the direction of the crudely built shack. "It just sounds better."

The subject made her uncomfortable, even though she understood what Benteen was saying. A fine line separated greed and ambition. One was a virtue, and the other was not. And ambition could easily beget greed.

Lorna turned her thoughts to a more positive topic. "You said you had the site picked out where we would build our house," she reminded him. "Where is it?"

"Do you see that knoll just ahead?" Benteen pointed to the sloping rise of ground they were heading toward. "That's where we'll have our house."

"A two story house, painted white," she added details to the dream image.

"With white pillars in front." He seemed to tease her.

"Yes, with pillars in front," Lorna agreed with a decisive nod, because it sounded so grand, and she didn't care that he was making fun of her. She turned the tables on him. "After all, it has to be a fitting structure if it's going to be the home of the Calder Cattle Company."

His throaty chuckle warmed her. When they reached the top of the knoll where their future home would be built, Benteen turned to study the view, the arm around her shoulders turning Lorna as well. The increase in elevation allowed them to overlook the sweeping bend of the river and the rolling expanse of plains.

"We're going to be pushed for time, with winter coming," he said. "The best we can do is throw up a log cabin near the river so we can be close to a water supply. But you'll have your house, Lorna. If not this year, then soon."

"After almost five months of living in a wagon, even a cabin sounds good," she admitted.

"There's a lot we have to get done before winter sets in. We have to build a shed for the horses we'll be keeping here to use, and a long-house where the men can sleep and eat." While he formulated his plans aloud, she listened to its scope and wondered how it could be done in such a short time.

While they waited for the herd to come, Benteen made constructive use of the time. He staked out the locations for the various ranch buildings and paced out their dimensions, putting Lorna to work gathering broken tree limbs for stakes.

She was carrying an armload when she noticed the horse and rider pause to eye the rude camp and its occupants before resuming their approach. There was something familiar about the rider, yet Lorna was positive it wasn't one of the drovers. Without taking her gaze off the rider, she partially turned her head to call to Benteen. "There's someone riding in. A stranger, I think."

Benteen straightened and turned to face the rider, casually unhooking the leather strap over the hammer of his holstered gun. He moved to stand beside Lorna.

As the rider came close enough for Lorna to see his face, her mouth opened in surprise. "It's Mr. Giles," she said to Benteen, but he had already recognized him and his gaze had narrowed with suspicion.

After the meeting with Barnie Moore, Lorna remembered the deceptive appearance she made in the clothes she was wearing. She could tell Bull Giles was trying to place her by the way he was studying her. She hid a smile and took off her hat, letting her dark hair tumble loose to fall about her shoulders. Amusement danced in the big man's eyes as his look swept over the slim fitting pants that showed the length of her legs.

He greeted her first. "I told you we might meet again, Mrs. Calder."

"You did, Mr. Giles," Lorna admitted. "But I didn't think you meant in Montana."

"I thought you'd be in Texas." Benteen picked up on her comment.

"It's been a few years since I was up here. I thought I'd take a look around." Bull Giles made it sound like a casual decision. His gaze traveled past them to the shack and the rude corral of sticks. "This is your claim, huh?"

"That's right." Benteen's head was tipped in silent challenge.

"Grass, water, enough broken country for shelter in the winter." Bull Giles enumerated the merits of the rangeland Benteen had chosen. "It's not bad."

"That's what I thought." Benteen remained aloof.

"I told Boston it was like this up here," the man stated.

"Are you here on Boston's orders?" Benteen questioned.

Bull Giles gave a mild shrug. "He indicated a curiosity about your destination. I guess he wanted to make sure you were out of his hair."

"I told him my plans. When you see him, you can mention that I don't like my word being questioned." Benteen remained stiffly alert, not relaxing his guard with this representative from the Ten Bar.

"You and Boston don't exactly get along too well." Bull smiled when he voiced the observation. "I don't think he's going to look on you with much favor when he finds out you signed his name, authorizing me to pay twenty head of steers as toll to those Indians."

"He just paid back some of what he took from my pa," Benteen replied.

"Those are strong words." Bull considered him thoughtfully.

"I've said them to his face."

Bull let the comment ride and asked instead, "Would you be objecting if I stepped down and watered my horse?"

"You're welcome to the water and the graze for your horse. You can camp here for the night if you like." Benteen extended the hospitality of the range. Someday the situation could be reversed and he would be the one far from his home.

"You can have supper with us, Mr. Giles." Lorna broadened the invitation.

"I'd like that. Thank you, Mrs. Calder." He tipped his hat to her, then rode his horse to the shade of the cottonwoods and dismounted.

"He's one of Boston's men, Lorna," Benteen warned in a low voice. "Don't get friendly with him or he'll stab you in the back."

She thought he was being unfairly critical of Bull Giles and boldly returned his hard look. "I don't believe Mr. Giles is anyone's man but his own. It's wrong for you to throw stones when you once worked for Judd Boston."

Benteen didn't look pleased by the comparison, but couldn't find a logical argument against it. So he chose another subject to show his displeasure with her.

"You change into a dress as soon as the wagons get here," he ordered, and turned away to resume staking out the bunkhouse.

When Barnie had seen her dressed this way, Benteen had only smiled, she remembered with an amused shake of her head. Because it was Bull Giles, he was reacting jealously and trying to make her feel that she was the one in the wrong for being dressed this way. And men claimed women didn't think logically. Amusement deepened the corners of her mouth as she carried the armload of broken branches over to where Benteen was working.

The wagons arrived in the middle of the afternoon in advance of the herd. After Lorna had changed into a blue calico dress, she helped with the setting up of a permanent camp. They'd all be living out of the wagons for a couple more weeks until the buildings could be constructed.

With Benteen around, she tried not to show any interest in Bull Giles, but the attempt only made her more conscious of the man. He lent a hand with the fire and gathered more wood for it in repayment of the hospitality. His saddle and bedroll were set off to one side and his horse was hobbled and turned loose to graze.

When the herd came into sight, Benteen rode out to meet the point riders and direct the Longhorns downriver. Lorna supposed that he considered she was adequately chaperoned with Mary, Rusty, and Woolie in camp. She liked Bull Giles — as a friend — and wished Benteen could understand that.

She noticed the water barrel was low and unhooked the wooden pail from the side of the chuck wagon. "Mary," she called to her friend. "I'm going down to the river to get some water." She followed the custom of always letting someone know where she was going when she left camp.

The grass grew tall and thick under the trees by the river. Her long skirts swished noisily through it as Lorna made her way to the small sand bar jutting out from the bank. She had to hold them out of the way when she bent down to dip the pail into the clear running river. A school of small fish darted like quicksilver out of the shallows into deeper water.

She let the bucket sink below the surface, automatically filling with water. When she raised it, cold water sloshed over the sides, splashing on her skirt. There was a warning crunch of footsteps on the gravel bar behind her. Lorna turned sharply, spilling more water.

"I didn't mean to startle you," Bull Giles apologized.

"I didn't hear you, that's all." She shrugged aside the brief moment of alarm.

With typical boldness, his glance wandered

over her dress and the thick, concealing folds of its long skirt. Lorna knew he was remembering the way she had looked in pants.

"I like the dress, but I was more aware that you were a woman in those pants," he stated with utter frankness.

"They were a necessity. The cattle spooked at my long skirt," Lorna explained because it seemed necessary that he understand she didn't flaunt convention without reason.

"Let me carry that bucket. It's too heavy for you," he insisted, and reached to take it out of her hand.

Lorna surrendered it to him, not because she wasn't strong enough to carry it. She had hauled a lot of water during those long months on the trail. But it was the gesture of a gentleman, and she liked the way he treated her like a lady.

"Do you think you're going to like it out here?" he asked. "It's going to take a lot of hard work."

"I know that." She walked to the bank and accepted the steadying support of his hand on her arm to climb up the slippery grass.

"It's gonna be lonely for a pretty thing like you," Bull stated.

His remark was an instant reminder of the woman in the sod house. Her chin was pushed forward in a silent determination that this country wouldn't do that to her.

"I'll probably be too busy to notice that, Mr. Giles," Lorna insisted. "As you said, it's going to take a lot of hard work."

"But a woman like you shouldn't have to work. You should be living in a fine house with a maid to do the work for you," he declared. "You're too delicate to be dirtying your hands."

She arched her neck to laugh from her throat. "I assure you, Mr. Giles, that I am neither delicate nor weak. I can ride as well as most men, and can shoot straighter than some. A woman likes to be challenged, Mr. Giles, not pampered. I would have thought you knew that."

"Then maybe I should let you carry the bucket." He smiled.

"It's a little late," Lorna mocked him. "We're almost there."

They were only a few yards from the chuck wagon and the water barrel secured to the side. Bull carried the bucket over and emptied it into the barrel.

"Thanks for carrying the water, Mr. Giles." Lorna continued to smile.

He folded his arm across his waist to make a mock bow. "My pleasure, Mrs. Calder."

There was no need to hold the Longhorns in a loose bunch at night. This range was going to be their new home. Benteen and the drovers pulled back when the herd reached the river to let them drink and scatter as they willed.

The remuda of horses was a different situation. Benteen had Yates throw up a rope corral to hold them. Tomorrow he'd choose the ones he wanted to keep for range work. The rest he would take to Deadwood to sell when they made their trip for winter supplies.

His mind was busy with the many things that had to be done when he rode into camp, but the sound of Lorna's laughter caught his attention. His jaw hardened when he saw her walking from the river with Bull Giles. The bucket Giles carried explained what the pair had been doing. Benteen wasn't fooled by the surface innocence. He was a man, so he knew how Bull Giles's mind worked. Without being told, Benteen knew Giles had seen Lorna go to the river for water and followed her. Cold irritation darkened his eyes because Lorna couldn't see the way Giles was easing his way into her confidence, inviting her to trust him. She didn't regard his flattering attention as a threat, but Benteen did.

Dismounting, he watched the pair separate. In grim silence he unsaddled his horse and turned it out with the rest of the string. He walked with the trailhands to the fire for the habitual cup of coffee and avoided any contact with Lorna. If her head could be turned by another man, then he didn't want her. But he was gritting his teeth when he told himself that.

Around the fire that night, Barnie Moore was the focus of attention. He was questioned about how much it rained and when, did the rivers flood and how bad?

"I'll tell you one thing." A cigarette dangled precariously from his lower lip. "When this ground is wet, it's like gumbo. You walk from here to the river and yore feet get so gobbed up with mud, they're three or four times their regular size. It dries as hard as a rock, an' ya need a hammer an' a chisel to get it off yore boots."

And they wanted to know about the winter. How cold it was and how much it snowed. When did it start and how long did it last? What sections of the range drifted free of snow? What about the blizzards, and what were the cattle's chances of weathering them?

"Ya might get yourself some of those Westerns," Barnie advised Benteen. "They got Shorthorn and Devon blood, but they're used to this northern weather. An' they got enough wild in 'em to fight for their young. They ain't like that blooded stock we seen comin' into Texas that turn tail and run from a coyote an' leave their calf to be his dinner."

There was a brief discussion about the relative merits of different breeds. Benteen listened with interest to all of them. He needed to expand the size of his herd, but he also needed quickly maturing beef to take to market. Barnie's suggestion of buying stock that had originated in the Northwest instead of relying solely on the Longhorns seemed to make sense.

"Barnie, you've had a chance to look over the range good," Ely spoke up, asserting himself in his quiet way. "Where's some good land for Mary and me to file on?"

"I can show you a couple areas," Barnie said. "But I think the best piece is north of here, right on the edge of the foothills. It's got a good flowin' river runnin' through it. If you want, we can ride over that way tomorrow and I'll show it to you.

"That'd be fine." Ely nodded.

"What about the wolves?" Shorty asked. "I heard they was bad."

"Those yellow-eyed devils are cunning." Barnie turned his head, shaking it slightly.

Rusty added another dry limb to the fire, sending up sparks to mingle with the starscape overhead. Lorna was listening intently to the conversation among the cowboys, taking more interest since she had started working with the cattle on the drive. Someone had rolled a fallen tree trunk up to the fire, and she was sitting on it, with her skirts tucked around her legs to keep out the night's chill. She didn't notice when Bull Giles paused by the fire to refill his coffeecup as so many of the other cowboys had done before him. Nor did she pay any attention when he drifted over to the log where she was sitting.

"I imagine you're getting bored with all this cattle talk," he murmured unexpectedly to her, and Lorna turned her head, discovering he was standing behind her.

When he crouched down, the shadow gathered him in. Lorna remembered the lucheon they had shared in Dodge City and the fun he'd made of the cattle talk going on around them. At the time, the subject hadn't been important to her. But her attitude had changed in the last half of the trail drive.

"I'm a rancher's wife," she reminded Bull. "Cattle are just as much my future as they are Benteen's. I'm not bored by all this talk. A wife should know something about her husband's business so she can discuss it intelligently with him."

"You don't mind if a cow comes first?" he asked skeptically.

"A cow may be a female, but I'm certainly not going to be jealous of one." A smile played with her mouth, because she remembered the time when she had resented the priority the animal received from Benteen.

From the edge of the camp, a steer snorted and lowed a curious sound. When Lorna turned to look, she recognized the brindle-colored steer that had always walked at the front of the herd. The light from the fire gleamed on the width of its horns.

"Would you look at that?" Shorty declared. "It's Captain."

"He's probably come to find out why nobody's ridden out for night guard," Zeke guessed.

"Yeah, probably got used to the company of humans an' now he's wonderin' where his friends are," Jessie suggested.

19

Bull Giles rode out at dawn the next morning. Immediately after breakfast, the men began work on the ranch buildings. It was a hive of noisy activity with axes felling the cottonwood trees along the river and horses dragging the unhewn logs to the building sites, where more cowboys worked spading up the sod to make dirt floors. It was organized chaos. And the brindle steer, Captain, stood on the knoll overlooking the scene as if he was supervising it all.

Within two weeks the primitive buildings were standing. The green logs were chinked with moss and mud, and the roofs consisted of branches covered with dirt. Zeke Taylor was the closest to being the carpenter in the group of cowboys, so he had built the bunks, chairs, and tables. They were as rough and crude as the buildings that housed them.

Half of the men left when Ely and Mary pulled out to take up their claim on the land Barnie had showed them to the north. Their cabin and barn would be up in an equally short time. Lorna didn't mind seeing them leave, because they would be neighbors even if they were thirty miles apart.

The covered wagon was partially dismantled to be converted for ranch use. Lorna took the white canvas top and hung it in the cabin to make a cloth wall partitioning off the sleeping area from the rest of the one room structure. As she set her personal possessions around their new home, she refused to compare its crudeness to the sod house of the farmer's wife in Kansas.

In September Lorna realized she was definitely pregnant, even though she'd experienced no morning sickness and felt in the best of health. When she told Benteen the stork would be visiting them in the spring, he promptly informed her, with considerable pride, that it was going to be a boy.

A week later, Benteen left with the wagon and thirty head of horses. Rusty, Jessie Trumbo, and Bob Vernon stayed behind, as did Lorna. Benteen didn't want to risk anything happening to her or their unborn baby by being jolted around on the wagon seat, completely ignoring the rough, nearly five-month-long journey she had just endured. So Lorna stayed at home while he purchased their winter supplies, filed their homestead claim with the land office, and sold the extra horses.

In addition to the supplies, he brought back yard goods so Lorna could make a few additions to their limited wardrobes and three hundred head of the so-called Western cattle. Texas horses were in demand by the northern ranches and brought top prices.

When he returned, he sent Jessie Trumbo, Rusty, Shorty Niles, and Vince Garvey back to Texas to gather another herd of wild stock to drive north in the spring. The brindle steer trotted after the chuck wagon, too anxious to get back on the trail. They took him along to lead the next herd north.

Barnie's adjoining claim served as an outlying camp from which he worked, checking on the cattle in his area.

The first winter was cold and blustery, with subzero temperatures common and days of heavy snowfall, with the first flakes falling in early October. It wasn't a severe winter by Montana standards. At Christmastime Mary and Ely came for a holiday dinner. Ely read the Bethlehem story from the Bible, then Woolie played Christmas carols on his harmonica and they all sang.

When Lorna's time drew near the first of April, Mary came to stay at the cabin and serve as midwife. Despite all the frightening stories Lorna had heard about childbirth in the wilds, she had an easy time of it. Benteen held their newborn son, Webb Matthew Calder, that first day of his life, and on the next, Benteen rode off with the rest of the men to start the spring roundup.

Bridle chains clanked as the small group of riders approached the collection of crude buildings forming the ranch's headquarters on an early May afternoon. They sat loosely in the saddle, swaying slightly with the rhythm of their trotting horses. The stirrups were long, so there was hardly any bend in the knee.

Haggard lines were drawn across Benteen's bronzed features from the brutally long days of the roundup, but his eyes remained keen and restless. Both winter losses and calving losses had been minimal, less than he had expected.

When he saw Lorna standing in front of the cabin holding the baby in her arms and waving eagerly to him, the sight revived his acute hungers. Her hair gleamed rich brown in the sunlight, and her parted lips were even and red against her smooth complexion. It warmed him like a fire in the night or a spring flower pushing its way through the crust of melting snow. It was something in her eyes or her lips or the turn of her body that churned the depths of his emotions. The heat of something rash and timeless burned him, the kind of thing that would make a man kill if he had to.

He swung out of the saddle and dropped the reins. For the moment, his hands stayed at his side as Benteen faced her and his son. The faint scent of her hair lifted to him. Her dark eyes were shining as they returned his steady look. There was a powerful hint of fire in her slightly pursed lips, a sweetness in them for a man.

Her voice, when she spoke, did not address itself to him but to the nearly month-old boy-child with its mass of black-down hair. "Didn't I tell you Daddy would come home today, Webb?"

All his muscles were drawn together, poised for movement. With her words, the needs Benteen held in check were released. His arm hooked itself around her waist, discovering its slimness through the heavy shawl, and drew her into him. He bent and kissed her. A fine sweat broke out on him as he felt the gathering insistence of her response.

Benteen knew the pressure of his arms and his mouth were too strong, too assertive of his rights to her. He broke it off, taking a step back, aware of the vibration all the way through him. There was something uncertain and questioning about the way she looked at him. Her lips were still parted and he looked to see if he'd left the print of his roughness on them. Maybe the impulses that drove him were dirt common.

He swung his attention to the baby and caught the little fist flailing the air. A smile edged his mouth as Benteen tried to curl the tiny fingers around his forefinger.

"How did it go?" Lorna asked, and he knew she meant the roundup.

"Good. He doesn't look like the squawling red-faced baby I held." Benteen took his son from her arms to hold him again.

"You have been gone awhile," she reminded him.

Cradling the infant in one arm, Benteen turned and scooped up the reins to his horse, looping them over its neck. He stepped a foot into the stirrup and swung into the saddle, all in one fluid motion. With his weight shifted to the back of the saddle, he set his baby son in front of him and spread his hand across Webb's chest and stomach to hold him firmly in place.

"Benteen, what do you think you're doing?" Lorna hurried to the side of his horse.

"I'm taking Webb for his first ride."

"But he isn't even a month old yet," she protested.

"He has to start sometime if he's going to

407

make a living off a horse like his old man," Benteen stated, and walked the horse out, aware that Lorna was following anxiously.

He kept the baby's head supported with his body and held his mount at a slow walk. When he'd been three years old, he'd been riding a full-grown horse without the assistance of an adult, so his father told him. Benteen saw no harm in starting his own son out early.

When he reached the crude barn-shed and dismounted, the cowboys gathered around the infant like moths to a flame. In their profession, it was rare to have any contact with babies or youngsters. Lorna stood back amused to watch these hard, rough-talking men cooing and talking silly talk to the baby in Benteen's arms. Woolie insisted Webb had the hands of a first-rate roper, while Bob Vernon claimed he could see the intelligence in the baby's eyes, although they were closed at the time.

Lorna stepped forward to take her son when Webb started fussing. Hats were swept off the cowboys' heads as they made room for her. The birth of the child had elevated her status from merely woman to mother. They treated her like a Madonna.

"There's coffee on the stove," she said to Benteen when he placed his son into her arms.

"I'll be there as soon as I've seen to

my horse," he promised.

There was something in him that made him take longer at the task than he had to, as if he needed to deny himself the thing he wanted most. When he lifted the latch to the log door and pushed it open, Benteen forced an indifference to his face. The cabin appeared empty as he stepped inside. His searching glance noticed the coffeepot sitting on the iron stove that heated the small space and cooked their food.

"Lorna?"

"I'll be there in a minute." Her voice came from behind the cloth wall.

His footsteps were drawn to it. When he lifted it, he saw her sitting on their bed nursing their son. Her eyes widened to show him a startled expression. Color ran richly across her cheeks as she started to interrupt the baby's feeding.

"Don't stop if he's still hungry." Benteen stepped around the curtain and let it fall into place behind him.

"He's very greedy sometimes," Lorna murmured.

Benteen looked down on the pair. The front of her dress was unbuttoned to free the taut fullness of her breast. Little fists pushed at its roundness while a small mouth sucked vigorously on the nipple.

"I didn't think I could stand calmly by while another male enjoyed the ripeness of your breasts," Benteen commented.

"He's nursing," Lorna murmured. "It's hardly the same."

"I should hope not," he said dryly, and lowered himself to sit on the edge of the bed beside them.

His hand reached to stroke his son's head, then traced a finger over the swell of her breast. He unfastened a few more buttons and pushed aside her dress to expose both breasts. She breathed in when he cupped the weight of her other breast in his hand and stroked his thumb over the rose-brown nipple. He was aroused by needs long unfulfilled.

"I'm going to be envious of my son for a while," he admitted, and she finally lifted her dark eyes to look at him. It was a wordless comment, steeped with flaring passions. There was a struggle within him before Benteen finally pushed aside his desire and drew away. "I think I'll pour myself that cup of coffee."

A trio of riders quietly sat their horses, poised on the crest of a hill more than a half mile from the ranch. Bull Giles pushed his hat to the back of his head and leaned on the saddle horn, studying the improvements that had been made since he'd last seen it. He looked complacently at the gaunt and narrow man in the middle.

"I told you Calder had the best range staked out for himself." He felt the coldness of the light gray eyes touch him, then swing back to the scene.

"It would seem that way," Loman Janes replied. Giles felt a rush of intolerance for the man's icy ways. "Moore's got the adjoining stretch of river, and Stanton's laid claim to a section on the north. Calder's got control of ... probably six hundred square miles already."

"Bein' first in a fight don't mean you'll be standin' when it's over. You ought to know that, Bull." Loman curled his lip over the words. "Calder may control the range. But who's challenged him?"

"You're talkin' about Benteen Calder — not the old man," Giles retorted.

"Ain't you heard that sayin' — like father, like son?" The Ten Bar foreman didn't wait for a reply as he glanced to the third rider. "Let's ride down and say our howdies."

The last member of the trio was a man named Trace Reynolds. He was a fair cowhand, a better tracker, and the best marksman in Texas. It was whispered that, for a price, someone could choose the target, but those kind of whispers followed any man who showed a proficiency with firearms.

Bull Giles straightened in the saddle, glad of Loman Janes's suggestion. Lorna Calder might be a married woman, but he hadn't been able to get her out of his mind. Wrong or not, he wanted to see her again.

When Benteen heard Lorna come out from behind the curtain, he kept his back to her and walked to the stove to add more coffee to his cup. There was a small sound from the baby and the soft reassurance of her voice murmuring to it.

Another sound intruded as quick, striding footsteps approached the cabin door. There was a sharp knock, which Benteen didn't want to answer.

It was immediately followed by Woolie's voice. "There's three riders comin' in. One of 'em's a big man. Looks like Bull Giles."

Benteen pivoted, throwing Lorna a sharp glance. She was kneeling beside the cradle Zeke had made. "You stay inside," he ordered, and walked to the door.

Before going outside, he took the gun and holster off the peg and buckled it on. He couldn't say his reason for arming himself. It was sheer instinct rather than any sense of threat from Bull Giles.

When he stepped out of the cabin, the three riders were walking their horses into the yard. Benteen stiffened, recognizing the pock-faced man in the lead. Without needing to look, his peripheral vision told him where Woolie was standing, backing him up. Zeke and Bob were at the shed-barn, checking a horse with a loose shoe and watching the riders as they stopped their horses facing Benteen.

"You're a long way from home, Janes," Benteen remarked. "Lost your way?"

"Mr. Boston's been hearin' a lot of things about this country. He thought maybe I should take a look at it," Loman Janes said.

"Giles turned in a good report when he got back, I guess." Benteen threw a glance at the big-chested man and caught him searching the cabin — for a glimpse of Lorna, no doubt.

"Mr. Boston has been thinkin' about expanding his holdings." Loman ignored the reference to Bull Giles. "It shouldn't come as a surprise to you, Calder. A lotta big outfits in Texas are lookin' north to this free grass. You didn't really think you were gonna keep this range all to yourself?"

"No," Benteen admitted. "I figure to have

neighbors. And it's expecting too much to think the vermin will stay away for long."

Loman Janes stretched his mouth into a curved line that showed a chilling smile. "An' sometimes you have to drive the snakes out before a place is fit to live in." He gathered the reins to his horse. "We stopped to see if it'd be all right to make camp by the river. We've traveled a piece and need to light somewhere 'fore it gets dark."

"You can camp there," Benteen granted permission. "Just don't go makin' yourselves too much at home."

The coldly mocking smile stayed on Loman Janes's face as he slowly reined his horse in a turn away from the cabin and Benteen. From inside, the baby cried, and Bull Giles squared his shoulders to stare at Benteen.

"Is that a baby?"

"My son," Benteen stated, and watched the muscles tighten in Bull Giles's neck.

"Your wife . . . is doing well, I hope," he tersely inquired after Lorna's health.

"Yes." Benteen continued to send his level gaze at the big man.

"Congratulations, then," he said thickly, and wheeled his horse alongside the Ten Bar foreman.

The trio lifted their horses into a shuffling

trot and aimed for a point at the river not far from the ranch buildings.

Woolie stepped up to stand beside Benteen. "What do you think?" he asked, because he'd never been much good at figuring out other people's motives.

"Like he said, it shouldn't be a surprise that Boston's looking north," Benteen replied grimly. "The big always want to get bigger."

"I've heard he don't particularly care how he gets there," Woolie offered.

"Maybe someone will set him straight," Benteen suggested, and sent a dry glance to Woolie.

The cowboy grinned. "Maybe."

As he turned to reenter the cabin, Benteen realized he hadn't been surprised to see Loman Janes. The idea that someone from Boston's outfit might show up must have been at the back of his mind since last summer when Bull Giles had wandered in. There was trouble coming, and he'd best be making his plans for it now.

He walked into the cabin and unbuckled his gunbelt, hanging it back on the peg. Lorna noticed his preoccupied look and slowly stopped rocking the cradle.

"Who was it?" she asked, pretending that she hadn't heard the conversation outside.

"Loman Janes, Judd Boston's foreman." Benteen walked to the canvas curtain and lifted the bottom. "It seems Boston has decided he wants some of this free grass."

She frowned when she saw him take out his knife and make a slashing cut a couple of feet long at the bottom of the curtain. "What are you doing?"

"I need to make a map," he said, and made a crosscut to end up with a rectangular piece of white cloth. He carried it to the table and spread it out. "Get me a pencil, will you?"

"A map of what?" She handed him one from her sewing kit.

"Of our ranch, and the range surrounding it."

There weren't any maps of the area, except the one in his head. He had tried to explore as much of the surrounding territory as the time away from the ranch would permit. He began sketching the information, translating it from his head to the piece of canvas cloth. He drew in the Stanton claim, and Barnie's along with his own.

After more than two hours' work, correcting distances and locations, it was beginning to take shape. He didn't notice when Lorna lit the lamp and set it on the table, or smell the food cooking on the stove.

"I can't keep this food hot much longer, Benteen, or it will be ruined," she finally interrupted him.

He was so engrossed in the map, he'd forgotten she was there. Then her words sank in, and Benteen leaned back in his chair and combed a hand through his hair.

"I've got it pretty well finished," he said with a tired sigh, and began rolling it up.

She began setting the table, while Benteen walked over to wash his hands in the basin. "Why did you need to make the map?"

"For the future."

Whatever plan he had in mind, it was plain that he wasn't ready to tell her. Later that evening, Lorna took a look at the map he'd drawn. Three areas were marked with a dotted line. She mentally filled them in and realized they formed a long rectangle with their ranch, Barnie's land, and Ely and Mary's place.

After breakfast the next morning, Lorna carried the pan of dishwater outside to throw it into the tall grass by the river. She heard the horses coming out of the trees a little ways downstream as she emptied the pan. She paused to look when the trio of riders appeared.

When Bull Giles noticed her, he hesitated,

then swung his horse away from the pair and rode over to speak to her. Lorna waited, regarding him as a friend despite the company he kept, and locked her hands around the circumference of the dishpan.

"Good morning, Mrs. Calder." He tipped his hat to her, but it seemed there was a wounded look to his eyes. They lacked their usual boldness.

"Good morning, Mr. Giles," she returned the greeting.

"You're looking well," he said. "I understand you have a son."

"Yes. Webb Matthew Calder." She beamed with a natural pride and love.

His gaze skimmed the slimness of her figure, nearly back to its previous proportions. "You don't look like you have had a child," he observed with a shade of his former candor.

"Thank you." She nodded slightly at the compliment.

There was more that he seemed to want to say, but he finally tipped his hat again. "I'd best be goin'," he said. "I'll see you another time."

When Bull Giles had separated from them, Loman Janes had halted his horse to watch the brief exchange. Something told him that this was information he needed to pass on to Judd Boston. It could be important.

418

20

That summer Benteen had Zeke, Bob, and Woolie file on the three pieces of land he'd marked out on the map with dotted lines. They provided buffers between his ranch and other outfits and protected his range as much as it could be. It was open and unfenced, which meant other cattle would drift onto his land, but hopefully he could keep that number down and prevent his range from being overstocked with cattle other than his own.

He filed on the three contiguous pieces of land with speculation in mind, too. First, it would already be under his control if he chose to expand his operation. If that wasn't feasible, then he could sell the claims for a handy profit to outfits coming north. He tried to cover all angles and still leave himself a back door.

More outfits were moving into Montana. Last week he'd seen the dust of a trail drive and ridden south to see if it was Jessie. But the herd had belonged to another Texas outfit. The animals were in sorry condition. Benteen hoped Jessie brought their cattle up in better shape.

There was a slight movement in the bed beside him, distracting Benteen from his thoughts. He could tell by the way Lorna was breathing that she wasn't asleep either.

"You're very quiet," he murmured. "What are you thinking about?"

"Range bulls." It was an absent, almost musing response.

Benteen quirked an eyebrow as he turned to look at her in the darkness. "Range bulls?"

"I thought that would get your attention," she said with a certain smugness.

He shifted partially onto his side and laid his arm across her waist to draw her closer. "Am I roaming too much to suit you?"

"You're gone a lot of the time." Her hand wandered over his tautly muscled arm. "It isn't so bad during the daytime because there's always so much work to do, but the nights become very long. I'll be glad when Webb learns how to talk so I won't have to carry on conversations with the stove or the trees." Her mood changed to abandon the subject of loneliness. "With that canvas hanging there, doesn't it remind you of sleeping in the wagon?"

"I guess it does," Benteen supposed. "Maybe we'll be able to build the house next year."

"I hope so," she murmured. "This roof leaks mud when it rains. Bugs and spiders are everywhere. When I got up the other morning, one had spun a web across Webb's cradle."

"I stopped to see Ely and Mary the other day, did I tell you?" He knew he'd forgotten. Lately he'd been doing a lot of riding, studying the lay of the land and exploring different parts to fill in the blank areas on the canvas map hanging on the cabin wall. "They're coming down in a week to visit. Mary's anxious to see the baby she helped bring into the world."

There was no response as she turned more toward him and began tracing the line of his jaw with her fingertips. Benteen frowned, finding her behavior curious.

"Didn't you hear what I said? Mary's coming." He had expected her to be overjoyed by the prospect.

She ran her finger over his lips, outlining their male curves. "I was thinking about range bulls again," she said, "and wondering if they are as potent as you are." When she lifted her glance from his mouth, there was amusement in her eyes at his puzzled expression. "We're going to have another baby."

A soaring lift of inexpressible pride and emotion filled him. Benteen spread his hand across her flat stomach where the life they'd created now lived.

"It's going to be a boy," he stated

huskily. "I can feel him."

"Benteen, it's too soon for any movement." Lorna laughed softly.

"It's going to be a boy, just the same," he insisted.

They had made love not twenty minutes ago, but he was growing hard for her again. He kissed her, moving his mouth over her lips and parting them with the hard insistence of his tongue. His hand took the weight of a full breast, shaping itself to its plumpness. He bent his head to kiss the milk-sweet nipple, then nuzzled the roundness of her breast.

Her hands pressed and urged him as her body writhed in excitement. She was eager to satisfy him, and be satisfied, as she was so many nights. She was warm and giving, hot and taking, all at the same time. When he mounted her, her nails raked his back.

A light sighing groan of pleasure came from her. "Be wild with me, Benteen," she whispered.

He shuddered, and his flesh's need became all entangled with his soul's need. This blending created grace and made perfection out of something bestial. They were not two, but parts of one thing, alternately thrusting together until the pressure left them and they lay content.

"Did you like it, Benteen?" Lorna asked in the silence.

She was warm-flanked beside him. "My God, what the hell kind of word is that for it?" He was irritated, unable to express in words how she affected him, and wary, too, of the power she had.

"You never say anymore," she murmured. "You used to."

A long time ago — when they were newly wed — before she'd said those words, "I'm leaving you." They haunted him still, a nightmare that wouldn't be forgotten. Even now he couldn't erase them from his memory.

"I guess that's what comes from being an old married couple." He made light of her observation. "You just forget to say things."

"I am not old, Benteen Calder," she retorted quickly. "I am nineteen."

"With a little one on the way," he reminded her. "You'd better close your eyes and get some rest."

In the following silence, he sensed a change in her. She was motionless, waiting for something from him, but he didn't know what. When it didn't come, she turned on her side, facing away from him.

Jessie Trumbo and the boys arrived with the

herd of Texas Longhorns the early part of August, on the same day that Mary and Ely came to visit. The reunion of old friends and trailmates turned into a party that lasted well after nightfall. The brindle steer, Captain, stayed close by.

"The world's about to go crazy," Jessie told Benteen that night. "It's like everybody back East an' in Europe is just discoverin' there's cattle in the West and fortunes to be made with 'em."

The newly arrived cattle were in fair to good condition. The weaker ones Benteen culled out to be sold with the steers ready for market when they made their fall roundup.

Demand was high, sending the prices up. Benteen turned most of the profits back into building and grading his herd. He sent Jessie and Rusty back down the trail to bring more Longhorns from Texas the next year, with the brindle steer tagging along behind the chuck wagon like a puppy dog. Bob Vernon went west to purchase more Western stock. And Barnie was sent to Minnesota to buy a pure-bred bull, a "pilgrim" to the open range.

The winter was a bad one. The temperatures plummeted and the snows were deep. In the middle of a February blizzard, Arthur William Calder was born, with Benteen's help. Calm through it all, he had jokingly assured Lorna that he had aided many a cow and horse give birth, and a woman couldn't be much different. After the healthy baby boy had its first feeding, Lorna had fallen into an exhausted sleep, so she hadn't seen Benteen's hand shake when he poured a glass of whiskey and downed it.

The spring thaw revealed the extent of the winter losses. Coulees were dotted with dead cattle, which Benteen and the men skinned for their hides. There were signs that the losses weren't solely attributable to winterkill. The wolves that had often serenaded the ranch on dark, lonely nights had taken their toll of cattle.

The big yellow-eyed wolves weighed upward to 150 pounds, with a lot of brains and cunning to go along with the brawn. Their source of food had been the buffalo herds. Bringing down a massive buffalo was routine to them, but the decimation of the plains herds forced them to turn to the cattle.

The Longhorns weren't exactly easy pickings for the wolves. Benteen found a few carcasses of wolves gored to death by a battling Longhorn. But working in packs, the wolf usually wore down its prey quickly — if winter had weakened the cow.

More bothersome than the loss to the wolves

and the winter was the number of cattle missing. Indians wandered on and off their reservations in Dakota, Montana, and Canada practically at will. With their buffalo herds eradicated by white men, the Indians felt justified in killing or driving off any cattle they found. Indian trouble was something Benteen didn't need.

In all, he'd lost somewhere around a thousand head of cattle, but there remained nearly ten thousand head with a Triple C branded on their hips, comprising his original herd and its offspring, the second, larger herd Jessie had brought, and the Western stock purchased. And it was just the beginning.

Ely Stanton worked with them on the spring roundup. At a noon break, he came over to stand with Benteen, surveying the morning's gather.

"Mary and me was talking before I left," Ely began. "We started out the same time you and Lorna did. All we had was about three hundred cows and you had . . . seven, eight times that. But all we got today is 'bout four hundred. An' look what you've done for yourself."

"You'll start increasing." Benteen knew the parity of growth was due to a lack of aggression on Ely's part.

"No." Ely shook his head. "A man's gotta

take a hard look at himself sometimes. I know about cattle an' the land, but I ain't got no head for the business side of ranchin'. I can be the best damned foreman that ever forked a saddle for somebody like you — and not worth a plug nickel for myself."

"Ely —" Benteen began on a deep breath of regret, because it was undeniably true.

"Mary and me talked it over, and we wanta sell out our claim to you — if you're interested," Ely interrupted. "You just buy up our claim like you're doin' with the rest of the boys. An' as for the cattle, you pay us for them when you can. We know you're good for it. An' if you need a good foreman, I'm available full-time."

"The job's yours, Ely, but" — there was a vaguely incredulous frown tracking across Benteen's forehead — "the ranch and livestock, you could sell to some other outfit for a hand-some price. You're offering to practically give it to me. You shouldn't do that."

"Like I said" — there was a rare gleam of amusement in the quiet man's eyes — "I got no head for business 'tall." Then he extended his hand to shake on the deal.

Mail was a rarity, but early summer brought a windfall of letters from Texas, some dated more than nine months ago. Lorna received two from her parents. One was a joyous acknowledgment of the birth of their first grandson, Webb Matthew, and the second was a Christmas letter. Lorna wondered if they had gotten her letter yet, informing them of their second grandson's entrance into the world and describing the fat-cheeked baby she'd named Arthur William after her father.

Her friend Sue Ellen had written, too. Lorna had laughed aloud at some of the passages where Sue Ellen hinted that she knew Lorna was enduring untold horrors in that wild, primitive land. She sounded certain Lorna had been at death's door when she gave birth to Webb. Included in the letter, Sue Ellen passed on some information from an article she'd read in a New York newspaper that some salesman had left in her mother's millinery store. It caught her eye because of the letter Lorna had written about the English lady she had met in Dodge City. The article said that the Earl of Crawford had taken ill and died while in the city before leaving for England, and that his widow, Lady Crawford, would be sailing for England, where his remains would be laid to rest at the ancestral home. Sue Ellen thought Lorna would be interested in learning about the "tragedy."

Lorna recalled the brief chat she'd had with Lady Crawford, and the kindness she'd shown when she sent her maid to Lorna's room with a small jar of lotion. It was all gone now, but Lorna had kept the jar as a memento of the incident to show her children as proof that she had met and talked to a real "lady" once. The story had a sad ending now. According to the date in Sue Ellen's letter, the Earl of Crawford had died nearly a year and a half ago.

The mail also included a hastily scratched note from Jessie Trumbo. He expected to leave Texas the last week of March with a mixed herd of three thousand. The Ten Bar was sending up two herds of that number. In addition, there were four other herds that he personally knew about heading for the Montana country.

The open range was going to fill up fast.

With the arrival of more Texas herds in eastern Montana, other changes began. Ranches needed supplies and cowboys needed a place to spend their wages. Miles City began to take shape as a cow town.

That September, a man named Fat Frank Fitzsimmons came to the territory with two wagons of supplies and whiskey. When one of his wagons broke an axle out in the middle of nowhere, he decided fate had taken a hand in choosing a location for his new store. Within two weeks he'd thrown up a crude building of sorts and was open for business. His sign read simply: "Fat Frank's — WHISKEY."

The first cowboy who happened by thought for sure he was seeing things. After two shots of whiskey, he informed Fat Frank that he was doomed to fail, since nobody came this way but once in a blue moon. Fat Frank immediately added another sign to his storefront, a smaller one, proclaiming "Blue Moon, Montana Territory." Whether the story about the cowboy was true or not, Fat Frank told it to everyone that chanced by and pointed to the Blue Moon sign. The tale made good telling around the campfire, and the word spread.

The place offered a closer source of supplies than Miles City. With that possibility in mind, Benteen rode to Fat Frank's store and saloon to look it over. The squat building made a strange sight, plopped in the middle of the plains with nothing around it for miles. The whiskey sign was like a beacon on that frosty October morning. His shaggy-coated horse pricked its ears at the sight and picked up the pace. It snorted in interest at the two horses tied to a rail outside, its warm breath making a hoary cloud.

Reading brands was a habit. When Benteen noticed the Ten Bar's mark on the saddled horses in front of the store, his gaze sharpened. He was aware the two herds they'd sent up the trail had arrived about the same time Jessie had. They had located their headquarters on some fair range to the east and north of him, but this was the first that he'd met up with any of their riders.

He dismounted and looped the reins around the hitching rack. There was no hurry in his measured stride as Benteen walked to the rough-planked door. His spurs made a muted jingle in the quiet. The door swung inward on rawhide hinges as Benteen walked into the store. His gaze made a sweep of the jumble of boxes and crates used to display wares in the front section.

From the back there was the low murmur of voices, the soft, drawling sound of Texans. Unbuttoning his coat, Benteen moved in their direction just as a fat man waddled forward to greet him. It was obviously the proprietor.

"Good morning, sir." It was a glad-handing voice. "Welcome to my humble establishment. The name's Fitzsimmons but everybody calls me Fat Frank." He patted his rotund dimensions with pride. "What can I do for you this fine day?"

"Your sign outside said whiskey."

"And it's real whiskey I've got, too," Fat Frank declared. "Not that watered-down rotgut you fellas call whiskey. Just step back here to the back of the store where I got me a little bar set up." Puffing with the effort of carrying around so much weight, he led the way. Benteen caught the sharp side glance the fat shopkeeper sent him and noted the shrewdness underneath the jovial facade. "You wouldn't be Benteen Calder, would you?" the man guessed.

"Yes." Benteen didn't bother to ask how the man had known. Saloons in the middle of nowhere, like this one, were always fountain-heads of gossip. And the man would have made it his business to ask about potential customers.

"I heard a lot of talk about you," Fat Frank admitted. "I been wondering when you'd be stoppin' by. You'll find my prices are fair, and I got just about anything you'll need. If I don't have it, I can get it. If your wife needs yard goods or ready-made clothes, just ask Fat Frank."

"I'll keep it in mind." Benteen didn't commit himself.

The back corner of the building was where the liquor was sold. A board laid across two barrels served as a bar, with open-ended crates behind it where the bottles were kept. There was a potbellied stove against the wall that bore a striking resemblance to the man's shape — round and huge, with spindly legs. Two crude chairs sat next to it, inviting customers to sit and warm themselves. In addition, there was a small table with two more chairs. They were occupied by Loman Janes and Bull Giles. Benteen nodded to the pair and continued on to the makeshift bar Fat Frank walked behind. Uncorking a bottle, he poured the whiskey into a shot glass, then pushed it to Benteen.

"On the house," he insisted when Benteen started to reach inside his coat to pay for the drink.

"Obliged." He nodded and took a swallow, feeling the pure fire burn its way down his throat.

"I told you it was the real stuff," Fat Frank reminded him.

"You did," Benteen admitted, and let his hand stay around the glass as he turned, angling his body toward the two other customers.

"You acquainted with Mr. Janes of the Ten Bar?" Fat Frank asked, as if prepared to make introductions.

"I am."

"I swear all you Texans know each

other." The shopkeeper laughed.

"Who's mindin' the Ten Bar with you up here, Janes?" Benteen inquired with semi-interest.

The gaunt-cheeked foreman idly rolled his glass in a half-circle on the table. "Ollie Webster is runnin' the Texas end."

"Good man." Benteen inclined his head in a silent admission of the cowboy's abilities. He'd worked with him a few times.

"There been much Indian trouble?" Loman asked.

It was a question from one cattleman to another, and Benteen treated it as such. "Some. They run off a few head from time to time."

"Poor, starving savages." Fat Frank shook his head. "More than half the supplies the government promised 'em never makes it to the reservations. And that scum up on the Missouri don't help the situation, selling them whiskey."

"What are you talking about?" Loman Janes asked, lifting his head with frowning interest.

"There's a pack of ex-buffalo hunters and woodhawks that's nested on the Missouri River." Woodhawk was the term supplied to men who chopped wood for the steamboats that trafficked the river. "They're an unsavory bunch. The minute they found out the

Canadian government was paying the Crees and Bloods some money every autumn, they been selling them rotgut and separating those savages from their money. I understand it's getting so the Indians spend most of the winter on this side of the border."

"I guess that explains why I lost more beef last winter than usual," Benteen murmured, and studied the liquor left in his glass, knowing the situation was likely to get worse before it got better.

"I thought you were new to this area." Loman Janes studied the fat man with close interest.

"I traveled some before my wagon broke down here. You see; you learn." The man lifted his pudgy hands in a weighing gesture and shrugged. "And it so happened that I ran into the leader of the bunch. I knew him a few years back when he was hunting buffalo in Kansas. He was a mean sort then. Now he's just plain bad. They call him Big Ed."

"Big Ed," Bull Giles repeated. "Big Ed Sallie? He's got a scar running clear across his right cheek?" He ran a finger diagonally across his own cheek from eye to chin.

"That's him." Fat Frank nodded.

"You know him?" Loman Janes glanced at Bull as the stoutly muscled man straightened from his slouched position.

"I hunted buffalo with him one season a few years back. I saw him get into a knife fight with another hunter — slashed him to ribbons." Bull took a sip of whiskey and seemed to hold it in his mouth before swallowing it.

"Indians are enough trouble when they're sober," Loman Janes remarked. "Drunk, it's worse." His glance raised to Benteen. "You got a lot more range to cover this winter than I do."

"Yeah." Benteen listened for something else in the comment, but didn't hear it. If the Indians started raiding the stock, this was one time size would be a hindrance. Loman Janes wouldn't have that problem with his smaller herd ranging over less ground. "I figured you'd be down in Texas, Bull, throwing together another Ten Bar herd to bring up the trail."

"I decided to stay the winter," Bull replied. "I had my fill of that alkali dust for a while."

Bull Giles never got along with anybody for very long. Benteen couldn't imagine him taking orders from Loman Janes all winter.

"You planning on working for Janes?" He came right out and asked.

Loman Janes responded. "I heard the wolves were bad, so I told Bull he could spend the winter cuttin' down their number, since he was going to be here. We're pickin' him up some supplies and ammunition."

All the Ten Bar cattle were getting their first taste of a northern winter, so it was a sensible plan to cut down on the number of predators stalking the cattle's range. Benteen had issued ammuniton to his men with orders to shoot any wolf they saw but those gray wolves could be as elusive as ghosts. Hiring a wolver wasn't a bad idea, but it could be an expensive one, since they got paid three times or more what a regular cowhand made.

That thought prompted Benteen to inquire, "Does Boston know about this?"

"I put it in the last report." Janes stiffened at the implication he didn't have the authority to do it without Judd Boston's okay.

Benteen finished his whiskey. "In your next report, give him my regards."

"Why don't you wait until spring, then you can deliver them in person?" Loman Janes suggested with a cool smile.

Covering his surprise, Benteen eyed the Ten Bar foreman. "Boston is coming here? Why?"

"He's going to open a bank," Janes informed him. "With all these Texans coming up here, he thought they'd rather do business at a bank owned by a fellow Texan than with these Yankees."

"As I recall, Boston was a Yankee himself when he came to Texas," Benteen remarked cynically. "Now he's claimin' to be a Texan, huh?"

"He's lived there longer than most," Janes defended the claim.

"I guess he has." Benteen stepped away from the bar and nodded to Fat Frank. "Thanks for the whiskey."

"Come back anytime and bring your wife," the owner invited.

Out of the corner of his eye, Benteen saw Bull Giles reach for the whiskey bottle that sat on the small table. The timing of it came right on the heels of the reference to Lorna. The big man still coveted his wife, which made Benteen wonder why Giles hadn't been around the ranch pestering her. But whatever was keeping the man away, Benteen wanted it to stay that way.

As he rode from the store, the cantering of his horse's hooves seemed to drum out the name Judd Boston. A Texas bank in Montana. It was a brilliant move. The man would end up making money on every outfit up here, not just his own. Benteen had to give the man credit. He was a smart and shrewd businessman, like him or not.

21

The winter was a mild one. The warm, dry chinook wind that came from the eastern slopes of the Rockies was blowing across the plains, melting the snow and exposing the cured grasses to the grazing cattle.

It was dark when Benteen rode into the ranch after taking supplies to Shorty out at one of the line camps. He unsaddled his horse and the packhorse, turning both of them into the corral. As he walked to the cabin, he studied the curling ribbon of smoke bending over to be whisked into the night by the chinook.

When he entered the cabin, Lorna was balancing a fussing little Arthur on her hip while stirring a pot on the stove. Webb was hanging on her skirt and sobbing. Benteen noted the harassed and impatient look on her face and smiled as he turned away to remove his coat.

"What's the problem, Webb?" He crossed the room, rolling up his shirt sleeves to wash his hands.

But his older son wailed louder and tried to climb up Lorna's skirt. "He wanted me to hold him." Lorna irritably tried to push the little boy from the hot stove.

It seemed dark in the cabin. Benteen glanced around and realized only one lamp was lit. "How come you haven't lighted the other lamp?" He poured water in the basin and reached for the chunk of lye soap.

"The kerosene's getting low. I'm trying to make it last."

"I'd like to see what I'm eating. Light it anyway and I'll ride over to Fat Frank's tomorrow or the next day and pick up some more."

"Webb, you're going to get burned if you don't keep away from this stove. Who is Fat Frank?" Both sentences came all in one breath, without a break in between.

"It's that little general store east of here." Benteen wiped his hands and glanced over to see his whimpering son still hovering close to the hot stove. "Can't you make your son do what he's told?"

"And hold little Arthur and cook your supper all at the same time, I suppose," Lorna flared, and dropped the spoon in the pot, leaving it unattended. "I'll just let supper scorch." She plunked a fussing Arthur in his

440

cradle, and he immediately let out an ear-piercing wail. She smacked Webb on his bottom and sat him on a chair, where he immediately began crying in earnest. Pausing, she lit the second lamp and set it on the table with an abruptness that made the glass chimney rattle. There were angry words in the look she sent Benteen as she swept past him to the stove.

"Is something wrong?" He tried hard not to smile at her display of temper.

"You never mentioned anything about a general store east of us, certainly not a man named Fat Frank."

"Didn't I?" He quirked an eyebrow in mild surprise, then shrugged and laid aside the towel he'd dried his hands on. "It must have slipped my mind. The place went up just this last fall."

"A lot of things have been slipping your mind lately." Lorna began dishing food onto the plates and setting them on the table. Webb was still crying. She shoved a spoon in his hand and pushed him closer to the table. "Be quiet and eat."

Sitting down, Benteen waited until she had returned to the table with the wailing one-year-old in her arms and sat down with him. "What things have been slipping my mind?" he asked.

441

"Everything." It was an all encompassing answer as she forced a spoonful of food into Arthur's mouth. "I don't know anything that goes on anymore. You have men working for you that I've never even met. You don't tell me anything that's going on."

"I didn't realize I was supposed to introduce you to every new hand I hired." He frowned. "Considering that the three men are vaqueros who came up with the herd last summer, it's a little late to be getting upset over an oversight. At the time, you were busy taking care of little Arthur and Webb. It hardly seemed important."

"What about that new Hereford bull you bought last September? Barnie was by today and said you're keeping it at Mary and Ely's." Lorna fought to hold the squirming child on her lap as Arthur tried to wiggle free. Her glance swept Benteen with an impatient look. "Can't you at least take your hat off at the table?"

"Sorry." He removed his hat and hooked it on a chair back.

"I thought you were going to turn that bull out with the cows," Lorna returned to the subject.

"That bull's too valuable to have one of those range-wild Longhorns kill him in a fight."

Benteen explained his reasons for isolating the purebred. "Ely's going to select a small herd of Western stock to breed to the bull this spring. That way he won't have to compete to have his own private harem."

"Webb, use your spoon," Lorna warned when she caught him eating with his hands.

"Don't want to!" He hid his hands behind his back.

"What's gotten into these boys?" Benteen frowned at the pair of defiant youngsters. "Can't you make them behave?"

It was the final spark to set off her temper. Lorna pushed away from the table and shoved a startled Arthur onto Benteen's lap. "Here. You can do everything else by yourself. You might as well raise your own sons!"

While Benteen was still trying to recover from the shock of her unexpected action and hold on to a squealing boy as well, Lorna grabbed her shawl and went storming out of the cabin. Webb started to slide off his chair, crying with alarm, "Mommy!"

"Stay right where you are," Benteen ordered in a harsh tone that stopped the tears instantly. He sat Arthur on Lorna's chair and stuck a spoon in his hand. "You're old enough to feed yourself." Then he stood up and pointed a warning finger at the two shocked and silent youngsters, staring at him with rounded brown eyes. "Eat your supper and neither of you move."

Long, angry strides carried him to the door Lorna had so recently slammed. Before he stepped outside, he sent one last look at his silent and unmoving sons, then closed the door behind him. Almost immediately he saw Lorna huddled against the corner of the cabin, her shoulders shaking with silent sobs. The rage that had filled him when she had walked out the door faded. She hadn't really left him and the boys. He came up behind her, his hands closing on her shoulders with a kind of fierceness.

"My God, what was the idea of walking out like that?" Benteen muttered thickly with relief. "Where did you think you were going?"

"It hardly matters, since I didn't go very far." Her voice quavered.

"You'd better come back inside. It's cool out here," he said.

"No. I don't want to go back in there yet." Lorna resisted his mild attempt to turn her around.

"I think you have a bad case of cabin fever," Benteen guessed.

She whirled around at the faint smile in his tone and faced him, all angry defiance and trembling resentment again. "That shouldn't come as a surprise. What else do I see but those four walls? I don't have anyone to talk to all day long but two little boys who can't even talk well. Every day it's the same thing. I cook, clean, and sew, haul water, wash clothes, and keep the boys out of mischief." Her chin was quivering. "I swore I wouldn't let this land get to me. I swore I wouldn't end up like that woman in Kansas. I was going to work and help us build a future here."

"That's what you're doing," Benteen assured her when she turned away and sank her teeth into her lower lip.

But his reply angered her instead. "How?" Lorna challenged. "By cooking your meals, taking care of your sons, and sleeping in the same bed with you! You can hire people to do that. It's obvious that's all you want from a wife."

His gaze narrowed in bewilderment. "I don't understand you."

"I think that's the problem. You don't," she agreed. "You leave in the morning and never tell me where you're going. You come back at night and never tell me where you've been or what you've been doing."

"I suppose I have Mary to thank for this, because Ely talks everything over with her."

Impatience rippled through him. "I make the decisions in this family."

"Without talking it over with me. I have absolutely no say in what happens. I don't even *know* what's happening."

"Why are you bringing this up now?" he demanded. "Why has it become so important all of a sudden?"

"Maybe because I was too busy when the babies were small to realize how little I knew about what was going on," Lorna suggested. "In case you haven't noticed, this happens to be the first winter I haven't been pregnant."

"If it's going to keep you from becoming a nagging wife, maybe we ought to change that," he snapped.

"I'll bet you'd like it if I calved every spring like one of your cows. Or do you want to keep me pregnant so I can't leave you?" The bitter accusation was a cruel one. Lorna instantly wanted to bite back the words. "I'm sorry, Benteen. I didn't mean that." She tried to retract them, but he stood rigidly in front of her, no expression showing on his hard features. "Benteen, you have to believe me. I love you too much to ever leave you. I am not like your mother."

"I left the boys alone," he said. "We'd better go inside and finish our supper."

446

"No." Lorna stood her ground, searching his unrelenting features. "All I want is for you to share your life with me. And I'm not taking one step until you tell me you believe that."

He looked at her for a long second, then scooped her off the ground and into his arms. "Believe this, Lorna," he said. "I'm never going to give you the chance to leave me."

Despite the possessive ring in his voice, it wasn't the answer she wanted. She knew, without being told in so many words, that he didn't want to need her. There was a part of him that didn't want to love her. That's why he allowed her to occupy only a small space in his life and not the whole of it. But she wasn't going to let it continue, even if it meant becoming a nag or a shrew.

Spring was twice as busy that year. The mild winter had given them a good calf crop. That and the continuing boom in the cattle market convinced Benteen to begin the construction of the house on the knoll. In addition to the branding crews, he hired men to dig the footings and ordered lumber from the mill. A well was drilled to supply the house with running water, and a crew of carpenters was hired.

The house began to take shape right before

Lorna's eyes. It was going to be more magnificent than she had dreamed it would be. Benteen consulted her on just about every detail. She was too excited by all their plans and the sight of the mushrooming structure to notice that he failed to keep her abreast of happenings elsewhere on the ranch. There were wall coverings to be chosen, furniture to be picked out, and draperies to be selected, carpets for the floors, and fixtures in the house. All of it had to be ordered and shipped in via train, steamboat, and finally freight wagon. If they were lucky, it would arrive when the house was finished.

When Jessie Trumbo arrived in late July with another herd of Longhorns from Texas, he beheld the sight of the two-story structure towering up from the plains. It was merely the outer shell, but it gave him quite a start.

Fat Frank Fitzsimmons lifted the stopper covering the container and squeezed his pudgy hand through the opening to take out two pieces of peppermint sticks. There was a twinkle in his eye as he turned to Lorna.

"It sure is a shame there aren't two good little boys in my store that I could give this candy to," he declared, and deliberately ignored the two boys that, a second ago, had been pushing at each other.

"I'm good," Webb piped up immediately.

Little Arthur stuck a finger in his mouth and blinked at the fat man with wide-eyed innocence. "Dood," he affirmed, despite the finger in his mouth.

"Well ..." The proprietor hesitated for a minute more under the anxious looks from the boys. "I guess you have been pretty good." He was too fat to bend over, so he leaned downward and gave a piece of candy to each of them.

"What do you say to Mr. Fitzsimmons?" Lorna prompted.

"Thank you." Webb had to take the stick out of his mouth to respond.

Little Arthur didn't think it was necessary. "T'ank oo."

"You're welcome." The fat man beamed and helped himself to a stick of peppermint before he covered the jar. "I'm still a little boy myself — a growing one." He patted his stomach and laughed.

"I don't think you should give them candy every time we come in," Lorna protested mildly. "They'll start expecting it."

"And they'll always want to come to *my* store when you shop. Bribe the youngsters and get their parents' trade." He declared his motive openly.

"You have certainly expanded since I was here in the spring," Lorna remarked, and glanced around at the improvements he'd made. A second room had been added on, which was now the saloon area and separate from the store. There were glass windows in the front and shelves to hold his goods. It seemed she could never enter a general store without judging it according to her father's.

"From what I've heard, you and your husband have been doing some building, too." He began packing her purchases in a box.

"Yes, we are building a home." She tried not to sound too proud.

"A mansion, by all accounts," he chided her modesty.

"It certainly seems huge compared to the one-room log cabin we're living in now."

"When will it be finished?"

"I was hoping we could celebrate Christmas in it, but I doubt if the furniture will arrive by then. We plan to move into it sometime this winter."

"It's only fitting that you and your husband have a grand home," Frank Fitzsimmons assured her. "Your husband is bull of the woods around here. I hear he's running upwards of twenty thousand cows on his range."

"Really," Lorna murmured, unaware the number was so large. She opened her cloth purse. "How much do I owe you?"

"I'll just put it on your account," he replied.

She hadn't known Benteen had set up an account at the store. It was something else he had omitted telling her, but she didn't let on to the storekeeper.

"Of course." She smiled thinly.

"I'll carry this out to the wagon for you." The fat man picked up the box, puffing at the slightest exertion, and waddled out from behind the counter. "Did someone ride in with you?"

"Yes. Mr. Willis is at the smithy's. One of the team threw a shoe on the way here," Lorna explained why Woolie wasn't with her now. She turned to the two boys, busily sucking on their candy. "Come on, boys. Let's go outside to the wagon."

In addition to the general store and saloon, the town of Blue Moon boasted a blacksmith's and wheelwright's shop, too, and two cabins to house the Fitzsimmons family and the smithy — a man named Dan Long. Traffic had worn away the grass in front of the two businesses, exposing the hard earth and creating a short street of sorts. Three sets of rutted tracks fanned out from it and disappeared over the rolling plains.

Their wagon stood outside, with only one horse standing in the traces. A blacksmith's hammer sounded out rhythmically in the summer afternoon.

"If you would put the box in the wagon, Mr. Fitzsimmons," Lorna requested, "I'll let Mr. Willis know that we can leave whenever he's ready."

"Of course, Mrs. Calder," he agreed.

While he puffed his way to the back of the wagon, Lorna took Arthur by the hand to walk to the blacksmith's shop. Webb skipped a few paces ahead of her, then stopped abruptly to point.

"Look at that wagon, Mommy!"

"It's a carriage, not a wagon," she corrected, seeing it almost at the same moment her son did. It was a fancy carriage, too, all enclosed and brightly painted. She had not seen anything remotely like it since leaving Texas. It more than piqued her curiosity.

"What's a carriage?" Webb frowned.

She laughed at his question. "You're looking at one."

"Oh," he said, and ran ahead for a closer look.

It gave Lorna an excellent excuse to satisfy her curiosity and venture nearer after Webb instead of going directly to find Woolie Willis. A pair of matched sorrels with flaxen mane and tail were in the corral adjoining the smithy's shop. They had to be the team that pulled the exquisitely built carriage. Lorna had a glimpse of seats covered with red leather, but Webb was trying to climb inside to see what it was like.

"You mustn't climb on other people's property," she admonished, and dragged him from the step-up.

"But I wanta see inside," he protested.

She heard footsteps coming around the carriage and saw a pair of booted feet before the man walked out from behind the vehicle. Her eyes widened in surprise, because she had expected it to be the owner of the carriage. Instead it was Bull Giles.

"Mr. Giles." She smiled widely in recognition. "It's good to see you again."

"Lorna." He took off his hat and held it in front of him. He seemed to stare at her for the longest time.

She was a little shaken by the raw yearning in his eyes and the liberty he had taken by using her given name. She tried to cover the sudden awkwardness she felt. "Did you just

453

arrive from Texas with another herd?"

Bull Giles seemed to straighten a little, and the look went away. "No. As a matter of fact, I didn't leave last fall."

"You didn't? I hadn't seen you in some time, so I just supposed . . ." She was at a loss for something to say.

"I saw your husband here last fall. Didn't he mention it to you?" He knew the answer even as he asked the question.

"He must have forgotten," Lorna weakly tried to defend Benteen.

"I'm sure he did," Bull Giles agreed dryly.

"I guess you've been working on one of the ranches," she realized. "For the Ten Bar again?"

"In a way. They hired me to spend the winter hunting wolves. Your husband knew that, too," he added deliberately, to let her know that Benteen had been well acquainted with his activities.

"I see," Lorna murmured. In the initial surprise of seeing Bull Giles again, she had let go of Webb's arm. His interest in the big man had quickly waned and he was back at the carriage, scrambling to climb inside. "Webb, come away from there."

"It's all right, Mrs. Calder. He can't do any harm," Bull said.

"The owner might not think so." She caught hold of Webb's arm again and pulled him down. Little Arthur started crying because he dropped his candy on the ground.

Crouching down, Bull Giles picked up the stick of candy and brushed the worst of the dirt from it, then offered it to the boy. When Lorna started to protest, he glanced at her and smiled. "A little dirt won't hurt him."

"Okay," she gave in. When she let go of Arthur's hand, he toddled unabashedly over to the muscled stranger. Once he had the stick of candy in his mouth, Arthur stayed there to study him.

"He looks a lot like you." There was a softness in the tough man's eyes when he finally lifted his glance from the boy to Lorna. "What's his name?"

"Arthur — after my father," she added for no reason that she could explain.

"Why can't I get in the carriage, Mommy?" Webb wanted to know.

"You can." Bull slowly straightened and moved to the older boy. "I'll lift you in."

"But —" Lorna began.

"It's all right," he assured her again. "One of the bolts was sheared off the other day. I brought it in to have Dan repair it."

A little frown ran across her forehead. "This

carriage belongs to the Ten Bar?"

"No," Bull laughed shortly. "Not even Judd Boston owns anything like this."

"But I thought you just said you were working for them." She was becoming confused.

"I did last winter," he replied.

"Well, then, who does this carriage belong to?" Lorna moved closer to the vehicle, which automatically brought her nearer to Bull Giles.

"I hired out a couple weeks ago to a party of English gentry, acting as a guide and escort. It belongs to them," he explained as his attention became riveted on her face. A small hand tugged on his pants leg, dragging his gaze downward to Arthur. "You want to sit in the carriage with your brother, don't you?" Bull guessed, and Arthur nodded vigorously.

"English gentry," Lorna repeated as he lifted Arthur into the carriage. "Do you mean they have titles?"

"Yes. Every time you say anything, you have to add 'your lordship' or 'your ladyship.' " He seemed to express Benteen's mocking derision of all the pomp that surrounded the European titled class.

It seemed impossible, yet Lorna couldn't help wondering, "One of them wouldn't happen to be Lady Crawford?" she asked.

His brow shot up in surprise. "How did you know that?" Then he appeared to doubt that they meant the same person. "She's an older woman, with yellow-white hair."

"That sounds like her." Lorna couldn't believe it. "I met her in Dodge City — the same day you and I had lunch. She was very kind. She even had her maid bring me some lotion to make my skin soft." She absently ran a hand over her cheek in a gesture of remembrance of the gift. "And you say she's a member of this party you're escorting?"

"From what I can gather, she's a chaperon or companion to one of the younger women who's engaged to the duke," he explained.

"I never did get a chance to personally thank her for the lotion." Lorna sighed, then laughed softly at herself. "She probably doesn't even remember it."

"I'll mention it to her," Bull said.

"It's hardly important." But Lorna hoped he would.

"Mrs. Calder?" Woolie Willis came around the carriage, leading the second horse of the team. "It'll just take me a couple of minutes to hitch this horse up and we'll be ready to go."

"We'll be there directly," she promised. As he led the horse to their wagon, Lorna turned to her two sons, bouncing on the carriage seats.

"That's all boys. We have to go now."

"Not yet, Mommy." Webb frowned and stubbornly moved out of her reach.

"Do as your mother tells you," Bull ordered. "Come on. I'll lift you out."

Neither child was inclined to argue with the big stranger. Arthur was the first to come forward and let the large pair of hands pick him up. He squealed with delight when Bull lifted him high in the air before setting him on the ground.

"Do me like that," Webb insisted when it was his turn to be lifted out.

Once Webb was set down, there was an immediate clamor from both boys for Bull to do it again. Lorna was afraid Bull might allow himself to be cajoled into a repeat, so she stepped in.

"No more," she refused, taking each of them by the hand. "It's getting late and we have to be back to the ranch in time to fix Daddy's supper." There were wrinkled noses and quiet grumbles, but no outright rebellion. "All the men at the ranch make such a fuss over them that they've become a little spoiled," Lorna admitted to Bull.

"They're nice boys." He rumpled Webb's dark hair with affection.

"I wike you," Arthur said, tipping his head

way back to look at the stranger.

"I like you, too," Bull replied with a slight gruffness in his voice.

"You're very good with children," Lorna remarked. "You should get married and have some of your own."

"That isn't likely to happen," he said, "considering the only girl I ever wanted to marry is somebody else's wife." His bold gaze made it clear that he was referring to her.

"Please don't say things like that, Mr. Giles," Lorna insisted awkwardly, because it couldn't be unsaid, or forgotten. "It makes it impossible for us to even be friends."

He breathed in deeply and released it in a quick sigh. "My apologies, Mrs. Calder."

All she could do was nod and murmur a "good day." With the boys in hand, she turned and walked to the waiting wagon.

22

Canvas tents were clustered together like so many giant mushrooms erupting out of the stark, lonely plains. Not far from the stretch of river where the tents and assorted wagons sat, a herd of horses grazed under the watchful eye of a wrangler. Long-eared mules and powerfully muscled draft horses browsed side by side with sleek thoroughbreds, intermingling and sharing the food feast in a classless way that the people occupying the tents regarded as unthinkable for themselves.

"Don't you find this all so exciting and adventurous, Lady Crawford?" declared Penelope Dunshill, daughter of the present Earl of Crawford and the future wife to the Duke of Middleton. The high-spirited brunette didn't possess any real beauty, but her vivacity made it appear she was attractive. "I want to mount my horse and gallop madly over this melancholy land." The instant the desire was expressed, she turned eagerly from the awesome expanse of rolling grassland to her companion. "Let's go riding."

"No." Elaine Dunshill adjusted the black parasol to the other shoulder to keep the sun off her relatively unlined face. "Even you would wilt in this heat, Penelope, and George has a lavish dinner planned for this evening so we all can sample the wild game he shot this morning. He will be greatly disappointed if his future bride is too enervated to enjoy it." That should have been sufficient argument against it, but for good measure she added, "Our guide is away from camp getting the carriage repaired. A person can become too easily lost in this country without a native to show the way. I suggest you lie down and rest for a couple of hours instead."

"If you insist." The long sigh that accompanied the agreement was an exaggerated show of unwillingness.

When they paused in front of Penelope's tent, her personal maid appeared instantly. Counting the guide, horse handlers, cook, maids, and valets, there was a retinue of twelve to serve the English party of six. Yet, they were supposedly "roughing it." Elaine smiled to herself each time the thought occurred to her.

It was practically the only amusement she found in this tour of the "real" American West. Con's death had diminished the role she played in London society and politics. She made a striking figure in black, a color she continued to wear even after the year's mourning had passed, but she was the wife of a dead earl, no longer sought for the influence she no longer had. Despite her personal and inherited wealth, she had been relegated to dowager status.

She chafed under the loss of power and prestige that had her playing companion and chaperon to an empty-headed girl who found more excitement in a mad gallop across the plains than in making money and manipulating people. The only alternative to her present position was to receive no invitations and retire to some country manor. And that would be infinitely more galling.

With her charge whisked into the tent by the maid, Elaine continued on, but not to her own tent. She wanted to have a word with her host, the Duke of Middleton, and find out how soon they would resume their travel. In truth, part of the appeal that had prompted Elaine to accept the invitation to come on this trip as her niece's companion had occurred when George – the Duke of Middleton – had mentioned they would be touring the northern territories, including Montana. Elaine had been intrigued by the possibility of chancing across her son,

Benteen Calder, and discovering whether he had made use of the potential she'd seen in him. But this territory was big, and so far she'd not heard his name mentioned. Not that it was important; she admitted to only an idle curiosity about him.

When she neared the center tent, Elaine noticed the horse and buggy out front, and recognized it as belonging to Judd Boston, a banker turned rancher. Their camp was located on his range, so he had become a frequent visitor. As a matter of fact, it was he who had recommended their present guide when George had dismissed the previous one for drunkenness. Although Elaine had little personal contact with the banker, she suspected that he was deliberately trying to keep their party on his land for some purpose of his own.

At the sound of voices coming through the canvas walls of the tent, Elaine had no qualms about eavesdropping on the conversation between this Judd Boston and her host. There had been occasions in the past when she had picked up valuable information in the same manner.

"I am confident this will prove to be a very profitable investment for you." It was the man Judd Boston talking. Although he claimed to be Texan, he didn't possess the accent. Elaine briefly thought it might be interesting to delve into his background. "This partnership of ours will be highly successful. There's a lot of money to be made in cattle, especially if a man has not only financial backing but also important connections in government. With your financial support and my connections, our company will have both."

"The Duchess Land and Cattle Company. It has a nice ring to it, doesn't it?" George declared in his haughty, boasting voice. "My future bride is so taken with this country. I'm certain she shall adore having a ranch named after her."

"An excellent engagement present," Boston agreed, but Elaine caught a trace of cynicism in his tone.

Now she understood his game. He had kept the party here in order to persuade the Duke of Middleton to invest some of his considerable fortune in his ranch, as so many other members of European royalty had done recently. Fools, Elaine thought. They had no knowledge of the vagaries of ranching in the West. Droughts, blizzards, disease, not to mention fluctuating cattle markets. Money could be made. Yes, a lot of it. But not as easily as men like Judd Boston proclaimed. Absentee owners and partners were begging to be fleeced and bilked of their moneys.

"This is prime range," Boston was saying. "You can search the whole of Montana and find none better."

From what Elaine had seen of it, there was a critical lack of water to sustain a large herd, certainly anything the size Boston had indicated he was bringing up the trail from Texas. Water had been the one asset Seth Calder possessed, but he had always been too conservative in everything he did. "Growing slowly," he had called it, and Elaine had seen the months slip into years with no discernible improvements in their standard of living.

"What was this you mentioned about three claims you — or rather *we* — would be able to assume?" George corrected himself and emphasized his participation.

"Before the government will deed land to an individual, it requires that improvements be made. As I mentioned, there are three claims that don't fulfill the requirements. I have a 'friend' in the land office that will throw out the claims at the proper time, leaving it open for us." There was a slight pause before Boston continued. "You realize, of course, that the information must be kept strictly confidential. We wouldn't want the owner of the Triple C to discover our plans and meet the conditions."

"I'll not breathe a word," George promised, at the same time slightly affronted by and enthusiastic about their clandestine activities. "You will join us for dinner tonight, Boston. That Mr. Giles you recommended is a marvelous guide. This evening we will be feasting on game that I personally shot — game that our guide led me to. I should like you to share in the spoils of the hunt and celebrate our new partnership."

"It would be my pleasure, sir," Judd Boston accepted the invitation.

"I am sure you would like to rest and freshen up before dinner." There was the sound of snapping fingers. "I'll have Barton show you where you may stay."

With the meeting brought to an end, Elaine assumed a strolling pace that brought her to the front of the tent as the valet lifted the netting to guide Boston out. She nodded to him and he politely tipped his hat, making a slight bow at the waist. While he walked away, she paused, aware the Duke of Middleton was alone in his tent, and debated whether she should speak to him as planned.

But the turn of events had stimulated her mind. It seemed much less imperative that the party resume its journey. So she returned to her own private tent and dismissed her maid. Merely as a mental exercise, she began imagining what she would do with a ranch in Montana – where and how money could be made. Most of the beef was sold for shipment to Eastern cattle markets, which put the rancher at the mercy of their prices. How could that be controlled? A rancher could sell directly to the U.S. government.

However, Canada was much closer – and they were building a railroad across the Rockies, she recalled, plus the outposts for the Mounted Police, and all those Indians on reservations to be fed. There was the vague memory of a poor relation working for the Canadian government, a second or third cousin of her late husband, the Earl of Crawford. She had met him briefly on that last, ill-fated tour through the West. He had tried to borrow money. Roddy – no, Roger Dunshill, that was his name. He worked as a purchasing agent.

Elaine laughed at herself. If Judd Boston only knew it, his new partner had valuable connections as well, but she had no intention of bringing the information to the duke's attention. Why should she make him a fortune? Eventually someone would see the market for cattle in Canada. It was a pity she wouldn't share in the killing that could be made.

Trying to fund two operations had stretched Judd Boston's recources thin. With the unlimited letter of credit signed by the Duke of Middleton and bearing his seal, he had all the money he needed. The partnership agreement didn't concern Boston at all. There were too many legal ways to drain away funds to be bothered about splitting profits.

Patience. It was only a matter of patience, and he'd eventually get everything he wanted. Including those three claims Calder had filed on. The man was so busy building his new mansion, he had forgotten to make the necessary improvements to retain his legal right to the claims.

Aromatic smells were coming from the cooking area, prompting Boston to take out his vest watch and check the time. In another twenty minutes it would be proper for him to present himself at the duke's tent, so he continued to wander among the wagons in no particular hurry while the sun went down behind him in a blaze of glory. He heard the sound of a carriage approaching the camp and turned to see Bull Giles driving a team of matched sorrels.

Boston waited until the carriage had stopped

and the big man had vaulted to the ground before walking over to meet him. Two of the horse handlers came forward to take care of the team. Bull Giles paused to inspect the carriage wheels.

"You here again?" Bull remarked dryly when Boston came up beside him.

"I told you I'd make it worth your while if you kept the duke and his friends in the area for a couple of weeks." He lifted a bag of coins from his pocket and dropped it into Giles's hand.

There was a weighing gesture of the hand before he slipped it into a pocket. "It just worked out that way," Giles insisted.

"To the mutual benefit of both of us," Boston murmured, and studied the man for a long second. "I don't understand you." Usually he could read any man, but Bull Giles didn't follow any accepted pattern.

"Is there any reason why you should?" the man asked with a trace of derision.

"No, I don't suppose there is," Boston admitted with a narrowed look. "But you were here before most of the others. You knew the potential of this country. You could have done the same thing Calder did. Today you could be building a big house just like he is. You have the knowledge and the ability, but you don't use it. Why?"

Bull shrugged indifferently. "I reckon I don't have your kind of ambition — or greed."

"Every man wants something." Boston wouldn't buy that. "What do you want?"

"To be left alone." Bull cast him an impatient glance.

"What's keeping you here?" Boston answered. "You usually drift on to another place." His head lifted as he recalled a remark Loman Janes had made. At the time, it hadn't held any interest for him. "It wouldn't happen to be Benteen Calder's wife, would it?"

There was the slightest pause before Giles challenged, "What would I want with another man's wife?"

But Judd Boston just smiled, his black eyes darkening with a knowing light. "I guess range accidents happen. Young wives can turn into young widows quick out here. Maybe that's it," he mused. "Or are you trying to get the courage to arrange for Calder to meet with an accident?"

"I never did like you much, Boston," Bull growled.

"Let somebody else do all the work, and you step into his shoes — and his bed. Not a bad plan, Giles," Boston conceded.

"I never said nothin' of the sort," he denied.

"But you're thinking it." His smile widened. "It could work."

"You've got an ugly mind." Bull swung away.

But it gave Judd Boston something to think about. Maybe it could be worked to his advantage, provided Giles did more than just think about it. Women did funny things to men, corrupting some who believed they were honest. It would be interesting to see what happened.

As Bull Giles entered the camp proper, he was seething with rage. He knew Judd Boston looked on the Calder range with envy. There was none better around. But the attempt to use him as a pawn to get Calder out of the picture struck him raw. It was true that he had thought about what would happen to Lorna if Benteen was killed or crippled, but it had only been out of concern for her. It hadn't been a death wish for Benteen.

A woman like her wouldn't look twice at a man like him. His steps began to slow as a painful tightness gripped his chest, twisting him up with the deep emotions the thought of her dragged from him. She was so beautiful with those dark eyes and hair as sleek and shiny as those thoroughbreds grazing out there. She had called him friend. That meant something, didn't it? She must like him. A groan tore from his throat.

He looked around to see if anyone heard that betrayal. Lady Crawford was just stepping out of her tent. With his memory of the meeting with Lorna so vivid in his mind, he immediately recalled that she had said she had met Lady Crawford before. He had promised to mention it to the woman.

Removing his hat, he stepped forward to intercept her. "Excuse me, your ladyship." He bowed slightly.

"Yes? What is it?" she prompted him to state his reason for stopping her, all regal and haughty.

"By chance, would you have been in Dodge City three years ago?" he asked.

An eyebrow lifted in quizzical surprise. "I was, yes, with my late husband."

"Perhaps you might recall speaking to a young woman and giving her a bottle of lotion for her skin," Bull suggested.

Her interest became genuine and sharply curious. "I do remember the incident. May I ask how you learned of it?"

"I spoke to the young woman, Mrs. Calder, this afternoon while I was getting the carriage fixed. She was most grateful for

472

your kindness to her."

"Mrs. Calder, yes, that was her name." She nodded, as if his mention of it had prompted her memory. "And she lives around here? What a coincidence!"

"Her husband owns one of the neighboring ranches," he confirmed.

Lady Crawford was quiet for a thoughtful moment. "Perhaps I could call on her," she mused aloud, then glanced at Bull. "Do you think she would mind?"

"I think she would be very pleased." He smiled at how pleased Lorna would be to see the woman again.

"It wouldn't be correct to arrive unannounced. Would you ride over to her ranch tomorrow and ask if I might call on her the day after?" she asked.

"I would be more than happy to do that for you," Bull assured her.

"And I will require that you escort me to her ranch the following day. I'll arrange it with the duke," she stated.

"Very good." He made another slight bow as she moved away.

With all the noise that went on at the building site, Lorna didn't pay any attention when she heard the rumble of a wagon outside their cabin. Webb came racing into the house and charged straight at her. Lorna grabbed the hot iron an instant before he bumped the board.

"Mommy, it's Aunt Mary!" he exclaimed breathlessly. "She's come to see us!"

Lorna forgot all about scolding him as she set the iron back on the stove and walked quickly to the door. Webb wasn't mistaken. Mary and Ely both were both approaching the cabin.

"Webb said you were outside," Lorna declared in surprise. "Why didn't you let me know you were coming? I could have baked a pie."

"There just wasn't time," Mary said, then looked at Ely. Both of them were wearing a smile that went from ear to ear. Lorna had the feeling that they were a young couple falling in love.

"Wasn't time?" she repeated, thoroughly confused by their behavior.

When Mary looked back at her, there was a misting of tears in her eyes. "We're going to have a baby, Lorna," she announced.

"You are!" Lorna was shocked and happy, both at the same time.

"Yes." Her chin bobbed up and down excitedly. "Isn't it wonderful? After all this time, we're finally going to have a baby."

"It's more than wonderful!" The next second she was hugging her friend as they cried and laughed together.

"I just couldn't wait a minute more without telling you," Mary said when she drew back to catch her breath. "Ely was worried about me riding all this way in the wagon, but I knew I'd bust if I couldn't tell you in person. We've waited so long."

"I'm so happy for you." Lorna wiped at the tears on her cheek, then reached over to squeeze Ely's hand. "I'm so happy for both of you."

She heard the cantering of hooves and looked up to see Benteen riding in. Lifting her arm, she waved excitedly to him. He spied Ely and reined his horse toward the cabin. She barely gave him a chance to dismount before she was telling him the news. When the congratulations died down a second time, Lorna suggested they all come into the cabin for coffee.

While the men were busy discussing ranch business, Mary leaned over to whisper to Lorna, "Is it true that Bob Vernon is getting married?"

"I hadn't heard anything about it."

"Ely hinted that he might be, and I thought Benteen might have said something to you,"

Mary explained her reason for asking. "It's because of a girl that he's been going to Miles City once a month."

"I knew he went there a lot," Lorna admitted. "But a lot of the men do. I hadn't realized he was seeing a girl."

"Not just any girl," Mary whispered. "She's a harlot, but I understand they are madly in love with each other."

Lorna searched herself but couldn't find any shock or moral indignation. Her view of life had changed a great deal. If Bob Vernon wanted to marry the woman, knowing her past, and she wanted to marry him, then it was enough.

"I think I'll suggest to Benteen that we let Bob have this cabin when we move into the house." She voiced the thought as it occurred to her.

Mary started to speak, but she was interrupted by Webb, who came tearing into the cabin again. He flung himself at Lorna with his usual abandon. "Mommy! That man is here — only he didn't bring the c'raige."

The last word escaped her. When she glanced to the door Webb had left standing open, Benteen was walking to the opening. There was something about him that reminded her of a dog bristling at the sight of an intruder. It made her move just a little more quickly to see who it was.

When she reached the threshold, Benteen had stopped a foot outside the door, blocking the way. Over his shoulder she could see Bull Giles swinging off his horse, and she realized Webb had been trying to say the word "carriage." Arthur was trotting out to greet him, then stopping shyly at the last minute and sticking a finger in his mouth.

Bull paused to smile down at him and rumple his hair. "How ya doing', Artie?"

Arthur turned on his stubby legs and ran to Benteen, but he was smiling, not at all afraid of the big man following him. Lorna glanced at Benteen. His rigid jaw was thrust forward, showing aggression.

"What brings you here, Giles?" Benteen challenged, not bothering with a greeting.

Bull's gaze flicked past him to Lorna, and she was conscious of a nerve twitching in Benteen's cheek. "I have a message for your wife from Lady Crawford."

Her lips parted in warm surprise and delight, but Benteen spoke before she had a chance. "Who's Lady Crawford?"

"You remember me telling you about her," she rushed to explain, moving to his side and touching his arm. An eagerness was in her eyes when she tipped her face up to him. "I met her in Dodge City and she gave me that jar of lotion."

There was a flicker of recognition in his face; then his eyes narrowed. "What's she doing here?"

"She's with a party of English gentry that are touring the area. Mr. Giles is acting as guide for them," Lorna explained. It seemed to silence Benteen, and she turned her glance to Bull. "You said she gave you a message for me? She remembered me?"

"Yes, she remembered meeting you," Bull said, answering the last question first. "She'd like to call on you, and asked if it would be inconvenient if she came tomorrow?"

"Tomorrow?" Unconsciously her hand tightened on the sleeve of Benteen's arm. "Tell her it's not inconvenient at all. She's more than welcome."

"Around two o'clock," Bull suggested.

"Yes, that will be fine," Lorna assured him, still finding it hard to believe that the woman wanted to call on her.

It would be her first opportunity to socially entertain someone other than Mary and Ely. She felt the excitement and anticipation growing and struggled to quell it. Just because she hadn't had any real social contact for several years, she wasn't going to become pathetically eager the way the woman in Kansas had been.

"I'll tell her that you'll expect her tomorrow, then." He nodded and turned to leave.

"Won't you come in for coffee?" Lorna invited, despite Benteen's unwelcoming attitude.

But it was Benteen who drew Bull's glance before he shook his head to refuse. "No. Thank you, Mrs. Calder." He walked to his horse and stepped into the stirrup, hefting his broad torso into the saddle.

As he trotted the horse away from the cabin, Webb tugged on her skirts. "How come he didn't bring the c'raige?"

"Probably because it was faster to ride his horse," Lorna reasoned, but she was conscious of the look Benteen sliced her.

"When did the boys meet him?" The question was fired low and quick.

"Yesterday," she admitted evenly, "when we went to Mr. Fitzsimmons' store. Mr. Giles was at the blacksmith shop getting a carriage repaired that belongs to the English party."

"You didn't mention it last night."

"It must have slipped my mind." There was a sweetness to her voice that said she was paying him back for all the things he hadn't

479

bothered to tell her. Actually she had failed to tell him because she had been bothered by the last comment Bull had made.

"What else has slipped your mind?" He wasn't amused. In fact, he was close to furious.

It wasn't her intention to make him jealous, and Lorna sighed tiredly. "Nothing, Benteen. Nothing else." Then she pulled herself together and smiled at him. "Will you be here tomorrow when she comes? I'd like you to meet her."

His gaze studied her, then swung to the rider leaving the ranch. "I'll be here when she arrives tomorrow."

It suddenly dawned on Lorna that Bull Giles would probably escort Lady Crawford to the ranch. He was the reason Benteen was going to be here. He wasn't interested in meeting Lady Crawford, and he hadn't agreed just to please her.

"You think Mr. Giles is coming tomorrow," Lorna murmured to let him know she was aware of his reason.

The look he turned on her was cool. "Don't you?"

"I am married to you, Benteen," she declared with quiet force.

"Then I want to make sure he doesn't forget it," he replied without any change in his hard expression.

23

A tall wooden structure towered above the unbroken tedium of rolling plains. Elaine sat up straighter in the carriage seat and leaned forward slightly to study it. Its proportions were grand, but anything less would have been dwarfed by the vastness of this empty land. The house was claiming dominion over the sprawling reaches of this wild country.

"Is that where we're going?" she called to Bull Giles to confirm the certainty that already burned in her heart.

"Yes, ma'am. That's the Triple C up ahead." He turned slightly in the driver's seat to answer.

"Did you say Triple C?" Elaine questioned sharply.

"Yes, ma'am. That's the brand Calder uses. The Triple C."

Settling back against the seat, Elaine kept a hand on the carriage side for balance as it rolled along the rough and rutted track leading to the ranch. Considering the remark Judd Boston had made, it seemed her son's ranch wasn't as secure as the house implied.

Lorna pulled at the neckline of her dress, trying to force it higher so not so much of her breasts would show, but her bustline had increased since having the boys. The bodice of the dress simply wouldn't stretch to cover the swell of her breasts.

Her eyes critically studied her image reflected by the mirror. Immodest or not, Lorna was going to wear it. This was her best dress. She refused to entertain her English guest wearing one of her plain, everyday dresses. Her fingertips traced over her cheek, testing its smoothness.

A second image appeared in the mirror, startling her. Benteen had come up behind her with cat-soft steps. His rugged, lean-jawed face was next to hers in the mirror. Their eyes locked together for a long second before Lorna turned around to face him. His hand moved to lightly stroke the curve of her throat while his gaze followed its path.

"Giles will appreciate the time you've taken to make yourself beautiful," he remarked cynically while his fingers continued their downward journey to wander over the exposed swell of her breasts.

"I didn't do it for him," Lorna insisted

sharply, irritated that he should say such a thing and all the while aware of the way her flesh tingled under his touch. "Besides, I don't even know that he's bringing Lady Crawford."

"He is," Benteen stated. "And he'll notice how you look."

"I can't help that," she protested as his fingers forced their way under the already strained material of the dress's neckline and followed its dipping line. "Why must you keep harping about him?"

"He wants to do what I'm doing right now with you." The flat of his hand spread across the small of her back as his fingers finished their climb to her shoulder. "He'd like to take you away from me. You know that, too."

His eyes challenged her to deny it, but she couldn't. "There isn't any reason for you to be concerned about that."

"Isn't there?" His hand applied pressure to bring her against the lower half of his body. "Then tell me you don't like him."

"But I do like him — as a friend," Lorna qualified her answer, but refused to lie about her feelings for Bull Giles.

"He'll use that someday, Lorna," Benteen warned. "That's why he's hanging around this area — because of you. Nothing else is keeping him here. You can't trust him."

"You're exaggerating." But there was a grain of doubt within her. "This isn't the time to talk about it anyway. They'll be coming any —"

"*They*," Benteen cut across her words. "You are expecting him to come."

"Benteen, please don't do this." He had no cause to be jealous, but she couldn't seem to convince him of it.

His fingers dug into her shoulderbone to pull her the rest of the way to him. There was a fire in his kiss, as if he wanted to sear his brand on her lips and mark her the way he marked all the rest of his possessions. When he lifted his head, her breath was coming quickly. She was angered and aroused at the same time. The contradiction showed in the fiery sparkle of her eyes and the swollen softness of her lips. Pivoting, Lorna turned to survey the damages in the mirror.

"There isn't time for that," Benteen said. "The carriage was approaching when I came in."

She whirled around, furious with him for destroying her calm when their arrival was imminent. There was a satisfied glint in his eye as he studied her. Closing her mouth tightly, Lorna brushed past him to walk swiftly to the door. She could hear the rattle of the wheels outside.

The carriage was just pulling to a stop when Lorna opened the door. An inner sense told her that Benteen was a step behind her. She squared her shoulders against him as she walked out from the cabin to greet her special guest. The boys were already running forward to meet the visitors. When Lorna noticed the grass stain on the seat of Webb's short pants, her irritation increased.

Bull Giles swung down from the driver's seat, his gaze running over Lorna. She was conscious of it, but she wasn't able to meet his eyes, not when she knew that Benteen was keenly observing both of them. It created a strain in her manner when she wanted to make a good impression on her afternoon guest.

She called Webb and Arthur to her side as Bull Giles moved to open the carriage door, offering his hand to assist the woman seated in back. When Lady Crawford stepped out, Lorna was struck again by the woman's regal bearing, an effect made more dramatic by the sheer silk blouse and long satin skirt, both jet-black. She looked older than she had the last time Lorna had seen her — age lines showed around her dark, nearly black eyes — but oddly no less beautiful.

As Lady Crawford moved gracefully forward to greet her, Lorna's instinct told her to curtsy, but Benteen's hand closed on the curve of her waist as if to check the movement. She stiffened slightly under his firm grip and remained erect.

"It's a great pleasure to see you again, your ladyship." Lorna welcomed the woman with a proffered hand that was briefly taken and released.

"Please. Let's dispense with the formalities on this meeting. I would like you to call me Elaine," she requested as her gaze swung pointedly to Benteen. "This is your husband?"

While his wife made the introductions, Elaine watched her son's face closely but she saw no recognition there. It wasn't surprising really, considering how small he had been and how much she had changed from a simple Texas girl to a member of England's ruling class. He showed a marked disinterest in her, yet she sensed a tension coming from him and wondered at its cause.

The two little boys were introduced to her. The heritage of Calder blood showed strongly in both of them, and Elaine remarked on it. Inwardly she was uncomfortable with the idea of having grandchildren. Growing old was something she fought, and the children were proof of her advancing age, regardless of the lies the mirror told.

"Mr. Giles." She partially turned to address the guide. "Would you fetch me the two presents on the carriage seat?" Certain of his obedience, she kept her attention focused on the couple, her glance straying more often to Benteen. "I brought you each a little something to show my appreciation for your hospitality today. I wasn't aware of your two children or I would have included a small gift for them."

"You shouldn't have brought us anything," Lorna protested.

"My wife is right. We must refuse," Benteen stated with a show of that stubborn Calder pride Elaine remembered so well.

"Nonsense." With an autocratic gesture she motioned for Giles to hand them their gifts. "They are merely token presents. A jar of lotion for your wife and some cigars for you. Mere trifles, I assure you."

Benteen grudgingly accepted the gift while his wife was much less reluctant. But Elaine's interest was caught by the glance he shot the guide, Giles. It was dark with suspicion and mistrust when Giles presented his wife with her gift. Elaine was quick to note the way his wife avoided looking directly at the guide. It seemed they were not quite the happy family unit that they had first appeared to be.

"Would you like to come into the cabin?"

Lorna invited. "I fixed some tea and cakes."

"I should like that," Elaine accepted, then paused to glance at the house being constructed on the rise of the plains. "I couldn't help noticing that you're building a new home. It's a very imposing structure. Perhaps later you might show me through it?"

"The carpenters are just starting work inside, so there isn't very much to see, but I'd be happy to give you a tour of it," Lorna agreed with an air of pride. "The cabin is going to seem very small and crude in comparison."

"Mommy, please, can we sit in the c'raige?" Webb pleaded, unable to contain his eagerness a second longer.

Lorna tried to distract him. "Wouldn't you like to come inside and have one of those fancy cakes I made?"

"I wanta sit in the c'raige," he insisted stubbornly.

When Lorna hesitated, Lady Crawford spoke up. "If the carriage can survive the journey over this rough country, two little boys aren't likely to harm it." Children had always been more of a nuisance to have around than anything else, so she wasn't sorry that they were more interested in the carriage than her.

"I know the boys wouldn't intentionally do anything —" Lorna began.

Bull Giles interrupted her. "I'll watch the boys for you, Mrs. Calder, and see that they stay out of trouble."

A brief but awkward silence followed his offer as Lorna glanced uneasily in Benteen's direction, but he said nothing. The corners of her mouth trembled with the effort it took to smile.

"That's very kind of you, Mr. Giles. Thank you," she accepted.

"Come on, boys, Let's go see the carriage." The two hurried to join him.

Lorna had been concerned about entertaining someone of Lady Crawford's class and breeding, yet the woman made her feel remarkably at ease over tea. The conversation flowed smoothly, except for the way Benteen held himself aloof from it. Lorna was conscious that Lady Crawford had noticed it, from the many times she let her gaze wander in his direction.

The happy voices and laughter of the boys carried into the cabin, an assurance that Bull was keeping them entertained. Lorna sensed that Benteen wasn't pleased by that. Perhaps she shouldn't have allowed them to stay outside, but Webb had acquired such a temper lately that she hadn't wanted to risk one of his stormy tantrums in front of Lady Crawford.

After waiting until she had deemed that her social obligation had been fulfilled, Elaine suggested they tour the new house. Her plan went awry when they went outside and both children wanted to accompany them to the building site. She thought they had been safely pawned off onto the guide, but it seemed she was wrong.

The interior of the house was a maze of skeletal timbers with chunks of sawed wood and stacks of lumber lying everywhere. To the small boys it was a giant playroom. Their running and shrieking seemed to add to the confusion. In spite of it all, Elaine could visualize exactly how the house would look, from the formal dining room to the serving area in the large kitchen. It had the potential to be magnificent by Western standards, and she knew it.

"This is going to be the study," Lorna explained as they completed the circling tour of the ground floor, which had brought them to the room off the large entryway.

There was a loud thud behind them, followed by a shriek of pain and fright from one of the boys. Elaine was the only one who didn't react with alarm as both Lorna and Benteen hurried to the younger child, screaming where he had fallen. His stubby legs hadn't managed to lift his foot over a board. It had tripped him, the fall scraping both knees on the rough wood floor.

Benteen started to pick him up, but Arthur wanted his mommy and sent up a fresh wail, stretching his clutching hands to her. She lifted the toddler into her arms and cuddled him close, rocking him slightly in silent comfort.

"Is Arthur hurt?" The older boy strained to see the injury. "Is he bleeding? Can I see?"

"He just scraped his knees," Lorna replied, then glanced apologetically to Elaine. "Would you excuse me?"

"Certainly," she agreed with alacrity. "Your husband can show me the rest of the house." She turned away to conceal the satisfaction that gleamed in her eyes and crossed the room to the massive fireplace. She listened to the sound of footsteps, separating Benteen's from those of Lorna and the children as they left through the front door.

"The stairway to the second floor isn't completed," Benteen informed her. "There isn't any more of the house to see."

Elaine tipped her head toward her shoulder to study him with a sidelong look. "You don't remember me at all, do you?" she murmured.

"I beg your pardon." There was a quizzical

lift of one eyebrow, yet his curiosity seemed forced. It was obvious his mind was elsewhere.

"I didn't expect that you would." Her gaze returned to the fireplace. "Your father used to keep a picture of me on the mantel. I often wondered how long he left it there."

When she looked at him again, she saw the whiteness under his skin as his facial muscles tautened with cold shock. Elaine wasn't surprised by the bitter hatred that blazed suddenly in his eyes.

"It was there until the day he died." His voice rumbled the answer, yet his control remained unshaken.

"Seth always was a hopeless romantic," Elaine declared on a throaty laugh, then let her gaze wander over the half-finished house. "Perhaps if he had built me a home like this, I wouldn't have left him. Is that why you're building it, Benteen? Are you afraid of losing your wife?"

"I don't know why you're here, but you can get the hell out!" His low-pitched voice vibrated with the effort to contain his wrath. "Go back to your fancy lords and ladies. You aren't wanted here."

"I haven't come to beg your forgiveness," she replied with a trace of amusement. "I don't regret running away from your father and leaving you. When I left Texas with Con Dunshill, I never once looked back."

"Do you think I give a damn?" Benteen challenged thickly. "I am not my father. You walked out of my life and you can stay out."

Her dark gaze studied him unmoved by his bitter hatred of her. "You aren't like your father," she agreed. "I knew that when I saw you in Dodge City. You are like me, Benteen. Just like me."

"You're an adulterous, scheming bitch. You don't even have the scruples of a whore." Contempt and derision twisted his features as he spat the accusations at her.

"And you are ruthless, ambitious, and intelligent — all the things you claim I am. In a man, they are qualities to be admired," she reasoned. "But if a woman possesses them, she is a scheming, gold-digging bitch. I plead guilty to all three. What now, Benteen? Aren't you just a little bit curious why I'm here after all this time?"

"Not particularly."

"You do want to know. You just don't want to admit it." She smiled with certainty. "So I'll tell you. Since my husband's death —"

"I assume you mean my father," Benteen broke in coldly. "He was your legal husband."

"Add bigamy to the charges against me,

then." She shrugged aside the technicality. "Since the death of the Earl of Crawford, whom I had been living with these past years as his wife, I have found English society too confining. I am not quite ready to sit on a shelf, as they would have me do. Ever since I saw you in Dodge City, the idea has been in the back of my mind that we'd make a great team, you and I."

"I'm not interested in a partner, and I certainly wouldn't pick you."

"I am an extremely wealthy woman, although I doubt if that's of any interest to you at the moment. But later, after you've had time to get over the . . . shock — shall we call it? — of seeing your mother again, there's a business proposition I'd like to discuss with you."

"I don't have a mother," Benteen stated flatly.

Her shoulder lifted in an expressive shrug of indifference. "I'd much rather be your partner, but we'll talk about that another time."

"There won't be another time, and I'm not interested in any proposition of yours — business or otherwise. I suggest you leave before I throw you out." There was no softening of his hard, embittered features.

"I'll leave." She smiled coolly. "There's just one more thing before I go."

"Then say it and be done with it," he snapped, showing the first rush of impatience.

"I believe you know a man named Judd Boston."

"What about him?" His dark eyes were guarded.

"It seems he has a friend in the land office who had told him about three claims that have not had the necessary improvements made to fulfill the requirements of the land act. All rights and title will be denied the present claimant, and Mr. Boston will be quietly taking them over."

"Very interesting, but hardly surprising. That's the way Boston works," Benteen replied.

She moved slowly toward him, gliding in rustling satin skirts. "Ah, but those three claims are yours, Benteen." The uncertainty of disbelief flickered across his face. "So you see, I can be very helpful to you — in many ways." Elaine smiled knowingly and laid her hand lightly against his cheek, stroking her fingers across it in a brief caress. "I'll be in touch in a few days, and we'll talk about that proposition."

After she walked by him to the door, Benteen remained motionless. The touch of her hand had brought a pain that splintered through him like shattering glass. For a split second he was a little boy again, wanting the warmth of a mother's hand and desperately wishing the beautiful woman in the picture would come back to him. That was before he realized his dream mother didn't exist.

Slowly he turned and walked to the front door, where she waited to be escorted to her carriage. Benteen didn't look at her. He tried to expel her existence from his mind. Although he knew her to be in her late forties, she didn't look it. She was too elegant and sophisticated to ever be considered matronly.

Many times in his youth he had planned what he would say to her if she ever came back. Some of it he had done — calling her names and denying her, ordering her out of his life. Yet, the sensation of her touch lingered on his cheek. He ached from it. But no one could see it. His hard features had been too well schooled in concealing the privacy of his emotions.

The southern exposure of the house had them walking into the sun. The sky was a huge chunk of blue, crowning the range in all directions. Benteen surveyed it with a slow, sweeping gaze, aware of the land's raw malevolence that could give and take by turns. The warning from his mother of Judd Boston's plans came whirling into his thoughts. He had been too confident, too sure of himself.

When they reached the carriage, Lorna was just coming out of the cabin with Webb at her side. Bull Giles followed her, carrying little Arthur in the hook of one arm. Despite the skinned knees and the traces of tears on his cheek, the toddler seemed quite happy on his lofty perch.

"You're a brave boy," Bull Giles was saying, neither he nor Lorna noticing the pair standing by the carriage.

"Just clumsy," Lorna laughed.

"Give him a chance to grow into his feet," Bull insisted. But when he smiled at Lorna, his glance encountered Benteen.

Beside him, his mother remarked, "Mr. Giles appears to be very much at home here. Is he a close friend of yours?"

"No." Benteen pulled all expression from his voice as he watched Bull set Arthur on the ground. The natural smile had left Lorna's lips, replaced by a more self-conscious one. "He's my wife's friend, not mine."

All is not well, Elaine thought to herself as Lorna came forward. She studied her son's wife with a little more interest. Lorna was an attractive, well-developed young woman. The hard work this country demanded from a female had kept her figure intact, despite the birth of two children. In the right clothes, she

497

could be stunning. There was intelligence in her eyes, yet she had retained a certain vulnerability. Elaine saw that Lorna still possessed a child's desire to trust, which made her easy to be deceived.

"I'm glad your child's injury wasn't serious," Elaine remarked when Lorna reached her, with little Arthur trotting to keep up.

"It was very minor," Lorna responded.

"It's been an enjoyable afternoon. I shouldn't have liked it to end on an unpleasant note," Elaine said.

"Are you leaving now?" Lorna inquired with mixed surprise and disappointment.

Elaine slid a brief glance at Benteen. "I must," she replied. When she moved to the carriage door, Bull Giles was there to help her inside.

Lorna came to the side of the carriage and took the boys by the hand to keep them away from the wheels. "I'm glad you called. And thank you for the gifts."

"You're most welcome." Elaine's glance slid past her to Benteen, standing silently. "We'll meet again," she said, then brought her gaze back to Lorna. "I'm confident of that."

As the carriage pulled away from the cabin, Lorna watched it for a few minutes, then turned to Benteen. "Why didn't you tell her good-bye?"

He seemed to drag his gaze from the sight of the carriage rolling onto the limitless plains. "I already had," he stated, and swung away from her and the boys.

"Where are you going?" She frowned at his abruptness.

But Benteen didn't answer as his long-legged strides carried him from her. She lost sight of him when he walked behind the shed-barn to the corral where the horses were kept. A few minutes later, she saw him riding out.

Over by the area they called the Broken Buttes, Benteen found Zeke Taylor dousing a cow with a bad case of screwworms. Kerosene fumes made the air pungent. Benteen reined his horse to a halt and stayed on the sidelines as Zeke untied the cow's feet and made a run for his horse. It was a zigzagging race, with Zeke dodging to avoid the hooking horns of the ungrateful cow when it charged him. After its initial rush missed him, the cow took off into the broken country, its tail sticking straight up in the air.

Zeke walked his horse over to Benteen. "Hot day," he said, and removed his hat to wipe the sweat from his forehead with the back of his arm.

"Find Woolie and Bob Vernon," Benteen

ordered. "Pass the word that I want the three of you to meet me first thing in the morning. You might want to shave. We're riding into town."

"It can't be payday already." Zeke frowned in an attempt to recall the number of days since the last one.

"It isn't." Benteen wheeled his horse to the side and spurred it into a lope.

Zeke sat there for a minute, wondering what was in Benteen's craw. He wasn't concerned by the failure to explain what he wanted with him and the others, but he usually offered a man some cigarette makin's.

Lorna had supper ready a little before dark. When Benteen didn't return, she went ahead and fed the boys and tucked them into bed. She kept the food warm another hour, then fixed herself a plate. She lost count of the number of times she went to the door and looked out into the night. Finally she took the food off the stove and changed into her nightdress.

With Benteen gone, she couldn't sleep. She sat in bed with her knees hunched up and her arms clasped around them, rocking a little in an attempt at self-comfort. Filtering through the chinked walls of the cabin were the muted cries of nightbirds. The loneliness of the place seemed to shiver over her.

The slowly building echo of horse's hooves began to separate from the thudding beat of her heart. It had to be Benteen. Lorna sprang from the bed and pushed aside the curtained wall to run barefoot to the door. She had a glimpse of a rider's silhouette against an indigo-dark sky before it was gobbled up by the shadow of the barn-shed.

Shutting the door, Lorna hurried to the stove and stoked its fire, then set the food back on it to warm. She heard the faint jingle of spurs as Benteen approached the cabin. The anxiety she had felt, not knowing where he was, changed to a kind of irritated relief when he walked in the door.

"I waited supper as long as I could," she said. "It'll take me a few minutes to warm it up for you."

He stopped inside the door to remove his gunbelt and hang his hat on the wooden peg. Without looking at her, Benteen raked a hand through his hair and crossed the room to the crude shelves that served as cupboards.

"I'm not hungry," he said, and reached to the back of the top shelf, taking down the bottle of whiskey and a glass.

It was the flatness of his voice coupled with the whiskey bottle that made Lorna stare. He walked to the table and dragged out a chair. With his feet propped on the table, Benteen uncorked the bottle and filled the glass half-full of whiskey. While Lorna watched, he downed most of it and stared at the map hanging on the cabin wall. She had never seen him like this before.

"Benteen, what's wrong?" she murmured.

His flicking glance barely met her eyes. "Nothing. It's late. You'd better go to bed." As he spoke, he refilled the glass with whiskey.

"But —"

"Just leave me alone," he demanded tiredly.

After a long moment's hesitation, Lorna didn't attempt to probe for an explanation of his behavior. She took the food off the stove and put the dishes away. Benteen didn't answer when she told him good night. She had the feeling he hadn't heard her.

It was a long time before she fell asleep. The lamp continued to burn, shedding light on the canvas partition. When she woke up the next morning, the pillow next to hers was smooth. She found Benteen slumped over the table, the whiskey bottle more than half-empty.

24

The four riders rode into Miles City at a shuffling trot. Benteen split away from Woolie, Zeke, and Bob Vernon as they turned their horses into the hitchrack in front of the land office. There were two ways of acquiring title to land under the Homestead Act. One required a five-year residence and improvements, while the second, called commuting, gave title after six months and payment of $1.25 an acre. Woolie, Zeke, and Bob were about to "commute" their claims. It had taken a chunk out of Benteen's ready cash, but it was a quick, sure way of stopping Judd Boston's plans.

Benteen dismounted at the newspaper office and tied his horse to the rack. A couple of soldiers from the fort walked by, but the dusty street was relatively quiet on the August day. He looked across the street to the row of angular buildings. The sign on one read "The First Texas Bank of Montana," the one owned by Judd Boston.

His spurs clinked as he walked into the newspaper office, breathing in the strong smell of ink. A mustached man seated at a desk looked up with an absent frown, then stood with a certain briskness.

"Can I help you?"

"Yes, I want to put an advertisement in your newspaper," Benteen replied.

The man reached for a paper and pen. His hands appeared to be permanently stained with ink. "Just tell me how you want it to read and I'll write it down for you."

" 'I, Benteen Calder, do hereby notify the public that I claim all the land . . .' " He described boundaries that encompassed more than a half a million acres.

After he had finished, the pen continued to scratch across the paper for a few seconds more. Then the newspaperman read it back to him to be sure he'd gotten it all. He looked at Benteen and gave a wry shake of his head.

"These damn things always read like a legal notice," he declared.

"Legal or not, they work," Benteen replied. "How much do I owe you?"

The advertisement was one of many land-grabbing tactics practiced in the West. Such claims of stock range had no basis in law, but ranchers observed such statements of owner-ship by fellow ranchers. Where no law existed, they created their own code. It was another occasion when the Golden Rule came into play: you respect another man's claim to boundaries, and he'll respect yours.

As Benteen left the newspaper office, he noticed a man hurrying into the bank at a running walk. He took his time untying the bridle reins and stepping into the saddle, but the man didn't come out. He walked his horse down the street to the land office where the Triple C horses stood slung-hipped in the shade. Reining his horse to the end post, he swung down. There seemed to be a heated discussion going on inside the building — angry voices carrying out to the street. Zeke was fixing to grab the short man behind the counter by the shirt collar when Benteen walked in.

"What's the problem here?" Despite the low pitch of his voice, the demand stopped all movement. The land clerk behind the counter was wet with a nervous sweat as he glanced uneasily at the three angry cowboys.

"This puny pen-pusher is tryin' to stall us," Woolie complained with a contemptuous fling of his hand.

"Yeah," Zeke chimed in. "The sonuvabitch is sayin' he can't find the records we filed on our land."

From the back of the building there was the

sound of a door being opened and closed. Someone had come in through the rear entrance.

"I'm not saying I don't have them," the agent said. "They seem to be mislaid. I can't take your money until they're found. Maybe if you came back later —"

"There he goes again," Zeke flared.

"Why don't you let us help you look for them?" Bob Vernon suggested.

"These are private government records." The agent shook his head. "I can't let just anyone go through them without authorization." A man appeared in the doorway to a back office and motioned to the agent that he wanted a word with him. He looked very much like the man Benteen had seen hurrying into the bank a few minutes ago.

"You know those records are here, Benteen," Woolie said. "You want us to take the place apart? We'll find 'em."

"I don't think it will be necessary," he murmured as he watched the two men conferring in whispers. A set of papers was passed to the agent. "I have the feeling it's already been straightened out."

The agent returned to the counter with the papers in hand. "Here's the records." He smiled tightly. "Just misplaced, that's all."

With the filing records verified, the cash payments were made and title given to the three 160-acre parcels. The cowboys promptly signed the land over to Benteen.

"I was a landowner for five minutes," Woolie declared. "Don't that call for a drink, Benteen?"

"Why not?" he agreed, but paused as the three cowboys headed for the door and the waiting saloon. Benteen glanced at the agent. "Be sure and give my regards to Judd Boston the next time you see him." The man paled and stammered around for an answer as Benteen walked out the door.

Montana's Ten Bar ranch house was made of logs and board planks, more compact and without the luxuries of its Texas counterpart. Judd Boston sat back in a cowhide-covered chair and contemplated the shape of one of the duke's cigars. Loman Janes helped himself to a shot of whiskey from the decanter sitting on the small round table.

"I'd sure as hell like to know how Calder found out about it," Boston muttered aloud.

"Are you sure Giles didn't know about your plans?" Loman questioned. "You know he's got ideas about that Calder woman. Maybe he's tryin' to get in good with her."

"The only way he could have known it is if the duke had told him. George swears he didn't discuss it with anyone else. The man may be a pompous ass, but he's not a liar." He clamped the cigar between his teeth and puffed on it. "I don't know how he got wind of it."

"Maybe you'd better send Webster a telegram tellin' him to hold off buyin' all those cattle you were fixin' on bringing up here until we find some range to put 'em on," Janes suggested. "This place won't support that number. If they made it through a winter, they'd still have it grazed to the roots in a year."

"Grass isn't the problem. It's water." Boston knew that from his experience in Texas. "And I'm not sending any telegram to Webster rescinding my order. We've still got time to find some land. It would have been straightforward and clean if we could have picked up those three claims of Calder's. I wish that land belonged to anyone but him."

"Why should we care?" A puzzled and wary look crossed Janes's face. The comment smacked of fear, and he had no time for a man who showed yellow.

"If I go after his land after that business with his father, he's liable to take it personal.

508

I've had my fill of vendettas."

"Vendetta? Never heard of it." Janes frowned.

"It's a killing feud between families." His name hadn't always been Boston, but that was part of the buried past. "Maybe I can buy a couple of his water rights."

"He'd be a fool to sell." Loman Janes shook his head at the thought. "Why should he? He's got no reason to sell when he can use it himself."

"He might if he suddenly needed money," Boston suggested, and thoughtfully tapped the ash from the cigar. "A man never knows when the sky might fall in on him. It could happen even when it's looking the brightest."

Loman Janes was relieved to hear that kind of talk. For a minute he thought he had misjudged Boston. He didn't respect a man who turned from a fight, but Boston was just being cautious. Loman knew about feuds. His family came from Tennessee, so he didn't see why Boston thought it was something to be avoided. But Boston was the brains of the outfit.

"What do you want done?" Loman asked, and downed the balance of the whiskey in his glass.

Boston took a puff on his cigar. "Got a match?"

Line camps were outposts of the ranch, forming an invisible perimeter to be ridden by cowboys unlucky enough to be assigned the lonely job. The Triple C was already too big to be manned solely from the central ranch quarters that the cowboys had already dubbed the Homestead. Since cattle had no notion of boundaries and had roaming tendencies, line riders formed a kind of living fence, patrolling between their camp and the next one up or down the line. They held in their own cattle and turned back the neighbor's.

It had been a while since Benteen had checked on Shorty. He rode into the prevailing wind, blowing hot, dry air from the southwest. He could smell the smoke from Shorty's campfire when he was still two miles away.

Benteen wasn't sure the exact moment when he realized the bruise on the southern sky wasn't gathering stormclouds. It was billowing smoke. The dry grasses of the plains had become a vast tinderbox, making them ripe for fire.

He whipped his horse into a flat-out run, racing straight for the growing clouds of black smoke. The red line of the fast-creeping flames was in sight when he spied Shorty trying to drive a crazed bunch of Longhorns across a creek. It was the only place that offered a natural firebreak for miles. Benteen swung his horse toward the creek to lend Shorty a hand.

Six of the steers took off, and they had to let them go in order to get the other forty-odd head across the creek. Once they had the cattle on the other side, they continued to drive them, gathering more animals as they went along — coyotes, rabbits, antelopes. A mile and a half from the creek, they left the herd to circle back to make another sweep for any cattle they may have missed.

A haze of smoke and ash filled the air to choke them. Benteen tied his bandanna around his nose and mouth to filter out some of it. The wind seemed stronger, the heat from the fire creating its own draft.

He shouted to Shorty, "I don't think the creek will stop it! The wind's too strong!"

Shorty nodded and pointed to Benteen's right. A finger of smoke was rising from the grassy bank on this side of the creek. From the smoke, a tongue of flame shot up and began devouring the dry grass.

"We'll never hold it here without help!" Benteen waved Shorty away from the creek.

About a mile away, a jumble of rocks had

been thrust from the earth. Its natural barrier would flank the wildfire on one side. Benteen pulled in his horse and brought it to a plunging halt. The bandanna had fallen to his chin.

"Here comes Barnie and Ramon!" Shorty called to draw Benteen's attention to the riders galloping into view.

"Shoot a couple of those steers," Benteen ordered, and reached for the rope tied to his saddle.

Shorty wheeled his horse after a small group of bawling steers trotting away from the smell of smoke. Benteen watched Shorty ride up to the first steer and drop it with a pistol shot through the back of the head. Almost able to feel the heat of the fire, Benteen glanced over his shoulder to see the steadily advancing red glow. The black smoke nearly blocked out the sun as it filled the sky, towering above them with ominous intent. He rode over to the two dead steers to lend Shorty a hand.

The steers were skinned on one side and ropes were tied to two of their feet. When Barnie and the Mexican vaquero, Ramon, reached them, all Shorty had to do was hand them each a rope. They galloped off, dragging the bloody carcass of the steer to the fire line. Benteen and Shorty mounted their horses and wrapped the free end of the ropes around their saddle horns and took off with the second carcass, dragged between them.

When they reached the narrow line of flames, Benteen jammed his spurs into the panicking chestnut and leaped the horse over the fire onto the hot and blackened ground. Running parallel with the flames, he was on one side and Shorty was on the other. The bloody-wet carcass was towed down the length of the flames, smothering it dead as it went.

The heat was blistering, drying the sweat from his body the instant it reached his skin. He choked from the smoke, his lungs straining for air. There was no thinking, only doing. The fire had to be stopped. The stench of burning blood and air was powerful.

Benteen and Shorty had to frequently change sides so the horses wouldn't be crippled by prolonged running on the burned earth. When it seemed they would ride in this fiery hell forever, the flames were out. Benteen unwrapped the ropes around the saddle horn and let it fall, leaving behind the charred remains of the steer. The four riders came together in a small cluster and let their trembling horses rest. Their faces and clothes were blackened with smoke and ash, its smell hanging heavy on them. Benteen took a long drink from his canteen. The water in it was hot, but it was wet.

"How many cattle do you figure we lost?" His voice was a croaking sound, and he took another drink.

"Fifty . . . a hundred head. Maybe more," Shorty answered. "I know there was a big bunch trapped in a draw."

Barnie was having trouble gathering enough spit to lick his cigarette paper together. Finally he gave up and carried it to his mouth, indifferent to the tobacco spilling out. He felt around in his pockets, then looked at the others.

"Anybody got a light?" he asked.

"You serious?" Shorty stared. "If you want to smoke, just breathe in, you stupid sonuvabitch."

Benteen was too tired to laugh.

Webb ran ahead of him to the cabin, hardly able to see where he was going with Benteen's hat falling down around his ears. He pushed the door open, then turned to wait.

"Mommy!" Webb called as the hat turned askew. "Daddy's home an' he's all black. Come quick an' see!"

The door was opened the rest of the way by Lorna, who came in response to her son's call. Astonishment wiped the slight frown from her forehead as she stared at him with her mouth opened.

"There was a prairie fire," Benteen explained his appearance. "We managed to put it out."

"Are you all right?" A little shiver broke the motionless grip of surprise. She moved toward him, her hands raising hesitantly to touch him. "You looked charred."

"It's just smoke and ash," he assured her tiredly. "It will wash off."

Her fingers came away smudged when she touched his shirt. Satisfied he was unhurt, Lorna grimaced at his blackened clothes. "I don't know if that shirt and pants will ever be clean again." She scooped the hat off Webb's head, but it had already left a blackened ring on his forehead. She shooed the little boy into the cabin ahead of them. "Stay clear of your father. I don't want you getting all dirty, too."

She handled his hat gingerly, hanging it on a peg inside the door. Her nose wrinkled at the strong smell of smoke and singed hair that clung to his clothes and skin. It tainted the air in the cabin. Little Arthur took one look at Benteen and let out a squawl of fright, trotting over to hide in Lorna's skirts.

"I know he doesn't look like him, but that's your daddy," Lorna assured the toddler.

"Wait until I get my face and hands washed."

Benteen sent a weary smile to his younger son and crossed the cabin to the washstand. As he filled the basin with water from the pitcher, he noticed the food cooking on the stove. "Supper nearly ready?"

"Yes. We'll eat as soon as you're washed." She picked up two water pails and started for the door.

"Where are you going?" Benteen half-turned.

"To bring some water for your bath," she answered without pausing. "It can be heating while we eat." Little Arthur hurried after, whimpering because the voice belonged to his father but he still wasn't sure it was him. Lorna stopped at the door. "Webb, mind your little brother until I come back."

Webb took his young brother forcefully by the hand and pulled him away from the door. Arthur immediately sent up a loud protest despite Webb's adultlike attempts to shush him.

The soap lather turned into gray-black bubbles when Benteen scrubbed his face. It took repeated soapings before the rinse water washed away clear. When Lorna returned with the buckets filled, he was blotting his stinging eyes. Arthur watched him with a thoughtful finger in his mouth; then a smile split his face.

"Daddy!" He pointed a wet finger at Benteen in happy recognition.

"That's right." Benteen draped the wet towel over a corner of the washstand and bent down to his younger son.

"Don't pick him up," Lorna ordered, dishing up their supper plates. "You've still got that ash all over your clothes."

"Sorry, fella." He rumpled the top of Arthur's hair and took hold of his hand to walk to the table.

After Lorna set the plates on the table, she went back to the stove to put kettles of water on to heat. Benteen and the two boys started eating without her. The food was nearly cold when she finally joined them.

"How did the fire start? Do you know?" she asked.

"No." There was a brief shake of his head. "We'll probably never know. Half a dozen things could have started it."

"Was it bad?" Worry began to set in now that he was safe and looking halfway human again. She had frightening visions of him fighting the fire while it blazed around him.

"Bad enough," he answered. "We won't really know until we've been able to check the burned area."

"I thought I smelled smoke in the wind. Was it to the south?" Her question received an affirmative nod. She shivered a little. "If it had kept burning, it could have reached here."

"'It's out. Barnie and Shorty are camping there to make sure no hot spots flare up," Benteen said to assure her there was no further danger.

"Do me and Arthur have to have a bath?" Webb asked, ready to make a face of protest.

"Not tonight," Lorna replied. "We're just going to clean up your smelly father." She glanced at his plate. "Don't forget to eat your potatoes."

When supper was through, Lorna dragged out the squat, oblong tub and positioned it in front of the stove. She alternated filling it with buckets of water and the heated water from the kettles. While Benteen shed his smoky clothes, she put the boys to bed. She carried the pile of smelly clothes outside and hung them over the clothesline that ran from a corner of the cabin to a tree so they could air.

When she returned, Benteen was sitting in the short tub with his knees bent, letting the medium-hot water soak his tired body. Fatigue drooped his muscled shoulders and closed his eyes. He was making no effort to soap himself down.

"You'll never get clean that way," Lorna remarked, and moved to the side of the tub.

"Do I have to wash behind your ears the way I do the boys?"

"Good idea," he murmured without opening his eyes, and lifted his hand from the water to give her the bar of soap.

"Let's start at the top and wash your hair first." It reeked of smoke as she knelt beside the tub. Her hand curved itself to the back of his neck, feeling the taut, sinewy cords. Reluctantly Benteen shifted his position in the water and yielded to the pressure of her hand that forced his head underwater. She lathered it hard with the strong soap. There was a wiry feel to the ends of his hair where it had been partially singed by the extreme heat. Lorna shivered inwardly again, realizing how very close he must have been to the fire. Then she was forcing his head underwater again to rinse out the soap.

Wiping the soapy water from his eyes, Benteen resumed his former position in the tub. "I think you did that on purpose to wake me up," he accused.

"I just want to be sure you're alive." Her voice had a husky pitch. She lathered a cloth to scrub his back.

His flesh was solid beneath her rubbing hand, even with the powerful muscles at rest. After bathing the boys so many times, it was a novel experience to have the full-grown width of a man's tapering back to wash. There was a slight play of muscle as he resisted the pressure of her hand, pushing against it. It became important to cover every inch of his spine and shoulders. Lorna didn't realize how much time she was taking to wash the back of one shoulder until she happened to catch the gleam in his dark eye. Suddenly self-conscious, she made a couple more swipes at it, then attempted to briskly hand him the soapy washcloth.

"Don't stop now," Benteen murmured. "I was just beginning to enjoy it."

"I think you can do the rest," she tried to insist.

"I'd much rather you did it," he replied, and leaned against the back of the oblong tub.

The look in his eyes made her warm. She felt a little bit naughty, pleasantly so, as she began soaping his flatly muscled chest with its dark crown of hairs. She stole a glance at his face and saw that he was enjoying it. His ease at having someone else bathe him made her wonder.

"Has anyone else given you a bath before?" Lorna asked with more than just curiosity. "Other than your mother, of course."

Benteen seemed to stiffen under her touch. With guilt?

"Why do you say that?"

"Because you don't act like this is the first time." Her scrubbing motions became brisk, a little jealousy showing as she washed the flexed muscles of his arm. "How about that time in Dodge City when you claimed you took a bath at one of the saloons? Maybe you had one of the ladies scrub your back." She remembered the brass token she'd found in his bedroll, and she began rubbing harder.

"Hey!" Benteen protested her roughness and caught hold of her wrist, water dripping from his hand. Her dark eyes were snapping when she met his puzzled gaze. "Whatever gave you that idea?"

"Does the name Miss Belle mean anything?" She hadn't forgotten the name printed on the token.

His frown deepened. "Not a thing. Why do you think it should?"

"Because I found a dollar token in your bedroll with her name on it, and portrait." Lorna confronted him with her knowledge and dared him to deny the evidence. "And you know you stayed out late both nights we were in Dodge City."

"Do you think I spent those nights in the

company of some other woman?" His eyes narrowed.

"How else did you get the token?" she challenged.

"It's accepted as coin. I probably got it back in change when I paid for the drinks I had at the saloon on one of those evenings," he said. "No woman gave it to me. I was trying to get myself drunk enough not to want you."

"Is that true?" She had drawn warily back from the tub to study him.

A hardness flickered across his expression. "I can't prove it, if that's what you're asking."

"You wanted to make love to me and I . . ." Lorna stopped, not wanting to remember why she had been so reluctant to have him touch her. It was best left in the past. "You could have gone to another woman to satisfy your needs."

"Perhaps." There was a grimness to his mouth. "But it so happens since the night I undressed my bride, I haven't been interested in the satisfaction some other female might provide. It seems you have done too good a job at that."

There was an underlying thread of anger in his voice that seemed at odds with his assertion. "Why does that upset you?" She frowned.

"Because . . ." His wet hand pulled her back to the edge of the tub as his other hand came up to grip the nape of her neck. ". . . I can't get enough of you." He breathed the words into her mouth, filling her with the heat of his desire.

His hands tried to draw her closer, attempting to arch her against him despite the barrier of the tub. A responsive need clamored within Lorna, turning her body pliant to his will while her pulse raced. His mouth traveled in a series of rough kisses over her face and throat. In a brief moment of sensibility, she felt the spreading dampness of her dress.

"You're getting me all wet," she murmured in halfhearted protest.

"Take it off, then." His fingers partially unfastened the back of her dress and impatiently pushed it off her shoulders so his lips could explore their round curves.

With trembling hands Lorna tried to unfasten the rest of it. "What about the boys?" She breathlessly reminded Benteen of the lack of privacy, willing to let it be his decision.

"They're sleeping." He barely gave her time to slide the dress down her hips before his hands were tugging at the chemise that hid her breasts from him. "Get in the tub with me," he insisted huskily.

"There's not room for both of us. It's too small." She attempted to laugh at his suggestion, but the stimulating caress of hands turned it into a moaning sound.

"You just come here and I'll show you how we can fit in it."

It wasn't until the next day that Benteen realized how close the fire had come to causing total devastation. The wind could have driven the fire across his entire range if they hadn't caught it early. Instead, it had taken only a portion of the southwest section. But it had hurt him. About thirty head of cattle had been killed outright by the fire, and another two hundred of his blooded breeding stock had been burned so badly they had to be destroyed.

When the last rifle shot faded into silence, Benteen looked at the scene of an entire herd put down and felt a helpless anger. It jumped along his jawline as he turned to push his rifle into the scabbard. The barrel was still hot.

"It could have been worse," Barnie reminded him in consolation.

"Yeah," he admitted gruffly. "It could have been worse." He swung into the saddle and turned the horse toward Shorty. "Make a sweep and drift the cattle into one of the other sections."

"Want me to build another line camp?" Shorty asked. The fire had taken the one he'd been staying in, as well as his few belongings that weren't on his horse.

"No. We'll wait till next summer when the grass grows back." He turned his gaze on the blackened stretch of plains. "When you're through here, move on back to the bunkhouse."

The sun was hanging low in the sky when he rode his horse up to the shed-corral and dismounted. His mood remained grimly somber as he unsaddled his horse to turn it into the corral. Everything had been going smoothly until his mother turned up – Lady Crawford, he corrected with curling bitterness. There had been nothing but trouble since. He shook that idea away as unreasonable. She couldn't be blamed for Judd Boston's attempt to have the three claims thrown out, or for the prairie fire.

There was a leadenness to his strides as he crossed the yard to the cabin. The table was all set for supper when he walked in. Lorna was at the stove, dishing up the food. She sent him a quick smile over her shoulder.

"I timed it just perfectly for a change," she said, and carried two plates to the table for the boys.

There was a shine to her face, an eagerness that he hadn't noticed recently. She seemed excited about something.

Benteen walked to the basin to wash his hands while she sat the boys at the table. "What's up?"

"Nothing," she replied, then added, "There's a note on the table for you."

Shaking the water off his hands, he partially turned to glance at the table as he groped for a towel to dry them. A small square slip of paper was on the table by his chair.

"Who's it from?"

"Lady Crawford. Mr. Giles came by with it this afternoon." Once she started talking, it all rushed out. "I thought it was just a note to thank us for the other afternoon, so I went ahead and opened it."

He stiffened, pausing in the act of drying his hands. "What did it say?"

"She wrote to say that she's staying at the Macqueen House in Miles City and asked if we could call on her Friday afternoon."

"Is that all?" His gaze narrowed slightly to study her expression.

"Read the note." Lorna picked it up from the table and carried it to him. "I can't think of any reason why we shouldn't accept the invitation. We'd be going there in a month or so anyway."

The message contained in the note was what Lorna had told him, and nothing more — with one exception. It was addressed to him.

"This isn't a social invitation, Lorna." Benteen folded it up and slipped it into his pocket. "She wants to speak to me on a business matter."

"What kind of business?" Confusion clouded her eyes. "Why would she want to speak to you about it?"

"She indicated she was interested in investing some of her capital in a ranching venture," he said, and walked past her to the table.

No more was said until Lorna had dished their plates and carried them to the table. "Are you going to meet her?" she asked.

"It depends." He shrugged. "I might not be able to get away."

"I think you should," Lorna insisted. "It's an honor that she —"

"Lorna." His teeth were ground together in the effort to speak calmly. "I don't want to discuss it any further. If I'm not busy, I'll go. But if I'm needed at the ranch, Lady Crawford will just have to look to someone else."

When she heard the knock on the door to her suite, Elaine smiled at her reflection in the mirror with satisfaction. She touched a finger to the high ruffed collar of her black dress, aware that it attractively concealed the lines in her neck. She waited until her personal maid came to inform her that a Mr. Benteen Calder was in the sitting room.

"Thank you, Hilda. That will be all. I won't be needing you the rest of the afternoon," Elaine dismissed her.

"Very good." She curtsied and silently withdrew.

By coming here, Benteen had already given her his answer. He would agree to her plans, and Elaine knew it. The note had been a test — to see if he was willing to make an effort to see her. If his hatred had run as deep as he claimed, he wouldn't be in the sitting room now.

When she entered, Benteen was standing at the window with his hat in his hand. She read the impatience and anger in his stance, the regret that he had come. Her smile came and went quickly so that she met him with a calm expression when he turned.

"Would you care for some coffee?" She waved a graceful hand to the coffee service on the table between blue velvet sofas. "Or there's something stronger in the cabinet, if you prefer."

"Nothing," he refused.

His dark eyes were running over her, probing, inspecting, and seeking. Elaine permitted a small smile to warm her lips and motioned for him to sit down while she lowered herself onto one of the sofas and arranged her skirts.

"You won't be sorry you came, Benteen," she murmured. "This is going to be the beginning of a new relationship for us."

"You said you had a business proposition you wanted to make," Benteen reminded her.

"Yes. Business," Elaine agreed. "By the way, I understand you have secured title to those three claims. Congratulations. I knew you'd take care of it. Mr. Boston isn't too pleased. He's buying a lot of cattle and suddenly has nowhere to put them."

"That's his problem."

"He might make it yours, but that's another matter entirely, and not at all what you came here to discuss." She leaned forward and poured herself a cup of coffee. "Would you be interested in obtaining a beef contract to purchase all the cattle you can supply at a price that would average above market value?"

"A contract with whom?"

"I can't tell you that — not yet," she chided him for trying to get such valuable information

529

from her. "It's my leverage to persuade you to become my partner in the venture. If I told you my connection, you might try to cut me out of the deal."

"My own mother?" he taunted.

"Yes. You could regard it as a way of getting revenge," Elaine reasoned. "It would never have worked between myself and your father. And he would have killed me before he would have let me take his son." There was a slight pause before she added, "I believe you wanted an explanation."

"And you have absolutely no regrets," Benteen challenged.

"Regrets? No." She shook her head. "The regret would have been much greater if I had stayed. I would have never forgiven you or your father for keeping me there when I could have become somebody." She sipped her coffee, delicately raising her little finger. "I am ambitious – just like you are, Benteen."

"How many cattle will I need for this beef contract you claim you can get?" He returned to the original topic.

"More than you own," Elaine replied. "That's where I can help again by financing the purchase of additional cattle."

"And?"

"And we'll split the profits on the contract fifty-fifty."

"It sounds fair." He leaned against the sofa back and studied her with half-lidded eyes. "But how do I know that at the end of the deal you won't take all the money and run away?"

"Because I have learned over the years that you can cheat on your husband, you can cheat on your lover, and you can cheat on the household account – but you never, never cheat on a business deal." Behind her facetious tone, she was quietly serious.

"What's to stop me from keeping all the money?" There was a slant of mockery to his hard mouth.

"That absurd code you men live by, and twist to suit your own needs. If you give your word on something, you won't back out," she stated confidently. "But you really have nothing to lose. I have to produce the contract and the money to buy the additional cattle. I'll make you rich, Benteen. Is it a deal?" She held out her hand.

There was a long moment when Elaine thought she might have pushed for an agreement too soon. Then he was moving, reaching out to enfold her hand in the largeness of his. He continued to hold it, studying her.

"Why? Is it just the money?" His voice

was low, demanding.

"It's the challenge of making it," Elaine replied. "I know it's supposed to be a man's prerogative, but it isn't exclusively yours."

"Why did you pick me? Why not someone like Judd Boston? Was it guilt?"

Elaine set her cup on the table and pressed her hand over the roughness of his. "I picked you because we are so much alike. There's no stopping us, Benteen." There was an avid quality to the husky pitch of her voice. "Well?"

"It's a deal, " he agreed, but without her enthusiasm. He was more guarded, still wary. Elaine wasn't concerned by that. It would pass in time. "Who's going to be buying the beef?"

"Your neighbor to the north. Canada." She explained about the railroad construction, the reservation Indians, and the outposts the Canadian government would need to keep supplied with beef. She was careful to be ambiguous about her connection through which she would arrange the contract.

"Where will you be while all this is taking place?" Benteen asked. "I suppose you'll be traveling on with your English friends back to London."

"No, I won't be returning to London. As a matter of fact, the Duke of Middleton and his party have already left for the Dakota

Territory." This time when Elaine poured more coffee, Benteen accepted a cup. "I'll be staying here. This venture is just the beginning for us."

"I thought you ran away to have some of the glitter and the gaiety of society," he baited. "Are you coming full circle back to a cow town?"

"It's full circle, perhaps, but I'm coming back in style," she reminded him. "Besides, the glitter and gaiety excites young, beautiful women – like your wife. It palls, if there is nothing to stimulate the mind." He hadn't liked the reference to his young wife. "It must be extremely lonely out there for Lorna. She needs someone to keep her company when you're away. When did you say the house would be completed?"

"This winter, although we'll probably be able to move into a portion of the house this fall." He drank down a swallow of coffee. "The cabin's becoming cramped with two small boys running around."

"But it won't seem nearly as empty as that house if your wife is alone in it," Elaine pointed out. Someone knocked at the door. "I've dismissed the maid for the afternoon. Would you answer it?" She sipped at her coffee while Benteen went to the door. There was a long moment of silence after he opened it. Elaine turned to look over the back of the sofa. "Mr. Giles. Come in."

Benteen stepped out of the way to allow the broadly built man to enter the sitting room. Bull Giles's glance swept the room as if looking for someone else before he stopped beside the sofa.

"What is it?" she prompted.

"You asked me to bring you that reply to your telegram as soon as it came in." He handed her the wire.

"Thank you, Mr. Giles." Elaine glanced at it only to ascertain that it was from her late husband's cousin in Canada; then she slipped it between the seat cushions. "That will be all for now."

After tipping his hat to her, he turned and walked out. Benteen shut the door and returned to his seat. "I thought he was guiding your English friends."

"I asked him to come to work for me," she replied.

"Why?"

"Because I have a use for him. It isn't wise for a woman to go out alone in this country without a bodyguard or escort of some kind. Mr. Giles suits my purpose."

"He's worked for Judd Boston in the past," Benteen said.

"Yes, I know. But his loyalties lie elsewhere now," Elaine assured him. "Is there a reason you don't like him?"

"No." His answer was clipped, which indicated he was concealing something.

The Big Dipper was swinging down to its midnight position when Benteen rode into the main ranch quarters. The big house on the hill was silvered by the moonlight, an imposing sight in this land.

A light burned in the cabin, waiting for his return. When he left that morning, Benteen hadn't told Lorna where he was going. A dozen times or more he'd been on the verge of turning his horse back to the ranch. There had been a hundred reasons to let his mother wait for him at the hotel and not show up. And there hadn't been a single reason that made sense for him to keep the meeting. Right up to the moment he knocked on the door, he hadn't made up his mind whether or not to see her again.

Doubts, uncertainties, distrust, continued to plague him about her, yet he had agreed to the proposed partnership in her business venture. As far as anyone else was concerned, that was the only connection between them for the time being — until he was clear in his mind about this woman who had borne him.

535

25

It was after hours and the bank was closed. Judd Boston sat behind the big mahogany desk in his private office and went over the day's transactions while Loman Janes prowled the room with an animal's intolerance for confinement. Boston peered at him once and continued with his paperwork.

"S'pose he don't come?" Loman finally broke the silence.

"He'll come." Boston didn't look up to answer. "Curiosity will bring him, just to hear what I have to say."

"It would have been simpler if you'd just had me fetch him here. Save all this waitin'," Janes declared.

Boston didn't respond. As good as Loman Janes was at his job, the man thought with his muscle. He would have welcomed an all-out war with Calder over possession of the range. It didn't occur to him that Boston needed the goodwill and support of his fellow ranchers if his bank wanted to keep their business. A range war meant people taking sides. Accounts would be lost, the bank business would suffer, and a lot of unwanted notoriety would come his way.

Sometimes his foreman's lack of imagination was irritating. When the prairie fire hadn't done as much damage as they had hoped, he had wanted to set another. The last thing Boston wanted was Calder's suspicions aroused. Some loss had been sustained because of the fire. It was time to create more losses through other means. And in ways that would be difficult to trace back to Boston. He needed cattle range — not a war.

There was a knock at the rear door of the bank. A gleam of satisfaction appeared in Judd Boston's eyes when he met Loman's glance. "Go let Giles in," he ordered.

A few minutes later Janes ushered the bull-necked man into the office. Boston sent him a brief glance and returned to his paperwork.

"Have a seat, Giles. I'll be through here in a few minutes," he said. "Pour him a drink, Janes." The wait was deliberate, giving Giles time to settle comfortably in the big leather chair facing the desk and have a drink of bonded whiskey.

"The king is in his counting house, counting out his money," Giles recited when Boston set the books aside and lit a cigar. "And the knave

. . ." He paused to throw a look at Loman Janes, but the meaning of the word escaped the foreman. "You wanted to see me, Boston?"

"Yes." He leaned back in his chair. "I admit I was surprised when you quit the duke's party. But I guess you wanted to stay close by."

"If that's all you wanted to talk to me about . . ." Giles set the unfinished glass of whiskey on the desk and made to rise.

"The Calder woman is still a touchy subject with you, isn't it?" Boston observed, and waved him into his chair. "Sit down. There's something I'd like you to do for me."

"I've already got a job, Boston." Giles sat back in the chair.

"Yes, I understand you're employed by Lady Crawford. The hardships of traveling proved to be too much for her, I was told." It seemed a curious and abrupt decision to Boston, but those English aristocrats had their own peculiarities. "She plans to rest here for a month or so before journeying on by more comfortable modes of transportation, I believe."

"If that's what you heard, I guess it's so." Bull Giles didn't commit himself one way or the other.

"Did you introduce her to Calder?"

There was a slight twist of his thin mouth. "I suppose the duke passed that information on to you. All I know is, she met Mrs. Calder before." He didn't mention the private meeting she'd had with Benteen in her hotel suite. That was something he still hadn't figured out.

"Unless you're at her beck and call every minute, I'm sure you have a lot of free time," Boston suggested. "The task I'd like you to do for me won't take you more than a day or two."

"What is this 'task'?"

"I understand you know a man named Big Ed Sallie." He leaned forward to leisurely tap the ash from his cigar.

A quick frown chased across his forehead as Bull Giles glanced from Boston to Loman Janes and back. "Yeah, I know him. What about it?"

"I want you to contact this Sallie and arrange a meeting between him and Mr. Janes."

There was a narrowing of his eyes as he demanded, "Why?"

"I don't see that it's any of your business," Boston replied, but he sensed that Giles wouldn't cooperate unless he was given a logical reason why he wanted the meeting. "Actually, it's a simple matter of bribery. As I understand, if anyone has influence over the Indians, it's Big Ed Sallie and his bunch of white renegades up on the Missouri. I'm hoping Janes will be able to persuade him to keep the Indians from raiding the Ten Bar."

"Is that all?" Giles questioned.

"That's a great deal, if it can be accomplished," Boston stated. "Can you arrange the meeting?"

"I can't guarantee it. It's been a while since I've seen Big Ed. But I'll give it a try," Giles agreed.

"This agreement is just between us, of course. Strictly private." Boston wanted it understood that Giles wasn't to mention it to anyone else.

"I can see that it wouldn't work if every rancher tried to buy off Big Ed. No one's got that much control over those reservation-jumping Indians. They're going to take somebody's cattle."

"Probably Calder's," Boston said. "Does that bother you?"

"No. Why should it?" Giles lifted his head to a challenging angle, denying that he had any special interest for the Triple C or its mistress.

"You never can tell, Giles. What's bad for Benteen Calder might turn out to be good for you," Boston suggested. "See what you can arrange, and get a message to me."

From the smell of Big Ed Sallie, he hadn't had any contact with water for years. The flopped brim of his hat shadowed the blue of his eyes without concealing their cunning shine. His shaggy, unkempt beard emphasized the jagged scar on his cheek where the hair didn't grow. He wore a buffalo coat, a reminder of his previous profession. Its fur had grown mangy and stank with the odor of whiskey, vomit, and man's sweat.

"Bull said you wanted to talk to me." When his lips pulled back to speak, they showed yellow teeth stained by tobacco juice. He turned his head and spat a yellow stream at the ground.

"I do," Loman confirmed. His icy gray glance slid past Big Ed Sallie to the band of cutthroats sitting their horses in a clump of trees. His glance swung to Bull Giles, who had guided him to this meeting place out in the middle of nowhere. "Your job's done. You can go."

Giles shrugged that it was Janes's funeral and backed his horse a few steps, then reined it in a half-circle to leave. Janes waited until the sound of trotting hooves had receded behind him while continuing to measure the renegade leader with his eyes.

"You must think you're pretty tough." The saddle creaked under Big Ed Sallie as he shifted his weight and rested both hands on the horn. "There's some that might be worried 'bout my friends waitin' over there for me."

"Why should I worry about them when I got a clear shot at you?" Loman called the attempt to bluff him.

Big Ed chortled in his throat, a gleam of respect showing in his eyes. "What is it you want?"

"It's gettin' close to that time of year when the Indians will be comin' to buy your whiskey," Janes began.

"It's illegal to sell whiskey to Indians. I don't know if I like you makin' such a charge against me." Big Ed cocked his head.

"Drunk or sober, an Indian's just as worthless," Janes said. "It's nothin' to me how they spend their money or what they trade for. It's when they go to raidin' ranches that I want to talk to you about."

"I ain't them red-faces' keeper."

"But you sell 'em whiskey, which makes you their friend," Janes reasoned. "If a friend was to tell them that cattle with a Ten Bar brand was no good, they might listen."

"They might." Big Ed thoughtfully rolled the wad of tobacco around in his mouth and spit again, not taking his attention from the pock-faced man.

"And if their friend was to say the Triple C

cattle are worth more than any others, it could be they'd take heed."

"How much are they worth?"

Loman Janes slowly reached backward and lifted the flap of his saddlebag to lift out a leather pouch. He juggled it in his palm a minute to make the gold coins inside rattle against each other; then he tossed it to Big Ed.

"And there'll be a bonus later on when we see how successful you are," Janes said.

"In other words, you're payin' me to rustle Triple C cattle?" Big Ed smiled.

"How could I do that?" he mocked. "You said yourself that you aren't those Indians' keeper. How could anyone blame you if the Indians 'happen' to raid Triple C cattle more than any other ranchers' in the area?"

"Yeah." Big Ed nodded, his smile widening into a grin. "That's right."

When Lorna heard the clatter of the buggy wheels outside the cabin, she ran smoothing hands over her hair and walked quickly to the door. She glanced over her shoulder at the two boys napping on the short cots, then stepped outside.

The buggy had stopped, but Bull Giles still held the reins. Lady Crawford leaned forward in the rear seat when Lorna approached, and inquired, "Where can I find Benteen?"

"He's up the hill." Lorna indicated the house with a nod of her head.

"Thank you." The woman sat back and waved a hand at Giles to order him to drive on.

The breath Lorna released came out in a troubled sigh. She turned and walked slowly back to the cabin door. As she paused on the threshold, her gaze strayed to the hill, where the black buggy stopped in front of the house. She saw Benteen come out and help Lady Crawford down. Then the two of them disappeared inside the house.

It wasn't the first such visit Lady Crawford had made. She'd been to the ranch on two other occasions. Neither time had she visited with Lorna at all, not even briefly. Benteen had explained that he was undertaking a business venture with her, but avoided telling Lorna any details.

But it was more than being excluded from their business conversations that bothered Lorna. It was Benteen's reluctance to discuss anything about Lady Crawford with her. Something was changing him. It seemed to have started that night he'd sat up drinking. He had become preoccupied lately, uncommunicative.

Sighing again, she turned and entered the cabin.

"The house is beginning to take shape quite nicely, isn't it?" Elaine remarked as they walked from the entryway into what would be the study. All the interior walls were up, dividing the house into rooms, and the finish work was under way. "Maybe your wife will be happy once you move into this house."

"What do you mean?" Benteen asked her sharply.

"It doesn't matter." She made a pretense of shrugging aside the thoughtless remark and let her fingers tighten on his arm. "That isn't what I came to talk to you about anyway. When do you anticipate the cattle will be delivered to the government post in Canada?"

"Jessie should get there next week." Benteen stopped and angled his body to face her. "Where did you get the idea Lorna wasn't happy?"

"Call it women's intuition, I suppose. We seem to be able to sense when another member of our sex is unhappy." She finally let her gaze meet Benteen's. "Your wife must have been very young when you married."

"Seventeen, almost eighteen. I wouldn't consider that too young."

"Naturally she was a virgin." When he averted his head, Elaine admonished, "You shouldn't have asked if you didn't want me to speak personally."

"I don't see that it has any bearing," Benteen stated curtly.

"No, men never do." She laughed softly. "You had some experience with women, so you knew what you wanted in a wife. Lorna didn't have that advantage. If she discovers she's made a mistake, she has no more choice than I had."

"There's been no mistake."

"I didn't mean to suggest there had been in your case," Elaine pointed out. "I was only speaking in generalities. Which reminds me. I'd like you to have dinner with me one evening next week. There are two gentlemen that I think you should meet."

"Who are they? Canadians?" He was quick to accept the change in subject.

"No. They are local politicians."

"I'm not interested in becoming involved in politics."

"There are degrees of involvement," she said. "Your father went to the extreme. I'm talking about playing with politics, manipulating people and events to your own interest. You should become familiar with some of the leaders in the territorial government."

"That government might as well not exist." He voiced a sentiment shared by the vast majority of citizens in the territory. "It is a system that the East dreamed up. And they have no idea what it's like out here. Everyone out here ignores it."

"It's feeble," Elaine agreed. "But when Montana achieves statehood, there's no reason why you and I can't have a hand in choosing the first governor. The game of politics is a challenging one that can be highly profitable for the ranch. Look at the beef contract. It never hurts to have influential people in government who owe you favors, Benteen."

"Perhaps." But he wasn't in full agreement on that point.

"The secret is to use them — not be used *by* them."

"You're good at using people, aren't you?" he observed with a narrowed look.

"I'm going to pretend that's a compliment." She smiled and took his arm again to let her gaze survey the room. "I believe this study is going to be my favorite room in your house."

The cabin was filled with the yeasty aroma of baking bread. Lorna sat with her back to the window, using the sunlight so she could see to hand-stitch a shirt for Arthur from the remnants of one of Benteen's.

Her concentration was broken by the knock

547

on the door. She quickly set aside the shirt to answer it, brushing at the flour dust on her muslin apron. But when she opened the door, it was Bull Giles, not Lady Crawford, who stood outside. She relaxed a little, not really disappointed.

"Are the boys here?" he asked.

It had become a habit for him to play with them during Lady Crawford's visits with her husband. Lorna's mouth curved at the irony of the situation. Lady Crawford spent more time with her husband than Lorna sometimes did. And Bull Giles spent more time with the children than Benteen.

"They're taking a nap," she explained, keeping her voice low. "Benteen didn't mention that you would be coming today."

"I brought them each a couple sticks of peppermint." He took them from his pocket and handed them to her. "You can give it to them after supper tonight."

"The boys will love it. Thank you, Bu . . ." She caught herself using his name and quickly corrected it. ". . . Mr. Giles."

"I'd like it if you'd call me Bull," he said quietly.

"That surely isn't your given name."

"No." A sudden twinkle sprang into his eyes. "If you promise never to tell anyone,

548

I'll tell you what it is."

"I promise." She crossed her heart in a child's vow of secrecy.

"Horatio."

"Horatio," she repeated, and felt the bubble of laughter in her voice.

"Disgusting, isn't it?" Bull smiled.

" 'Bull' does suit you better," Lorna agreed, able to smile now that he was.

" 'Lorna' suits you just fine, too," he murmured. When she withdrew from the implied intimacy of his tone, Bull changed it and made a show of sniffing the air. "Is that fresh bread I smell?"

"Yes. I have some loaves baking in the oven."

"Nothing tastes better than hot bread straight out of the oven," he declared.

She laughed quietly. "It should be done in about fifteen minutes. Why don't you come in and have some coffee?" Lorna invited.

"I'd like that, if you're sure it's all right." Bull waited, giving her a chance to reconsider her impulsive offer.

Lorna flashed a glance beyond him at the house on the hill. If Benteen wouldn't tell her anything about what was going on, maybe she could find out from Bull.

"Of course it's all right." She opened the door wider and stepped to the side to let him in. "Have a seat."

While she went to pour the coffee, Bull walked to the chair by the window and picked up the sewing she'd left on the seat. "What are you making?" he asked.

"A new shirt for Arthur. You can put it on the table for now." She paused to peek in the oven at the baking loaves of bread.

He unfolded the shirt and held it up. "It sure is small. My hand won't even fit in the sleeve." He wiggled the three fingers that he was able to slip into the opening.

"Your hand's a lot bigger than his arm." She exchanged the cup of coffee for the shirt.

Bull repositioned the chair so he was sitting parallel to the window and facing the door. His gaze traveled to the two small boys sleeping soundly on the short cots in the far corner of the room.

"I was never around kids very much. I've grown kinda fond of those two," he admitted, and took a sip of the hot coffee.

"They like you a lot, too."

"That Webb is going to be quite a horseman when he grows up. He can practically ride by himself now."

"It isn't really surprising. Benteen took him for his first ride when he was less than a month old." Lorna smiled as she remembered the day.

The mention of Benteen brought her thoughts back to her purpose. "Of course, the ranch has kept him so busy lately he hasn't been able to devote very much time to teaching Webb to ride. He's had to be away a lot because of this business venture with Lady Crawford."

"I know he's been out buying a lot of cattle to fill that Canadian contract," Bull agreed. "It looks like those two are going to make nothing but money."

Lorna had known Benteen had been purchasing cattle and that Jessie had taken a herd to Canada to sell, but she hadn't connected the two to Lady Crawford.

"To tell you the truth, I am a little surprised at how well Benteen is getting along with Lady Crawford. He used to have a low opinion of so-called aristocrats. They're actually becoming friends, I think."

"It really shouldn't come as a surprise," Bull said, studying Lorna thoughtfully. "She's still a beautiful woman. Any normal man would enjoy her company."

"Yes, she still is beautiful" — Lorna's agreement came easily until she read another implication in his words — "although she is considerably older than Benteen."

"Do you think that makes a difference?" he asked with apparent innocence.

"A difference in what?" She was wary, not liking the turn this conversation was taking, yet unable to stop it or direct it onto another course.

"In whether Benteen would be attracted to her," Bull said.

"Do you mean as a woman?" Lorna frowned.

"Yes, as a woman."

She tried to laugh, but the sound had a hollow ring. "Bull, you aren't trying to suggest that they have more than a friendly relationship, are you? That's silly."

"Why?" he wanted to know.

"Because Benteen and I are married." The reason sounded weak.

"It isn't likely a married man would have an affair." But his statement didn't sound like an agreement.

"Benteen wouldn't." She turned to the stove. "The bread should be done." Just as quickly, Lorna pivoted back to face Bull. "Why are you saying these things to me? Why are you trying to create doubts in my mind?"

He held her gaze for a long moment, then stood up to walk to the stove and fill his cup. "Because I've seen them together and you haven't. I've seen the way they look at each other. Whatever it is that's between them, I'd stake my life that it isn't strictly business.

There's something else," he insisted. "And I guess I wanted you to know that there's something more going on. I don't like the idea of somebody hurtin' you."

"I see," she murmured, because there wasn't anything else she could say.

His suggestion that Benteen might be having an affair with Lady Crawford left Lorna stunned. It was a possibility that hadn't occurred to her. The woman was beautiful, elegant, and sophisticated, but Lorna had assumed because she was older than Benteen that he wouldn't regard her in a sexual way. Yet, wasn't it a possible explanation for the way he'd been behaving lately? Why he didn't want to talk to her about Lady Crawford? She tried to reject the idea as preposterous, but it wasn't so easy.

With movements that were automatic, she reached for a towel to protect her hands and removed the tin loaves of bread from the oven. She hardly noticed the way Bull watched her, and she was completely unaware of the frown of hurt confusion on her face.

"I probably shouldn't have said anything," he sighed. "I hope you won't hold it against me."

The look of deep concern on his brutish features prompted her to smile faintly in reassurance. "I don't, Bull." Again she unconsciously used his name.

The door opened, flooding the cabin's interior with sunlight. Benteen's angular build was outlined by it, poised one step inside the cabin. Then he moved out of the glare of the sunlight to hold the door open.

"You left the buggy unattended, Giles." His voice was harsh. "She's ready to leave."

Bull deliberately paused to take one last swallow of coffee before passing Lorna the cup. "Thanks for the coffee, Mrs. Calder."

He walked to the door Benteen was holding open for him, his stride unhurried. The air was charged like it was just before a storm.

When Bull drew level with him, Benteen ordered, "Don't ever set foot inside this cabin again."

There was no response from Bull. His only reaction was a slight break in stride before he continued out the door. Lorna trembled with anger, but she waited until Benteen had closed the door to unleash it.

"How dare you give an order like that?" She tried to keep her voice down, but it vibrated with the fury of her temper. "I invited him in here for coffee. This is my home, too. I can entertain anyone I please."

"No, you can't," Benteen snapped. "Not him."

"Why? Because he's a man," she retorted. "Is it any different than you and Lady Crawford spending all that time alone?"

"You're damned right that's different!"

"Why is it proper for her and not for me?" she demanded.

"Because I said so."

"That isn't good enough!" Lorna hurled angrily. "I'll not be told what to do or who I can have for a friend. Certainly not by you!"

"I happen to be your husband," he reminded her.

"How odd that you should remember that at this particular time," Lorna remarked with biting sarcasm.

"What is that supposed to mean?" Benteen glowered.

"It means you usually only remember that you have a wife when you're hungry, the children are crying, or you feel the urge to make love," she retorted. "Any other time I might as well be a chair, for all the notice you give me."

"Are you saying you aren't happy?"

"No, I'm not happy. Who would be in my place?" Lorna said, thinking of the way he shut her out and wouldn't let her share in his plans.

"That's too damned bad, because you're just going to have to live with your mistake. So don't get any crazy ideas in your head about changing things. This is the way things are going to be, so you might as well learn to live with it."

In the next second, Benteen was slamming the door. Lorna's first impulse was to run after him and demand to have an explanation for that remark, but the banging door had awakened the boys. By the time she had dealt with their cranky whines, Benteen was riding away from the barns.

She stared after him, a determined glint in her eyes. He was wrong. Regardless of what he wanted, there were going to be some changes. If he chose not to include her voluntarily, then it was going to be involuntarily.

She wasn't one of his men to be given orders — or one of his cows to be branded and bred once a year. She was his wife, and he was damned well going to have to realize that.

26

When cattle walk through grass, they push it down behind them in the opposite direction they're walking. A horse pushes the grass forward in the same direction it's going. Reading sign is something a cowboy learns early in his career.

Since the prairie fire had blackened the land and burned out the line camp in the southwest section, Shorty had been shifted back to the central headquarters. He was out riding in the northeast quadrant when he cut the sign of twenty head of cattle being driven away from the ranch by four riders.

Being roundup time, it was possible cowboys from a neighboring ranch had ventured onto Triple C range looking for strayed cattle and were driving them home – except they were riding unshod ponies. The trail was fresh and easy to follow, not more than an hour old. Shorty swung his horse alongside it and pushed the snip-nosed bay into a slow lope.

He scanned the muscular Montana land ahead of him and occasionally looked at the trail to be sure it didn't take any abrupt turns. He wished for his rifle back in the bunkhouse, but it got in the way when he was tending cattle. His pistol was loaded, and he had a spare in the saddlebag. He didn't expect the thieving Indians to make a fight of it. Usually they just scattered across the plains and regrouped elsewhere, then slunk back like a pack of coyotes to raid again.

The country was getting rougher as the trail wound around the jutting base of a butte. When Shorty rounded the point, a bunch of cattle with Triple C brands were spreading out to graze on sun-cured yellow grass. He yanked back on the reins, setting the bay on its haunches.

One minute, there was stillness broken only by the grunting breath of his snorting horse, the jangle of bridle chains, and the groan of his saddle leather. There was no sign of Indians, horses, or riders.

In the span of seconds it took Shorty to absorb the scene, the air was ripped by shrill whoops. There were five of them, coming at him from all sides. As he grabbed for his gun, Shorty wondered how he had missed cutting the fifth rider's sign. He must have been lying to the side.

There wasn't any cover. He was trapped,

flat-out in the open, and they had rifles. His gun hadn't cleared leather when he sank his spurs into the bay and raced it for the middle of the bunched cattle. Explosions rent the air as bullets whined all around him.

He was in deep trouble and he knew it, with three pressing after him from behind and two screaming savages angling at him from the front. It was a cool September day, but sweat was streaming down his forehead as he snapped off three shots at the Indian coming from the right front. The Indian slumped, and Shorty had his opening.

Then something jerked his arm. A second later, it felt like a fist had plowed into his back. The force of it shoved him forward onto the bay's neck. A weird numbness seemed to go through his limbs. He didn't feel like he was in the saddle at all. Blackness was closing in, narrowing his vision. He couldn't seem to breathe or sit up.

The bay mustang was running for all its worth. Shorty's head was resting against its stretched-out neck. His blurring eyes saw the riders giving chase. For a confused second he was sure one of them was white. The last thing he remembered was wrapping the reins around his wrist and wondering why he couldn't feel it.

The clothes hanging on the line rigged from

a corner of the cabin to a tree were cool to Lorna's touch but they were dry. She checked the pair of pants that had once belonged to young Joe Dollarhide, but there was no trace of the mildew she had discovered when she unpacked the trunk they had been stored in.

When she glimpsed the horse and rider out of the corner of her eye, Lorna turned her head to look, thinking it might be Benteen. Her attention was first caught by the uneven gait of the bay horse, favoring the right front leg. Then it was the motionless body of the rider slumped against the horse's neck.

For an instant Lorna stared until it sank in that the rider was hurt. She dropped the clothes and picked up her skirts to run across the yard toward the shed-barn to intercept the horse. Ten minutes ago, she'd seen Rusty outside the bunkhouse. Lorna yelled for him to come.

The lathered horse shied its head when she grabbed for the reins. She murmured something to the animal and moved to the limp rider. It was Shorty Niles. When she touched his right shirt sleeve, her hand came away sticky with blood. A bullet had creased his thigh, laying open his pants leg and turning the material dark with blood. Lorna stretched to put an arm around his waist to tug him from the saddle, and discovered the wetness of more blood on his back.

With a sudden shock she realized Shorty could be dead. She knew a moment's fear when she cradled his face in her hands, mindless of the blood she smeared on his cheek. Relief trembled through her at the faint pulse her fingers found. She tried again to pull his deadweight from the saddle. Then there was another pair of hands to help her as Rusty arrived on the scene.

"He's alive," Lorna murmured as she struggled to unwrap the reins bound around his wrist.

"Somebody pumped some lead in him, though." Rusty grunted with the effort of dragging the body out of the saddle.

Lorna moved quickly to help him hold Shorty up. With Rusty on one side taking most of the weight, she draped an arm behind her neck and braced his body with her shoulder, so they could half-drag and half-carry him.

"We'll take him to the bunkhouse," Rusty stated.

The bunkhouse was alien territory to Lorna. It was unheard-of for a woman to venture into the sacred domain of the cowboy. When Rusty kicked open the door, she was assailed by the odor of sweat, cow manure, and the licorice

561

scent from tobacco plugs. It was a filthy, untidy mess with dirty clothes sitting stiffy on the floor and pages from catalogs tacked to the walls. Lorna saw lice scurrying for cover as Rusty pulled back a cover on one of the cots.

"This is worse than a pigsty," she declared in choked disgust. "We're taking him to the cabin." When Rusty started to argue, her temper blazed. "You heard me! We're taking him to the cabin right now!"

Grumbling under his breath, Rusty hoisted more of the burden onto his shoulder and headed for the door. As they stepped out, two cowboys rode in. Vince Garvey and Woolie peeled out of their saddles and came to take Lorna's place.

"What happened?" Vince demanded.

"He's been shot," Rusty answered. "She wants him in the cabin."

"I'll get a place fixed for him." Lorna hurried on ahead.

Even if there had been time to fetch a doctor, there was none for fifty miles. Lorna cleared off the table so Rusty could operate on it and rounded up all the clean bedding she could find. There was a brief argument when Rusty tried to insist she had to leave because Shorty's wounds necessitated undressing him, but he buckled under at her forceful determination to stay. She sent the children outside with Woolie and did what she could to help Rusty, holding the lantern for more light and dabbing away the oozing blood so he could see. Except for a few nauseous moments when he cauterized the wounds and she smelled the burning flesh, Lorna handled the bloody ordeal quite well.

After his wounds were bound and dressed, Vince and Woolie carried him to the big bed behind the canvas curtain. Not once had Shorty regained consciousness or showed any movement. The pallor of his face seemed emphasized by the whiteness of the muslin sheet.

"It's up to the good Lord now," Rusty declared as he looked from his patient to Lorna.

"I think there's some coffee on the stove," she said.

"I could use it. My hands don't feel too steady right now."

Rusty was lacing his coffee with a shot of whiskey when Benteen walked in. Vince and Woolie had already filled him in on the situation.

"How is he?" he demanded as he walked to the bed to see for himself.

"He's breathin'," Rusty answered. "But that's about all I can say. He was shot up pretty bad."

"He never said anything at all? Not a word about who did it?"

Rusty shook his head. "He never made a sound."

Turning from the bed, Benteen crossed to the stove and poured a cup of coffee. Webb had slipped silently into the cabin behind Benteen. He stood on tiptoe peering at the cowboy in the bed.

"Mommy, is Shorty going to sleep here?" he asked.

"Yes, until he's better," she replied, aware of the sharp look Benteen sent her.

"But where will you and Daddy sleep?" Webb frowned.

"Daddy can sleep with you and Arthur. I'll put some quilts in a chair and sit up with Shorty." She took him by the shoulders and pointed him to the door. "Go outside and play while I get supper ready."

In the predawn hours, Shorty drifted into semiconsciousness. His mumbling wakened Lorna as she dozed in the chair next to his bed. She moved to quiet him and moisten his dry lips with a wet cloth. Benteen came soundlessly to the bed and leaned over it.

"What happened, Shorty?" His murmured

question brought a brief lifting of the cowboy's eyelids.

"Indians . . . run off . . . stock . . . ambushed me." The mumbled words were faint, most of them unintelligible, but Benteen got the gist of the story.

"Indians." Lorna looked at Benteen with vague alarm. They'd stolen cattle before, but there had never been any attack on the men.

Shorty curled his fingers into Benteen's shirt. A bewildered frown clouded his pain-filled expression. ". . . thought . . . white man . . . with them." He closed his eyes tightly. ". . . must have been . . . wrong."

"Sssh." Lorna became concerned that it was taking too much of his strength to talk and firmly took his weakly clutching hand from Benteen's shirt. "It's all right, Shorty. You just rest."

There was a slight nod as he seemed to relax. She smoothed the covers over him, then turned to Benteen.

"What do you suppose he meant about the white man?" she asked.

"I don't know," he muttered with grim impatience. "He shouldn't have gone after them alone, but you can't tell Shorty that. He'd take on an army to prove he's as big as anyone else."

For five long days and nights Lorna nursed him through fever and bouts of delirium. There were times when Shorty became violent and Benteen had to hold him down to keep the wounds from being ripped open. Lorna fed him broth when he was conscious and force-fed it to him when he was not. But Shorty managed to pull through the worst of it. Rusty declared that the cowboy was too damned ornery to die.

Benteen didn't attempt to question Shorty about his reference to a white man being a party to the rustling until the fever and delirium passed. But Shorty couldn't shed much light on it.

"Everything was just blackin' out on me when I caught a glimpse of him — or thought I did." Shorty was agitated by his own vagueness. "I can't swear one of the riders was white, Benteen. The more I think about it, the more I think my eyes was playin' tricks on me."

"It happens," Benteen agreed.

"I'm sorry. It just never occurred to me they'd be watchin' their backtrail. I'd a-been more careful about followin' 'em."

"Remember that, if there's a next time. And don't try to take them on alone. That's an order," Benteen added for good measure; then his mouth crooked in a playful angle. "Get some rest. I want you out of my bed and back in the bunkhouse where you belong."

Before Shorty was moved to the bunkhouse, Lorna attacked it. She started by moving everything out, then washing down the walls, floors, and bed frames with the strongest solution of hot lye water she could make. Over the cowboys' objections, she boiled their clothes and bedding and laid them out in the September sun to dry.

When she was finished, the bunkhouse came close to sparkling. Every bone and muscle in her body ached, and her hands felt raw from the burning lye soap, but she looked on the results with satisfaction.

Her pleasure wasn't shared by Vince when he stepped into the bunkhouse and wrinkled his nose at the sharply clean smell. "It just don't seem like home anymore." He mumbled the complaint and shuffled past Lorna to his bunk.

When she mentioned the remark to Benteen, his reply was equally disapproving of her actions. "You didn't expect to be thanked for interfering, did you?"

Lorna realized she was fighting alone in a man's world.

When Jessie Trumbo returned from the

Canadian drive, he reported being harassed by Indians during the trip. He figured they had run off twenty head of steers and ten horses, but no one was injured. After the incident with Shorty, Benteen gave orders for the men to work in pairs and carry their rifles with them. The same day Jessie returned, Zeke Taylor accidentally shot himself in the toe, and complained bitterly about ruining a good pair of boots.

The black buggy didn't stop by the cabin. Lorna watched from the window as it went directly to the house on the knoll. Her lips thinned into a straight line. Turning, she grabbed up the black shawl and swung it around her shoulders.

Webb was running to the cabin to tell her of Mr. Giles's arrival when she walked out the door. He was thrilled when he discovered they were going to the house to see him. Lorna was walking too fast for little Arthur to keep up, so she straddled him on her hip and carried him, while Webb cantered ahead on a make-believe horse.

Bull Giles showed his surprise at her approach. Usually he came to the cabin to see the boys; Lorna didn't bring them to see him. Arthur wiggled to be put down. She let him slide off her hip to the ground and scamper to his big friend.

She didn't stop to speak to Bull, and ignored his questioning look that followed her when she swept by the buggy to climb the steps to the front door. The husky sound of Benteen's laughter greeted her, its warmth sending a shiver down her spine as she paused in the entryway. Her feet were drawn to the study, where the sound had originated. The door stood ajar, permitting Lorna to see inside.

Benteen was standing fairly close to Lady Crawford, so stunning in black with her dark eyes and silvered blond hair. It was a second before Lorna noticed Benteen was filling a glass Lady Crawford was holding. Liquid foamed from the bottle in his hand to fill a second long-stemmed glass.

She could hear the murmur of their voices but couldn't make out what they were saying. They were both smiling. Pain began to spread through Lorna. As Benteen partially turned to set the bottle on a wooden crate in the room, Lady Crawford cupped a hand to his cheek to turn his face back toward her. The action was so natural and familiar that a protest screamed inside Lorna. For a split second she glimpsed a taut yearning in Benteen's features. Jealousy seared through her.

Her hand shoved the door the rest of the way open as she stepped forward with an angry tilt to her head. "Is this a private celebration, or can anyone attend?" she challenged.

Benteen made no attempt to hide his grim displeasure at her intrusion, but Lady Crawford turned and smiled at her with brazen ease. "Do come join us, Lorna," she invited. "We were about to drink a toast to our first success."

"A toast?" Her feet hardly seemed to touch the floor as Lorna swept into the room to cross to Benteen's side. "Is that champagne? How wonderful," she declared with icy brightness. "I've never tasted it before. Do you mind?" She took the glass from Benteen's hand without waiting for his permission. She sipped at it and pretended to like the dryly sour effervescence. "It's quite good, isn't it?"

"Actually it is a poor year, but it was the best they had," Lady Crawford replied.

"I'm not experienced about such things," Lorna admitted freely, and passed the glass back to Benteen. "Forgive me for not allowing you and Lady Crawford to toast the first delivery of cattle on your beef contract." She wanted to let him know that she was aware of the nature of his joint venture with Lady Crawford, even if he hadn't told her the details.

His fingers were curled tightly around the glass, his knuckles showing white. "Are you going to dash the glass into the fireplace after the toast?" Lorna inquired. "That's how it's usually done, isn't it?"

"Very rarely," Lady Crawford replied, and sent Benteen a private look over the rim of her glass when she held it to her reddened lips.

"Was there something you wanted, Lorna?" Benteen asked.

"Merely to say hello to Lady Crawford." She fixed a bright smile on the older woman. "I wouldn't want you to think I was being rude."

"My dear, I would never think that," Lady Crawford assured her.

"Would you mind leaving us now, Lorna?" It was an order, not a request. "We have some business to discuss."

A tremor of mutiny quivered through her, but it ended on a note of sarcastic surrender. "I wouldn't think of intruding on a business discussion."

With a proud nod of her head to the English widow, Lorna exited the room. She didn't slow down until she was outside the house and descending the steps. Her eyes were stinging with dry tears. She blinked to ease their rawness and missed the last step, stumbling to her knees.

"Damn, damn, damn," she swore under her breath, getting tangled in the long skirts when she tried to stand up.

"Are you hurt?" Bull Giles crouched in front of her and reached forward to grip the upper part of her arms.

"I'm fine. I just tripped." Lorna kept her gaze down as he helped her up.

"You're trembling," he accused, and Lorna realized she was vibrating with a mixture of anger and hurt.

"I'm okay, really," she insisted.

"You'd better let me help you to the cabin." Bull started to put his arm around her shoulders for support, but Lorna spread her hands across his broad chest to stop him.

"No really . . ." Her protest died when she lifted her head and saw the undemanding adoration burning in his eyes. "Don't look at me like that, Bull," Lorna whispered.

"It was seein' Benteen in there with her, wasn't it?" he guessed. "The man's a fool. If you ever want to leave him, Lorna, just say the word and I'll take you and the boys anywhere you want to go. I'll look after you. You know that."

"Don't." She shook her head. "I could never leave him."

His big callused hand brushed the side of her

face in an involuntary caress. The deep, gentle longing was there in his eyes for her to see. It changed the harshness of his blunted features into vulnerability. There was a faint noise, but it didn't have any significance to Lorna until she heard the savage bite of Benteen's voice. "Get your hands off my wife!"

Lorna whirled around to face him. He towered above them on the steps. She whitened when she saw his hand on the butt of his gun. Suddenly a woman's hand closed around his wrist to check any attempt to draw it from the holster.

Benteen's hot gaze shifted to the woman at his side. "Get him out of here before I kill him."

Lorna's feet seemed to be rooted to the ground as Lady Crawford descended the steps with an unhurried grace. Lorna stared at Benteen, feeling the violence that emanated from him like a living thing.

"Help me into the buggy, Mr. Giles," Lady Crawford ordered calmly.

Lorna hardly noticed her two small sons hurry over to stand beside her and wave to Bull as the buggy rolled away. When Benteen turned on his heel to stride into the house, a shudder racked through her body.

"What's the matter, Mommy?" Webb asked.

"Nothing, dear," she lied. "Let's go back to the cabin, shall we?"

The silence at the supper table that night was so heavy it nearly suffocated Lorna. Benteen had barely said one word to the boys, and less than that to her. The food was tasteless. She ended up pushing it around on her plate without eating it.

After the table was cleared, Benteen spread his paperwork on it and turned up the lamp. It seemed impossible, but the tension increased. Lorna put the boys to bed earlier than usual, but a day of hard play had them quickly falling asleep. There was mending to be done, but Lorna couldn't tolerate the thought of sitting in the chair near Benteen to share the light of his lamp.

Sleep was the farthest thing from her mind, but she went behind the canvas wall and began undressing for bed. At least the cloth might serve as a barrier to block out the tension that filled the rest of the cabin.

Her dress was lying across the top of the trunk. As Lorna stepped out of her long slip, the curtain was yanked back. She stiffened at the cold look on Benteen's face.

"What do you think you're doing?" he demanded.

"I'm tired and I'm going to bed." She tossed the slip on top of the plain calico dress.

"And do what? Dream about running away with Bull Giles?" Benteen challenged.

Lorna was startled by his question. "Did you hear him say that?" She blurted out the question because she hadn't thought he had come outside in time to overhear their conversation.

"It was just a guess." His lips were pulled back to show the even row of white teeth ground together. "But an accurate one."

"Not really, since it was Bull who —"

" 'Bull,' is it?" He seized on her familiarity. "Not 'Mr. Giles' anymore."

"Stop it, Benteen," she protested irritably, and half-turned, not wishing to continue this embittered argument.

His hand grabbed her forearm to spin her back. "How many times has he held you in his arms?" he demanded.

"He hasn't," Lorna denied.

His other hand brushed her cheek the way Bull's had. "I suppose that was the first time he touched you, too," he mocked.

"It was, but I'm certainly not going to try to convince you of that," she declared, and jerked away from the derisive caress of her face.

"How many times has he been here when

I've been gone?" He twisted her arm to pull her closer while his cold eyes narrowed on her.

"That question doesn't deserve an answer," she spat, and turned her arm sharply in an attempt to break his painful grip. "Let go of me. I want to go to bed."

His fingers closed on the straight neckline of her thin chemise. With a downward stroke of his hand, he ripped it off as Lorna breathed in sharply from shock. She struggled frantically when he scooped her naked body into his arms, kicking and hitting at him with desperate little sounds coming from her throat. The bruising grip of his arms didn't hold her long as he dropped her onto the bed.

"Isn't that what you wanted?" he growled.

For a stunned moment she lay there looking up at the labored movement of his chest, unable to believe he hadn't intended to rape her again. It was that kind of violence she saw in his face. Just when she was about to accept she was wrong, he lowered himself onto the bed, using his weight to pin her to the mattress. Twisting and writhing, Lorna tried to throw him off her, clawing at him with her nails.

He caught her hands and forced them above her head, holding her wrists easily in the shackling grip of one hand. Helpless now,

Lorna turned her face from him and closed her eyes tightly. The fight went out of her as she began breathing in silent sobs and tried to shut her mind to the violation of her body.

Yet the hand stroking her was not cruel and the hard mouth moving along the hollow of her collarbone was not brutal. He held the weight of her breast in his palm and began moistening its firm swell with warm kisses. She trembled with uncertain desire when he took the nipple into his mouth and rolled his tongue around it until it hardened to an erect nub. His teeth nibbled at it, sensuously tugging at it.

Her breath started coming in tiny pants, reluctant with passion that might be misspent. Lifting his head, he watched his hand explore where his lips had been. His weight shifted partially off her.

"Has he touched you like that, Lorna?" Benteen murmured.

"No," she moaned.

Her wrists twisted under his pinning hold, but he wouldn't release them. His hand began wandering over her rib cage and across the flatness of her stomach. Then he was bending to explore her navel, her toes tingling with the sensation his tongue created. He ran his hand over her naked flank, gliding to her knee and curving behind it to raise it. When his fingers began making a teasing trail along the inside of her thigh, the small sound that came from her throat was an articulate expression of arching desire.

"Can he make you feel like this?" Benteen asked, and rubbed his mouth against the corner of her lips.

"No. No," she insisted, and tried to slide her mouth under his, but he avoided the attempt.

"Tonight, Lorna," he murmured against her throat, "I'm going to make you want me so much that you'll never look at any other man as long as you live."

"I don't want anyone else," she whispered.

Her hips moved against him in a silent urging. It seemed he was listening as he shifted to remove his pants with one hand but he wouldn't release her arms. Her skin flamed with the heat of his body when she felt the nakedness of his muscled legs. She arched willingly against him, but he continued to resist giving her the satisfaction her body craved.

With his hands and his mouth, he explored every inch of her from fingers to toes, stroking and nibbling until there wasn't a part of her that didn't tingle. When he finally mounted her, it was a mating of the mind, the flesh, and the soul. There was a purity to it that brought tears to her eyes and an eroticism that left her limp.

27

"Tell me now" – Benteen tightened the arm encircling her waist – "that you can leave me and run away with Bull Giles."

"I couldn't do it before, and I certainly couldn't do it now," she admitted, and let her hands play over his chest, now that she was finally allowed to touch him.

"But he's suggested it."

"Yes, but that's only because of you – because he thought you were hurting me." Lorna shifted in his hold so she could see his face.

"Hurting you?" Benteen frowned. "What gave him that idea?"

"The way you and Lady Crawford behave together. I saw it for myself today." There was a trace of accusation in her voice – but only a trace. It was difficult to believe he could be having an affair with another woman after the way he'd just made love to her. Yet there was still the evidence of her own eyes.

"Saw what?" There was a narrowing of his gaze.

"The way she touched you. It wasn't any different than the way Bull touched my face," Lorna said.

His chest lifted on a deep breath; then he was removing his arm from behind her and turning to sit up on the edge of the bed. This physical as well as mental withdrawal from her seemed to confirm what Lorna hadn't wanted to believe.

"Is . . . is she your mistress, Benteen?" She had to know.

There was a short, heavy laugh from him, followed by a shake of his head. "No, Lorna, she isn't my mistress." He combed a hand through his hair. With his back to her, she couldn't see his face. "She's my mother."

"What?"

This time, Benteen turned his head to look at her. "She's my mother."

It seemed incredible. Lorna scrambled out of bed and pushed her clothes off the top of the trunk. Raising the lid, she rummaged through the contents until she found the framed picture. She stared at the young blond-haired woman with dark eyes. It was true.

"Why didn't you tell me?" She swung around to stare at Benteen.

"Because . . . I wasn't sure if I wanted anyone to know." Confusion etched deep lines in his face. "I hated her. You know how much I hated her."

She moved to the bed. "And now?"

"Now . . . I don't know what I feel." He sighed heavily. "She's a stranger — a fascinating stranger."

"Why is she here?" That sounded too blunt, too unfeeling. "I mean . . . she must have wanted to see you again. Is that why she came?"

"She claims I've been on her mind since she saw me in Dodge City and that she wondered if we could get together again," Benteen indicated. "She's here, so I guess it's true." A faraway look entered his eyes as he stared into a dark corner. "When I was a young boy, my pa used to tell me she'd come back someday. I wanted to believe him. I used to dream about her. After a few years, the dreams became nightmares — she'd come back, promise to never leave me, then laugh and fade away while I cried to her."

For the first time, he'd opened a door for Lorna and let her see inside him — his anguish and his loneliness — this man who had always seemed so self-sufficient, so strong. But he had human needs, too. Lorna climbed onto the bed and knelt on the mattress.

"Why haven't you talked to me like this

before?" she asked. "Why did you keep all this to yourself? Didn't you think I would listen or care? I don't understand why you haven't let me get close to you."

His gaze swept slowly over her as the slashed corners of his mouth deepened in a faint smile. "Why didn't you sit on the bed like that on our wedding night?" he countered. "It might have given me a hint of what I was letting myself in for."

Lorna realized she was unashamedly naked, but there wasn't an inch of her that he wasn't intimately familiar with. She looked again at the framed picture she was holding.

"What does that have to do with what I asked you?" She lifted her glance to frown.

His smile was more pronounced as he took the photograph from her and set it aside. Then his gentle hands were firmly pushing her onto the mattress while he stretched out full-length on his side, facing her, as naked as she was. His fingers reached for the face she turned toward him and trailed over her temples, pushing the tendrils of silk-brown hair aside.

"I thought I had married a well-brought-up young lady who was warm and giving and happy. When I discovered on our wedding night that she was also passionate, I was that much more pleased by my choice," Benteen murmured while his fingers continued to trace over her face, touching her nose and following the line of her cheekbone. "I thought I had a wife I could safely love."

"You aren't making any sense." Lorna searched his velvet dark eyes and the warm expression on his angular features. The little scar near his eye stood out as a white line on sun-bronzed skin.

"Yes, I am." He smiled. "It wasn't long before you began challenging me. You didn't simply accept things the way I thought you would. You argued, you defied me. But more than that, you began crawling inside me. Instead of a tame little wife, I had a stubborn little rebel who wore man's pants and insisted on getting involved in my life." He let his fingertips run lightly over her lips. "Lorna Calder was a handful that I didn't know how to handle. You can be very irritating."

"Not half as irritating as you can be."

"That's because you were demanding too much. You started to mean too much to me. Suddenly it wasn't safe to love you anymore. If I gave you too much of myself, what would I have left? So I tried to keep some things back. I tried to fence you in, but you kept cutting the wire."

"Benteen Calder – building fences?" she

584

chided the absurdity of the idea that an open-range man would put up wire. "If it's a fence you want to build, then build it around us. Put both of us inside it, then I won't have any reason to tear it down."

"Not even to get out?" he asked quietly.

"I never should have threatened to leave you," Lorna admitted. "That was a young girl's foolishness. All I ever wanted was for you to love me – and to let me love you. But you wouldn't tell me what you were thinking, feeling, or dreaming." His hand was on her throat. She took hold of it and carried his palm to her lips. "I know your body almost as well as my own, but you haven't let me know what's in your heart."

"I love you, Lorna. One way or another, you've managed to leave room for little else," he declared huskily. "God help me, but I love you."

When he kissed her, the world was filled with light. She murmured his name over and over against his hard lips. They were equally strong in spirit, pride, and will, forged by a land and a time that recognized only strength, but love made them unconquerable.

Elaine studied her son with a keen interest. There was a new ease about him, a freeness of manner that hadn't been present before. He had always projected the image of a man sure of his purpose, but now there was an added confidence.

When he finished conferring with his foreman, he dismissed the man and crossed to the fireplace where she was standing. There was a preoccupied look to his expression, his thoughts still focusing on the discussion with the quiet, angular cowboy. Elaine didn't pretend she hadn't been listening.

"I didn't realize you were having trouble with the Indians. When did this start?" she asked.

"We've always had trouble with them, but this year seems to be worse," he admitted with an absent frown. "A couple weeks back they shot up one of my men when he caught up with them."

"You didn't mention it to me." An eyebrow was raised at this discovery. She thought he had been keeping her informed of all that went on. Obviously he still didn't completely trust her.

"It didn't concern you."

"But it concerned you, so therefore it was of interest to me," Elaine insisted. "So does this matter with the Indians. If you are suffering losses —"

"Every rancher expects to lose a certain number of cattle to the Indians. It's part of doing business," Benteen replied.

But he didn't mention that he'd already lost more than the normal percentage, and the season was young. Ely had been checking with some of the other outfits, but they had hardly been bothered at all. It wasn't logical for the Indians to pick on one ranch. There was always a chance, though, that it was just bad luck. Somehow it didn't seem likely. Yet, if they were deliberately selecting Triple C cattle, the next question was: Why?

"How many cattle have they stolen?" Elaine questioned.

"I'll know that when the roundup is finished." He was sure the number was going to be high. "That's where I'll be for the next few days, so you won't be able to contact me. Lorna and the boys are coming, too."

"You're taking your wife and children? I suspected that you didn't trust her, but I didn't realize you felt you had to watch her every minute," she remarked with feigned surprise. "If that's the case, you're better off without her."

"That isn't the case," Benteen replied evenly. "By the way, she knows we're related."

"You told her?" There was a pleased note in

her voice because it marked progress.

"Yes, I told her."

"I'm glad." Elaine smiled and reached out to clasp his hand. "I think she was resenting the time you spent with me, and I don't want anything to interfere with that. I have a great many plans for the two of us."

Benteen studied the smooth hand that covered his. He wanted to believe the affection in her touch, but he was bothered by the possessive quality of it. That should have reassured him the gesture was genuine.

"I'll walk you to the buggy." He took her hand and slipped it inside the crook of his arm.

Slipping her hat off, Lorna let it hang by the throat strap down her back. Her gaze studied the shimmering aqua color of the pretwilight sky, pearlized by the downing sun. The smoke from the campfire drifted upward in the still air, a group of tired cowboys scattered around it. There were so many memories of the trail drive contained in the scene — the same smells, the same sounds, the same tired bodies.

A series of discordant notes was played on the harmonica, drawing her glance to Woolie sitting cross-legged on the ground with Webb on his knee. He was patiently attempting to teach Webb to play a song on the harmonica.

One of the *vaqueros* had whittled a wooden horse, which little Arthur was galloping over the ground.

Her coffeecup was empty, so Lorna refilled it from the pot warming by the fire. She took a quick sip of the bitterly black coffee and wandered over by the chuck wagon, where Rusty was working. He glanced at her, taking in the cup in her hand.

"Thought you didn't like my coffee," he said.

"I guess I've acquired a taste for it." She shrugged lightly and smiled.

"It seems like old times to see you struttin' around in a man's pair of pants." His glance raked the lower half of her body, a twinkle lighting his eyes. "You filled em' out a bit more. The shirt, too. There's no mistakin' you for a boy anymore."

"I should hope not." Her laughter was soft, not minding his teasing remarks.

"Speakin' of boys, those two of yours are havin' themselves a high time."

"I know." She cast a fond look at the two boys. "They're convinced this roundup is being staged for their entertainment."

"That's fer sure." Rusty seemed to test the air, distracted by a watchfulness that was wakened inside of him. "It sure is still."

Lorna looked at the sky, clear except for

some clouds on the far horizon. "I hope it doesn't rain in the night. The boys want to sleep outside like the rest of you." They'd brought along a tent, a small one erected on the edge of the camp circle.

"If it does, you can always throw 'em in the cooney," Rusty said. "They'll stay high and dry there. Slept in it myself on many a rainy night."

"Don't tell Webb that. He'll insist on trying it out," Lorna warned, then spied Benteen walking into camp with Ely Stanton. "I'll talk to you later."

As she angled across camp, the two men stopped to talk about something. Lorna could tell by Benteen's expression that the subject was a serious one.

"Is something wrong?" she asked when she reached them.

When Benteen opened his mouth to speak, she knew he was about to deny it. He held her gaze for a second; then the shutters came down.

"So far, the tally is running about five thousand head short," he admitted.

The number staggered her. She knew the Indians had run off some cattle, but this was more than "some." "Do you think the Indians are responsible?" She was incredulous. "But what would they do with that many? I thought they only stole what they needed to eat."

"That's what they've done in the past," Benteen said.

"It's for sure if they're stealin' to sell or trade for goods, somebody's puttin' 'em up to it." Ely shook his head. "It isn't like 'em to do things on this kind of scale. A dozen head of cattle would keep them supplied with firewater all winter, and probably a couple of warm blankets, too."

"Maybe it isn't the Indians," Lorna suggested.

"It's Indians sign we've been cuttin'," Ely said.

"Remember when Shorty was delirious from the fever?" Lorna turned to Benteen. "He mumbled something about a white man."

"I asked him about it later," he admitted. "When he was blacking out, he thought he saw a white man riding with the Indians, but he was sure he had just imagined it."

"What if he didn't?" she asked.

"What white man would be riding with Indians?" Ely didn't put much stock in the idea. "For that matter, what white man would the Indians let ride with them?"

For a long minute his questions went unanswered. "There might be one," Benteen offered finally with a thoughtful look.

591

"Who?" Ely frowned.

"That ex-buffalo hunter up on the Missouri that's been trading with the Indians. His name's Sallie. Bull Giles knows him." The last was added absently, his mind already running ahead.

"Bull knows him?" she repeated. Benteen had said it as if it meant something, but she didn't see any significance in it.

It was possible there wasn't any, but Benteen was recalling the scene in Fat Frank's place when the renegade's name had first been mentioned. Bull Giles had been there with Loman Janes. Janes was the Ten Bar foreman. The Ten Bar needed water and range. In Texas, Judd Boston's tactics had been to overstock and drift off a few head of his father's cattle. The aim had been to put his father in a financial bind, which had ultimately worked. Was he making a similar but more subtle play here in Montana for part of the Triple C range?

Benteen tried to dismiss the thought with a vague shake of his head. It wouldn't work — not with the Canadian beef contract he had. This five thousand head was a substantial loss, but he could financially weather twice that number. It would merely set back his timetable of expansion. Besides, Bull Giles was working for his mother.

"Is that coffee any good?" His arm curved naturally around Lorna's waist. "I could use a cup."

"It's Rusty's coffee, if that answers your question." She wasn't concerned that he hadn't told her what he was thinking or explained the reference to Bull Giles. The situation had changed. She was confident that, in time, he would tell her. It was Ely's presence that had kept him silent, not hers.

As they walked to the fire, Woolie was playing a melancholy version of "Shenandoah" to show Webb how the harmonica was supposed to sound when it was played right. When the last note wavered into the night, Webb eagerly wanted his turn. Lorna couldn't help smiling at the way he tried so hard to copy Woolie, right down to wiggling his hand, but he was either sharp or flat and never on key.

"Why don't you give it up?" Zeke protested. "You said you was gonna make a first-rate roper out of him, Woolie. He sure can't hurt a man's ears with a rope."

"Wanta bet?" Woolie laughed. "Go get the rope I made ya, kid, and rope that critter over there."

The plaited rope was shorter and narrower than what the cowboys used. It was little-boy-sized, especially for Webb. The cowboys had been instructing him in the rudiments of the art of roping for over a year. He had the idea, although most of the time his coordination was not all that good.

Encouraged by the rest of the cowboys, Webb got his rope and set out in pursuit of an unusually slow-running Zeke. The quiet scene was destroyed by shouts and laughter and mis-thrown loops. Arthur tried to join in the fun, but he kept tripping over cowboys' legs.

So much attention was focused on the little boy chasing the bowlegged cowboy that the restless stirrings from the remuda went unnoticed. With coffeecups in hand, Lorna and Benteen were standing to one side of the fire, laughing with everyone else at the antics of their sons.

The *vaquero* Ramon shouted a warning, breaking across the laughter to bring the camp alert. Benteen heard the pounding of hooves and the snorting whicker of panicked horses an instant before the remuda plunged out of the gloaming and charged into camp. He felt Lorna's instinctive movement toward the children and grabbed her, throwing her out of the path of the stampeding horses. Whipping off his hat, he waved it wildly at the herd and whistled shrilly between his teeth to divert them. The ones in front shied from him, but they were crowded by the others. It was a churning mass of horseflesh and dodging cowboys.

"Indians!" someone shouted. "They're running off the cattle!"

Shots were being exchanged opposite Benteen's position. It was the side closest to the herd, which meant the men were firing at the raiders and being fired on. The first rush of the horses had passed, leaving gaps that would allow him to cross to the fight.

Stampeding the remuda had been a diversionary tactic to create chaos in the camp while the cattle were run off. Benteen sent one glance at Lorna, huddled tightly against a wagon wheel. Her gaze was frantically searching the confusion for Webb and Arthur. He was saying a silent prayer for them himself, but he knew his men. They would have put the boys' safety over their own lives.

"They got the boys out of the way. Don't worry about them!" he shouted to Lorna. "Just stay where you are."

Waving his hat at on oncoming horse, Benteen dodged forward when it shied. He managed to run through the tangle of bedrolls and saddles, trying to keep one eye on the loose horses and the other on the fight in progress.

"Grab some of those horses!" he shouted to

Vince Garvey. They couldn't let all the horses scatter, or they wouldn't be able to mount a pursuit.

The camp was crossed. Benteen reached the four cowboys, returning the gunfire of a fleeing band of Indians. He was conscious of the weight of the pistol in his hand without being aware he'd drawn it. The hat was back on his head. The air was tainted with the smell of gunsmoke. He had time to snap off two shots before the raiders were out of range.

Automatically he reached for more bullets to reload. "Start throwin' saddles on those horses!" He threw the order at the camp, but a half-dozen cowboys were already doing that very thing. Benteen glanced to see who was with him as he pushed new bullets into the empty chambers. Barnie was nearest him. Both turned simultaneously, heading for the horses at a running trot. "What about the boys? Do you know if they're okay?" Benteen asked as he shoved his pistol back in its holster.

"Saw Zeke scoop up Webb. I think Rusty grabbed the little tyke," Barnie answered. "One of them raiders with the Injuns had a beard and a buffalo coat."

Benteen cursed himself for exposing Lorna and the boys to this kind of danger, only there hadn't been any reason to suspect the Indians would raid a manned herd. It had seemed logical to believe his family would be safer in the company of twenty armed cowboys than left alone at the cabin. But he hadn't counted on the Indian raids being instigated by a white renegade, either.

Only eight of the horses from the scattered remuda had been caught. No time was wasted sorting out saddles and owners. Zeke handed Benteen the reins to a big Roman-nosed chestnut the instant he entered the camp.

"Where's Webb?" Benteen stepped a foot into the stirrup.

"Just returned him to his mamma," Zeke answered.

Benteen's gaze swept the camp, a jumble of men on foot and on horseback. He was briefly torn by a desire to make certain his family was unharmed, yet each minute's delay meant the cattle were being driven that much farther. If he wanted to recapture the bulk of his herd, immediate pursuit was imperative. It was half-dark now.

The decision was made before his boot found the other stirrup. "Let's go." He gave the order, but it was his action the men followed, letting him take the lead on the big chestnut.

When Benteen made that mad dash between

horses to the other side of camp, Lorna scrambled to her feet and pressed herself flat against the chuck wagon. There was so much running, shouting, and shooting going on that she couldn't separate it all.

The worst of it was over in a flurry of moments that seemed eternally long. The confusion went on as cowboys snared the stragglers from the remuda and began swinging the big, heavy saddles like they were pillows.

Lorna pushed into the chaos, frantic to find Webb and Arthur. Shoving the bunched haunches of nervous horses out of the way and ducking the tossing heads of others, she forced her way to the place where she had last seen the boys. Everyone was running, moving in and out of her vision. She was breathing in panicked breaths and struggling to control it.

"Here, ma'am," a voice said.

She hardly had time to recognize Zeke before he was thrusting Webb into her arms. It was relief that collapsed her knees rather than the four-and-a-half-year-old's weight. Her fingers gripped his arm while her hand trembled over his face and hair. He had a stunned, wide-eyed look at all this commotion of horses, riders, and gunshots.

"Are you okay?" Her voice trembled, although she tried to appear very calm. There was a lump in her throat and the dampness of tears in her eyes. She kept them open wide.

"Yeah." He nodded. "I wasn't scared, Mom. Honest."

"Of course you weren't." Her smile quivered.

"Were you?" he wondered.

"A little," she admitted, and hugged him with a mother's fierceness, then forced herself to draw back. "Where's your brother? Do you know?"

He shook his head. "I dropped my rope. Zeke said I could find it later."

"Yes, later." Lorna nodded and began looking around. "First we have to find your brother."

The stampeding horses had scattered the campfire, taking away the light it would have afforded. Behind her, there was the digging of hooves, and Lorna glanced over her shoulder to see eight riders gallop into the graying night. She guessed Benteen was with them, although she couldn't distinguish the riders.

Their departure left a degree of quiet in the camp as the remaining cowboys attempted to restore some kind of order and search for horses that might have lingered nearby. Lorna gripped Webb's hand tightly as she stood up. She took a step, not certain where to look first for Arthur.

When she saw Rusty moving woodenly toward her carrying the child in his arms, a second wave of relief flooded through her. As he came closer, she sensed something wasn't right. Rusty's face was nearly as white as his whiskers. There was a sunken, hollow grief in his eyes. A pounding fear began to beat in her, growing louder and louder with each step that brought him nearer.

Her glance fell to the boy-child lying so motionless in his arms. His eyes were closed, his face innocent with sleep, but he didn't have his finger in his mouth. She tried to smile — tried to say his name and wake him up.

"I'm sorry." Rusty's voice wavered hoarsely. "It was a stray shot . . . or a ricochet." A tear slipped from his eye as he bowed his head, his shoulders shaking silently.

"No." Lorna shook her head, trying to be very firm. "He's just . . ." But as she reached to lift Arthur from his arms, her fingers felt the sticky warmth of blood.

A clawing, wild pain ripped her chest apart. She gathered his limp little body into her arms and pressed him close, as if to give him life again, as she had once before when she carried him inside her. With shattering disbelief she scanned his beautiful face for some small sign of life.

"No. No." She wasn't conscious of murmuring the protest over and over again. Pressing her cheek against his, she closed her eyes and rocked back and forth.

"God in heaven, but it isn't right," Rusty declared thickly.

"What's the matter with Arthur?" Webb tugged on her pants leg, but Lorna was beyond hearing him.

Rusty sniffed loudly and wiped briskly at his nose. "Come with me, son." His voice was gruff, but not unkind.

Slowly she sank to her knees and cried softly, barely making any sound. She just sat there, holding him tightly and rocking, unaware of the hush in camp, the soft-walking cowboys with pain in their eyes, and the darkness that filled the sky.

It was left to Rusty to answer Webb's questions and put him to bed. "Why is Mommy holding Arthur and crying?"

"Because he's going away." He tucked the quilt around the little shoulders.

"Am I going too?"

"No, you gotta stay here and take care of your mother."

"But where's Arthur going?"

"Away. Far away. But you'll see him by and by," Rusty said. "Now, close your eyes."

"Can we look for my rope in the morning?"

"Yes. In the morning, but first you have to sleep." He sat with the boy until sleep came, then stole quietly out of the tent.

A fire was burning brightly, keeping a lone vigil with the woman holding her child for the last night. Rusty gathered up a quilt and walked over to put it around her shoulders. She gave no sign of being aware of him. Rusty felt very old. He'd seen too much. He lifted his eyes to the night sky. The endless sky. Cowboys and sailors saw too much of it, whether it was the rolling plains or the sea they rode. He'd seen too much of it.

It was early dawn when Benteen approached the camp. They'd finally caught up with the main herd being chased north by the Indians. There had been a brief running gun battle before the raiders gave up their prize. Outside of two minor crease wounds, none of his men had been hurt. It had taken them another two hours to get the cattle bunched and quieted down. He'd left the rest of the men with the herd in case another try was made for them.

At first, it was the uncanny silence of the

camp that struck him. There was no grumbling among the riders as they drank their morning coffee. Then it was the way their eyes shifted away from meeting his.

When he spied Lorna wrapped in a quilt and rocking little Arthur, his tiredness lifted. He swung down from his horse at the chuck wagon and let the reins drag the ground. As he took a step toward Lorna, Rusty moved into his path. A frown flickered across his face at the old cook's rheumy-looking eyes.

"Ain't no easy way to say it," Rusty began. "One minute I had him safe . . ." His shoulders lifted. "A stray shot . . ." Then he glanced in Lorna's direction. "She's been sittin' with him like that all night."

There was a roar of pain inside him. Benteen pushed Rusty out of the way and covered the ground to Lorna with long, reaching strides. When he stopped in front of her kneeling form, his breathing was labored and deep. His eyes burned from the vision of his lifeless son. He swayed, undermined by an agonizing grief.

When he felt her gaze lift to him, his mouth opened, but no words came out. He lowered himself into a crouch before her. His hands and arms felt so empty.

"You can cry, Benteen," Lorna murmured. "It's all right."

He pressed a hand across the front of his eyes and gritted his teeth together. "I'm sorry." Guilt weighed on him – for unknowingly putting them in danger, for not being with her.

"Did you get the cattle?" she asked.

"Yes." It was a brutally painful admission.

"You had to go after them, Benteen," she said in a calm voice. "There was nothing you could have done for him if you had stayed. You had to go."

When he finally lowered his hand, there were tears in his eyes. He looked at her for a long minute, then reached for their son. "I'll take him now, Lorna." His voice was thick.

Reluctantly she relinquished him into Benteen's keeping and watched as he carried him to the chuck wagon. She knew Benteen was saying his last good-bye to Arthur.

It was a sad and solemn procession that set out for the headquarters with the body of the small boy wrapped in a quilt and carefully laid in the back of the chuck wagon.

28

Lumber from the new house was used to make little Arthur's coffin. The carpenters would have done it, but Zeke insisted it was his right. He'd made the cradle Arthur slept in as a baby and nailed together the cot that had been the boy's bed. He'd make Arthur's final resting place, too.

The grave was dug under the shade of the cottonwood trees by the river where he had played so many hours. Galloping Triple C riders had located a traveling preacher trying to save some sinners at Frank Fitzsimmons' place in Blue Moon. They hadn't wasted time with explanations – just dragged him out of the saloon and shoved him onto his horse.

A cowboy could be put under the earth with a simple spoken introduction to his Maker. But in their thinking, the little boy – Mrs. Calder's little boy – needed some proper words said. It was a way of showing their deep respect and loyalty for Benteen, too.

Word of the tragedy had spread beyond the boundaries of the Triple C. Besides Mary and

Ely and the cowboys, there were a couple of neighboring ranchers, Frank Fitzsimmons, Lady Crawford, and Bull Giles among the throng of mourners at the grave site.

It was a crisp, tart morning with a stiff breeze rustling the dried brown leaves of the cottonwood trees. There was more than grief and the mourning of a loved one in the air. The cold breath of revenge had brought its scent, visible in the guns strapped to Benteen's hip and to the hips of his men. Saddled horses with rifle scabbards filled stood waiting at the corral.

The minister took note of this when he finished his prayers, with a request for forgiveness. "And may God have mercy on the souls of those who perpetrated this deed. Amen."

First Benteen, then Lorna stepped forward to throw a handful of dirt into the grave. One by one, the cowboys began filing past. Lorna's eyes were bright with tears, but she kept her shoulders squared. Benteen stood straight and tall beside her. The minister came quietly over to offer his condolences.

"My deepest sympathies to both of you," he murmured.

"Thank you, Reverend Worth," Lorna replied with a faint nod of her head. "My husband and I are extremely grateful that you are here."

"It is my work," he insisted.

"We would like to build you a church as . . . as soon as all this is over . . ." She faltered slightly. "This country is in need of churches . . . and schools. I'm sure Mr. Fitzsimmons will be happy to help you choose a site."

"You are most generous, Mrs. Calder," the reverend declared. "And you, Mr. Calder."

Benteen acknowledged the remark with a short nod of his head. The *vaquero* Ramon approached the grave and hesitated, glancing at Benteen and Lorna. After a moment's indecision he approached them and bowed slightly with quiet dignity and respect. Reaching inside his jacket, he took out the little wooden horse he had carved for Arthur and presented it to Lorna.

"I found eet, señora," he said. "You would wish to keep eet, no?"

"Yes." She accepted the return of Arthur's toy, gripping it tightly for a moment. "*Gracias,* Ramon."

The *vaquero* bowed again and moved away. Benteen's arm tightened around her waist. She stood a little taller, strengthened by his silent support. Mary hugged her and cried. Then Benteen's mother, Lady Crawford, came, a black veil covering her face. She embraced Lorna in a gesture of sympathy and turned to Benteen.

"You can't really mean to go after them." She sounded impatient, but the veil concealed her expression. "What will you prove? It won't bring back your son, Benteen."

"No." Even though he agreed, it didn't change his decision.

"You are being foolish," Elaine insisted. "Send your men after them, if you must, but don't risk your own life. What if you are shot and killed? You should be thinking of your wife and your other son — of this ranch and what will happen to it if you die, instead of following this stupid code of a man's honor and pride."

"You don't lead men by staying behind where it's safe," he said grimly. "And you don't stand by while cattle are stolen and your son is killed and do nothing about it."

"Let someone else do it." Her agitation was apparent. "It's a matter for the law to handle."

"There isn't any law out here. You're looking at the only justice there is. 'Just-us.' "

"Lorna . . ." She turned to appeal to her.

"Benteen's right," Lorna said with an unsteady voice. "If he doesn't stop them, who will? Maybe someday that won't be true, but it is now."

With a quick turn, Lady Crawford moved stiffly away. Bull Giles paused in front of

Benteen. His eyes were red-rimmed with grief, but they burned, too, with a dark anger. Bull worked his jaw for a silent minute, trying to find the right words.

"If you'd see clear to loan me a horse, Benteen," he said, "I'd like to ride with you."

"We're not going after Indians," Benteen said. "We're going after Big Ed Sallie and his bunch."

"I can show you where to find them," Bull stated.

"Tell Barnie I said to saddle a horse for you." Benteen accepted the offer to ride with them, hearing all the explanation he needed.

When Bull Giles left, they stood alone by the partially filled grave. Benteen shifted, angling toward Lorna. She felt the vague movement of his hand on her back and lifted her face. Her eyes clung to him with naked love and anguish.

"I won't say good-bye, not to you," she whispered, and borrowed the phrase from the Texas border country. "Just . . . go with God."

The pressure of his hand pulled her to him. His mouth was hard on her lips, promising to return, promising a life tomorrow, and promising a love that would endure as long as grass grew green in the spring. Her eyes stayed closed when the kiss ended, her lips trembling apart on a breath. The muted jingle of his spurs marked the strides that carried him from her to the waiting horses.

Saddle leather creaked and hooves shuffled. Lorna opened her eyes to watch the band of riders leave. Benteen swung his horse toward her and held her gaze across the distance, then reined it north. She lost sight of him when the other riders fell in behind his horse.

At Lorna's invitation, the minister stayed for an early lunch, then escorted Mary to her home. Lady Crawford was brittlely silent, taking little part in the table conversation. Within minutes after Reverend Worth and Mary had departed, she left Lorna with the dishes and disappeared in the direction of the Homestead.

Rusty and the recuperating Shorty had taken charge of Webb, which left Lorna with empty minutes to fill. She'd already had her time of tears and prayers. She needed another outlet to work off her pain. She began by sorting Arthur's things in the bottom of a trunk. From there, it graduated to a general packing.

As she folded a dress and laid it on top of one of Benteen's shirts, the cabin door swung open. Lorna paused only long enough to glance over her shoulder and identify his mother, then began folding another dress.

"Is this why you encouraged Benteen to

leave?" Lady Crawford challenged calmly. "So you could run off while he was gone?" Lorna slowly turned, stunned by the suggestion. "I can't say that I blame you for wanting to leave. I've noticed how fond you are of your children. Losing your son in such a brutal fashion was undoubtedly the last straw. You can take my buggy. Just leave it at the livery in town."

"You are mistaken. I am not leaving and I have never had any intention of leaving," Lorna correctly stiffly. "This ranch is my home. Do not presume that because you could not tolerate this kind of life, every other woman feels the same."

"I don't presume that," she replied. "But you've been unhappy here. I've seen that. No one should have to fight and struggle, and live like this, especially a woman."

Lorna's fingers curled into the worn dress in her hand before she tossed it briskly aside. She walked over to grip Lady Crawford's arm and direct her to the map drawn on the piece of canvas.

"Do you see that? Do you know what it is?" she demanded.

"It's a map of sorts." The woman shrugged her indifference to it.

"It's a map of the ranch and our future," Lorna stated, and released the black-sleeved

611

arm to walk to the map. "These are the hundred-and-sixty-acre tracts that Benteen has claimed." She pointed them out individually. "He has declared ownership of all the rest as stock range." She faced his mother. "That's why I'm here, working with him to build this ranch. If you had stayed with his father, maybe the two of you could have built a place like this in Texas. When you left him, he lost heart in trying. All he cared about was hanging on to the place until you came back. Benteen told me that."

"Seth was never half the man that Benteen is," his mother stated. "He couldn't separate dreams from reality."

"You start with a dream, then build a foundation under it. This ranch was a dream the day we set foot on it and walked up on that hill where the house is standing now," Lorna said. "I'm beginning to realize that all your life you have been taking, grabbing for all you could get. Just exactly why are you here?"

"Maybe I discovered it wasn't enough." Her head was held high.

Lorna tipped her head to the side, seeing a beautiful shell and not much inside it. "I think you would have been glad if I left Benteen," she realized.

"That's nonsense," Elaine denied. "I have

nothing against you. A man has need of a wife. Benteen is no different."

"A wife. You make it sound like the woman is a nonentity, to serve but not to speak. That's what you wanted me to be." In the beginning, it was what Benteen had wanted from her, but Lorna didn't mention the past. "What is it you want from Benteen? It isn't a son. You won't even claim him openly."

"It isn't practical."

"No," Lorna agreed with a measure of sadness. "If you admitted he was your son, then you'd have the problem of explaining your marriage to the Earl of Crawford when you were legally wed to Seth Calder. You'd not only forfeit your inheritance from his estate, but your title as well."

"Why should I give it up?" Elaine challenged. "It would be foolish."

"Yes, it would be."

"I don't believe you understand the situation." Elaine gathered herself to stand a little taller. "With my money and influence, I can make Benteen a powerful man in this territory."

"I have no doubt that you can," Lorna admitted. "But I don't think that's what he wants from you."

"You are obviously implying that it's a

mother he wants. Since we are being candid, I will freely admit to you as I have to him that I don't regret leaving him. The maternal instinct that is supposed to be so strong in women has eluded me. I can't be what I never was." There was no apology in her statement.

"Then stop trying to arouse a son's love for you," Lorna demanded. "If you have any feeling for Benteen at all, don't use him this way. Be his business associate, his financier. Be his friend, but don't let him go on wondering if the mother he's always wanted has come back to him."

There was no response to her plea as Lady Crawford turned away and appeared to wander leisurely to the trunk Lorna had packed. She picked up the dress that had been tossed aside.

"Why are you doing all this packing?" She acted as if none of the previous conversation had transpired.

"I've decided to move all our things into the house," answered Lorna. "There are two rooms we can live in until the rest of it is finished."

"I see," she murmured, and laid the dress down. "I'll fetch two of the workmen to carry these trunks for you." She exited the cabin in an unhurried, gliding walk, leaving Lorna to wonder if anything had been accomplished.

Benteen brought his horse out of a lope into a sidestepping trot when he spied the crude buildings nestled against the bluff that sat back from the river. The other riders crowded together as they slowed their horses.

"That's it." Bull Giles confirmed they were looking at their destination.

Benteen's nerves were whetted to a fine edge as he surveyed the site. The trees had been cleared away, making it impossible to approach without being seen. The main building, the trading post, was butted up against the bluff. A shed with a corral sat forward on the right, and there was a shack sitting across from it. Any attempt to ride straight up to the post could trap them in a crossfire. The bluff eliminated any approach from the rear. The buildings were located with defense in mind. He stopped his horse. So far, they hadn't been seen.

"How many are there?" He shot a look at Giles.

"There were seven with him the last time I was here," he admitted. "Can't be many more than that in his bunch."

Unwilling to leave the range completely unmanned, Benteen had split his forces, which left him with ten riders, twelve counting himself and Bull Giles. He turned in his saddle.

"We're gonna have to divide up and hit 'em

615

from two sides. Barnie, you take five men and make for that cabin. The rest of you can follow me," he ordered.

"You reckon on circlin' around to the corral?" Bull asked.

"That's the idea," Benteen answered briskly.

"I'll come with you, then," he said.

Barnie swung his group of men close to some trees and waited while Benteen led the rest of them in a wide circle, hugging the riverbank. There was some movement around the buildings, but it seemed normal activity.

They were nearly in position when Benteen heard a shout from the buildings, followed by the bellow of a Sharps rifle. He laid his spurs to the speedy grulla and broke from the trees at a flat-out run. The hooves of the other horses pounded alongside him, racing for the corral. The sound of the Sharps had been a sobering reminder that most of the renegades were ex-buffalo hunters and excellent shots. Given time to pick their targets, they'd drop whatever was in their sights. The secret was going to be not giving them time or a stationary target.

The air was split open by the explosions of gunfire. Figures were scurrying around the clearing, taking up their positions. They were thirty yards from the corral before they were spotted, all of the concentration previously directed at Barnie's group. A bullet tugged at Benteen's coat sleeve. Puffs of smoke were coming from the shed. Benteen started emptying his gun as lead whistled around him.

There were a half-dozen horses in the corral, whinnying and racing in a panicked circle. When Benteen reached the fence, he swung off the grulla and hit the ground at a run. He ducked behind a water trough to reload and check the spare pistol tucked in his waistband.

A bullet caught Vince's horse. Benteen watched the horse sink as Vince threw himself free and flattened along the ground to scramble for cover. He threw a glance at the cabin and saw Barnie had made it. His mouth was dry and he licked the nervous sweat from his upper lip. Bull was weaving and ducking his way through the horses in the corral, making for the wall of the shed. Benteen peppered the doorway to give him cover fire.

Water splashed in his face, kicked up by the bullet splatting into the trough. A second shot splintered the wood, but he had the man spotted then. He fired before the man squeezed off the third shot, hitting him in the chest. The rifle was thrown in the air as the man was knocked backward by the force of the blow.

A barrage of bullets showered the water trough. Benteen left it at a crouching run and scrambled under the bottom rail of the corral to join Bull. A horse veered in front of him. He used its protection to reach the wall. Instinct had him shelling fresh bullets into the gun to keep it full. Powder smell settled around him.

He heard Bull say beside him, "It can't be any worse inside the shed than out."

"Let's find out," Benteen agreed.

Woolie and another cowboy were flattened on the corral ground, pouring lead into the shed. Benteen signaled them that he and Bull were going inside. They edged along the wall to the doorway.

"I'll take the left," Bull said, and Benteen nodded.

They went through the opening at nearly the same time, Benteen throwing himself low and shooting up, while Bull swung around the frame and let fly with both guns. When the dust and the smoke settled, one of the three men on the floor was groaning and Benteen was getting up. Bull kicked the gun out of reach of the one still alive and rolled him over with the toe of his boot. He was gut-shot.

"The other two?" Benteen asked, breathing harshly.

"Dead."

He edged toward the window, careful not to show himself. A voice boomed from the trading post. "Paulie? Hey, Paulie!"

Crouching low, Benteen darted to the other opening that looked onto the clearing and the cabin. He felt a wetness along the ribs. When he slipped a hand inside his coat, it came away red with blood. A bullet had grazed him. He didn't know when it had happened.

Bull came up beside him to peer out. "How's Barnie doin'?"

"They've still got the cabin."

Suddenly a renegade made a break from the cabin, racing across the clearing for the trading post. Both Benteen and Giles squared around the opening, squeezing off shots while a hail of bullets spattered from a side of the cabin. The man gave a little leap, then sprawled facedown in the dirt. He twitched once, then didn't move again.

"Barnie's got the cabin," Bull stated.

There was a noise in the doorway behind them. Benteen swung around, his gun cocked.

"It's me." Woolie dragged a wounded cowboy into the shed, one of the *vaqueros*. "Vince and Bob are at the corner of the shed. Diego's been hit in the hip." He paused to lean against the wall and ease the *vaquero* down. "We gonna rush the post?"

Benteen spied a lantern hanging on a peg by the door. It was more than half-full of kerosene. He slipped it off its hook. "We're going to burn them out. Tell Barnie."

While Benteen scraped a match over his pants to light it, Woolie darted to the window and called to the cabin with the others. He was breathing hard when he came back. "Barnie will go with your move," he said.

"Give us some cover fire." Benteen waited another second until the wick was burning strong.

The air was filled with the roar of gunfire as he stepped out of the doorway and hurled the lantern at the front window of the trading post. When he ducked inside, a bullet whapped the frame, sending slivers of wood into his cheek. He heard the crash of the lantern and the whoosh of flames.

"Get ready. They'll be comin' out," he warned the others.

There were three in the trading post. It didn't take them long to choose which way they wanted to die. The three renegades burst out of the door with guns blazing. One's coat was on fire, but he was rolled to the ground by a shot. A second man was knocked back into the flames, screaming once. The gun was shot out of the third man's hand, the bearded one in the buffalo coat.

"That's Sallie," Giles said.

"Hold your fire!" Benteen shouted around.

As the Triple C riders emerged from their cover and began stalking the unarmed man, Big Ed Sallie made panting, staggering attempts to find an opening to run through. His eyes were rounded until the whites were showing. He was a panicked animal with no more places to hide.

"What's this all about?" he pleaded. "Somebody tell me what this is all about?"

"You know what it's about, Sallie." Benteen kept his gun leveled on the man.

"No. I swear I don't." His breath wheezed through his voice, shrill with panic. "You jest came ridin' in here, shootin' up the place."

"Have you forgot that Triple C herd you tried to run off two nights back?" Benteen challenged. "My son was killed in that."

"I was here. I swear I was right here." Behind him, the flames were roaring through the wooden structure, their hissing, popping sounds making a hellish backdrop. "I never stole anybody's cattle. Not the Triple C. No one's."

"He's lyin', boss." Vince Garvey pushed to the front of the tightening circle of cowboys and tossed to the ground a cowhide, carrying the Triple C brand. "This was dryin' on his fence."

"I trade with the Indians. I bought it off them," he explained frantically while blood dripped from the wound in his hand.

Bull Giles shouldered past Benteen, his ugly features curling with hate. "Let me talk to him. Sallie and me speak the same language." He pulled his knife and reached down to slash off a strip of rawhide. Handing it to Barnie, he said, "Tie up his hands." A second strip of rawhide, he took to the watering trough.

"No." Big Ed Sallie started to struggle. "No!"

Two cowboys jumped forward to help Barnie, overpowering the renegade and forcing his arms behind his back. When they were tied, Bull strolled back with the wet piece of rawhide. He smiled at Sallie as he removed the renegade's hat.

"I don't have to tell you about rawhide, do I, Sallie?" He began to tie the wet strip around the man's head, despite his attempts to dodge and duck away. "When it's wet, it stretches fine." He pulled it taut and tied a knot by the temple. "But when it dries, it shrinks. It'd pop your skull plumb open, Sallie."

"No, don't," he cried in fear. "It was all your doin', Bull. You was the one who set me up."

"You mean with Janes?" he demanded.

"Yeah." Sallie nodded wildly.

"But that was just to pay you to keep your

Indians away from Ten Bar cattle." Bull eyed the man with callous regard. "Maybe we should tie another piece of rawhide around your neck and see whether you strangle before your head cracks open."

"No. He paid me to sic the Indians on the Triple C," Sallie insisted.

"He did, huh?" Bull mocked.

"Dammit, yes!" he cried angrily. "It wasn't my idea. Don't make me die like this!"

Bull slowly turned to face Benteen. "I set up a meeting 'tween him and Janes. Boston said it was just to buy protection and keep the Indians away from the Ten Bar." Bitterness and pain twisted through his face. "I didn't know . . ." He choked on the words.

Benteen had seen Bull too many times with Arthur to doubt the man's grief. He felt anger at the confession, but it was tempered by cool reason that said Bull had been used merely as a go-between.

"I've never killed a man for being a fool," Benteen snapped.

"What do you want done with him?" Barnie jerked his head toward the renegade.

"Hang him."

29

Nervous sweat ran from his pores as Judd Boston sat behind his desk in the bank's private office. He kept dabbing at the moisture beading on his upper lip and forehead until his fine linen handkerchief was damp. He looked again at the clock and the tic-tic-ticking of the pendulum that seemed to prove time was running out.

At the knock on the door, he grabbed the gun from his desk drawer and forced himself to speak calmly. "Yes?"

"It's me — Janes," came the muffled reply.

Returning the gun to the drawer, he got up quickly to unlock the door. He locked it back when Loman Janes walked through.

"You wanted to see me?" Janes said.

"What in bloody hell did you tell that renegade?" Boston exploded. "Can't you carry out a simple damned order and get it right?"

Janes stiffened at the unwarranted attack, his light gray eyes growing cold. "I told him exactly what you told me to. Why?"

"*Why?*" Boston raged. "Because Benteen

Calder's son was shot and killed when those Indians tried to run off the herd the other night! That's why!"

"That's hard luck." Loman shrugged. "But he shouldn't have had the kid along on a roundup. What's it to us, anyway?"

"Us! There is no 'us'!" Boston flung his hand in the air to dismiss the idea. "I'm the one that gives the orders! And you seem to foul them up!"

"Now, you wait a minute." A deadly quiet was settling over Loman Janes, an ugliness sweeping into him.

"No, you wait a minute!" Boston slammed his fist on the desk. "I told you I wanted no war with Calder! The orders were to take his cattle and leave him alone! I should have known when that rider of his got shot up, you had messed things up."

"I don't like being talked to like this," Janes warned.

"I pay you. I'll talk to you any damn way I please," Boston hurled angrily. "You don't think Calder is going to let his son die without going after the ones who did it, do you?"

"So? Let him chase the Indians back to Canada."

"My God, you must think the man is as simple-minded as you are," he declared with

625

contempt. "What happens if Bull Giles talks? What if he mentions arranging that meeting between you and the renegade?"

"If it's Giles you're worried about, I can shut him up," Janes said, still glowering under the insults.

"By killing him, I suppose," Boston snorted. "What if it's already too late?"

"Then I'll get rid of Calder. That's what we should of done in the beginning, then we wouldn't be wonderin' where we're gonna put all them cattle."

"You can forget about the cattle. I've sent Webster a wire instructing him to unload them and get the best price he can." He moved to his desk and dabbed the handkerchief to his forehead again.

"You did what?" The gray eyes narrowed to cold slits.

"I told him to sell," Boston repeated, and began moving papers around on the desk. "We're going to have to pull back, lie low for a while, and hope to hell all this blows over."

"What about Calder? Ain't you goin' after his range?"

"Forget about Calder. We're leaving him alone." Boston snapped the order.

"You're scared to take him on face to face, aren't ya? That's why ya hired me to do your dirty work for you. 'Cause you ain't got the goddamned guts to do it yourself," Janes spat.

Incensed, Boston struck him across the face with the back of his hand. "That's enough out of you!"

Janes's hand trembled on his gun. "You ever do that to me again and I'll kill you."

Boston drew back, staring at the faithful dog that had suddenly showed signs of turning on him. He pivoted away. "Go back to the ranch. And try not to foul up anything else," he added sarcastically.

For a long second Janes wavered with indecision before he went to the door and turned the lock. As he opened the door and breathed in, he smelled the fear in the air. He cast a look at the sweating man by the desk. He felt nothing but contempt for Judd Boston, who talked big and tough until someone threatened him, then cowered like a whining pup with no teeth.

"Better lock the door, Boston. The boogeyman might get ya," Loman Janes taunted with a snicker. He didn't bother to shut the door when he left.

He heard it close and the key turn, and it deepened his disgust. When he reached the street, he untied his horse from the hitchrack and swung onto the saddle. Instead of riding out to the ranch, Janes angled his horse down the street to the nearest saloon. It didn't matter what he'd been told to do. He'd get to the ranch when he damned well pleased.

There were three other Ten Bar horses tied outside the saloon. Janes put his horse in alongside them. He needed a drink to get the bad taste out of his mouth, and he needed to think. And he wasn't all that good at thinking. He was a man of action and reaction, black and white.

Somebody was banging away on a piano as Janes entered the saloon. Stepping to one side of the doorway, he paused to look the place over. Raucous laughter came from a back corner. Off to the side, a poker game was in progress. A half-dozen cowboys were standing at the bar. Smoke hung over the room like a haze, mingling with the smell of alcohol.

A cowboy at the end of the bar accidentally kicked a tarnished cuspidor sitting on the floor and cursed. "Somebody better move this damned thing before I spit in it." He turned and spat a stream of yellow juice onto the floor.

Janes spotted Trace Reynolds and another Ten Bar cowboy halfway down the bar. He crossed the saloon and shouldered his narrow body in to the bar beside them. "Whiskey," he told the bartender.

"Didn't know you was comin' to town,

Janes," the Texan Reynolds drawled with mild interest.

"I had to talk to Boston." Janes didn't say he'd been summoned. "Might be trouble with Calder." He lifted the glass and threw part of the contents down his throat, then slid a cold gray look at the cowboy with the oiled holster.

"Boston step on his toes again?" Reynolds asked with an easy smile.

"Ya could say that." Janes finished his drink and ordered another.

The town sat before them, a sprawl of dark shapes with squares of light spilling from them. Benteen straightened in the saddle and winced from the smarting wound in his side. With the nest of renegades wiped out, that left only the man that hired them. He glanced at his little band of riders – Jessie, Woolie, Bob Vernon, and Bull Giles. The rest he'd sent to the ranch with the wounded.

"Woolie, ride ahead and see if Boston's buggy is behind the bank," he ordered. "We'll meet up with you in front of the land office."

With a nod, Woolie swung his horse away from the main road to enter town by one of the back streets. The darkness soon swallowed him up, with only the receding sound of his horse's hooves marking his path into the night.

Benteen nudged the tired grulla forward, letting it settle into a slow walk. The rage had gone out of him. The fight at the river had slaked his thirst for revenge. Now it was just a job to be finished. He was hard-caught in a pattern that didn't leave him any alternative. It was the way of things until time changed them, if it ever did.

Lorna had been on the porch that ran the length of the two-story house, conferring with the crew foreman of the finish carpenters when she'd seen the straggling band of cowboys ride into the ranch, some of them slumped in their saddles. She had murmured a quick excuse and hurried down the knoll to meet them. Their numbers were fewer than those that had left. Alarm had rushed through her when she failed to see Benteen among them.

Rusty and Shorty were already on hand to help the wounded from their horses when Lorna reached them. Shorty had kept muttering, "I shoulda been there."

Cornering Barnie, she demanded. "Where's Benteen? Where's the rest of them?"

"Nothing to worry about. He's all right," Barnie had assured her. "They went into town after Boston."

Webb had caught at her hand, troubled by

the sight of all his injured friends. "What happened, Mom? How did they get hurt?"

"They were in a fight." At that point it had become impossible to wait patiently at the ranch until Benteen returned — if he returned. She had to be there when it was over. "I'm going into town." Her announcement hadn't come as any surprise to Rusty. "Can you manage?"

"I can manage, but you ain't goin' in alone. Benteen would have our hides for that. Barnie will hitch up the wagon and ride into town with you."

"Can I go, too?" Webb had pleaded.

"No." She had lost one son in a shooting fray. She would not now risk the life of her only child.

Loman Janes threw the money on the bar for his drinks and pushed away from the rail. His pointed glance prompted the other three members of the Ten Bar outfit to follow suit. "Reckon it's late."

There was a reluctant shuffling of boots and rattling spurs as they trailed after him to leave the saloon. Janes paused on the board sidewalk outside to instinctively take in the activity on the street. As he was hitching up his gunbelt to a more comfortable position on his narrow hips, he saw the four riders coming down the street slow and easy-like. There was no mistaking Bull Giles's broad hulk or the tall, loose-riding form of Benteen Calder.

Janes stepped out of the light spilling from the saloon and into the shadows close by the wall, hissing to his men to come away from the door. The sight of the two men together seemed to confirm Boston's fearful suspicions, Janes realized. With Boston running scared, it was time to take matters into his own hands. Calder had come into town hunting trouble, but what he didn't know — Janes smiled coldly to himself — was that trouble had found him first.

"Hank, get across that street into the side alley by the land office. Young, get to a window upstairs." Janes began dispersing his men with whispers. "Reynolds, you take that next doorway. It's Giles and Calder we want. Concentrate on them."

It was cut and dried to Loman Janes. When you wanted a man dead, you killed him. Only a gunslick looking for a reputation walked out on the street and challenged a man. Most gunfights came two ways — either with pistols drawn in the heat of an argument or with a planned attack on your enemy.

Benteen's gaze, always restless, traveled over

both sides of the streets. A cowboy entered a saloon ahead of them on the right. At the end of the block, a man crossed the street. Figures moved in the shadows outside the saloon, but all the activity seemed normal. Benteen was thinking ahead — to the bank and Judd Boston, if that's where he was. There was no sign of Woolie yet.

The curly-haired blond cowboy turned his horse up the side alley that would bring him onto the street by the land office. The buggy had been parked behind the bank, and a light had been burning in a rear window.

Woolie noticed the cowboy leaning against the corner of the building at the head of the alley. He didn't think much of it at first. The cowboy could have stepped into the alley to take a leak before riding home, but his stance was all wrong and he seemed to be watching the street. The ground was soft under his horse's feet, so it made little sound. A furrow of unease ran across Woolie's forehead. What was the man hanging around for if he wasn't taking a leak or havin' a smoke? As he came closer, he saw the glint of a gun barrel and had enough of a look at the man's face to recognize him for a Ten Bar rider.

With a yelled warning, Woolie drove his spurs into the horse's flanks and charged straight for the cowboy. He saw the man jerk his head around in surprise, then try to turn and bring his gun around, but Woolie's horse was shouldering into him and knocking him against the building. Woolie fired his gun at the man as the horse raced past him, and cursed when he missed.

When the yell came from the alley, Benteen yanked on the reins. A coldness went through him in quick, successive waves. Suddenly all the sounds were loud, all the smells were strong, and all the images on the street became sharp. In the split second of reaction time, he was swinging his horse out of the center of the street just as a shot cracked the air. Then all hell broke loose.

On horseback, they made high-placed targets for the men in the shadows. Lead was whining all around him as Woolie broke into the street with his gun blazing to answer the fire from sidewalk areas outside the saloon. Benteen's horse staggered as he peeled from the saddle. A bullet slammed into his left shoulder, spinning him into the shadows of a building's front. He scrambled behind a wooden barrel, his left arm hanging limp.

His pulse was striking hard in his neck, his breath coming short and fast as Benteen scanned the opposite side of the street and tried to locate his own men. There was a lull in the firing, no more shooting blindly. Riderless horses cantered down the street to escape the noisy fracas. His left arm was useless, so he tucked his hand inside the waistband of his pants.

Jessie was sprawled flat on the ground between a horse trough and the raised board sidewalk. There was the scrape of a boot behind him. Benteen sent a short look to the sound. Bull Giles was dragging a leg as he tried to sit up in a recessed doorway. He couldn't see Woolie or Bob Vernon, but there weren't any bodies in the street.

If Woolie hadn't warned them, they would have been caught flat-footed. Chances are they'd all be lying in the street now. Benteen's gaze returned to the buildings on the opposite side of the street, searching for shapes in the night. He noticed a strange thing. All the windows in the second story of the saloon had lights in them − all but one. It was dark, and the window was open. Benteen could see the curtain blowing out. He fired three rounds into it and saw a man slump over the sill, a gun falling from his hand.

But he'd also given away his own position. Bullets whacked into the barrel and sprayed the building just above his head, pinning him down. Then Bull opened fire along with Jessie, aiming for those bursts of flame across the street. Benteen made a break for the alley, crouching low against the building. There'd been a man waiting there to ambush them, so he came around the corner, expecting to be met. The cowboy was slumped forward on his knees, a hand holding the back of his bare head as he groaned and made an uncoordinated attempt to rise.

"My head . . ." he moaned, "I feel funny," and slithered to the ground, unconscious.

There was the rattle of a buggy coming down the street. Benteen flattened himself against the alley wall. Confusion traveled through him when he recognized the man in the bowler hat and business suit driving the buggy. Judd Boston.

From across the street, Loman Janes's voice called, "Get out of the way! We got Calder pinned down!"

Boston stopped the buggy in the middle of the street, sawing on the reins to hold his nervous horse. "You fool! You imbecilic fool!" Then he stood up in the buggy and faced the other side of the street. "Calder! This is not my doing! Janes is acting on his own! I had nothing to do with this — or anything else!" He proclaimed his innocence for all to hear.

"You yellow bastard!" Janes growled from the shadows.

Two shots were fired, one on top of the other, and Boston fell back onto the buggy seat, the horse bolting. Benteen took advantage of the runaway vehicle's distraction to make a dash across the street. He reached the other side and ducked down behind a rain barrel.

His shoulder was throbbing, wetness trickling down his arm. Licking his dry lips, he remained poised and listening to pinpoint the location of his adversaries by sound.

Boston was either dead or out of it, but it wasn't over. As much as he disliked Loman Janes, Benteen felt a certain degree of respect for the man. He had his standards and he'd stick by them to the end. He'd brought the fight to Benteen, and it wouldn't be over until one of them was dead.

A wave of dizziness washed over him and he shook it off. There was a scurry of movement. Benteen swung away from the barrel, squared toward the sound, and fired. He quickly moved to the left toward the building. His shots had missed, but they had driven a man away from the protection of a wide door frame. It was the gunhand Reynolds. He fired from the hip at Benteen's moving target. One sliced a hot iron along his thigh. His leg started to buckle as

Benteen fired at the man's shape, briefly out-lined. The hammer clicked on an empty chamber, but Reynolds was falling.

A cold smile of satisfaction had curved Janes's lips when the rig with Judd Boston had bolted down the street. The bastard had been putting all the blame on him to save his own skin, and he got what he deserved.

All Janes had was a glimpse of the figure that crossed the street in the wake of the buggy. He was sure Calder had been positioned some-where close to the alley. It had to be him. Giles had got it in the leg and couldn't possibly run. The other three were up the street.

He had made a hunting search of the shadows where Calder had to be hiding and decided he had to be using the rain barrel. It hadn't occurred to Janes to warn Reynolds that Calder had made it to this side of the street. His sole interest had centered on getting rid of Calder, then Giles.

There was a gap between the two buildings behind Janes just wide enough for a thin man to squeeze through. He had faded into it to slip around the buildings so he could slip up on Calder from the side.

He had circled the building and was sneaking up the side when he heard the sudden sharp exchange of gunfire and the thud of a body falling. He paused to listen, guessing that it had been Reynolds who got it.

With his left arm useless, reloading would be too slow. Benteen leaned against the building and slid the revolver into his holster, reaching for the spare gun in his waistband. Across the street, he saw Bull Giles standing sideways behind an upright post, but he couldn't see where any of the others were.

Benteen didn't have the vantage of Bull Giles's position. At first Bull wasn't certain the outline he saw at the corner of the building was a man. It moved slightly. The cold realization ran through him that the narrow shape belonged to Loman Janes. Somehow he'd slipped behind the building to sneak up behind Benteen.

Bull's glance swept back to Calder, wondering if he was aware he was being stalked from behind. It was impossible to tell if he knew, although Bull suspected he didn't. He opened his mouth to shout a warning, but nothing came out.

If Benteen died, Lorna would be a widow. The ugly thought came to him unbidden. He clamped his mouth shut, hating himself.

He had left it too late for a warning. Janes was coming away from the corner shadow to make his ambush of Calder.

Benteen began to inch along the side of the building, his ears straining for sounds other than the loudness of his own breathing and the rush of blood through his veins. There was a sudden movement across the street as Bull stepped from behind the post, exposing himself.

"Janes!" Bull shouted the challenge and fired.

A gun cracked behind Benteen, and he whirled to face Loman Janes. In the span of slow seconds, he thought of Lorna and home as he fired his gun. He watched Janes's gun kick up from its first shot that went wide with Benteen's turning. The barrel steadied on him again as Benteen fired the second time and heard his shot strike home.

There was a quick, small cough from Janes. Surprise went through his eyes as he began to tip backward. He fell against the rain barrel and slowly slid to the ground.

The echoes of the shots faded away and the street became quiet. It was over. Fatigue ran deep into his bones. With the pistol still in his hand, Benteen gripped his left arm, throbbing from the wound in his shoulder. He swayed and staggered into the street. Dully he was

aware of people filtering cautiously out of buildings, but all he wanted was to go home — to Lorna.

A wagon clattered up the street. Benteen stopped in irritation to let it pass, but its team was halted before it reached him. His weary gaze thought it watched Lorna springing from the wagon seat. When her hands touched his face, he realized it was really her.

"What are you doing here?" The rasping tiredness was in his voice, but his eyes were alive to her.

"I couldn't wait any longer." She was checking him over, inspecting his wounds with her hands and her eyes.

"Take me home," he said.

"I'm taking you to the doctor first," she insisted.

Then he remembered something that was important — the way Giles had stepped out and drawn Janes's fire after the man had sneaked around the building.

"I think Giles took a bullet meant for me," he said. "Go see how he is."

"But —"

"I'm all right," Benteen assured her.

Lorna half-turned and ordered, "Barnie, get him to a doctor." Then she hurried across the street.

Bull was lying on the ground, propped against the sidewalk. There was a ghastly pallor to his face, and his left knee was soaked with blood. His right arm was held awkwardly across his stomach while blood stained his sleeve.

When Lorna knelt down beside him, Bull looked at her and smiled weakly. "He sent you here, didn't he?"

"Yes," she admitted, and bent to look at the wound in his knee. It was a shattered, pulpy mess.

"It looks like it was a good thing I got some practice drivin' a buggy for Lady Crawford. That's about all I'll be ridin' from now on," Bull said, acknowledging it was a crippling wound.

"We'll get you to the doctor. It's amazing the things they can do nowadays." But she knew that he was right.

"You love him, don't you?"

"Yes." It was the way she said it, the look in her eyes, that convinced him.

"You'll always be a special woman to me, Lorna," Bull said quietly. "But I reckon that's all."

"You'll always be very special to me – and to Benteen, too, I think," she added. Townspeople began gathering around. Lorna motioned to two strong-looking men. "Help me get him to the doctor."

30

When Benteen awakened, there was sunlight streaming through the window. He had trouble focusing his eyes, the room kept blurring. There was a sharply antiseptic smell around him. It was a minute before he realized he was on a cot in the doctor's office. He tried to move, and a stab of pain seared from his shoulder, evoking a grimacing groan.

"Lie still." It was Lorna's voice, and her hand that gently touched his arm.

His gaze wandered over the face that was now within his vision. She was dark — and vivid, her lips red and warm for him. He caught the fragrance of her, so fresh and wild.

"I thought you were going to take me home," he reminded her.

"The doctor thought it would be a good idea if you spent the night here. He gave you something to sleep while he dug out the bullet." She showed him the slug that had come from his shoulder. "Do you want to keep it?"

"No. You can throw it away." He pressed a hand to his bandaged shoulder. "I don't need anything to remember this by."

Lorna couldn't have agreed more, and gladly tossed the bullet in a waste receptacle. She didn't want to ever live through that moment again when she had seen Benteen staggering across the street.

"What about the others? Giles. Woolie." Concern tracked across his expression, drawing heavy lines.

"Woolie's horse was shot out from under him. He has a broken leg. Jessie was creased in the arm, and Bob Vernon got shot in the hand." Lorna listed the injuries, then hesitated on the last one. "Bull had his knee shattered. The doctor says he'll be all right, but he'll never be able to bend it again. It'll be stiff."

Benteen sighed, but said nothing, aware of the debt he owed the man. "Is Boston dead?"

"Yes."

"It's crazy," he murmured on a faraway note. "They always say people who live by the gun die by it. Boston did his taking with legal papers, not bullets. A nonviolent thief. But he died violently just the same."

There was a light rap at the door. Lorna turned, not leaving his bedside. "Yes?"

The door opened and Lady Crawford swirled into the room in her long black satin skirts. She was the model of composure as she crossed the room to the cot. Black gloves gripped the pearl handle of her parasol.

"So you were the one doing all that shooting last night," she said to Benteen in mild accusation. "I complained bitterly to the management about the disturbance. It did little good, of course." She paused briefly. "How are you feeling?"

"I'll feel better when I'm back at the ranch," Benteen said, and linked his fingers with Lorna's.

"I'm sure your wife is capable of nursing you, although I don't envy her the task," Elaine stated. "As for myself, I'm leaving for Helena. The territorial governor has invited me to spend a few days with his family. It should prove to be a valuable trip, I believe."

"Yes, it should be," Benteen agreed, but Lorna caught the resignation in his voice.

"Perhaps you'll be well enough to go with me another time," Elaine suggested absently. "There's a lot of groundwork that needs to be done, and I'm certainly not needed here, when you have Lorna to take care of you."

"That's true," he agreed again.

"Unfortunately, it will be a few days before Mr. Giles is up and around, so I'm forced to travel alone. Hopefully he'll be able to resume his duties in a couple of weeks. I looked in on him briefly," she admitted.

"I'm glad to hear he'll be getting better." Benteen glanced at Lorna, no longer feeling threatened by her friendship with Bull Giles, as he had proved last night when he'd sent her to him.

"I'm sure you don't feel like talking business," Elaine continued. "And I have a great deal of packing to do. I only stopped to let you know where I'll be. I'll contact you when I return."

Lorna was beginning to understand his mother's seemingly cool attitude, so brisk and efficient. A mother would be concerned about her child's illness or injury, and reluctant to leave him when he was unwell. But Lady Crawford was showing neither emotion. Purposely. She felt a surge of admiration and respect for the woman.

"By the way . . ." Elaine paused in her turn away from his bed. "I have lodged a formal complaint with the Canadian government on your behalf, because of the cattle stolen by Indians from their reservations. I am quite sure that you will soon be recompensed for your losses."

Benteen raised an eyebrow to register mild surprise and pleasure. "That's good news."

"I thought you'd say that." Elaine smiled. "I

must go. Take care of yourself."

With parasol in hand, she glided to the door. Lorna unlinked her fingers from Benteen's grasp. "I'll be back in a minute," she promised, and hurried after Lady Crawford. She carefully closed the door behind her.

"Did you want something?" Lady Crawford inquired with a regal tilt to her head.

"I wanted to thank you," Lorna admitted.

"Thank me?"

"Yes, for what you did in there — the impression you left with Benteen." She regarded the woman warmly, because it had been a very generous thing to do.

"Yes, well . . . you were quite right, you know," Lady Crawford said, and made a study of smoothing the gloves on her hand. "There is one thing that I can't give him . . . but there are other dreams that I can fulfill."

"Thank you," Lorna repeated.

"Nonsense." She dismissed the expression of gratitude. "Don't forget, I shall profit enormously from the association."

She moved toward the front door before Lorna could say anything else. But it had all been said. Lorna slowly turned and went back into the room where Benteen was. She found him sitting on the edge of the cot, swaying unsteadily.

"Chase Benteen Calder, what are you doing?" She hurried over to help him.

"We're going home, aren't we?" he said, then turned a questioning eye on her. "What did you have to talk to Lady Crawford about?"

"It was nothing." Lorna helped him on with his shirt. "She returned something, and I wanted to thank her for it."

Three weeks later the first shipment of furniture arrived for the new house. Included was the big desk for the study. Lorna halted the workmen and had them uncrate the desk and carry it into the study. She hung the map on the wall behind it, and put Benteen's ranch papers in the drawers. There were a couple of chairs that belonged in the living room, but she arranged them in the study in front of the huge fireplace.

When she heard Webb galloping across the porch to greet his father at the steps, Lorna slipped out of the room to meet him in the entryway. His shoulder was still stiff and sore from the wound, and he was leaner, but there wasn't any doubt that he was back in full control of the Calder Cattle Company.

Webb was riding on his hip. Benteen swung him to the floor as they entered the house. His gaze went to Lorna, sweeping over her in that intimate way that always sent her pulse chasing after itself.

"Supper ready?" he asked.

"I haven't even started it," Lorna admitted, then laughed and grabbed his hand, tugging it like a child. "There's something I want to show you."

With barely contained excitement, she led him to the study doors, opened them, and stepped into the room. She made a whirling pivot to watch his reaction as his gaze traveled around the room.

"Part of the furniture arrived after you left this morning. I've had the workmen busy ever since, uncrating it and getting it arranged," she explained.

"The map." He noticed it and smiled at her. "I like that." He wandered over to the cavernous stone fireplace. "The mantel needs something."

"I was thinking that myself." She bit at the inside of her lip, then walked calmly over to a desk drawer and took out the daguerreotype of his mother when she was young. "Would you want to put this on it?"

She handed it to him, and watched him study it. There was a rush of conflicting emotions across his ruggedly planed features. His chest lifted on a deep breath as he looked at her.

"No." He slowly shook his head. "Put it away somewhere if you want."

There was nothing left of the old dream, or the old bitterness. Lady Crawford and the image in the picture were two different things, separated in his mind. Lorna crossed the room and put her arms around his middle.

"You knew that, didn't you?" Benteen murmured against her hair.

"I hoped that all the ghosts were gone," she admitted. "She couldn't be what you wanted."

A chuckle came from his throat. "Can you imagine Webb calling her grandmother? She'd be horrified." He lifted his head to look at her, linking his hands at the small of her back to mold her against the lower half of his body. "Speaking of Webb, you don't think you could persuade your son to go out and play for another hour?"

"An hour?" she murmured provocatively. "You're not bragging much."

"You sassy little —" He wasn't allowed to finish the rest, as she pulled his head down to kiss him.

Epilogue

From free grass to fences,
A lotta things have passed,
But one thing that's for certain
This Calder range will last.

1902

In the early morning light, Benteen led the two saddled horses to the camp. When Lorna saw him coming, she shook the coffee dregs from the tin mug and left them in the wreck pan by the chuck wagon. It wasn't as good as Rusty's coffee had been. She smiled briefly at the thin man named Bogie who had taken his place. She missed the irascible, white-whiskered cook. There wasn't anyone to tell her where she should look for the "wildflowers" growing. He had died peacefully in his sleep one night — just slipping away. She regretted that she hadn't told him how much she liked him, but it always seemed there was time.

Conscious of Benteen's gaze on her, Lorna shook off the faint sadness and smiled. His eyes darkened as they ran over her. A pair of pants fit snugly over her hips, softly curved hips created for a man's pleasure by the wise Maker. The denim material was new and stiff, making a rustling noise as she walked to meet him. She was just as slender and beautiful as the day he'd married her, although considerably more experienced, Benteen thought with a hint of a smile.

He handed her the reins to a blaze-faced roan, observing, "I think you come on these roundups just so you have an excuse to wear pants." He liked her in them, but it wasn't something he intended to admit to her.

"I think you asked me to come just so you can see me wearing them," Lorna returned saucily, and hopped to step her foot in the stirrup, swinging easily into the saddle.

It was a movement Benteen watched over the seat of his saddle, enjoying the way the material stretched to outline her firm buttocks. She continued to stir him, as nature had intended from their first mating.

Benteen mounted his horse. "I should have made you take those things off the first time you put them on instead of thinking it was going to be a temporary thing. Give a woman an inch, and she takes a mile." But he smiled when he said it. "You do know everyone in the Stockmen's Association talks about the way you ride around like a man?"

"I don't know why they should talk," Lorna declared. "I'm not the only woman who rides astride."

"But you're the only one who does it wearing pants," he pointed out, and turned his horse toward the gathering pens. "All the rest have split riding skirts."

"Are you trying to tell me what to wear, Benteen Calder?" she challenged.

"It wouldn't do any good. You'd do just as you damn please, the way you've always done," he replied dryly.

"Not always," Lorna corrected, because there was a time when other people's opinions had mattered. "This land taught me to be independent."

They rode out to where the cowboys were making the spring gather. The Hereford cattle being rounded up had shiny white-faced calves at their sides. The gate was opened so another small bunch could be driven in to add to the growing number inside the pens. Benteen and Lorna reined to one side to watch.

The Triple C brand was a burned mark on the rust-red flanks of the cows. Lorna felt a sense of pride and achievement whenever she saw it. She cast a brief glance at Benteen, while the bulk of her attention remained on the wild rangeland that they owned.

"Do you feel like a cattle baron?" There was a smile in her voice — she was aware the term irritated him.

"Nobody ever says 'cattle baron' without saying *greedy* cattle baron.'" He rose to her

baiting tone. "It's something I'll never understand. It's always the homesteading farmer
with his little wife who gets all the sympathy
and support for the hardships and struggles
he's gone through. They always make out that
the big cattle ranchers are some kind of feudal
lords. They don't take into account the
struggles and hardships we endured to have
what we now possess."

"You told me a long time ago it's human
nature to want what someone else has," Lorna
reminded him.

"Yes. But someday people will have to
recognize the cowboy. Nobody had a lonelier,
harder job, not even the farmer. The hours are
long, the working conditions usually poor, and
all he has for company is a horse. We were here
before there were towns and people – when
there were just prairie dogs and Indians. We
built something where there was nothing, and
now we're condemned for it." There was
disgust and impatience in his voice.

"That's because they think we are somehow
to blame for the high price of beef at the
stores," she said. "When they're trying to feed
their family, they aren't interested in the bad
years we've had – the droughts, the blizzards."

"The winter of 1886-1887 was the worst,
coming right after a summer drought that left

the range in bad shape," Benteen remembered with a grim look. "A lot of ranchers went under after that."

Lorna recalled the year that had nearly crushed them along with so many others. After deep snows fell in late November, the chinook had come in early January to give them hope. But it had turned bitter cold. The partially melted snow had turned into an armor of ice that hooves couldn't break through to reach the grass. Frozen and starved cattle had died by the thousands.

It had been a severe blow. The previous year, they had branded nearly ten thousand calves at spring roundup, but after that killing winter there were only twelve hundred calves branded. A lot of ranchers had gotten discouraged and quit or lost their financial backing.

Benteen had figured the tremendous loss of cattle would create a shortage of beef at the market and drive the price up. He took what cash reserve they had and partially restocked the herd. Then he'd sent Shorty Niles to Canada to purchase some draft horses and turned fertile bottomlands into hay. Shorty had come back with the horses and the farmer's daughter as his wife.

The gamble had paid off, and there was hay

to feed the cattle if there was another such severe winter. Ranching became combined with part-time farming.

"Mr. Calder!" Jessie Trumbo's fifteen-year-old son came riding up, one of a handful of second-generation Triple C riders.

Ely and Mary Stanton's firstborn was a girl named Ruth Ann. Woolie Willis had married a little red-haired schoolmarm, and Bob Vernon had eventually married his dance-hall girl and had a seventeen-year-old son working the roundup. Barnie Moore, Vince Garvey, and Zeke Taylor were all married with growing children. There was a sense of continuity and belonging, an established order that lent a feeling of permanence to things.

Benteen turned his horse toward the approaching rider and waited until Dick Trumbo had pulled his cantering horse down to a plunging walk. "What is it?"

"Pa wants you to come. It's Captain. He's dead." The boy was already wheeling his horse in a circle to lead the way.

A murmured sound of regret came from Lorna as she reined her horse to follow after Benteen. The old Longhorn had led the trail drives up from Texas until the influx of settlers had finally closed it off. They had retired the brindle steer to pasture some years ago.

About a half-mile from the pens, they saw Jessie. He had dismounted and was standing at the rim of a coulee. His hat was in his hand, a gesture of respect for the loss of a comrade. Little remained of the steer. Scavengers had picked the carcass clean, leaving a partial skeleton, a few pieces of loose hide, and a set of long twisted horns.

It was a sober-faced Jessie who looked up at Benteen. "It's Captain. I'd know those mossy horns anywhere."

The announcement was followed by a long silence that Benteen finally broke. "We'll take the horns back to the ranch." His glance went to Lorna. "They belong above the mantel."

She nodded a mute agreement. The steer had played a vital role in the building of the ranch. It was fitting that his memory be honored — and that of his breed.

"Dick, climb down there and get those horns," Jessie gave the order to his son. "Take them to the chuck wagon."

The young rider swung off his horse, dropping the reins. He went down the embankment at a sliding walk to reach the carcass and its horned skull.

"These horns must be five feet across or more," he declared as he hefted a tip and realized they were nearly as long as he was tall.

Jessie walked to the side of his horse and mounted. "There aren't many of his kind left on the range," the cowboy observed. "I sure do miss seein' them. They sure weren't slick and pretty like those Herefords."

His comment didn't need any explaining to Benteen. The Longhorn was essentially a wild breed of cattle that had been domesticated — or as tamed as they'd ever get. But it was the wildness that made them special, a kind of freedom that was part of their nature, like the horns. They could fend for themselves; they didn't need anybody looking after them.

"I don't think any cowman is happy to see their herds disappearing," Benteen agreed. "It's a case of circumstances. With land costs and taxes being what they are, you can't hold a Longhorn on the range until he matures. You need a breed that ages fast, so you can get him to market. A rancher can't afford to have a Longhorn grazing a range for six years when a Hereford is ready in less."

"Yeah, I know all the arguments." Jessie nodded. "The range is too valuable, so the breed's gettin' phased out. I guess there comes a time when we all get phased out. I reckon he had his time of glory, though."

He touched his hat to Lorna, then reined his horse away to resume his roundup activities. It was a moment before they turned their horses from the coulee and started back to the gathering pens, walking their horses. Lorna watched Benteen scan the range, its vastness pulling his gaze and stretching it out until it hurt.

"It still bothers you to see fences, doesn't it?" she murmured.

"It isn't something any range man would choose, but it was forced on us," he said. "Just like getting paper title and lease rights to all this land to keep all the little ranchers from taking it away. It isn't just fencing others out. Cattle have become too valuable to be allowed to stray. A cowman can't afford to buy a prime bull and have him servicing somebody's else's cows instead of his own. It's a combination of economics and circumstances that killed the open range."

"And the cowboy," Lorna murmured. It had been hard for so many of them to make the transition. They'd made their living off the back of a horse with a rope in their hand. Then it had changed, and they were expected to cut hay, dig holes for fenceposts, and string wire.

As they neared the pens, a pair of riders was leaving. Lorna recognized her son with a mother's ease. Webb Calder had grown into a tall, rawboned young man with brown, nearly black hair and dark eyes. Since birth the cowboys on the ranch had treated him like one of their own, never doing his work for him, but always showing him how to do it right. He was young yet, but he already showed signs of independent thinking.

"Webb has been hinting that he wants to move into the bunkhouse," Lorna remarked. "I think he's trying to break it to me gently that he's grown up."

"You can tell him to stop hinting," Benteen replied. "The governor and his family are coming for a visit the first of the month. I want Webb there."

"I had forgotten." She grimaced slightly. "Elaine would be busy organizing everything if she were here."

It was still difficult to accept that she had died three years before, taken swiftly by a heart attack. Lady Crawford had been such a woman for making entrances and exits that it always seemed to Lorna that she had left too abruptly. It hadn't been her style at all. They had received a telegram from Bull Giles in Washington, where Lady Crawford had journeyed on one of her many political missions.

"She was an extraordinary woman," Benteen murmured. To this day, everyone believed her association with Benteen had been purely a financial one. He was content to leave it at that. It had eventually become a close relationship, based on deep respect rather than affection, something that few people would have understood.

"It's been a while since we've heard from Bull. I wonder how he's doing?" Lorna thought aloud.

"From what I've heard from other ranchers, his hotel in Denver is making quite a name for itself. He's catering to the upper crust, I understand," Benteen said. "He had a lot of practice over the years as Elaine's male secretary, bodyguard, and . . . friend."

"They were an unusual combination — beauty and the beast," she said, but affectionately.

It had been an odd alliance. Bull, who had always been so argumentative and resentful of authority, had trailed along with Lady Crawford wherever she went, taking her orders and running her errands, yet he never truly bowed his head to her. There had been a strange equality between them. When Lady Crawford had died, the bulk of her wealth had been left to Bull Giles. In a sealed letter left for Benteen, she stated that she had already helped him to acquire great wealth of his own while she was alive, so she didn't feel she was obliged to leave him anything on her death.

"You never really minded that she left most of her fortune to Bull, did you?" Her side glance wandered over his profile, handsome in its strength and male vigor.

"No." It was a rather bland look Benteen gave her. "She was never truly my mother and I was never her son. Any obligations we had to each other were canceled out a long time ago — along with the bitterness."

"I'm glad."

He reined in his horse, and it sidled against her roan. "I remember the way you cried the day we left Fort Worth. Are you sorry we came here?"

Lorna was taken aback by his question. "How can you ask that? No, I'm not sorry. This is my home."

"But you'd like to see your parents again, wouldn't you?"

"Yes." She didn't try to deny that. "In Mother's last letter, she said Daddy wasn't feeling too well."

"Maybe this fall we can go back for a visit," Benteen suggested.

For a long second she could only stare at him. It had been something she had wanted to do for several years, but she knew he had no desire to go back. When he'd left Texas, it had been for good.

"I'd like to go," she said simply.

"We'll plan on it," he said. "I might buy a couple of bulls while we're there." His mouth slanted in a mocking smile. "When a wife stops complaining, a man doesn't mind doing things for her."

"Tell me, Benteen, are you sorry you don't have a quiet little wife who waits patiently at home?" The warm gleam in her eye challenged him.

"I'm sure it would be different if I had a wife who knew her place," he murmured dryly.

"But I do know my place," Lorna stated. "And it's right here beside you."

> We built this Calder range
> To last five times a score
> It's a legacy we're leavin' —
> Of pride and something more.